THE MIDNIGHT FOX

By

James H. Davis

To Josephine. Who else?

CONTENTS

ACKNOWLEDGMENTS

To Vivienne and Andrew,
many thanks for your advice and input.

Comets are for princes. There are no comets in the sky when a beggar dies.

- William Shakespeare

CHAPTER 1

Wednesday 4th September, 2007

Holly Winter always stood out from a crowd. She was tall, blonde and beautiful and knew it. Any man who managed to make eye contact with her received in return only a slightly amused look from her powder blue eyes. That was her stock in trade, amusing her wealthy clients and being paid handsomely for her services. Indeed, in her short tenure escorting, as it is called these days, wealthy and lonely gentlemen had already provided her with a nice apartment in Islington and the Mercedes SLK she had always coveted, both gifts from her infatuated Arab clients. She specialised in Arabs, even to the extent of acquiring a rudimentary knowledge of the language; there's nothing wrong with self-improvement, she believed.

Habitually a night creature, she was definitely not in her element at eight o'clock in the morning among the heaving mass of humanity in a London Tube. The sight of daylight at the top of the escalator brought a feeling of blessed relief.

Bond Street station, between Oxford Circus and Marble Arch was the nearest to her destination; she could have taken a taxi, but her instructions had been clear – use the Tube, taxis leave trails, and the rendezvous time was eight thirty, sharp.

The man – one of Sid Green's enforcers – who had given her those instructions and paid her in fifty-pound notes had frightened her. Holly, being in the business she was, did not frighten easily, but there was something about this one, best do exactly as she was told. It was simple enough after all. Park your car outside a particular house the previous night, go to it at eight thirty sharp and drive away. Nothing risky about that, was there? Piece of cake, really.

Ursula Kaminski drove the Black Mercedes S Type into the car park at Marble Arch and found a space on the floor above the one where she had parked the green BMW the previous evening. It was exactly 8.05 by her watch. She knew each floor was covered by CCTV, and anyone seen parking one car and driving off in another would be noticed and she did not want to be noticed.

Using the stairs, she went down one floor, found the green BMW and opened the boot. Inside was the wooden croquet box Kramer had put there. The name stencilled on the side read 'Jacques of London', the brand leader she had been told when she bought it. She then dumped the original contents into a skip as instructed, Kramer only being interested in the box, which now contained a block of plastic explosive connected to a detonator, battery and a mechanical timer which, according to Kramer was simpler and more reliable than any electronic device. There was also a hessian sack of six-inch nails which she was to place on top of the explosive after arming it.

It was set to detonate at 8.45, forty minutes from now, and required two steps of arming. The first was to remove the strip of plastic which disabled the contacts of the timer and the second to throw the switch which connected the battery.

The box was to be placed on the rear seat of the car to enable easy access to it when she had to arm it. Simple really, pull out the plastic strip, throw the switch, get out and walk away. Nobody would pay any attention to a croquet set left on the rear seat of a BMW in London W1.

She had been assured it was safe to move. Until the plastic strip was removed and the switch thrown it was as safe as a piece of soap.

It did not give her any comfort to know she had also been told to handle it like a baby. She had never handled a baby but she knew that they did not like to be dropped.

The box was not heavy, with rope handles on each end to facilitate lifting and being of a fatalistic nature she also knew, if anything went wrong, she would not feel a thing. It would be curtains for Ursula.

Nothing went wrong. She moved the box, donned the blonde wig, which together with large shades should beat the CCTV, and drove out into the Park Lane traffic.

Daisy Clowser, although a sound sleeper, never needed an alarm clock when she was in her London apartment. She had Heinz, so named because of the multiplicity of colours in his coat. He was a twelve-year-old street cat who had taken up residence with her one cold winter seven years ago and became a house cat. He was also a very particular cat, who liked punctuality and had a perfect sense of time. Every morning at seven o'clock his paw would tap her arm with just a hint of a claw. Any tardiness on her part would result in persistent tapping with a little more claw until she came to her senses and got up to let him out onto her balcony where his outdoor litter tray was kept, as he preferred to conduct his affairs in private. On weekend mornings when she was not working, she would also put his food down at the same time and return to her bed to grab a couple of hours' extra sleep.

Today was Wednesday which meant a regular nine o'clock management meeting to which nobody was expected to be late. Said office being in St. James meant a thirty-five-minute drive from her apartment allowing for traffic and time spent finding a parking space in a nearby car park. Normally she'd have taken the Tube but today she needed the car in the afternoon.

After feeding Heinz, she took a shower, followed by a coffee and fruit muesli breakfast, before checking her emails and taking a look at Google News for any world-changing events. As usual the trouble spots in the world were still in trouble, other than that, there was nothing to interest her.

By ten past eight she was leaving the apartment. Heinz was asleep on her bed and would stay there until the cleaning lady came during the morning, at which time he would be allowed onto the balcony until she was leaving, then take more food and continue sleeping until Daisy returned.

Daisy lived in a five-storey apartment block off the Bayswater Road. Residents' parking provided her with a coveted parking space for her Porsche Boxster. It was warm for September and the sky was blue so she decided it was a roof-down day, or so she thought until she reached her car and saw her front offside tyre flat to the rim.

Being of a practical persuasion she could actually change a tyre but Porsche in their infinite wisdom held their tyres in such high esteem, they neglected to provide a spare. Engine in the back, luggage in the front, and in the unlikely event of a puncture the owner could ring a hotline anywhere in the world and receive assistance within the hour. She didn't have an hour and cursed the wisdom of the people in Stuttgart. She was also cursing her own luck and was lost in thought as she considered her options when she received a light touch on the arm and became aware of someone beside her.

'Morning Daisy, trouble?'

Mary Grey's appearance was like manna from heaven. She was the slim and attractive brunette with the greenest eyes Daisy had ever seen, who lived in the apartment below her. Besides being a good friend, she was most importantly in the light of her present predicament a taxi driver. Her shiny black cab was parked beside the Porsche.

Skipping the usual formalities, Daisy pointed at the offending part. 'Mary, look at my bloody tyre.'

Mary examined the tyre with an expert touch. 'Nothing to see, Daisy, probably just a faulty valve.'

'I've a management meeting at the office at nine o'clock, can you take me there?'

Mary shook her head. 'Sorry Daisy, no can do, I've a pick-up at eight forty-five, I can't be late, he's a regular and a great tipper.'

'Where's your pick-up?'

'Shakespeare Mews, do you know it, just behind the Connaught?'

Daisy didn't know it, but she knew the Connaught and said, 'Great, can you drop me off? I can hoof it from there in fifteen minutes.'

Mary thought for a moment before saying, 'You're a bloody nuisance. Okay, let's go.'

Holly, who had had made good time, was in advance of her rendezvous time, which had been explicit. *'Remember, girl, 8.30 sharp, drive away at 8.30 sharp, don't look back and forget you ever met me. Now that's not a lot to ask for a grand in fifties, is it? So get it right.'*

She knew if she wanted to continue working in London and keep her looks, she should do exactly as she was told.

It was not lost on Holly, paying a grand to reserve a parking space was not an everyday occurrence, but in her line of business she met some weird people and had learned it was never in her interests to speculate too much into their affairs.

Having ten minutes in hand allowed her to drag her feet a bit. As she made her way down New Bond Street, she browsed some of the more delightful window displays, a practice she would normally enjoy but today her heart wasn't in it, as unease, even fear began to grip her. This was mob business, she was thinking. Maybe the space was needed to make a hit. Where would that leave her? She would be an accessory before the fact or something like that. Difficult to prove but big trouble just the same and certainly not good for business.

Best not think about it, more likely it's a drug deal that requires a drive up, stop beside a car, give or take the white stuff and drive way, no big deal really, the Toffs pay a lot more than a grand for their happy packs. Anyway, even if it is a hit, better do what she's told or she could be next.

Her Cartier showed 8.29 as she turned into Shakespeare Mews. *Nice, classy little place,* she thought, and convenient for the West End, maybe six or so small houses on one side facing the high wall of a hotel car park. She had been told to park outside the house with the green shutters which was the largest in the mews and the only one with a garage. She had parked there after dark the previous evening, but now seeing it in daylight she was impressed. Probably stables in Victorian times but now as the agent would enthuse, 'Chic and desirable, that's a million plus, thank you very much.'

Holly liked the idea of living in a place like this. Her apartment in Islington was Chic in its way, but these were Chicer, if such a word exists. Maybe she should review her business plan and upgrade her clientele.

Her SLK was where she had parked it, and at 8.30 precisely, she drove off, and did not look back. She had a bad feeling about this and had her bags packed and a ticket booked for the Euro Tunnel. She planned to spend the next few months on the Côte d'Azur and not listen to the news or read the newspapers. Better not to know whatever happens next.

Ursula Kaminski's criminal career had been – that is up to now – successful and profitable to herself and her associates. She put that down to careful planning and taking care of all the little details. Born into a working-class family – Polish father and Czech mother – in Czechoslovakia during the Soviet occupation, she grew up, like every Czech girl, aspiring to be a famous tennis player like Martina Navratilova.

Although she had all the necessary attributes for the sport, a quick mind with lighting reflexes, and a killer serve, even after a promising junior career, she was not deemed good enough to be selected for entry to the elite tennis academy. This was a bitter blow. She knew full well she was good enough but did not have the correct family background. This made her vengeful towards the so-called elites, and after finishing university with a law degree, she joined the StB – the much-feared secret police – where, if you were deemed capable and loyal to the State, you could succeed, no matter what your background was. Before long she had the opportunity of settling a few scores, which she did.

It was in the StB she learned the importance of tying up all the little details and cutting off any loose ends. Tasked with sniffing out dissidents, she soon found she had a natural ability to frighten people until they happily told her their innermost secrets. This became her forte and earned her quick promotion, together with all the perks handed out to loyal employees of the State. She had a nice apartment in a good area of Prague, a car and access to tax-free stores reserved for the special few.

The good times came to an abrupt end when the Soviet Union collapsed and the satellite countries fell like a house of cards. In February 1990 the StB was closed and all the employees were banned for life from working in government or police. Their files, many millions of pages, were gradually thrown open to the public.

She knew, sooner or later these files would be read and throw up her name too many times: the citations she had been so proud of would now incriminate her.

With her future prospects in the new country being non-existent, she would have to look elsewhere if she was to continue her comfortable lifestyle. Knowing her CV would not impress potential employers in the west, she reached the conclusion her skills would be equally useful to the criminal fraternity.

Amid the confusion of the split between the Czech Republic and Slovakia she and several colleagues from the StB were able to source misplaced military ordnance for which there was a ready market in various trouble spots in the world.

That was the start of her smuggling career – she preferred to call it Logistics – and over the next sixteen years she became an expert at it, setting up a number of safe routes for the illegal movement of weapons and drugs. She still planned each operation with the same meticulous care, taking care of all the little details and from time to time having to clean up the odd loose end.

As she drove to the rendezvous, she let her misgivings disrupt her focus on the task ahead. This morning's job was full of loose ends, everything had to be done in such a rush. There had been no time for attention to detail. Two rare moments of carelessness on her part had brought this about, one chance in thousands, and this was the result. Still if it must be done, it will be done.

It was 8.30 when she turned into the mews and saw the SLK drive off. *Good,* she thought. The man who had arranged this had done his job.

Kramer had set up the meeting, which took place in a Clerkenwell pub. There, she met the man Kramer simply called the Fixer, who had agreed, for a substantial amount in cash, to provide the BMW and arrange for the space to be occupied until the last minute.

A quick look around told her the mews was empty and she carefully reversed into the empty space. She wore gloves, even though she expected the car to be a burnt-out wreck, so nothing to worry about there. She leaned back and opened the lid of the box, removed a glove to enable her to pull out the plastic strip and throw the switch. *Done. Now close the lid. Don't worry about leaving a fingerprint, or DNA, the explosion will incinerate any evidence.* She got out, locked the car and keeping her back to the CCTV camera walked away, dropping the car keys into the first drain she came to.

As she waited for the lights to change at the Bayswater Road junction, Mary spoke to Daisy through the open partition window. 'It's handy I ran into you, Daisy. I know it's weeks since my birthday, but everyone's on holiday in August so I usually leave it for a month. I'm having a few drinks with some friends on Friday, can you come?'

'Love to,' Daisy said, smiling broadly. 'We had a great night last year, where and when?'

'The Kings Head in Moscow Road, about eight, that okay?'

'Eight's fine, look forward to it.'

The lights changed and Mary joined the flow of traffic going towards Marble Arch.

Leaning forward Daisy asked, 'What age are you this time?'

'Twenty-nine,' Mary said, as she cut across three lanes at Marble Arch and entered Park Lane.

Laughing, Daisy said, 'Hang on a bit, I thought you were twenty-nine last year?'

Mary's green eyes in the driver's mirror had a mischievous grin when she said, 'I was, I decided to stop counting for a few years at twenty-nine, it keeps you younger.'

'Good idea.' Daisy reckoned that, although Mary had the face and figure to pass for the age she owned to, she must be nearer forty-five.

Mary took a left into Upper Brook Street but was stopped by the first set of lights, when she turned and said, 'I was going to pop up and see you tonight, but seeing as you're here, I have a favour to ask you.'

Unusual, Daisy thought and said, 'Fire away.'

Turning to face her, Mary said, 'You're a detective, right?'

Shaking her head, Daisy replied, 'A detective? Not really, Mary, I'm not in the police or anything like that, but why the question? Do you need a detective?'

The lights changed and Mary took a right into Park Street before answering. 'I'm interested in a company and I need to know who the owners are. I tried Companies House yesterday, but couldn't find a listing.'

'I can look up a company for you, no problem, what's the name?'

'Daisy, if you're not a detective what are you?'

'I work for a firm which investigates corporate risks, mainly overseas.'

Mary laughed. 'Bullshit, Daisy, you're a detective. I drive a taxi, remember; I know the signs.'

Daisy, wondering what the signs were, said, 'Investigator, Mary, there's a difference. I can help you with the company, what's the name?'

Taking a left into Mount Street and joining slow-moving traffic Mary replied, 'I've written it down. I'll give it to you when I stop.'

Taking a longer look at Mary's face in driver's mirror Daisy asked, 'You all right, Mary? You're looking a bit peaky this morning.'

Mary with a wane smile said, 'I'm okay, just a bad night's sleep, that's all.'

Daisy said, 'Ghosts from the past, eh. I get them myself sometimes.'

Mary's reply was almost inaudible. 'More like voices from the past, one voice in particular.'

Deciding not to press the point Daisy asked, 'This big tipper, what's he like?'

Mary's face brightened as she replied, 'Oh, Mr Abdullah, he's nice, insists on me collecting him. I must be outside his house, when he opens the door, at eight forty-five Monday to Friday.'

'Punctual to a fault, eh,' Daisy said. 'What happens if you're late, stuck in traffic?'

Mary crossed the junction at St. Audley Street and took the inside lane before she replied. 'I'm always a few minutes early, traffic is never a bother, I know all the back doubles. It's only pests like you with flat tyres are the bother.'

'Maybe he's just an anxious type,' Daisy said. Then as the thought struck her, 'It could be he's stuck on you, has he ever asked you out?'

Indicating she was taking the next on the left Mary said, 'Yeah, I think he's nervous about something and no, he's never asked me out, nosey, not yet anyway, but I think he may be building up to it.' She turned into a small mews, found a space halfway up and stopped.

Looking through the windscreen Daisy gave the half a dozen houses the onceover, before asking, 'Is this where your client lives?'

'Yes,' Mary said, pointing. 'The one with the green shutters and the garage.'

'Nice, your client is certainly not one of the world's needy. I'm surprised he doesn't have a liveried chauffeur.'

Mary took a folded envelope from her wallet before saying, 'I wondered about that too. I think maybe he prefers me.' Avoiding Daisy's eyes, her normally calm persona for once a little flustered, she handed her the envelope. 'I've written the name on this.'

Daisy was smiling as she took it, thinking, *Mary caught at last!* Unfolding the envelope, she read the name written on the back and said, 'Zentek Aviation, what's your interest?'

'It's half a minute to my pick-up time, I must dash, I'll catch up with you later.'

Putting the envelope into her pocket, Daisy said, 'Okay, what about the fare?'

'Forget it, Daisy, look up Zentek Aviation for me, see you later.'

Daisy got out and watched the taxi go the few yards to the house and stop outside the garage, behind the green BMW. It was almost eight forty-five – they had made good time, a fifteen-minute walk would see her to the office before nine.

Being by nature and profession an inquiring person, some might even go so far as to call her downright nosey, she loitered the few moments it took for the door to open in order to get sight of Mary's potential beau.

Looking at her watch, she saw it was seconds to eight forty-five when the door opened and a smiling man stepped out. His slight stoop and greying hair gave him an academic look. He wore a good suit, easily. Daisy knew the difference between Next and Savile Row. She approved; all in all an attractive fellow, good luck Mary. Turning away she started to walk towards the New Bond Street exit but only managed a few steps when she was aware of a great roaring in her ears and felt the air being sucked out of her lungs as a mighty force lifted her violently off her feet and threw her face down on the cobbles.

CHAPTER 2

Daisy's ears roared. Acrid air burnt her throat and lungs as she gasped for breath. There was an eerie silence. She coughed, but there was no sound. She was deaf. Managing to lift herself on hands and knees, she continued coughing and wheezing, her mind in turmoil. *God,* she was thinking, *what was that?* Her face felt wet. Drops of blood splashed the cobbles. Probing her face gently with her fingers she found a deep gash on her forehead which was wet with blood. Wiping her hand on her jacket she checked her ears; no blood, nothing ruptured then. She pinched her nose and blew to clear her ears. The roaring eased but she was still deaf.

Looking up the mews, she said aloud, 'My god, that was an explosion!' Flames and black smoke formed a chimney in front of the taxi. The green shutters were gone. She pressed the sleeve of her jacket hard onto on the gash on her forehead before gingerly getting to her feet. She knew the drill, no sudden moves. She remained perfectly still and waited for her head to get off the waltzer before attempting to walk.

Daisy had seen her share of bombs during her service in Northern Ireland and knew full well their lethal effect when the explosion propelled shards of metal and glass in every direction. Anyone close to it suffered horrendous injuries and Mary was bloody well right on top of it. As she started to stagger towards the taxi the words of Macintosh, a veteran at bomb disposal, came to mind: *Don't play the hero girl and rush to the scene, that's what they want isn't it? They often leave a second bomb, or in the case of a car bomb there's the fuel tank to think about, it doesn't always go up immediately, not until the fire reaches the fuel lines, you're not going to help anyone if you catch it.'*

Putting the thought out of her mind, she staggered to the taxi. The windscreen and all the windows were blown out. Mary was slumped forward in her seat, covered in fragments of glass, her arms hanging by her sides, the seat belt supporting her weight. Her eyes were open, staring, her face a mass of blood. There were no signs of life. She franticly pulled at the door handle. It was jammed. Panic must have given her extra strength, for after using a two-handed pull and straining every muscle in her body it burst open. She found the carotid artery in Mary's neck and to her relief found a faint pulse. She was alive, but for how long?

The BMW's entire roof and rear window section had been torn off, leaving only jagged pillars. The upholstery – burning fiercely – was producing a gagging stench. As the heat seared her face, she saw the boot and lower part of the car was still intact. If the fuel tank had already blown the entire car would have been engulfed. She knew it was only a matter of seconds before the fuel lines ruptured and the tank would become a fire-bomb. *That would surely finish Mary, not to mention yours truly if you hang around,* she thought. Being well aware that if Mary had internal injuries, moving her could prove fatal but leaving her there was not an option. She had to get her out of that seat and quick.

Leaning over Mary she found the seat belt fastener and released it. Then getting a firm grip around her thighs she lifted her legs and swung her bodily around until she faced the door. Mary never uttered a whimper as she got her into a semblance of a fireman's lift and eased her clear. She was only able to stumble a few yards when a blast of scorching air hit her as the BMW was engulfed in flames. Ignoring the searing heat on her back she staggered a few more yards to get clear before dropping to her knees and easing Mary off her shoulder as gently as she could.

Mary began moaning and trying to move as Daisy got to her feet. Now, she could hear perfectly, the second explosion must have unblocked her ears. She heard sirens; they were close. Pulling off her jacket she made a pillow and was about to put it under Mary's head when her eyes opened and she struggled to move. Gently lifting her head, she slid the jacket in place, saying, 'Try not to move, Mary, help is on its way.'

Mary coughed, her chest heaving as she fought for breath and gasped, 'Daisy, the green car, there was a flash... Jesus, Daisy, you look a mess.'

Daisy's heart sank when she saw a circle of blood spreading on Mary's shirt. *Oh God,* she was thinking, *I must stop her moving.* Holding her firmly by the shoulders she said, 'I'm okay Mary, there was an explosion, now try not to move.'

Mary, her eyes wild, whispered, 'Daisy I can't feel anything, I'm cold. God, I think I'm done for.'

Still holding her, Daisy said, 'Don't try to talk, Mary, they'll be here in moment.' The sirens were closer.

Mary persisted. 'Daisy, listen, you must listen. You must meet Harry, you can trust Harry, tell him, I heard his voice, he's alive... Delia, Delia...'

'Who's alive, Mary?' She put her face close to hear Mary's last whisper; when she looked the green eyes had closed. She felt her neck, there was still a pulse. An ambulance, siren screaming, blue light flashing, screeched to a halt beside her.

Kaminski found a coffee shop a short distance from the mews and took a seat at an outside table. The waitress was about to make her sales pitch from an enormous menu, when she was cut short by Kaminski's look. 'Just an espresso and an ash tray please.'

After scribbling on her pad, the waitress hurried away.

Kaminski looked at her watch. It was 08.43, only two minutes to go. Then she would find out if Kramer was as skilful as he claimed.

The waitress reappeared with her coffee at the exact moment the bomb went off. Not spectacular as explosions go, just a loud crack followed by a chimney of black smoke shooting into the sky.

'Bloody 'ell, what's that?' The waitress turned quickly to look at the smoke, forgetting her tray from which the coffee and ashtray slid and crashed to the ground.

Giving the startled girl her look, Kaminski said, 'I wonder. Probably just a gas leak, some people have no sense of smell, now will you get me an espresso and an ashtray?'

The waitress, still shaken, retrieved the ashtray and put it on the table before hurrying inside.

Kaminski lit a Marlborough and looked at her watch again. Impeccable timing, maybe the old ways were the best after all. She speed-dialled a number on her mobile; two rings and it was answered.

'Yes?'

'The package has been delivered.'

'Good.' The line was cut.

CHAPTER 3

Within minutes the mews was full of emergency services vehicles. The BMW was covered in foam. Mary was on a stretcher surrounded by paramedics.

Daisy, walking wounded, was seated in an ambulance, her cuts and bruises being attended to by a paramedic. After cleaning and dressing her wound he checked her for broken bones, listened to her heart and lungs and tested her blood pressure. Then after shining a light into her eyes he said, 'You're the lucky one. Nothing serious, but you've taken a bad knock, that cut will need stitching and you'll need to be checked for concussion at the hospital.'

'I'll live then,' she said, and tried to look out the window, but her view was blocked by another ambulance. Turning to the medic she said, 'The taxi driver is my friend, will she make it?'

As he swabbed her forehead with an antiseptic wipe the medic said, 'She's alive but only just. Bad internal bleeding, they're trying to stabilise her before moving her.'

Daisy felt her stomach knot as she remembered the spread of blood on Mary's shirt. God knows how much damage she'd done pulling her out of the taxi, but at least now she had a slim chance, she'd be surely dead otherwise.

'Hold your head still a mo,' the medic said, as he inspected his work. Satisfied, he said, 'That'll do you for now. Here, take a look,' holding up a small mirror.

Taking the mirror, she saw, other than the dressing on her forehead, her numerous scratches, now cleaned up and dabbed with some yellow stuff. She looked okay.

Although feeling far from cheerful she smiled, saying, 'Thanks, good job.' Returning the mirror, she asked, 'Do you know if the Arab gentleman is alive?'

The medic, his face grim, shook his head. 'An Arab, was he? His face was a proper mess. He was dead when we arrived, took the full blast, but you're okay to move, we'd better get you to A&E.'

'Thanks, but I feel okay,' she said, standing up. 'I'll wait outside for my friend.'

Stepping out of the ambulance before the medic could respond, she stood by the door watching the professionals at work. Each following a specific and well-ordered procedure. Mr Abdullah's body was covered by a forensic sheet. The area around the BMW, the taxi, and up to the place where she and Mary were found was cordoned off by blue and white tape. Two fire appliances were already leaving the mews, their work done. A smaller emergency control vehicle stood by for the remaining specialists. Two police minibuses, the uniforms still inside, were awaiting orders. A second ambulance was waiting. Mary was still surrounded by medics; a drip had been attached to her arm and an oxygen mask covered her face.

Standing by the ambulance with her clothing little more than bloodied rags, she received some curious looks before a serious-faced WPC hurried over.

'You must stay in the ambulance, miss,' she said.

'I need some air. Who's the senior officer here?' Her steady look and abrupt manner achieved the desired response.

'Detective Chief Inspector Sandys,' the WPC said, pointing. 'Over there in the grey suit.'

DCI Sandys was not a familiar face to Daisy.

Taking her arm, the WPC said, 'As you can see, miss, everyone is occupied, now will please you go back into the ambulance?'

With a raise of her eyebrows Daisy responded, 'Only a DCI. I would have thought a major incident like this would bring one of the big fish down from their ivory tower.'

Serious Face beckoned another WPC, who strode over. Seeing she was outnumbered Daisy was about to return to the ambulance when a black Jaguar appeared and stopped next to the blue and white tape. She recognised the stocky figure of the man who got out and stood surveying the scene, as a former colleague, one Commander J.J. Farmer, the head of the SO15 Counter-Terrorism Squad.

To the WPC blocking her retreat Daisy said, 'Be a dear, Officer, and ask Commander Farmer to come over, tell him it's Daisy.'

'Daisy who?'

'Don't worry about that,' she said. 'The commander only knows one Daisy, I'll wait in the office.'

When she climbed back into the ambulance the paramedic had gone. In less than a minute the WPC returned and took the seat opposite her.

'The commander is being briefed, he sends his greetings and asked me to tell you he'll be over in a few minutes.'

Smiling, Daisy said, 'Did he tell you to guard me with your life?'

Her stern look softening, the WPC said, 'He said nothing of the sort. I'm to look after you. Is there anything you need?'

'Thanks, there is. My jacket and briefcase are somewhere – the jacket's buggered, but if you can find my case, brown leather, I'd appreciate it.'

'I'll go look, don't go away,' the WPC said, and with a hint of a smile, she was gone.

After a few minutes the WPC was back, her serious look now replaced with a friendly smile as she put the jacket and briefcase on the seat beside her. 'Here you are, miss. The commander won't be long, is there anything else you need?'

Daisy smiled, saying, 'Thanks a lot. I'm okay. I'm sure you have things to do so I promise to sit quietly until he comes.'

The WPC hesitated for a moment, then said, 'If you're sure,' and climbed out.

Daisy took her mobile from the jacket pocket and checked it. Surprisingly it was still working. She was about to call her office when the ambulance shook and Commander Jack Farmer climbed in and took the seat opposite.

Dressed in a fine houndstooth-patterned suit in his favourite brown – one of his little vanities – he once told her he liked to stand out among his colleagues in their sea of blue. A Cornishman, in his mid-fifties, Farmer was a late starter when he joined the police in 1988. After serving fourteen years in the RN, he retired with the rank of chief petty officer and joined the police. He not only had a natural ability for the work but as a result of his former career, had gained an invaluable insight into dealing with, or as some disgruntled rivals might say, manipulating, the officer class. This ensured him accelerated promotion and an MBE when he became commander. Standing at five eight, just above the regulation height, he weighed 190 pounds with not an ounce of fat. His square features and shrewd grey eyes were topped by a head of steel-grey hair, now receding. Farmer with his weather-beaten appearance – thanks to his passion for sailing – looked more like his namesake than a policeman. This belied the fact that he was one tough and successful cop.

Looking her over, he growled, 'Jesus! Daisy, look at the state of you, what in hell are you doing here?'

Daisy raised her hands, saying, 'For once Jack, I'm just an innocent bystander, but thanks for your concern about my health. I've been checked over by the medic and other than the wreck you see I'm basically undamaged.'

Farmer snorted. 'You were never innocent, Daisy, and always the one to stick your neck out. What can you tell me?'

Daisy related the events of the past hour, starting with the puncture.

Farmer, who had listened without interruption until she had got to her arrival in the mews, raised a hand. 'So, the dead man lives in that house and the lady on the stretcher is one Mary Grey, a taxi driver. You're saying she collects him every weekday morning at 08.45 sharp and takes him somewhere, anything else?'

Daisy nodded. 'Yes, Mary told me he was nervous about something and would never open his door until she arrives.'

Farmer, shifting himself in his seat, said, 'Okay, she stops and lets you out, then what?'

'We got here just before 08.45. After letting me out, she parked outside the garage, behind the green BMW.'

Farmer nodded. 'Green you say, good, at least we have the colour, we'll get the rest from the chassis numbers, what then?'

'I waited until the client appeared.'

'Why?'

Shrugging, Daisy said, 'You know me, Jack. Mary told me she thought he fancied her, I wanted to take a look at him.'

Farmer grunted. 'You were always the nosey one. I hope you got a good look at him; we'll need to ID him.'

'I did. He opened the door just seconds before 08.45. I checked my watch.'

'Great punctuality but lousy security. Then what?'

'I watched him. He was smiling, obviously happy to see Mary. You've never met Mary, Jack, she's a real stunner.'

'Great,' Farmer said. 'If she lives through this, we can make up a threesome. What happened next?'

'Funny, Jack.' Daisy wasn't smiling.

Farmer leaned forward, and with his voice softening said, 'A joke, Daisy, sometimes helps ease the tension in these situations.'

'I must remember that.' Still stone-faced, she continued. 'The

21

client opened the taxi door, and I walked, only a few steps and bang. I hit the cobbles with my face as you can see.'

'The DCI told me you were both found a few yards from the taxi, how did she get there?'

Daisy nodded. 'Remember Northern Ireland, Jack? It's not my first car bomb. I wasn't sure if the BMW's petrol tank had blown. Mary was still in her seat, completely out of it, facing the burning car. If it went up, she'd be finished for sure.'

'You got her out?'

'Yes, I got the driver's door open; she was alive then.'

Farmer, shaking his head, said, 'So, you got her out, it would have been better if you left it to the experts.'

'That's what the book says, Jack. If I had left her, she'd be dead for sure. I'd only carried her a few yards when the tank exploded.'

'And you hit the cobbles for the second time.'

'Not quite,' Daisy said. 'I managed a few more yards to get away from the heat. 'Shortly after, the cavalry arrived and you know the rest.'

Daisy neglected to mention Mary's brief recovery and her words, after all they were private, between friends, nothing to do with the bomb. *Or were they?* she wondered.

Farmer pointed a finger. 'That was a bloody dangerous thing to do, don't you ever learn?'

Daisy knew Farmer's gruff manner was his way of concealing his emotions. Behind this façade he was at heart a kindly man, although he often put the fear of God into his subordinates, every one of them would follow him through hell-fire.

Daisy asked, 'Was it worth it, Jack, is Mary still alive?'

'I'll go and get an update,' he said. The ambulance shook again as Farmer climbed out and went over to the medics.

Daisy followed. This time the WPC standing by the ambulance

made no effort to stop her. Farmer and the lead medic were talking. Daisy didn't need an update, when she saw the sheet had been pulled over Mary's face. The drip bottle gone.

Farmer saw her, put his arm on her shoulder and gently guided her back into the ambulance. 'Sorry, Daisy, she's gone. They did their best, but they reckon she copped a piece of shrapnel in the chest. They couldn't stop the bleeding.'

Daisy nodded dumbly and climbed back into her seat.

Neither spoke for a moment before Farmer dug into his pocket and found a silver flask. 'You need a snifter. Here, take a drop of this. It's Glenmorangie.'

Shaking her head, she said, 'Thanks for the thought, Jack, but I'm not in shock, you know I've seen worse than this.' She took a slug anyway.

'Look, Daisy you'd better get yourself off to the A&E and have yourself stitched up and checked out.'

'No need to tie up an ambulance, a car will do fine,' she said.

Farmer grunted, 'I'll sort it,' and climbed out.

Alone in her seat Daisy tried to gather her thoughts. Farmer was gone and there was no longer any need for bravado. She was aware of the flask in her hand beginning to clank against the metal side of her seat as she shuddered uncontrollably. Her feet felt like ice. Forcing the flask to her lips she took another long slug, burning her throat, already seared from the toxic smoke, but it worked and the shuddering stopped. She'd seen car bombs before, but never so close, or so personal.

Daisy shook her head and stood up, 'No time for feeling sorry for yourself, girl, you're alive with things to do, leave the grief for later,' and climbed out of the ambulance to see Farmer returning with the DCI.

Daisy gave him the once-over. He was a head taller than Farmer, with a complexion which never saw much sun, but he moved easily like an athlete and when his calm grey eyes appraised her, she knew she was being catalogued for future reference. Without doubt, an astute fellow. He wouldn't be working for Farmer if he was anything less than the best. She returned his look with equal candour.

'Len, this is Daisy Clowser, a former colleague. I may have spoken of her.' Pointing to the stretcher he said, 'The dead woman is her friend, name of Mary Grey. Daisy, this my best man, DCI Len Sandys.'

Sandys held out his hand. 'The commander has mentioned you one, or twenty times, Miss Clowser, told us how big your boots were. I would have preferred to meet you under better circumstances. I'm sorry you've lost a friend.'

Taking the offered hand – which was dry, with a strong grip – Daisy said, 'So am I, Chief Inspector.' Then turning to Farmer, she said, 'My boots, Jack, what did you say about my boots?'

Farmer snorted. 'Not a bloody thing. Len, Daisy needs treatment for her face and a general check over, her head hit the cobbles. She needs a car and a driver.'

'No problem. If you feel up to it, Miss Clowser, WPC Denton can take you,' pointing to the WPC who was with her in the ambulance.

'Forget the miss, Chief Inspector, I'm Daisy. I'll be okay. Can we get on with it, Commander?'

'I'm done, Daisy,' Farmer said. 'You go and get yourself fixed up.'

'Before I go, Jack, a question for the chief inspector. Who exactly was Mr Abdullah? This doesn't look like any random car bomb to me. More like a targeted hit – 08.45 he steps out of his house as usual and at precisely the same time the bomb goes off. That's surely no coincidence now, is it?'

Sandys looked at Farmer questioningly.

Farmer nodded. 'Tell her what you know, Len.'

'I take your point, Daisy, it looks like he was the intended victim.

His passport was in his pocket. Saudi Diplomatic in the name of Prince Rahman ibn Abdullah. Occupation, academic.'

Farmer groaned. 'Jesus, a bloody prince, that's all we need. Show Daisy the passport, she saw his face.'

Sandys went over to one of the forensic team and returned with the passport in an evidence bag. Removing it, he opened it on the photo page.

Daisy took a long look at the face which was frontal and serious looking. Remembering the smiling man greeting Mary, her eyes welled as she said, 'Younger looking, but that's the man I saw.'

'That's good enough for now,' Farmer said. 'We can verify his ID with fingerprints and DNA if necessary.'

'What about Mary Grey's next of kin?' Sandys said. 'We'll need to inform them before the press gets hold of this.'

'Do you know them, Daisy?' asked Farmer.

Shaking her head, she replied, 'No Jack, she lived alone. I've met a few of her friends, but she never mentioned her parents or any relatives I can think of. I'm sure she had someone living in Spain, she went there a lot.'

'Likely the taxi company knows something; we'll get someone on it.' Farmer was interrupted, as his mobile shrilled like an old police car bell. Looking at the screen he pulled a face and said, 'I'll take this in my car, don't go away.'

Daisy saw two medics were about to move Mary's stretcher to the waiting ambulance and on impulse hurried over, saying, 'Please wait.'

The medics paused, giving her a strange look before catching Sandys' eye, who nodded his approval. They stood back as she knelt beside the stretcher, gently pulling back the sheet. Except for a few scratches, which had been cleaned up and were almost invisible, Mary could have been sleeping; her face relaxed, her beautiful green eyes closed forever.

Daisy looked at her friend for a long moment and besides tears, a fury welled up within her and she swore to herself, whatever it took or cost she would not stop until she settled accounts for Mary. Gently placing the sheet back, she got to her feet just as Farmer was returning.

'That's enough for now, Daisy. WPC Denton will take you to the Bayswater Clinic. It's the nearest and there's no waiting. Get yourself patched up, you can make a full statement later.'

'Bayswater!' Daisy asked. 'What's wrong with St Thomas's?'

'The press will expect that,' Farmer said. 'They'll be waiting there. We want to keep this under wraps until the Foreign Office decide what to do about Prince Abdullah.'

CHAPTER 4

They watched the car leave the mews before Sandys said, 'You're not thinking she might be involved in any of this, Guv?'

'Daisy? Not likely, she's as straight as they come. But she was at the scene and we have to verify her story. She told me her car had a puncture and the taxi driver was a friend and neighbour, who gave her a lift as far as the mews.'

Taking out his notebook and pencil Sandys said, 'You have her address? I'll have a DC go and look at the car.'

Farmer nodded. 'Better have a mechanic look at it as well. She lives in Portchester Mansions, Lancaster Gate. Her car is in the car park, it's a Porsche.'

Looking thoughtful Sandys said, 'That's an expensive place to live, and she drives a Porsche. A rich lady, is she?'

Farmer smiled. 'Rich, that she is, Len. Right now, she's the managing partner in Casey Clay Clowser, a family firm that's been associated with HMG for over a hundred years. They own a building in St. James Street that's worth millions. Before that she was with SO12 as you know.'

Scribbling in his notebook Sandys asked, 'Then why the clinic?'

'Daisy asked the same question. I told her she'll be treated quickly and be away from the press for a while.'

Sandys snapped his notebook closed before asking, 'Was that the real reason?'

Shaking his head Farmer said, 'No, I've just taken a call from Mr Peter Isaacs. Security Advisor to the PM is only one of the hats he wears, he has a number of others and he's not a man to cross. I told him she was at the scene. He knows her and wants to talk to her. It was he who suggested, in fact insisted, she go to the clinic.'

They walked over to where Prince Abdullah's body lay. Dr Simpson, the police surgeon, was covering him up, saw Farmer and stopped. Simpson, an old hand who had seen a few bomb victims in his time, explained, 'This poor fellow was hit in the chest; one piece went straight into the heart, he wouldn't have felt a thing. The lady had the same type of wounds. The bastards who planted this bomb meant to kill people, Commander. It was probably packed with nails. I've seen the like before.'

'Any reason why we can't move him?' Farmer asked. 'The sooner we get any debris out of him the better, every piece has to be looked at by forensics.'

Snapping off his surgical gloves the doctor said, 'There's nothing more we can do here. I'll have him out of here right away, you'll have my report in a few hours.'

As they spoke the BMW was being lifted on to a low loader. A second truck was waiting to remove the taxi which was now covered in white plastic sheeting. A forensic team of two men and two women, wearing white hooded overalls, were waiting to begin their search. PCs were knocking on doors. Curious onlookers were being held back at each end of the mews.

Farmer, turning from the scene to Sandys, asked, 'Any witnesses other than Daisy?'

Sandys, pointing up the mews, said, 'Yes. Two traffic wardens were entering the mews from the Adams Row end when the bomb went off. They were blown off their feet, but no serious injuries, just a little shocked. They were taken to St. Thomas.'

Farmer looked up and down the mews before saying, 'They'd have used a switch-car, to save the space, bring the BMW in at the last minute, too risky to leave a primed bomb overnight.'

Sandys nodded his agreement. 'We'll get statements from everyone living in the mews and the traffic wardens. Someone may have noticed a car parked there all night.'

Farmer, pointing to a CCTV camera at the far entrance to the mews, said, 'Better have that camera checked, also any CCTV in the adjacent streets, we might see a face.'

'We're already on it, Guv,' Sandys said. 'I'm going to take a look inside the victim's house. No need for keys, the door's been blown off its hinges.'

Looking at the shattered doorway Farmer said, 'Good, look for any personal contacts, we need to inform his family and Mary Grey's if she has any. Maybe the taxi company will have a name.'

'Guv, you said Mary Grey was a neighbour of Daisy's, in Portchester Mansions.'

'That's what she said.'

'An expensive place for a taxi driver to live, don't you think?'

WPC Denton drove the unmarked car back along the same route Mary had taken less than an hour ago. Daisy, in the seat beside her, wondered why she was being taken to the Bayswater Clinic. The reasons Farmer gave were plausible enough, maybe he was telling the truth, she would soon find out.

Turning to her driver she said, 'What's your name, Officer?'

Keeping her eyes on the road she replied, 'WPC 682 Denton, miss.'

Smiling, Daisy said, 'I know that already, I mean, your first name?'

'Sally, miss.'

'Forget the miss, Sally, my name is Daisy and I was once a WPC just like you. Have you been to the Bayswater Clinic before?'

Shaking her head, Sally said, 'Never heard of it before Commander Farmer gave me the address.'

'Did he tell you to wait?'

'No miss – sorry, Daisy – he said you'd be taken care of.'

Daisy knew all about the Bayswater Clinic. Situated on three floors with a basement car park, the building had an Indian restaurant on the ground floor and a private passenger lift to the upper floors, where there was a private hospital, complete with a state-of-the-art operating theatre to be used by medical specialists who were drafted in as and when required. There were also secure suites of rooms for the patients' – be they willing or unwilling – rest and recuperation. There were no name plates to excite the curious and the restaurant besides providing the perfect cover, often sent up delicious meals without knowing the recipients were sometimes prisoners of the State. Patients – as they were always called – were delivered via the car lift and if they were lucky left the same way on their two feet.

Sally turned into Queensway, passed Whiteleys shopping centre and turned into a side street. They were expected. Halfway up the street a smiling nurse accompanied by a burly porter in a bulging white jacket were standing by an open car lift. They waved them in.

Daisy gripped Sally's arm, saying, 'You said you didn't know this place.'

'I don't,' Sally said. 'Commander Farmer said they'd be waiting; they must have the car number.'

Daisy felt a sudden urge to get out and run, but resisted it, after all she was the innocent party and there would definitely be no four-hour waiting time.

The street doors closed automatically and the lift descended into the car park which was surprisingly spacious, with room for perhaps twenty cars. The porter stood in front of the car ensuring it stayed in the lift.

The cheerful nurse helped her out and after giving her the once-over said, 'Why, it's Miss Clowser, isn't it? How nice. Are we in trouble again? We'll soon have you fixed up.'

Daisy smiled at the nurse's enthusiasm. 'Thank you for asking, Mrs Hollis, but for once I'm just an innocent bystander who needs some minor repairs.'

Mrs Hollis's smile broadened. 'Of course you are, Miss Clowser, all our patients are innocent.' Then, turning to Sally, who was still in the car, she said, 'We'll take good care of Miss Clowser, Officer, there's no need for you to wait, we'll contact Commander Farmer when she's ready to go home.'

Sally was about to protest when the porter closed the doors and the lift ascended.

Mrs Hollis guided Daisy to the only other exit to the car park, a passenger lift which required a card swipe to open the doors. Fast and silent, it whisked them to the clinic which occupied the entire second floor.

Daisy, clutching her briefcase and blood-stained jacket, was led to what she knew from past experience was the reception to the operating theatre. It was bare of furniture except for a trolley-bed with a table beside it and a single chair. The wall clock told her it was 9.40. *Oh my god* – her stomach knotting at the thought – less than an hour ago she was chatting to Mary in the taxi.

'Let me take your things, dear.'

Slipping her mobile from the jacket pocket, she handed over her briefcase and jacket, saying, 'Chuck the jacket, there's nothing in the pockets.'

'It might clean up,' the nurse said after inspecting the jacket like it was some vital piece of evidence.

Daisy grimaced. 'Not in a million years. Anyway I don't need any reminders of this horror.'

'As you wish, dear,' she said. 'I'm sure we can find you something to go home in.' Putting them on the table she continued, 'And the mobile, they're not allowed in this area, they upset the equipment.'

Equipment my foot. No outside calls, you mean, Daisy was thinking, as she handed it over.

Putting the mobile in her pocket, Mrs Hollis pointed to the chair, saying, 'Now sit down and let's see what the damage is.'

Daisy tried not to wince as Mrs Hollis carefully removed the dressing from her forehead and inspected the wound.

'That's a nasty deep gash, my dear, needs stitches, but don't worry about a scar, our Doctor Webber is a real artist, after a few weeks you won't see a mark.' Giving Daisy's blood-stained jeans and shirt a critical look, she shook her head. 'We can't have you going into theatre in those. Wait a moment,' she said and left the room; returning in less than a minute carrying a folded bundle, which she handed to Daisy. 'Here you are, dear,' she said cheerfully. 'Change into these for the theatre, you can leave your underwear on. Once you've changed sit on the bed. I'll be back in a mo.' Taking Daisy's belongings, she left.

Daisy found the bundle contained a hospital gown, cotton socks and an elasticated cotton hat. 'All this for a few bloody stitches,' she grumbled to herself as she undressed and manipulated herself into the gown, which tied at the back, put on the socks and hat, then sat on the bed and waited.

Mrs Hollis returned with a tray of medical supplies, which she put on the table, then after adjusting the head-rest, she helped Daisy onto the bed, settled her head on the pillow and began busying herself with cotton wool and alcohol cleaning up the various scratches before dabbing them with stinging iodine.

Daisy's eyes watered but she resisted a yelp; it wouldn't do to show any kind of weakness.

'The wasn't so bad now was it?' Mrs Hollis scrutinised her work. Satisfied, she released the brake on the bed and pushed it through a pair of double doors into the theatre.

The room was glaringly bright and had a strong smell of antiseptic. A daylight lighting unit hung from the centre of the room under which Mrs Hollis manoeuvred the bed. A trolley load of electronic equipment, complete with screens and printers stood to one side. A second trolley full of medical supplies waited at the end of the bed.

'I'll tell Doctor we're ready for him,' she said and left the room.

Within minutes Doctor Webber arrived and carefully scrubbed up at the sink before looking her over. He was a big man, his white coat tight on his broad shoulders, but his hands were gentle as he moved her head for a better view. 'Been in the wars, have we?' He pressed his fingers on her temple. 'Not too bad though, we'll soon have you right as rain.'

Daisy, normally the first with idle chat, was suddenly at a loss for words and just watched as he went back to the sink and scrubbed up again before snapping on surgical gloves. She was thinking, what is it about hospitals and doctors that strikes one dumb? Or was it this particular hospital and the memories of her last visit?

She watched Mrs Hollis preparing a tray of instruments, including two syringes. She hated injections, particularly to the head. They were the worst, but as the alternative was pain, she must remain stoic. Stiff upper lip and all that rubbish, who was she fooling?

When Mrs Hollis's tray was ready, she donned a surgical mask and nodded to the doctor, whose face was now also hidden behind a mask. Taking a syringe, he tapped the needle several times. Satisfied, he smiled down at Daisy and said in a kindly voice, 'Just a few stitches, Miss Clowser, but we mustn't have any pain now must we? A couple of pricks and you won't feel a thing. The first injection is an antibiotic as a precaution, you never know what you picked up from the street, then a painkiller for the head.' He nodded to Mrs Hollis, who took Daisy's arm and rubbed in something wet.

Daisy was aware of Doctor Webber, still with his cheerful banter taking her arm and felt the prick of the needle, not so bad really. She then felt a wonderful calmness sweep over her. Doctor Webber was saying something, but his words drifted away.

CHAPTER 5

Daisy felt she was floating, her body totally relaxed, wiped clean of tension, without even a twinge of pain. A soothing friendly voice was talking to her. Somehow, she felt she must please her new friend or this wonderful feeling would be lost. She must not lose her new friend. It was simple really, just to chat, to tell him all about yourself and your recent activities.

'Tell me about your friends. You must have a lot of friends, Daisy, a good-looking girl like you?'

Eager to please, she chatted away about her friends, babbling away about her little irritations with one or two, particularly Walker and his aversion to marriage.

'And Prince Abdullah,' the voice gently interrupted. 'Did you know him before today, was he one of your friends? A special friend perhaps.'

She spoke of Mary's conversation in the taxi; even Mary did not know her client was a prince.

'Your puncture, Daisy, tell me about your puncture.'

There was nothing she could say about the puncture; it was just a puncture.

'Now tell me about the green BMW, Daisy. Did you know it would be there, waiting to explode? Did you go with Mary, your friend, knowing she would need your help? That would be a courageous thing to do.'

She was sorry to be so unhelpful but she knew nothing about the BMW.

'Daisy, you've been extremely helpful. One last question, were you given anything to trigger the bomb, your mobile phone perhaps? That would be able to act as a trigger now wouldn't it?'

She couldn't tell him anything about a trigger, she was sorry but she knew nothing.

'Thank you, Daisy, you should have a little sleep now.'

She knew, as he was talking, she was drifting away from her new friend. His words became gibberish as she desperately tried to hold on to that wonderful moment, but some inexplicable force was pulling her away.

South East Spain

In the shaded terrace of the La Gamba restaurant, the ceiling fans were spinning valiantly to provide some relief from the scorching sun. Veleta was eating his lunch, the Catalan dish of calamar a la planxa with black rice and a side salad, when Garcia the restaurant manager hurried to his table.

'Señor Veleta, there's is a call from London for you, a man, he says it's urgent.'

Veleta, who did not like to be interrupted during his meal, asked, 'Did he give a name?'

'He said to tell you it's Frank, señor.'

'I'll take it in your office, can you keep this warm for me? I'll be as quick as I can.'

Garcia's office was on the first floor of La Gamba, an up-market eatery, one of Veleta's many businesses in Spain.

Seating himself in Garcia's leather chair Veleta lifted the receiver. 'Veleta?'

'It's Frank.' The accent was London.

'Frank, can I call you back? I'm eating my lunch.'

'I'm sorry Harry, it can't wait, it's about Mary.'

'What about Mary?' Veleta's voice had dropped to a whisper.

'The police have been here; she's been in an accident.'

'What kind of accident?'

'She was waiting for a client when a car blew up beside her.'

'What hospital is she in?'

The phone went silent for a moment. 'Hello, Frank are you there?'

'Yes, I'm here. Look Harry, I'm sorry but there's no easy way to say this, the police told me Mary died at the scene.'

'You're sure of this?'

'I went to St Thomas's, they confirmed it, I'm sorry.'

Veleta, his face ashen, hung up and slumped back on the chair.

Frank heard the dial tone. *Jesus,* he thought. He was one of the few people alive who knew Mary Grey well enough to know who she was related to.

It was after four when Kaminski joined the shortest of four lines at the busy reception of St. Thomas's A&E. The waiting area was crowded with people of all shapes, sizes, and colours, some sitting patiently in the rows of chairs, talking to friends or reading, or plugged in to some portable device. Others just standing or talking on mobiles or sipping beverages from styrene cups. A display on one wall informed them the average waiting was three hours and twenty minutes. White coats, male and female paraded in and out at regular intervals. They all had that busy look.

Kaminski was third in line and uneasy when she saw two uniformed cops, a PC and WPC standing by the doorway. Cops always gave her the same uneasy feeling. *Can't be anything to do with me,* she was thinking. *Probably here to keep order,* although it was early, for troublesome drunks or druggies.

The TV news reporting on the bomb had been vague. Three casualties, believed to be one man and two women. The man and one of the women had died as a result of their injuries. The third casualty, who had been a passenger in the taxi, was taken to St. Thomas's A&E. She stood patiently in line for a further ten minutes before being spoken to.

'How can I help, dear?' The badge on her uniform gave her name and title. Hortense – Admittance Nurse.

Producing what she thought would be a suitably anxious look Kaminski said, 'I hope so, I'm worried about my cousin, we were supposed to meet for lunch and she didn't turn up, which is unlike her. She hasn't called and I can't contact her on her mobile. I saw on the TV, there was an explosion in the West End this morning and there were three causalities. I'm sure she was in the area about the time of the explosion, can you check her name for me?'

'Let me see.' Hortense checked her screen. 'What's her name?'

'Schmidt, Helen.' Kaminski spelt it. Hortense checked a list.

'No dear, we don't have a Schmidt registered in today's input.'

'What about the people injured in the explosion?'

'Ah, the explosion.' Nurse Hortense's voice lost its sharpness. 'I'm sorry dear, but the two people, a man and a woman, were DOA. They went straight to the mortuary.'

'Do you have their names?' Kaminski adopted an equally soft tone.

Nurse Hortense shook her head. 'Sorry, they're not on my system.'

'What about the third casualty, could she have been my cousin?'

'What third casualty?' Nurse Hortense's voice rose a pitch. 'There was no third casualty.'

'According to the six o'clock news there were three casualties.'

'You can't rely on the news; I've been here all day and no one has been admitted from that incident.'

'The dead woman might be my cousin, who should I talk to?'

'You'll have to talk to the police, it's up to them. I should speak to the constable over there.'

The last thing Kaminski wanted was to be noticed by the police. Shaking her head, she said, 'Thanks, I'll leave it until tomorrow,' and walked towards an exit in the opposite direction.

Bloody reporters, Hortense thought.

Daisy awoke feeling thoroughly relaxed and refreshed. Looking around, she saw she was in a tastefully decorated room and in a proper bed. She lay still, trying to collect her thoughts. She clearly remembered Doctor Webber leaning over her, the prick of the needle and then she was dreaming. She tried to recall the content of the dream but it was already gone. The more she tried the less she could recall, *But that's the way they do things here, isn't it?* she was thinking. Okay they might patch up your wounds, remove the odd bullet, but the real purpose of this state-of-the-art medical centre is to get answers, from reluctant citizens, and are they good at it, too right they are. They just shoot something into you, ask the questions and get all the answers. Well she hoped they were satisfied, the cheeky bastards, but she couldn't complain, she had used the facility on a number of occasions in the past and no doubt medical advances had made it even more efficient. Totally illegal of course, but where's the proof? She herself couldn't remember a thing.

A smiling Mrs Hollis came in carrying tea and biscuits on a silver tray. Putting the tray on the bedside table she said, 'Here you are my dear, you must be starving.'

Then helping her to an upright position, she fluffed her pillows and pulled a mobile tray across the bed to put the tray on.

Daisy took a sip, it was excellent tea, nothing but the best in this hospital. Her watch read 4.30. It must have definitely stopped this time; she couldn't have been out for seven hours.

'What time is it, Mrs Hollis?'

Looking at the watch pinned to her uniform Mrs Hollis said, 'Four thirty, my dear.'

'Blood hell!' Daisy said. 'You mean I've been out for seven hours?'

Mrs Hollis nodded. 'Doctor Webber believes in a minimum of seven hours' sleep after a head injury; it allows the brain time to settle back to normal.'

Daisy sniffed. 'To be washed, you mean.'

Mrs Hollis, a picture of innocence, raised an eyebrow. 'Whatever do you mean, dear?'

'Never mind, Mrs Hollis, where are my clothes?'

Mrs Hollis patted an invisible crease on the bed before replying. 'They were a mess, dear, we sent out for a new set in your size. Not McQueen I'm afraid, our budget doesn't run to that. Marks & Spencer.'

Mess my arse, Daisy was thinking. *Sent off to forensics for analysis, you mean.*

As she turned towards the door Mrs Hollis said, 'When you've finished your tea you can get dressed, your clothes are in the bathroom. You can take a shower if you wish. Press the bell when you're ready.'

'Ready for what?' Daisy asked.

'I'm sorry dear, I should have said; Mr Isaacs would like to talk to you.'

'Peter Isaacs is here?'

'Yes, he arrived half an hour ago. If you need anything press the buzzer.'

'Thanks, I'm sure I can manage. Where's my mobile and my case?'

'Mobiles are not allowed, dear; your briefcase is with your clothes in the bathroom.' Mrs Hollis beamed and left.

Daisy dunked a biscuit in the tea and tried to work things out as she ate the soggy mess. *Why the heavy hand?* she wondered. She was well known to Farmer and Isaacs, they should have given her the benefit of the doubt, but then what would she have done if the roles were reversed? Probably nothing different. If there was the slightest doubt, friendship did not enter into the equation. Trusting relationships have only led to the cock-ups of the past and she knew Peter Isaacs hated school ties.

Pushing the tray away she got out of bed. No wobbles or dizziness. *Great,* she thought, *get on with it, you'll soon find out what's what.*

She dressed in her new clothes, which fitted surprising well. Maybe she should give Marks & Spencer a look sometime, she thought as she checked her briefcase by turning the right-hand catch counter clockwise and saw the LED flashed green, indicating it had not been opened. The case had a mini-tape recorder, built in, with a miniature microphone concealed in the leather work on one side. Only a thorough examination would discover them. Turning the catch the opposite way set it to record. It was voice activated. She set it to record and pressed the buzzer for Mrs Hollis. She was ready to meet Peter Isaacs.

Mrs Hollis accompanied her as far as the lift which served the third floor only.

'Thank you for looking after me, Mrs Hollis.' She knew the nurse was never involved in nor indeed knew too much about the seedier side of the business. Mrs Hollis was a thorough professional. Her role never went beyond patching up the unfortunates who came her way and giving them succour, but she would have been well briefed on her clientele and anything she might see or hear in the course of treatment was to be reported and then forgotten.

'It was so nice to see you again, Miss Clowser, take care now.' She pressed the button and the lift ascended.

Inside the lift there was a convenient vanity mirror built into the panelling. Looking at herself Daisy saw, other than the plaster over the stitches, the other scratches were cleaned up and hardly noticeable. She also knew there was a camera behind the mirror and her photo file had just been updated.

On exiting the lift, she saw the floor layout had changed since her last visit. What used to have been an open-plan reception area was now an anonymous corridor with half a dozen doors off it, all of which were closed. She was surprised by the young man who was waiting for her. Fresh faced with a mop of auburn hair, his grey eyes were smiling as he proffered his hand. She normally found the Minders to be dour, unhappy souls.

'Angus, Miss Clowser, delighted to meet you.' With the exception of Sir or Ma'am for the chief, first names only were used on the third floor.

'And you, Angus,' taking his hand, which was a good hand, strong and dry.

'The chief is waiting in the conference room, I'll show you.'

Looking around, she said, 'You'll have to, this place has changed since my last visit.'

Angus, with an easy smile said, 'You know how it is these days, cutbacks everywhere, we have to share with another department who insists on privacy. New rules, visitors must be accompanied at all times.'

With a shrug she said, 'No problem, I know the drill, you're to be my shadow.'

'Something like that. Just forget I'm beside you, you'll soon get used to it, I'm ignored by everyone.'

She smiled. 'I'll find that hard to believe, Angus, you're cheerful and good looking, an unusual quality for this facility.'

'Thank you, Miss Clowser,' he said, blushing to the roots of his hair.

'You're welcome,' Daisy said, 'and forget the miss, Angus, it's Daisy, let's not break the first name rule and let's not keep Peter waiting.'

CHAPTER 6

The conference room was spacious, windowless and bug proof thanks to the inbuilt Faraday Cage system, whereby the walls, ceiling and floor were shielded with a lattice-work of fine wires which prevented any wireless transmission in or out. A long table, with six chairs on each side plus the chairman's position took up one end of the room. There was a desk at the other. The only other furniture was a glass-topped sideboard standing along one wall.

As they entered Peter Isaacs was seated at the desk, speaking into what she recognised as an office STE secure telephone. On seeing them enter, he said something too softly for them to hear, ended his call and stood up, advancing towards her, his hand outstretched.

'Daisy, how nice to see you. It's been far too long, how are you?' Holding on to her hand, he looked her over. 'Not too bad I hope.'

Daisy returned the inspection with a critical gaze. Peter Isaacs had aged little in the twelve years she had known him, a few more grey hairs in his straight jet-black hair which he wore perhaps a touch too long for a senior government official. Perhaps a little fuller in the face. It suited him, she thought, he always was too thin. His crooked hawkish nose which had been rearranged at some time in the past gave him what she had always considered a *piratical look*. All in all, an interesting character and still the snappy dresser, she saw. Today he wore a well-cut three-piece grey suit in a subtle bird's eye set off by powder blue shirt and a fine silk tie. Some might consider him a bit of a fop, but how appearances can be deceptive. His easy look missed nothing and his ability to think on his feet and go straight to the heart of a problem always kept him ahead in whatever game he was involved in. A fact she knew from experience when, but for his actions on that faithful night in Armagh she'd be dead.

Squeezing his hand, she replied, 'I'm fine now, Peter, a bit surprised to see you here though, I thought you were out of this kind of thing.'

Releasing her hand, he said, 'Oh, I am, well out of it. Like you, after the Good Friday agreement, I moved on. These days I'm a sort of general dogsbody trying to save the PM the embarrassment of finding out what the security people are up before the press does.'

'So, you spy on the spies, is that it?'

Isaacs shrugged. 'A bit more than that.'

Daisy laughed. 'Knowing you, Peter, a lot more. I would think by now, you are one of those powerful people who can click fingers and make things happen but officially doesn't exist.'

With his crooked smile Isaacs moved towards the table. 'I can certainly make things happen, Daisy, but as you know, finger clicking is not my style.'

Following him, Daisy said, 'Then, perhaps you can explain why I was brought here. I thought this place was solely reserved for serving officers of HMG and enemies of the realm. As far as I'm aware, I'm not in either category.'

Isaacs pulled the chairman's chair out. 'Of course, you're not, when I was told you were involved in this morning's incident and you had sustained some injuries, I thought it best to bring you here for speed and privacy.'

Meeting his gaze, Daisy said, 'I'm not involved in anything, Peter, as I'm sure whoever you use these days to interrogate the unconscious, will have confirmed by now.'

Isaacs feigned surprise. 'I have no idea what you're talking about,' he said, taking the chairman's position and indicating the chair on his right.

Pulling the chair out and putting her briefcase on the floor by her feet, she sat. 'Of course you don't, and I also suppose you run a dry ship here.'

Seeming eager to move on, he glanced at the wall clock and with a smile said, 'A drink? Of course, how remiss of me, I believe there's a bar of sorts. If memory serves you like your Scotch half and half?'

'Exactly,' she said. 'In a tall glass with no ice.'

Isaacs, turning to Angus, who had been standing by the door during this exchange, said, 'Do the honours, Angus, I'll take the same and have one yourself.'

Angus went to the sideboard and busied himself with bottles and glasses before putting the drinks on a silver tray and carrying it to the table. Then with a flourish he placed a silver mat and a whisky and water beside her, then one for Isaacs and himself before sitting opposite her.

'Thanks Angus,' she said, before raising her glass. 'Here's to crime.'

Isaacs nodded and raised his glass. 'And punishment.'

Angus followed suit nodding his head cheerfully.

Isaacs contemplated his glass for a moment before saying, 'I won't hide the fact, Daisy, this morning's business is a bit of worry. Death of a diplomat, a Saudi prince no less.'

Daisy took sip of her whiskey before replying. 'Saudi Arabia is awash with princes, Peter, many of whom use London as their summer playground and generally make a nuisance of themselves. They've even been known to kill each other.'

Isaacs nodded agreement. 'True, but we have been half expecting something like this.'

'How come?'

'GCHQ has intercepted up a number of signals. Chatter, I believe they call it, which indicates, one of Bin Laden's bankers is moving a large sum of money in Swiss francs to London for an operation.'

'You think this was it?' Daisy asked.

'It's a possibility of course. I was expecting something bigger, like the 7/7 bombings.'

Slamming her glass down, Daisy barked, 'Bigger! It's bloody well big enough, Peter, a dear friend of mine is dead because of this Saudi prince, she was a lovely person full of life, but I'm sure, in tomorrow's newspapers the prince will get the headlines and my friend will get hardly a mention.'

Looking decidedly uneasy, Isaacs replied, 'Sorry but that's the way it works, Daisy, and don't think me unfeeling. I'm sorry you lost a friend, but the fact is big news buries the little people. What was it the bard said? *"There are no comets in the sky when a beggar dies, comets are for princes".'*

With a scornful laugh Daisy said, 'Isn't a public-school education a wonderful thing, Peter? So tell me, you've had enough time to get the skinny on Abdullah, what was his problem?'

Isaacs shrugged. 'That's the worry, he doesn't appear to have any problems, our people in Saudi with sufficient high-level intelligence contacts have found nothing. Abdullah is off everyone's radar. He's an eighth son, not in line for any government position and not in anyone's way. It's early days yet but in fact all we have learned about him came from the taxi company. Every Monday to Friday at 08.45 precisely a taxi is waiting for him, which takes him to the British Museum.'

Daisy checked her glass, surprised it was not cracked, and took a sip. 'Mary told me he's obsessed with punctuality, she must be there when he opens his door, she assumed he was nervous about something.'

Looking at Angus, Isaacs asked, 'What else do we know about that?'

'Not a lot, Chief. I spoke to DCI Sandys about the taxi company. According to the manager, he has been following the same routine for three months and insisted on Mary Grey being the driver.'

Daisy asked, 'I take it they checked with the museum?'

Angus nodded. 'Yes, he has a reader's ticket and reads old manuscripts until 12.30, then he has an hour-long lunch in the restaurant, works again until four o'clock and leaves.'

Nodding, she said, 'Did they find out where he goes?'

'Yes, he's known to take a taxi from a nearby rank and go to the mosque in Kensington.'

'Which tells us something,' she said. 'He's not nervous about picking up a strange taxi and going with a driver he doesn't know.'

'Good point,' Isaacs said. 'What's your initial take on this?'

Daisy laughed. 'Is that why you brought me here, Peter, to make use of my brilliant powers of deduction pro bono?'

Isaacs smiled. 'Without flattering you too much, Daisy, while we were working together, I have found your methods, although thoroughly unorthodox, sometimes even bordering on the downright illegal, produced results. Yes, your input is always appreciated.'

She thought about it for a moment before saying, 'The first thing which comes to mind is, a car bomb is not a good choice for an assassination. Historically most attempts have failed to kill the intended target, killing instead innocent bystanders, which in this case was my friend and could have been me.'

'If Abdullah was punctual to a fault, as has been reported, they could guarantee his presence at 08.45,' Isaacs said.

Shaking her head, Daisy said, 'I don't buy it, Peter. They could never have guaranteed that. He could have had an urgent call of nature, or a telephone call, or any number of things which might delay him. We don't know anything, other than he wanted the taxi to be outside when he opened the door. Maybe he himself wasn't always punctual.'

Isaacs nodded agreement. 'So, to be sure, they would have needed to see him and detonate the bomb remotely.'

'Exactly,' Daisy said. 'Once the debris is analysed, they'll be able to say how the bomb was constructed.'

Isaacs nodded. 'To sum up then, you're saying, if there was a remote Abdullah was the target and if not, it was a random attack.'

Tapping her fingers irritably on the table Daisy said, 'Peter, you're not getting it are you? There were two victims, remember. You said yourself Mary was always outside, waiting, she was never late.'

One eyebrow lifted as Isaacs leaned back in his chair and said, 'Really, Daisy, I can't believe anyone would go to all this trouble to kill a taxi driver, do you?'

'Unlikely, but nothing should be ruled out. Even people as decent as Mary can have enemies who might want to kill her. Remember she was a taxi driver, she may have overheard a passenger talking or something like that.'

Isaacs considered this before saying, 'You're right of course, we can't rule anything out, and she did try to say something to you before she died, didn't you say?'

Got you! Daisy was thinking and took a sip from her glass before replying, 'No, I didn't say, however did you know that, Peter?'

Looking a bit shifty he said, 'I'm not sure, you must have told Farmer.'

With a mischievous smile she said, 'Perhaps I talk in my sleep, is that it?'

Isaacs lifted his glass and looked at the Scotch before taking a sip. She knew he was conjuring a suitable reply; she also knew he was an excellent poker player which also made him a plausible liar when the situation required it. She did not expect him to admit to anything, but he surprised her again. He raised his glass to her.

'Touché, Daisy, now what was it she said?'

Knowing that this was as close to an admittance as she was going to get, she told him.

47

'Nothing that made any sense. "Harry," then a gasp for breath, then, "You can trust Harry," then, "He's alive, his voice, tell Harry," then, "Delia, Delia." I asked her who's alive but all she could do was mumble something that sounded like Brown, or it might have been even just escaping air as she passed out.'

'Do any of the names mean anything to you?'

Shaking her head, she said, 'Not a thing, I've never heard her speak of a Harry or Delia.'

Isaacs let this sink in before saying, 'So, if there's no remote we must also consider a random attack. We had two bombs in Northern Ireland last year. The Real IRA were behind those.'

Shaking her head, Daisy said, 'IRA? I don't think so, Peter. It doesn't have the right feel for it. Firstly, why would they bother bombing an insignificant mews like that and remember, there was no warning was there? Even the die-hard fanatics phone in a warning. No, it's too much of a coincidence that it exploded at exactly the moment Abdullah stepped out of his house to be random, but I agree, it's best to keep an open mind. At this stage there's not enough input. I take it the borders are being watched?'

'Since 09.30, every air and seaport is covered.' Isaacs finished the last of his drink and contemplated his empty glass. 'Every known face will be held for questioning.'

Angus, taking the hint, took the glass and crossed to the sideboard.

'No thanks, Angus, I've to brief the PM later. Daisy?'

'Nor me,' Daisy said. 'I have to go to my office, before they sound the alarm.'

'Hmm, Angus, will you pop downstairs and ask Dr Webber if Daisy can be discharged?'

'Yes Chief,' Angus said, turning to leave.

'And Angus.'

'Chief?'

'This meeting with Miss Clowser never took place, no notes in the file, you understand.'

Making a knowing casting of the eyes Angus said, 'Got it, Chief,' and closed the door.

Once they were alone, Isaacs stood up and looked down at her, in deep contemplation, before saying, 'How long have we known each other, Daisy?'

Feeling a bit ill at ease Daisy stood up and faced him. 'Long enough for you to know I can be trusted, Peter, which begs the question, why was I given the treatment downstairs?'

Isaacs put his glass on the tray, his eyes focusing on it for a moment before replying.

'The thing is, Daisy, it's nine years since we worked together, and as you know I like to be sure of things, one must have no doubts about the people we work with, we've had too many embarrassments in the past. If I remember correctly you were quite happy to use the same methods when you thought it necessary.'

Daisy shrugged. 'True, but since when am I working with you?'

Isaacs returned to his seat, saying, 'Look, Daisy I want your help on this, sit down and listen.'

'I'm listening,' she said and sat.

Isaacs, tapping the table with his index finger, said, 'Okay, I want to rule Dissident IRA in or out and I need your input, you spent enough time among them to know all the players.'

Leaning towards him Daisy said, 'Peter, the last time I messed with those bastards I took five bullets and it was only due to your actions I got away with my life. I've so many metal pins in me, I can't go through an airport scanner without setting off the alarm.'

Looking concerned Isaacs said, 'I'm really sorry to hear that, you should have told me. I'll get you a special pass from the Border Security people.'

His show of concern may even have been genuine, Daisy thought; one could never be sure with Isaacs.

'I've already got one, thank you,' she said, smiling at his discomfort. 'Anyway, as far as the IRA are concerned, they knew me as Maggie Maguire, who died from her wounds, and I would like them to continue believing that. There are still a few fanatics out there who would love to settle accounts with me, if they knew I was still alive. That kind of trouble I can do without. If you want to know if this was a Dissident IRA operation, I suggest you have Jack Farmer talk to the Fisherman. I've heard they got quite close during the peace talks.'

Isaacs eyebrows raised as he thought about it. 'The Fisherman, you think he's still able to control the dissidents?'

'Maybe not the real hot heads, but I've no doubt he'll be having them watched and know what they are up to. If any dissident unit is active in London he'll know, in fact I'm quite sure he would have tipped Jack Farmer off beforehand. He needs to keep the peace more than anyone. Of course, there may be some rogue unit he doesn't know about yet but I would say that's unlikely.'

Nodding agreement Isaacs said, 'You may be right, I'll talk to Farmer.'

'Do that,' she said. 'If he rules out dissidents, then we have either a hit on Abdullah or a hit on Mary Grey.'

'Exactly.' Isaacs stood up and walked a few paces to the wall and back before continuing. 'And knowing you, no doubt you will want to find who's responsible and settle their hash as you used to say. The thing is, Daisy, I don't want you muddying the water, if you must be involved, we should work together.'

Smiling sweetly, Daisy said, 'Exactly what water would I be muddying, Peter? What else do you know about this?'

Isaacs gave her a thoughtful look and returned to his seat. 'The fact is, Daisy, besides the chatter I mentioned, we've received reliable intelligence relating to a shipment originating in Afghanistan, which includes heroin and what we believe to be weapons to be used in London. Today's operation may have nothing at all to do with al-Qaida but we can't rule anything out. It's even possible your friend the taxi driver did overhear something important and had to be silenced. By killing an important fellow like Abdullah at the same time they would divert attention and your friend would be just considered collateral damage. My source thinks the shipper in question is part of a drug trafficking ring using an established route between Pakistan and London. We've got the Drug Squad looking at all the known Narcos.'

Daisy considered this for a moment before replying. 'What if the weapons are already here? Don't you have your own spies?'

'Of course, we do,' Isaacs said. 'Since the 7/7 bombings two years ago, we've had agents in the mosques and known meeting places. Thankfully, they were successful in thwarting the attempts to smuggle liquid explosives on flights to the US last year. They're still in place but to date, nobody's heard a whisper. We're at a dead end, Daisy, and need all the help we can muster, which is why, if there's the slightest possibility today's events have any connection with these smugglers, I want you involved.'

'I'm already involved, aren't I?' Daisy said. 'You didn't think I was going to allow my friend's killers to get away with it, did you?'

Isaacs shook his head and smiled. 'No, I suppose I didn't. I want you to report directly to me. I'll clear it with Farmer and anyone else who needs to know as the situation arises.'

'You'll give me full authority then. I can use my own people?'

'You can use anyone you like so long as absolute discretion is observed.'

'Everyone who works for me is the soul of discretion, most are still covered by the Act.'

Pushing his chair back Isaacs stood and said, 'Good, that's settled then.'

Standing beside him Daisy said, 'Not quite, Peter. Besides my fee and expenses, I'll expect an OBE, when I sort this out.'

'Hmm, I'm sure it can be arranged.' With a puzzled look, Isaacs continued, 'I thought you were against such things.'

With a mischievous smile Daisy said, 'I was and still am. I was just testing your influence. Now what exactly do you want me to do?'

'It's your game, Daisy. I want you to find those bastards and I'm not fussed about how you do it.'

The grim look on his face reminded Daisy of the Peter Isaacs she knew of old, a man whose idea of justice was not meted out in a court of law. 'Right then,' she said. 'For starters I want you to find out everything you can about Abdullah and ask Jack Farmer to speak to the Fisherman. The sooner we can rule the dissidents in or out of this the better. Also tell Farmer I'm working for you and expect his full cooperation.'

'And you?'

'I'll start by looking into Mary Grey's background.'

The door opened and Angus reappeared and said, 'Dr Webber is satisfied with Miss Clowser's condition.'

Turning to Daisy, Isaacs said, 'Thanks for the chat, Daisy, and keep me informed, Angus will take you wherever you want to go.'

'He can take me to my office before they put me on the missing persons list.'

'Before you go there's one more thing.' Isaacs produced a mini-tape from his pocket and said, 'Your briefcase is clever, but Angus was able to open it and remove the tape, before resetting it, thus giving you the green light.'

Glaring, Daisy snatched the tape. 'Have I ever told you what a shit you are, Peter?'

Isaacs smiled. 'On more than one occasion, it goes with the job. May I ask you what you intended to do with a recording of our conversation?'

'Nothing at all, Peter, I always record my meetings as an aide memoir.'

'And I suppose you know, making a recording here is a breach of the Official Secrets Act.'

Laughing as she headed for the door, Daisy said, 'What's a breach between friends, Peter? I'll be in touch.'

CHAPTER 7

Daisy was travelling on the Bayswater Road for the third time that day, this time Angus was driving in the direction of Marble Arch. She approved of his choice of vehicle, a Mini Cooper S, but not the Union Jack painted on the roof.

'You've never done any undercover work, have you Angus?'

'No. Up until now, I've been an analyst, and general dogsbody for Peter Isaacs, but I've had the training of course,' he said, as he zipped across the three lanes at Marble Arch to exit on Park Lane.

Tapping him on the arm, she said, 'A word of advice, Angus, if you're doing any liaising for Isaacs with working agents, a car like this will attract attention, you need to be invisible.'

'No problem, I can get one from the pool.' He was on the outside lane when he got his first order.

'Take the next left,' Daisy instructed.

Despite the horns blaring and the screeching of brakes he cut across the traffic and just made the turn into Upper Brook Street.

Still gripping the sides of her seat, she said, 'Nice driving, Angus, you an aspiring racing driver or what?'

Angus grinned. 'I do a bit of saloon car racing at Brands Hatch and Donnington, but might I suggest a little more warning on the turns, Daisy?'

Daisy laughed. 'I'll try, Angus, wouldn't want to wreck your pride and joy, now take a right into Park Street and find Shakespeare Mews, it's off Mount Street. I want to take another look at the scene of the crime.'

It was after six when they pulled into the mews. All of the emergency vehicles had departed. There seemed an unnatural quietness about the place after the happenings of the morning.

'Stop there,' Daisy said, pointing to the spot where Mary had dropped her off and had given her the name of the company she was interested in. *Damn,* she thought, she had forgotten the name and now it escaped her. She remembered putting the envelope into her jacket pocket. It must still be there, but where was her jacket? She had told Mrs Hollis to dump it.

'Angus, can you call Mrs Hollis on whatever number you use and ask her to keep my jacket in a safe place? I left something in the pocket.'

Getting out, she looked up and down the mews. This time from an investigator's point of view. Even in the fading light she could see the cobbles outside Abdullah's were blackened from the explosion. A uniformed PC stood by the doorway, which by now had a new unpainted door fitted, the green shutters were nowhere to be seen. She wasn't surprised. No doubt the original door, the shutters and any other fragment of evidence were already in the Met Police forensic department at the Elephant & Castle.

The PC saw her and gave her the official once-over. He looked bored and tired.

Daisy saw there were CCTV cameras mounted at each end of the mews, and two street lights, one at each end. Abdullah's house was exactly in the middle, the darkest part of the mews. Hopefully there might be some video from last night to work with, she thought.

Angus interrupted her thoughts. 'Mrs Hollis sends her apologies but your jacket has gone off with the medical waste. She doesn't hold out much hope of finding it, but she'll try.'

'My fault anyway,' she said, again trying to recall the company name, but it wouldn't come. *Leave it,* she thought, *let it come naturally.*

A patrol car pulled into the mews and drove slowly past, the driver giving them a hard look before stopping beside the PC on guard. A passenger – another uniform – got out and after a few words they both turned towards them and gave them the *we're watching you* look. Then after a few more words they swapped places, the first PC getting into the car. *Changing of the guard,* Daisy was thinking, as the patrol car drove off.

Turning to Angus she said, 'Angus if you wanted to detonate a car bomb with a remote where would you watch from?'

Angus looked behind at the entrance and then towards the north end before asking, 'Where were you standing, Daisy?'

'Just over there,' she said, pointing a few yards from where they stood.

Angus, after a long look said, 'And the mews was empty, you're sure?'

'Absolutely sure, I had a clear view.'

Angus pointed. 'According to the initial report, that street facing us is Adams Row. It would have to have been that store, on the opposite side, there's a straight-line view from there.'

Daisy agreed. 'I'm sure by now, Jack Farmer will have considered that possibility and checked it out, we'll know for sure when forensics have done their bit.'

'What if they find no evidence of a remote?' Angus asked.

After a moment's thought Daisy said, 'In that case they relied on the timer. We know the bomb exploded at eight forty-five. That, as I explained to Isaacs, is the reason I doubt it was IRA, because all the Provo bombs I've seen, and I've seen a few, were always set to the hour.'

'Maybe the timer wasn't all that accurate.'

Shaking her head, Daisy said, 'It would have to have been bloody inaccurate, Angus, like fifteen minutes in the hour and I don't buy that. No, we'll just have to wait for the forensics.'

Then, after giving the mews a final look, Daisy said, 'Okay, I've seen enough, let's get to my office before everyone has gone home,' and got back into the car.

Angus got in and started the engine. 'St. James Street, right?'

'Yes, number forty-one.'

They drove past the new PC who gave them hard look, before writing in his notebook.

'He's taken your number, Angus,' Daisy said.

Angus grinned. 'No worries, if he looks it up, it's my sister's car.'

Jack Farmer had a spacious office complete with fitted carpet, a kidney-shaped rosewood desk and a conference table, on the fifth floor in New Scotland Yard. Seated beside the desk, DCI Sandys was briefing Farmer on progress, notebook in hand.

'Some progress, Guv,' he said. 'We have the registration number of the BMW, the number plate was found among the debris.'

Scribbling on his pad, Farmer said, 'You've traced it?'

Sandys flipped a page and said, 'Yes, to a car dealer in Leytonstone, Guv. I paid him a visit.'

'And?'

'One Bertie Smails, he's got form, small-time thieving, shop and warehouse breaking, last convicted fifteen years ago, served two years of a three-year sentence.'

'What's his story on the Beemer?' Farmer asked.

'It was on his forecourt up until Monday, ticket price three thousand. According to Smails, he received a phone call on Monday, a man's voice, London accent. He had seen the car and wanted to buy it immediately. He gave instructions for the car to be left on the first-floor parking in Brent Cross Shopping Centre. He was told to leave the keys under the front wheel on the driver's side, with the papers inside. Within two hours a biker delivered the full amount in fifties. We're trying to trace the biker. I have someone contacting all the known operators but so far we've come up with nothing.'

Farmer grunted. 'Not surprising is it? They wouldn't have made it that easy for us.'

Sandys agreed. 'No, a lot of the bikers operate on the black and put notices in newsagents and local stores.'

Making a note on his pad Farmer said, 'So, Smails delivered the car and like a good honest citizen he has the new owners' details as required by law.'

'He was given a name and address over the phone which was a total phoney.'

'When did he deliver the car?'

'Monday at six p.m.'

'You saw the money?'

Taking a thick envelope from his inside pocket Sandys said, 'I have the money, three grand in fifties.'

Farmer leaned forward and said, 'How come?'

Sandy's smiled. 'I told Smails it was evidence.'

Farmer's fist balled as he said, 'Good, serve the bastard right. Send them over to fingerprints, they might get a match. What about Abdullah's house?'

'Forensics have finished there. They've taken his laptop for analysis. We should know something in a few hours.'

'Did anyone see the switch-car parked in the space overnight?'

Sandys with a shake of his head said, 'Nothing from the traffic wardens but the owner of a house further up recalls seeing a black car parked there when she closed her curtains at about ten o'clock.'

'Shit,' Farmer said. 'That's all, a black car, no make or description?'

Sandys shook his head and said, 'The lady's in her eighties and doesn't drive herself, a low black car was all she remembered.'

'What about the CCTV?'

Sandys flipped a page and looked at a sketch of the mews before replying. 'There are two cameras, watching the mews, one at each end.'

'And?'

'There was nothing on the tapes since Tuesday evening.'

Farmer gasped. 'Nothing at all?'

'Both of the cameras had their lens blocked with paint.'

'Fantastic, didn't anyone notice on the monitors?'

Closing his notebook with a snap, Sandys said, 'Nobody actually monitors them, they're connected to time-lapse recorders and the tapes are wiped every week, if there's no reported incident. So, all we know is what the neighbour saw, nobody saw the BMW arrive nor the switch-car leave.'

Farmer made another note before saying, 'Great, a low black car. I'd better give it to the press anyway, someone might have seen it. These bombers are no amateurs, we'll have to hope forensic comes up with something.'

'Any progress there?' asked Sandys.

'I spoke to Ernie at Elephant & Castle,' Farmer said. 'He's putting everyone on the night shift, expects to have something on the bomb by the morning. What about the taxi driver?'

'Nothing much to report, Guv,' Sandys said. 'I ran a record check on her, no convictions of any kind. We've paid a visit to the taxi company. The day controller confirms she had a regular pick-up at Abdullah's every weekday at 08.45. That's been going on for about three months.'

'What about next of kin?'

'They didn't know of any. We have her wallet but there's nothing in it other than some cash, her driving license, and a couple of credit cards.'

Farmer thought about it for a moment before saying, 'We know she lives in the same block as Daisy. Did you find her keys?'

Sandys shook his head. 'No, Forensics have sealed the taxi.'

'They must be still in it,' Farmer said, and pushed a sheet of paper across the desk.

Taking it, Sandys asked, 'What's this, Guv?'

'It's an email from Peter Isaacs, read it.'

DCI Sandys read the brief message. 'Effective immediately Daisy Clowser is working with his department for the duration of this investigation, be so kind as to give her any assistance she requires.'

Handing the sheet back Sandys said, 'Unusual, Guv, can he do that?'

Farmer stabbed the email with a blunt finger. 'Too right he can, Mr Peter Isaacs is a law onto himself and has the ear of the Prime Minister, the Home Secretary and the Minister of Defence. This is a polite request, Len, normally he doesn't bother with such niceties.'

Sandys pulled a face. 'You're saying he can get away with hiring a PI?'

'In this case yes,' Farmer said. 'She's is not your ordinary PI. Her firm has been working with SIS long enough to almost make them an adjunct of the Ministry of Defence.'

'At least you know her, Guv, you said yourself she was good.'

Farmer smiled. 'Yeah, she's good. She has friends in high and low places and somehow or other gets the job done; however dirty it turns out to be. I've worked with her in Special Branch. Daisy may be blonde and innocent looking but she's as tough as old boots and smart with it. There's no down side for me. If she fucks up, which is unlikely, it's down to Isaacs and if she helps clear this up, we get the credit, no down side at all.'

'Isaacs is dealing with the Foreign Office and SIS?' asked Sandys.

Pushing his chair back and standing, Farmer said with a grim smile, 'Yes, all the balls are in the air, there's nothing more we can do until tomorrow. Right now I have to go upstairs and make a statement to the press, after which we'll go for a pint.'

CHAPTER 8

Angus turned into St. James Street and was lucky enough to spot a parking space being vacated no more than fifty yards from number forty-one, which he grabbed.

'Lucky, Angus,' Daisy said. 'Thanks for the lift. Since you're parked, why don't you come up and have a look at our operation. You never know, working for a man like Peter Isaacs you might need a job sometime.'

Angus laughed. 'He's not that bad, Daisy, but thanks for the offer, it'll be interesting.'

When they reached number 41 Angus stopped to read the engraving on the brass plate, which was worn from constant polishing over the past century. *Casey, Clay & Clowser, established 1903* was all it said. Nothing to indicate the type of business the firm conducted.

Inside the lobby he saw a number of similar plates which did state their owner's business. There was a chartered accountant, two law firms and a computer forensics company. There were two lifts, one with the legend CC&C only.

'We have the top two floors. The only official access is by this lift,' Daisy said, pressing the single button.

The brushed steel interior of the lift was lit by defused lighting and again had only a single button. There was also a key pad with a LED display.

Angus looked at it with an enquiring lift of the eyebrows.

Pushing the button, she said, 'This takes visitors to the fifth floor.' She explained, 'My office is also there. All the serious work, including

62

IT is on the sixth floor, hence the secure access.' The lift hummed.

They exited into an ash-panelled reception area, furnished with matching leather chairs and deep pile carpet. Again, the use of defused lighting gave the reception a warm, welcoming feeling. It was more like the executive suite of a FTSE 100 company than a detective agency.

A thousand years away from his cramped offices in Horseferry House, Angus thought. His allocated square of carpet was measured according to rank. Fitted carpets were for the gods.

The reception desk was empty. 'Bertha leaves at five thirty,' Daisy told him, neglecting to mention that Bertha was six foot two and weighed over one hundred kilos and his name was actually Albert. A former sergeant in the parachute regiment, his job was to discourage any unwelcome visitors.

On the wall facing the lift were three portraits of serious-looking men in the military garb of the late nineteenth century. 'The company's founders,' she said. 'The one in the middle is my great-grandfather.'

A corridor ran right and left to a number of rooms with closed doors. There was no sound of any activity. Turning right she led him to a door at the end of the corridor. Angus followed her into a spacious office with windows overlooking Piccadilly, again expensively, but tastefully furnished. A large L-shaped walnut desk – free of any clutter with the exception of an intercom-cum-STE secure telephone unit – stood in front of the windows. Two leather chairs stood in front. There was a conference table and chairs and a bookcase. The only other furniture was an old Milner safe. The three framed drawings were Picassos.

Dropping into the leather chair behind the desk she pushed a button on the intercom. It was answered immediately by a female voice with a trace of Yorkshire in it. 'Daisy, you've just caught me, where in hell have you been all day?'

'Thanks for waiting, Alice. I have a guest; any chance you can rustle up some coffee and something to eat if there's anything left in the fridge? I haven't eaten all day.'

Releasing the button, she turned to Angus. 'Coffee all right or would you like something stronger?'

'Coffee is fine. I have to drive. Your staff work late?'

'Alice would stay all night until she knew I was all right. She'll be here in a minute, sit down.'

Angus dropped into one of two leather chairs and tapped his fingers on the walnut. 'I must say you're not slumming it here, Daisy.'

Having herself worked in government offices Daisy understood his wonder and explained. 'We have a rich and powerful clientele, Angus, sometimes even the odd brush with Royalty and as our fees are exorbitant, we can't have them walking into anything that might be considered Mean Streets.'

'The nameplate in the lobby says established 1903?'

'That's right. The first partners, including my great-grandfather, were intelligence officers during the second Boer War. When they returned to England, they decided to set up a detective agency modelled on the American Pinkertons. To start with they rented two offices, including this one.' Pointing to the Milner safe she said, 'That there is their first piece of office equipment. Over the years the firm expanded, taking the top two floors. The partners bought the building in 1948 after a particularly good year, property prices not being like they are today.'

'What about your partners, is there still a Casey and Clay?' Angus asked.

'The first three generations are dead, with the exception of my father and George Casey who are retired. I'm fourth generation, there's only Arthur Clay and myself left and he's over sixty.' She was interrupted by the arrival of Alice pushing the door open with her shoulder as she carried a tray loaded with a pot of coffee and a plate of sandwiches, cups and saucers plus a bottle of Glenmorangie and three glasses.

Alice Godley, who had one of those ageless faces which could make her anywhere between forty and sixty, was a head taller than Daisy. Her dark hair, kept short and expensively razor cut contrasted sharply with Daisy's blondeness. She moved easily, like the athlete she once was when she won two silver medals in the '80 Olympics.

Putting the tray on the desk, she went to Daisy's side to inspect her face at close quarters. 'I thought you were supposed to be done with this kind of thing, girl,' she said, before giving Angus a hard look and asking, 'Who's your friend?'

'It's nothing serious, Alice. 'I hit the pavement and needed a few stitches, that's all, and this is Angus, he works for Peter Isaacs. Angus, meet Alice Godley, the real boss around here.'

Angus eagerly held out his hand. 'It's great meeting you at last, Alice. John Hay, our instructor, has often sung your praises, bemoaning your departure. According to him you had the best analytical mind in the service.'

Alice snorted. 'Then it's a pity the bastards didn't say so when I was working for them.' But her hard look slipped as she shook hands.

Putting her hand gently on Daisy's shoulder, her tone softened. 'I know what happened to you, Daisy. Jack Farmer called and told me the taxi driver was a good friend. I'm really sorry, Daisy.'

Daisy felt her eyes well up as repressed feelings flooded back. 'Thanks Alice,' she mumbled as she opened a drawer and found a Kleenex. Dabbing her eyes and blowing her nose violently, she composed herself by remembering the words of another instructor. *You'll see plenty of grief in this job, girl. Don't let it get personal or you'll be no good to anyone. Leave the grieving until the job is done.'*

Avoiding Angus's concerned look, she tossed the Kleenex into the bin beside her desk and said, 'Can we eat? I'm famished.'

Alice poured coffee into two of the cups. 'Help yourself to the sandwiches, they're smoked salmon.' She then poured herself a generous slug of Glenmorangie and raised the glass. 'Cheers, here's to crime, now fill me in on your day.'

Alice listened without interruption as Daisy related the events of the day between bites, leaving nothing out, including her thoughts on the seven-hour induced sleep.

Sipping her Scotch, Alice said, 'You were obviously given something to make you relax completely, it's common practice for a head injury.'

Daisy chewed her last bite before replying. 'That's what Peter Isaacs claimed at first.'

Alice, with a look of surprise said, 'Don't tell me he admitted drugging you.'

Pushing her plate away, Daisy said, 'Not in so many words, but I'm sure he did, not that I can remember anything about it.'

Alice shrugged. 'You'd have done the same given the opportunity, it's a safe and sure means of getting to the truth, and as you have agreed to work for him, you'll have to accept his devious ways and forget it, but why you want to work for that bastard again I can't imagine, it's a pity the fall didn't knock some sense into you.'

Daisy took a sip of coffee before replying. 'You know, Alice? Peter Isaacs may be everything you say, but I've always found him to be a straight shooter and by all accounts he now has the clout to make things happen, so it was a simple enough decision to make.'

Turning to Angus, she asked, 'You'd agree with me on that, wouldn't you Angus?'

Angus, pausing mid-sandwich, just nodded cheerfully.

Putting the cup down, Daisy continued. 'Look, Alice, a dear friend has been murdered, and I could have been killed as well, so for me that makes it bloody personal. These bombers didn't care about the innocents they maim or kill. Whoever they are they must be stopped.'

Alice smiled. 'Very laudable, Daisy, but are you sure that's the real reason or could it be you're just a wee bit of bored with corporate life at Triple C?'

Daisy shook her head in denial. 'Alice, that's unfair. Of course it's not the reason. You're forgetting you were with SO12 for years longer than I was, aren't you bored sometimes?'

Shaking her head, Alice replied, 'Definitely not. I was an analyst, remember, never sharp end. You, madame, revelled in it.'

Daisy poured half a finger of the Scotch into her coffee and stirred it thoughtfully. 'You know there might be just a grain of truth in what you say, Alice, but I've told Peter Isaacs I'd help, so that's that, now let's talk details.'

CHAPTER 9

Hampstead Garden Suburb, is a leafy North London enclave much beloved by billionaires and oil-rich Arabs. People who could afford to buy their mansion, spend millions on renovation and buy the house next door for their servants and bodyguards. The suburb is not immediately associated with the criminal classes, although, from time to time, there have been a number of supposedly wealthy owners rudely awakened at six a.m. by the Fraud Squad and taken away to assist in their enquiries.

Kaminski pressed her remote and waited for the five-bar gate of number 10 Twilight Avenue to swing smoothly open. A short gravel drive led to a circular turning point at the front of the house, where she parked the Mercedes.

Number 10 was a relatively modest detached property for the area, only five bedrooms and no servants' quarters, but it was at the end of a quiet cul-de-sac and the garden backed onto the Heath. As long as your means of transport was of sufficient quality, nobody paid any undue attention to one's comings and goings.

The house was available fully furnished, for short lets at certain times of the year. Kaminski, who needed a house for Kramer's visit, rented it through a reliable third party and paid the minimum three months' rental in advance, although she only needed it for a month.

Thomas appeared in the hall the instant she opened the door. A hulk of a man with an oversized head covered with tight blond curls – which he claimed were natural – and a neck like a tree trunk. He was Kramer's driver-cum-minder and fitted the stereotype perfectly –

big, mean and none too clever. His only redeeming features in Kaminski's eyes were his excellent knowledge of London and his extensive connections with its underworld figures, some of whom he had worked for in the past. Thomas was also surprisingly enough, a good housekeeper and cook, which dispensed with any requirement for outside domestic help.

Blocking her path and standing too close to her in his annoying way, he growled, 'It was good then.'

She had to crane her head to look up at him, which she knew was what he wanted, his power thing. Recoiling, she ignored the question. 'Where's Kramer?'

Giving her a look that should have frightened a ghost, he said, 'He's waiting in the study.'

Kaminski, who wasn't afraid of ghosts, nor much else for that matter, made no move to step aside. 'He doesn't like waiting,' she said, holding his gaze.

Thomas contemplated her for a moment, like a hungry bear undecided as to which piece of her to rip off first, before turning his back on her and walking towards the kitchen.

As she entered the room, she saw Kramer was exactly where he had been when she left for the hospital; slumped in a leather swivel-chair watching the various news channels on the TV, with a glass of brandy on his side table. Kramer consumed a lot of brandy but she had never once seen him the worse from it. The ticker at the bottom of the screen read '*Breaking News – car bomb in London street*'. Hearing her, he flicked the remote and muted the sound before turning the chair to face her.

Kaminski knew little about Kramer; in fact, she knew nothing at all about his original background and had learned less during the three years she'd been working with him. All she knew was, he was a secretive and ruthless man with money and contacts; one who was respected even by the hard men they associated with.

Rumours about him abounded, but no one knew anything about his origins or nationality; anyone who pried too deeply was apt to receive a visit from Thomas, who liked to hurt people. She judged him to be in his late sixties, but still fit and hard. Five-nine, no flab, barrel chested with a head which rested on his shoulders seemingly without a neck. His hair was close-cropped and iron-grey contrasted with black bushy eyebrows and black eyes; eyes which at that moment were giving her a piercing look.

'About time, what did you find out at the hospital?' Kramer spoke English with a distinctive accent; she couldn't place it, but it was a voice you would recognise in the dark – not that you would want to be with Kramer in the dark.

Kaminski went to the sideboard and poured herself a brandy before replying. 'All they would tell me, there were two deaths, one male, the other female, but no names until the next of kin is informed.'

'It said on the news there was a third casualty, a female, what about her?' Kramer lifted his glass and took a sip.

Kaminski settled into the armchair opposite him. 'They knew nothing about a third casualty. If there was one, she wasn't admitted to St Thomas's.'

Putting his glass down with a bang, he said, 'It's not good, Kaminski, is it? We don't know for sure which female died and since the second female is still unaccounted for, she must be important to them. We must find out if it's safe to proceed.'

For a brief moment, Kaminski's thoughts reverted back to the unfortunate episode which caused this trouble and she was mindful that, for the first time she had seen a moment of panic in Kramer's behaviour when it was obvious to everyone in the room that the taxi driver had recognised him. Emboldened by that thought she said, 'Just how safe are we, Kramer? What about your Fixer? Doesn't he know too much already?'

She was keen to remind him the Fixer was his idea. Kramer's story, which she didn't believe for one moment was: Thomas, who knew how these things get done in London, knew exactly how to contact a Fixer and set up the meeting in Clerkenwell which provided the BMW and the switch-car. Kramer also claimed, it was Thomas who located the C4 explosive and detonator and arranged for her to collect the mechanical timer.

She now felt sure, although he never discussed it, Kramer had lived in London in the past. After claiming their operation had been compromised and they must act immediately or abandon everything, he told her his plan, which was pretty desperate considering the time frame. As it was her moment of carelessness which was responsible for the breach of security, she had to go along with it. She was all right with that. Kramer paid well and there was always a hefty bonus in her Cayman Islands account after each operation. After all, she herself was a ruthless woman and not one who was squeamish or easily frightened.

'He's not a worry,' Kramer said. He won't talk. He's a professional, and he doesn't know either of us, he only knows Thomas and he's not going to mess with him.'

Kaminski sipped her drink and pushed further. 'What about the old man who set the timer? He must know by now what it was used for and he's seen my face, twice. Do we need to worry about him?'

Kramer gave a harsh laugh. 'He won't talk either, if he did, he'd be in it with us. Besides, they'd be looking for someone else, wouldn't they?'

'That would be Harry?'

Kramer stood abruptly and looked down at her, his face ugly. 'You're asking too many questions, Kaminski. Everybody's got a past, sometimes it catches up with you. In this case it's my bad luck. Right now, we need to know exactly who died this morning. Just be mindful of what's at stake.'

Never show fear to this man, Kaminski thought, and stood up to face him. Casually slipping her hand into her jacket where she kept a switch-blade, she said, 'There's sure to be a press conference before morning, then we'll know for sure. And, I know exactly what's at stake, we can kiss our business in Pakistan goodbye, if we don't play ball with Iqbal and deliver his shipment.'

Lowering his voice to a more conciliating tone Kramer said, 'I'm here, Ursula, at great risk to myself because Minihane insisted on it. Maybe it's just as well because considering Iqbal's intentions, I was thinking you might have qualms about this.'

With a brittle laugh she replied, 'Qualms, definitely none, whatever his intentions are is his business. It's dealing with fanatics that bothers me, they're so fucking happy to die, it makes them unreliable.'

Kramer eased back into his seat and reached for his glass. 'You're right of course, we'll need to be extra careful dealing with Iqbal. He's not beyond a double-cross, but in this case, I think not. He's got too much to lose. When is his shipment due at Tilbury?'

Crisis over, Kaminski thought and released her knife before sitting down. Reaching for her glass with a steady hand she knocked back the remains of the brandy. 'Tomorrow, it should be through customs and in Park Royal by Friday. Brooks will see to it, he's on duty all day.'

Kramer looked into his brandy for a moment, then said, 'Brooks knows nothing of its contents?'

'I told him it was heroin as usual, it won't be inspected,' Kaminski said.

Kramer emptied his glass and stood up. 'Excellent, remember, just to show Iqbal he can't fuck with us and have free use of our network, I negotiated a cash settlement of a million Swiss, cash, so it's not entirely a waste of time. As for the woman, I agree, we don't have any choice but to wait until morning. Now drink up and we'll go see what Thomas has for our dinner.'

South East Spain

Veleta's yacht was moored in the marina next to the restaurant. Although he owned a number of houses in the area, he preferred to live on board. He had not returned to his meal but was in his stateroom, where he had been since Frank's call, slumped in his chair in front of the full-width window overlooking the bow. From there he had a fine view of the gently swinging masts of the many yachts in the marina, with a backdrop of the mountains beyond. A view he normally enjoyed, but now, his eyes blurred with tears, he saw nothing. The news he had just received had shocked him to the core and he was not a man to be easily shocked.

Mary Grey had always played a major part in his life and now she was gone. He wiped his eyes as more tears welled. *How fucking cruel life is,* he thought. Evil survived and angels died. There was a slight tremor in his hand as he lifted the glass to sip his brandy, but when he saw the bottle on the table beside him – which had been full when he started – was now two-thirds empty and the clock on the wall read 18:00 hours, he realised he'd been slumped there for four hours. *Enough,* he thought, slamming the glass down. Getting stupid drunk was not going to solve anything and certainly would not bring Mary back. Pushing himself out of his chair he made his way to his bathroom and washed his face before going back to the restaurant.

Garcia, who was in his office when Veleta entered, saw the look on his boss's face, but said nothing.

'I need to make a private call, Fernando,' Veleta said.

'Si señor.' Garcia opened his desk drawer and produced a mobile which he handed to Veleta. 'This one is safe, señor,' he said.

Taking it, Veleta said, 'Good, I'll need it for a while,' and returned to the boat. It was still only five o'clock in London. He knew Frank Stubbs worked until six every weekday. He punched in the number. After six or more rings he got an answer.

Frank's voice sounded weary when he answered, 'Hello?'

'You have keys to the flat?' Veleta said.

'Yes, Harry.'

'Can you go there now and collect something for me?'

'I can leave in thirty minutes, what is it?'

Veleta explained in detail.

'What do you want done with them?'

'I expect to be in London by Friday morning at the latest. Keep the items until I arrive. I'll call you with the details tomorrow. Any problems, call me on this number,' reading out the number from the label Garcia had stuck on the back of the mobile.

'Right, I'll wait for your call.' Frank heard the dial tone. He knew now was not the time for small talk.

Veleta made another call, this time to a number in Alicante. The Costa Blanca was still teeming with tourists at this time of year and the man he called would be able to do his bidding. His instructions, in fluent Spanish, were precise and he accepted the exorbitant price requested for the service without a protest. He was guaranteed a result by the following day.

CHAPTER 10

The plate of sandwiches was empty. Alice poured the last of the coffee into their cups and replenished her glass.

Daisy leaned back on her chair and did some thinking for a few moments before speaking. 'As I see it there are three options to consider: One, the bomb was a random Dissident IRA attack, just bad luck Abdullah and Mary were there.'

'I don't know,' Alice said. 'There's been no IRA activity on the mainland for several years.'

'There were several bombs in Northern Ireland in the past year which were attributed to the Real IRA, but if I remember rightly in each case there was always a coded telephone warning to the press,' said Angus.

'Correct, there's always a warning, but none this time,' Daisy said.

Alice nodded. 'It also strikes me, the odds of a random car-bomb exploding at exactly the moment Abdullah steps out of his front door is a tall order, plus the fact that their car-bomb was parked outside his front door. That had to be prearranged by parking a switch-car there overnight. It's all a tad too sophisticated for IRA.'

'Agreed,' Daisy said. 'But it can't be ruled out completely, which is why I suggested to Isaacs, he ask the Fisherman.'

Alice took a sip from her glass as she considered this. 'Good idea, he would certainly know.'

Angus looked from one to the other before posing the question. 'Who exactly is the Fisherman, Daisy?'

Giving him her sternest look, Daisy said, 'An old and reliable contact, Angus, before your time and not to be mentioned again.'

Angus nodded.

'Okay,' Alice said. 'IRA can be ruled in or out quite quickly, what's your second option?'

'Abdullah was the target, and they used a remote to trigger the bomb.'

'Forensics will be able to confirm this,' Angus said.

Draining her glass and contemplating the empty for a moment before pushing it aside, Alice said, 'In which case, you don't need to get involved, you can leave it to Isaacs and Farmer.'

Raising her voice and slapping the desk, Daisy said, 'No bloody way. As I've already said, my friend was killed by whoever planted the bomb, which makes me involved, no matter what. Besides, Isaacs is worried about an ongoing threat which may be connected to this. He wants our help.'

Alice thought about it for a moment. 'Which makes you official.'

'Exactly, which is why I agreed,' Daisy said.

'And what if there's no evidence of a remote?' Alice asked.

Daisy drained the last of her coffee before replying, 'For Abdullah to be the target, there has to be a remote. If they relied solely on the timer, how could they guarantee he would step out at that exact moment? All it would take is for him to have a phone call or an urgent call of nature and their plan would fail.'

'He was punctual to a fault and they knew it,' Alice said.

Shaking her head Daisy said, 'No, we don't know it, according to the taxi company Abdullah wanted Mary to be waiting outside when he came out, it's not the same thing. He may have varied his timing by a few minutes; if so, to be sure, they would have to use a remote.'

Alice eyed her empty glass for a moment and then said, 'Okay, so, to repeat, if we rule out IRA and they don't find evidence of a remote?'

Daisy leaned over to replenish Alice's glass and said, 'Have a roady, Alice.'

As she spoke, the memory of Mary Grey's beautiful eyes closing for the last time and her final words filled her brain and a thought that had been lingering in the back of her mind suddenly crystallised.

'You know, guys,' she said. 'I think there's a third option.'

Alice smiled her appreciation and sipped the Scotch before saying, 'A third option?'

'Yes, there is. Mary could have been the target. She ticks all the boxes, she was always there several minutes before 8.45. The BMW was parked in front of her parking spot. Her windscreen would face the explosion full on. She could never survive the explosion.'

'Now, you're being just a wee bit fanciful, Daisy,' Alice said. 'Why go to all that trouble to murder a taxi driver, when it would be a lot easier to hail her, give her a remote address where she could be shot or stabbed and pass it off as a mugging that went wrong?'

Daisy considered this and nodded. 'As usual you have a point, Alice, but there's also the possibility that if, Mary was the target, and whoever's behind this didn't want anyone looking too closely into her life, killing Abdullah also, would provide the perfect smoke-screen.'

'That's your three options,' said Angus. 'If we find evidence of a remote the target is Abdullah, if there's no remote it's most likely Dissident IRA. I'll buy either. Mary Grey is pretty unlikely.'

'Unlikely or not we can't rule it out,' Daisy said.

Alice stood up. 'It's past seven and as nothing further can be resolved before you see the forensics report. I'm going home to my husband. What do you want me to do, Daisy?'

'For the next few days look after the shop, reschedule my meetings and tell the team you're in charge until I return.'

'How many days exactly?'

'As long as it takes, Alice, I'll be in and out.'

Alice gave her a long look. 'Just be mindful, Daisy, these people are killers, once they find out, which they will, you're looking for them, they'll come for you. Remember the drill, keep your mobile switched on. We can track you if you sound the alarm and make sure you carry your Beretta. Take care.' She lifted her tray and headed for the door.

When they were alone Angus spoke. 'What plans do you have for me, Daisy?'

Daisy, who preferred to work alone, but mindful of the young man's feelings said softly, 'At the moment Angus, nothing. If it turns out to be IRA, you can be a great help to me, we'll have to dig into the old files. Give me your mobile number and I'll call you.'

A dejected Angus produced his card. 'What about if I be your driver? I'd like to be on the outside for a change.'

Daisy smiled. 'I'll bear that in mind, Angus. Unfortunately the people I would need to talk to would clam up in front of a witness.'

'Don't you need a ride home?'

Smiling warmly, she said, 'It's okay, I'll take a taxi and thanks for looking after me, Angus. I won't forget it. Come, I'll see you out,' she said, leading the way to the lift.

Returning to her office and mindful of Alice's warning she went to the Milner safe, spun the dial, opened it and removed her Beretta automatic wrapped in soft chamois, a box of cartridges and a thick manila envelope and placed them on her desk.

Ejecting the empty magazine, she inspected the gun with a practised eye, snapping the slide back to check the action. Satisfied, she carefully loaded ten rounds of .40 Smith & Wesson into the magazine. She had trusted this gun with her life and had often wondered if she would ever fire it again outside the range. *Let's hope this is not the time,* she thought as she slipped the gun into a belt holster and clipped it on under her jacket, which concealed it perfectly.

The manila envelope contained an Irish passport in the name of

Margaret Maguire, issued in London and still in date. On the first page was a younger but not so different photo of herself. The envelope also contained a current Visa and American Express card and an international driving license in the same name. She looked at the passport for a long moment before shaking her head and putting everything relating to Margaret Maguire back in the safe, thinking, *Maggie can stay dead for the moment*. She had always trusted her instincts, and in this case, they told her this was not IRA. Before closing the safe she removed two bundles of cash – one in euros and the other sterling.

She put the cash in her briefcase, rang for a taxi and went downstairs. Within fifteen minutes she was going down Park Lane for the fourth time that day. As the taxi turned into the Bayswater Road her mobile rang. She saw the caller was Jack Farmer.

'Hello Jack.'

Farmer, his west country accent more pronounced over the telephone, said, 'You all right, Daisy?'

'Thanks for asking, Jack. I'll live. Anything new?'

'It's early days. Daisy I thought you were a smart girl, just how did Isaacs persuade you to work for him?'

Daisy laughed. 'He promised me an OBE, how could I refuse?'

Farmer snorted 'That's bullshit, Daisy. I know you too well. You're after vengeance, my girl, and you want Isaacs' cover for any shit you get up to.'

'You could be right, Jack. I'm glad you called, we need to meet.'

'We certainly do. Can you come over first thing? I'll send a car for you.'

'Sure, what time?'

'Eight, is that too early?'

'It'll be fine.'

'Good, now listen, the reason I called is there's to be a press conference in half an hour from now when Prince Abdullah's death will be announced. His family have been advised. We haven't been able to find any next of kin for Mary Grey. I can't name her until her family, if any, are informed. We haven't found her keys yet or I'd have sent a PC.'

'Did you check with the company she works for?' Daisy asked.

'Yeah, London Quality Taxis, and no, they didn't have anything. Can you get into her apartment?'

'I can,' Daisy said. 'She kept my keys and I have hers.'

'I thought as much. Can you have a look at her address book?'

Daisy – mindful of Mary's last words – was eager to look through Mary's papers, and asked, 'This is official police business, right?'

'As official as you like,' Farmer said.

'Good,' Daisy said. 'If I find something, I'll call you. One more thing, has Isaacs asked you to speak to the Fisherman?'

'No, I haven't spoken to Isaacs yet. What about the Fisherman?'

'Are you still able to speak to him?'

After a moment's silence Farmer said, 'It's possible, why?'

'If this is Irish, he would know.'

Farmer snorted. 'You want me to ask him straight out, just like that?'

'Why not? He's got as much to lose as anyone.'

'I guess you're right. Okay, I'll call him.'

CHAPTER 11

It was after eight o'clock when Daisy reached her apartment. As usual, she found Heinz on her bed, where he made a big show of stretching luxuriously before following her to the kitchen for his dinner. After putting his food down, she thought of her own dinner but decided it could wait. Farmer needed to contact Mary's next of kin before the story got into the newspapers. Finding the keys, she went downstairs.

The door of Mary's apartment opened onto a spacious living room, which was familiar to Daisy. Not only was she a regular visitor but the layout was an exact copy of her own: Living room, kitchen-diner, one-bedroom ensuite, a guest bedroom, bathroom and a small balcony overlooking the street. It was tastefully but sparingly furnished with a sofa and two easy chairs. A TV was standing on a unit which also contained a disc recorder and sound system. There was a shelving unit which contained books, CDs and DVDs.

Daisy couldn't recall Mary ever talking about her family, in fact now that she thought about it, Mary had never discussed her private life at all, which in itself was unusual. *Maybe she was an orphan. Best find her address book and have a look.* After flicking through the bookcase without success, she realised she should have asked Farmer if he'd looked through her Nokia, if it survived the blast.

There was a phone answering unit with a portable handset. She scrolled through the index, mostly familiar names, none of which looked like a relative. One entry was not a name, just the initial H. Could it stand for Harry? 'Mary's last words were to Harry.'

It was 00.34, a Spanish number. Daisy wrote the number in her notebook. Checking the call log, she saw the 'H' number was dialled at 07.23 today. Scrolling through the calls received log she found only three calls – all Private and today – timed at 09.20, 09.45 and 10.02.

Maybe it was the 'H' number returning her call. *Interesting*, she thought. All the other names in the list were complete or abbreviated in such a way as to be easily recognisable, why only 'H'? She should call the number later.

A search of Mary's bedroom only yielded a confirmed airline reservation to Alicante, Spain, in a week's time, and a passport. Mary had told her she was going to Spain for a couple of weeks. Mary's date of birth was on the passport. Daisy noted it in her pad. Mary was forty-five. Still thought Daisy, she could easily have passed for the twenty-nine she claimed to be.

The kitchen-diner was spacious and expensively fitted out. Daisy had often wondered how Mary managed on a taxi driver's wages; maybe her friend in Spain was rich or then again based on the little she really knew of Mary, she could have been an eccentric millionaire.

So far, she had not yet found any bills or financial statements. She kept her own housekeeping accounts in a folder in her kitchen, maybe Mary did the same. She flicked through a shelf of cookery books and kitchen equipment manuals. One of them was a springback folder with a picture of Delia Smith the TV chef on the cover and titled DELIA'S INSTANT MEALS.

Mary's last word had been, "Delia, Delia." 'God, poor Mary.' Thinking of it, her eyes welled again. She knew those last moments with Mary were going to haunt her for a long time. Finding a paper towel, she wiped her eyes and composed herself but her hands shook as she pulled out the file and opened it.

There were no recipes for instant meals in the folder, instead there was a two-inch-thick wad of yellowing newspaper cuttings, from single columns to folded pages, each dated and neatly filed in an A4 plastic insert. A label on the first insert read: *Gloria* 1986. Wondering who Gloria might be, she flicked through the cuttings and shook the folder. A photograph fell out.

Unlike the cuttings, it was not old. There was a date written on the back – 26th August '06 – and what she recognised as the same Spanish number from the phone index. The photograph was of a smiling Mary standing at the stern of a yacht. She was wearing shorts and a bikini top and looked happy. It was a large and expensive yacht, with its name and port of origin clearly visible. *The Lady Mary*, the home port Murcia.

Standing beside Mary, his arm around her shoulder, was a tall, dark-haired man. A pair of mirrored Pilot sunglasses covered his eyes. He had a deep tan and strong mouth and chin. His dark hair and sideburns were flecked with grey.

What a dark horse Mary was to keep her handsome and obviously rich friend a secret, Daisy thought, and wondered how many more secrets Mary had kept from her. Maybe the cuttings would tell her.

Laying the folder on a worktop, she began reading. The oldest cutting, which was a full page of the *Daily Herald*, with the headline: **Goddess of the Silver Screen, Marilyn Monroe is Dead!** A picture of the star's most iconic pose in the *Seven Year Itch* filled most of the page.

A small article at the bottom right was titled: **Sidney Vane hanged in Pentonville.** The date was the fifth of August 1962. Daisy checked her notebook. That was Mary's date of birth. Probably just a keepsake – lots of people are given newspapers from the day they were born, but they usually frame and put them on display.

Mounted in the second page was a faded black and white wedding photo. The bride, with shoulder-length blonde hair and a wicked smile – looking stunning despite her simple white dress – stood a touch taller than the groom who was a darkly handsome fellow with calm eyes, dressed in army uniform. The three stripes on his arm made him a sergeant and among the war service medals pinned on his chest, Daisy recognised the silver one with the head of King George VI on it. *A military medal – a hero then,* she thought. There was no caption and she wondered who the couple were. The mount next to it which had come unstuck, must have held the photo of Mary on the yacht.

The rest of the cuttings, also from the *Daily Herald,* followed a pattern: robberies, carried out by a gang of expert safe-blowers. Daisy speed-read as she paged through.

From 1976 to 1986, a series of high-value robberies took place in London. Safes and vaults were blown – always at midnight. The gang used a harmless, but loud, decoy bomb placed in close proximity to the robbery site, which masked the sound of the vault door being blown. Because of this MO, the perpetrator was soon dubbed the Midnight Fox in the popular press.

Over the ten years, their haul amounted to several million pounds. Big money even by today's reckoning, she thought as she read. The gang's last robbery was in 1986 and netted them 10,000 Krugerrands. *Strewth,* Daisy was thinking. *Even in 1986, that haul must have been worth millions.* She was about to read the last cutting, which was dated two weeks after the Krugerrand robbery and headlined **Crime Boss Found Dead in Thames**, when she heard a key turning in the door. She slipped the photo of Mary into her pocket, closed the file and returned it to the shelf. *Who the hell else has a key?* she thought.

She came out of the kitchen just in time to see the back of a man as he closed the door. When he turned and saw her, his eyes widened in surprise. In a voice that sounded like gravel pouring out of a bucket, he said, 'Who in hell's you? What's your business here?'

The man had the build of a bouncer, and a nose which had been rearranged at some time. His watery grey eyes looked at Daisy with deep suspicion.

'I might ask you the same question,' Daisy said, trying to sound more confident than she felt.

Moving towards her, he growled, 'I asked first.'

Daisy stood her ground. 'I'm here on official police business, looking for Mary Grey's next of kin.'

Still looking belligerent, he said, 'Okay then, show me your warrant card.'

Daisy wrote a number on her pad and handed it to him. 'I don't have one, but if you're worried, ring this number and ask to speak to Commander Farmer at Scotland Yard. He'll vouch for me. Now it's your turn, mister. Who are you and what's your business here?' Daisy felt comforted by the feel of the Beretta under her coat.

The man looked at the number and either recognised it or accepted the situation. 'I'm Frank, the manager of Mary's taxi company.'

'You have a surname, Frank?'

Not meeting her gaze, he answered, 'Stubbs.'

Daisy sensed the big man's unease and took the initiative. 'Good, now let's see some ID.'

Frank fumbled in an inside pocket, produced a wallet and removed a driver's licence.

Daisy glanced at it, wrote his name, date of birth and address on her pad and handed it back.

'What's your business here, Mr Stubbs?'

'The police have been to the office and told me what happened. Terrible shame. Lovely girl, Mary was, always cheerful, best driver we had.' Tears welled in the big man's eyes. He pulled out a colourful handkerchief and blew his nose violently. 'Sorry about that.'

Either he was genuinely grieving, Daisy was thinking, or he should be on the stage.

Putting his handkerchief in his pocket, he continued. 'She left a set of keys with me; I came to go through her papers to try and find some relative to call – none of the other drivers knew if she had any close family.'

Now feeling compassion for him, Daisy said, 'Mary was my friend too. I live in the apartment upstairs and was with her when she died.'

Looking less menacing, he said, 'You said you were a cop.'

Daisy shook her head. 'No, I said I was here on police business, which is true, but I'm not a cop and I'm also trying to find Mary's relatives.'

The big man's shoulder's relaxed and he said, 'That's all right then, isn't it? Did you find anything?'

His obvious relief of her not being a cop was not lost on Daisy as she replied, 'Nobody I didn't know already, no relatives. Did you know she had a friend living in Spain?'

Frank nodded. 'Yeah, she used to visit someone several times a year, but she kept shtum about who it was. You said you was there when she died, how come?'

Daisy told him everything that happened.

Frank, after listening without interruption, asked, 'Is that when you got those?' pointing to her plaster and scratches.

'Yes, I managed to get her out of the taxi before the second explosion but it was too late.'

Giving her a thoughtful look, Frank asked, 'Did she say anything?'

'A few words,' Daisy said. 'Do you know anyone called Harry?'

Daisy was sure there was a brief reaction to the name, before he said, 'Can't say I do, what did she say?'

Shaking her head, she said, 'Sorry, the words were for Harry. Look, I'm finished here. We'd better lock up and go.'

Frank shrugged. 'Yeah, I suppose,' and turned towards the door.

She followed him out and locked up, then walked Frank to the lift and waited with him.

'What about the funeral? The drivers will want to be there,' he asked.

'I don't know,' Daisy said. 'Let's hope someone close to her comes forward, otherwise I'll have to organise it when her body is released. Do you know if she was religious?'

The lift arrived. Stubbs held the door. 'She was born a Catholic, but I don't know if she went to church. Let me know about the funeral,' he said and stepped in.

The doors had closed before she remembered he still had a set of keys. She should have taken them and was about to take the stairs to intercept him when she heard the lift reach the ground floor. She'd call on him tomorrow.

Returning to her apartment she opened the door to the balcony and let Heinz out, then put a chilli con carne in the microwave for herself and opened a bottle of Dom Brial.

Sipping the wine, she looked again at Mary's photo and her thoughts drifted to the Delia folder. The collection of news stories chronicling the Midnight Fox robberies was labelled *Gloria 1986*. The last robbery was in 1986, but who was Gloria and what was her connection to Mary?

Mary would have been twenty-four in 1986. Maybe she was a member of the Gang. That would explain her being able to own the apartment downstairs.

Frank Stubbs's age, according to his driving licence, was sixty-one. He'd have been seventeen when Mary was born. He had said Mary was born a Catholic. She may have told him, or he could have known her from birth. If so, he was lying about not knowing any of her relatives. That is not to say any of them are still alive, but if Stubbs already knew this, what was he looking for in the apartment? She'd better read that Delia file again. Mary had made a great effort to name it before she died, it must be significant.

After finishing her meal, she returned to Mary's apartment. There was no sound of life anywhere in the building. She let herself in, closed the door and without putting on the light opened the French doors and looked over the street. It was quiet. *Why the worry?* she thought. She was still on police business and entitled to be here, but some instinct urged caution. Best read the file again and then make a more thorough search of the apartment. If Frank Stubbs was looking for something, what was it?

The kitchen, which was on the garden side of the apartment, had a window which was not visible from the street. She had enough light from the living room window to manage the two steps down the kitchen level. Closing the door, she put the light on.

Everything seemed to be exactly as she had left it an hour before. The line of books was still on the shelf, that is, with the exception of the Delia folder. It was not where she had put it, in fact it was not there at all. She searched through all the books. It was definitely gone.

She examined the apartment door. It had two locks – one a Yale, the other a Chubb mortice. Neither showed any signs of tampering, but remembering the news stories in the Delia file about the gang of safe crackers, who could probably open any door, it did not mean keys were used. Frank Stubbs had keys and was looking for something, probably he came back and took the file. If he did, he would certainly deny it, but why did he want it? All the events it described were ancient history, or were they?

She checked all the windows and found one in the small bathroom unlocked. Climbing onto the toilet seat she was able to look out and see it was on the corner of the building out of sight of the street and there was four-inch waste pipe running alongside it, with a tree offering further screening it from the street. It was a definite possibility for an agile visitor, but unlikely, she thought, that kind of skill wasn't needed by today's crims, peddling drugs being the softer option.

She began a thorough search of the apartment, delving into every cupboard and every drawer, including the undersides, in case something might be taped to it. She emptied the contents of all the containers in the kitchen, searched the clothes in Mary's wardrobe, even the mattress on Mary's bed, and found nothing. After an hour of this she was sure there was nothing to be found.

After locking up she returned to her apartment, poured herself a coffee and settled herself into a chair at the dining table which also served as her desk. Being blessed with an excellent memory, particularly when it came to dates, she began writing on a legal pad. She knew the first date was the day Marilyn Monroe died, fifth August 1962. She also knew a man called Sidney Vane was hanged in Pentonville Prison on the same day which was also the day Mary Grey was born. Did Mary keep the page as a reminder of her birthday or was she interested in Sidney Vane? As all the other stories were about a gang of safe breakers, Vane, although he was hanged fourteen years before the first robbery, may have been linked to the robbers.

And then there was the Crime Boss found dead in the river, what was his name? She didn't have time to read the article when Stubbs interrupted her but she remembered the date.

Mary's last words had been: "Harry – you can trust Harry... tell him... he's alive I heard his voice... Delia... Delia" – and then her last gasp, was it just, a gasp or was it a name? She tried to recall the scene, but all she saw were Mary's green eyes closing for the last time. *Leave it,* she thought, *it's been a tough day, it will come.* It was at *that* moment she remembered the name Mary had written on the envelope, Zentek Aviation. She wrote it on the pad. Mary said it was a company, easy to check, a job for Alice this time.

Looking at the list of dates she had dragged from memory, she was confident enough that she would be able to recreate the Delia file if she visited the national newspaper archive in Colindale. A job for tomorrow, she resolved, directly after meeting Jack Farmer. She was now surer than ever, the solution to this case involved Mary Grey and the Midnight Fox gang. For every robbery they had used a decoy bomb. In this case it looked like the unfortunate Prince Abdullah had been the decoy.

CHAPTER 12

After taking a couple of sleeping pills Daisy had eight hours of uninterrupted sleep and despite a few aches in her bones and a mild throbbing from the wound in her forehead she felt refreshed. As usual Heinz performed his stretching exercises at the end of the bed before jumping down and heading for the door to be let out onto the balcony.

After showering she examined her face in the bathroom mirror. The scratches were healing nicely. She gingerly peeled off the dressing covering her stitches as instructed by Mrs Hollis. The seven stitches holding the wound in a thin line seemed to be doing their job and there was no sign of infection. She cleaned the wound before painting it with Betadine and replaced the dressing. To ease the throbbing, she swallowed two Panadols and stayed in her pyjamas while she made her breakfast. Today it was two croissants and coffee in the microwave and a fresh bowl of water and crunchies for Heinz.

The intercom rang at exactly 08.00. Farmer's car had arrived, and within thirty minutes she was being shown into Farmer's office at New Scotland Yard. He was on the phone, listening with the odd grunt, but smiled when he saw her and waved her to a chair in front of his desk, which she dropped into.

'Thank you, sir, that's very helpful,' Farmer said and hung up.

He stood up and walked around the desk to inspect Daisy's face. 'You don't look too bad this morning, Daisy,' he said and gave her a peck on the check. 'You were lucky, a bit closer and you'd have had the full blast.'

Looking up at him, Daisy said, 'You're cheerful this morning, Jack.'

'And I should be, that was the Fisherman I was talking to, you remember him?'

'Of course, I do,' she said. 'I see you've already forgotten it was me who suggested that you speak to him.'

Farmer gave her a satisfied smile. 'That's the way it works, Daisy, isn't it? You do the work. I take the credit. You prefer to stay in the shadows. I have the public to deal with.'

She shrugged. 'That's fine by me, Jack. I don't want any truck with either the new or the old IRA. The Fisherman's a big man these days, isn't he? What did he say?'

Farmer returned to his seat and snorted. 'He was always a big man, and lucky for us he's someone we can do business with. He told me categorically there was no Irish involvement in yesterday's bomb, which means we now have two options: Abdullah or Mary Grey, my money's on Abdullah.'

Daisy slapped the desk. 'Don't bet your house on it, Jack. For it to be Abdullah, we'll need to find evidence of a remote, otherwise I don't buy it.'

'Wrong, Daisy,' he said. 'The man was punctual to a fault; we checked it with the taxi company, according to them he was always on time.'

Daisy disagreed. 'Nobody's that punctual, Jack. Any little thing could have delayed him for a minute or two. The only one who was always there at 08.45 was Mary Grey. For me to buy Abdullah, we need the remote. What's the story on the forensics? That should tell us something?'

'Ernie and his team have worked all night; I'm going over there next.'

'Can I tag along? I haven't seen Ernie for years.'

'Why not? Isaacs said you were now part of the team.' He pushed a button on his intercom to be answered instantly by a female voice.

'Sir?'

'Have my car out front, I'm going to Elephant & Castle.'

'Yes sir.'

Turning to Daisy he said, 'That'll take five minutes. I take it you found nothing on Mary Grey?'

For a moment Daisy considered telling him about finding the Delia file, Franks Stubbs' visit and the file's disappearance, but decided she wanted to do a little digging herself first.

Instead she said, 'No luck, Jack. I checked her address book and had a look through her papers, but didn't find any relatives, just friends I already know. Did you find her Nokia?'

'Not yet, it's probably still in the taxi.'

As he spoke the intercom buzzed and the female voice said, 'Your car's outside, sir.'

The forensic laboratory for the Metropolitan Police was located in an anonymous industrial building in an equally anonymous side street off the Old Kent Road in Elephant & Castle. Surrounded by a high wall protected with coiled razor wire, its only oddities among the other buildings in the street were the CCTV cameras and floodlights covering every part of the yard.

Farmer's driver had a remote for the gates which swung smoothly back on his command. A line of unmarked cars were parked in their allocated space in front of the building. Farmer's driver parked in one of the four visitor spaces.

After Farmer signed Daisy in, they walked through an open-plan laboratory – where white coated men and women were working at various instruments – to the conference room.

Daisy saw DCI Sandys was already there, drinking coffee and looking through a pile of photo enlargements on the table. With him she recognised Ernie Watters, head of forensics.

Unlike the usual dour type associated with scientists, Ernie was a positively cheerful fellow, and greeted them smiling, with an outstretched hand.

'Morning Jack, how's your luck?' Without waiting for a response, he turned to Daisy and gave her a hug. 'Daisy my love, I'd thought you'd gone out of my life forever, what's happened to your face?'

'Just an argument with the pavement, Ernie,' she said, laughingly returning the hug.

'Nobody tells me anything,' said Ernie. 'How come you're hobnobbing it with the hoi- polloi.'

'She's working with Peter Isaacs' mob for this job only,' Farmer growled as he poured himself a coffee from a Thermos jug. Help yourself to coffee, Daisy,' he said, before leaning over to inspect the photos. 'Looks like you've had a busy night, Ernie, what have we got here?'

Pouring herself a coffee Daisy dropped into the nearest available chair. *Best listen and learn,* she thought.

Picking out two of the photographs Watters said, 'We've been here all night but we've made progress. I'll go through the results. Here are the chassis and engine numbers of the BMW. It's a 1988 300 series metallic green.'

Farmer gave the photos a glance before handing them back. 'Good detail, but we've already traced the car. We found a number plate at the scene which turned out to be the genuine article. I take it you received the three grand in fifties that was paid for it?'

Watters nodded, saying, 'We have. The bills haven't been checked for prints yet, the bomb being the priority.'

'Dead right,' Farmer said. 'What about the bomb?'

Ernie, nodding enthusiastically said, 'First thoughts were, car bomb equals IRA, but now I'd be inclined to rule out IRA. The explosive was commercial plastic C4 and the timer was mechanical. The IRA have used Semtex ever since Colonel Gaddafi gave them tons of the stuff. Even after the so-called arms decommissioning there must be plenty unaccounted for.'

'Agreed,' Farmer said. 'We've already ruled them out, what about the timer?'

Ernie shook his head and picked up one of the photos. 'Again, not IRA. They've used electronic timers since the early nineties.' Pointing to the photo he said, 'Look at this piece, this a from a mechanical timer.'

Farmer, inspecting the enlargement said, 'What am I looking at, a cheap alarm clock?'

'A clock certainly, but definitely not cheap,' said Ernie, pointing to an enlargement of a brass sprocket. 'See this edge? This baby's been hand cut by a master craftsman, not stamped out in mass production.'

'So, we have a rich bomber and a dead Arab, that figures,' Farmer said and passed the photo to Daisy.

Not being an expert in things mechanical, she gave the print a long enough look to show interest before asking the question foremost in her mind. 'What about a remote, Ernie?'

Shaking his head, Ernie said, 'We found no electronics, Daisy. When a remote is used there's always fragments of electronics.'

'A quality timer like that, should be pretty accurate,' she said.

Nodding agreement, he replied, 'To a few seconds I would guess.'

'According to the taxi company Abdullah stepped out every morning on the dot of 8.45,' DCI Sandys said.

Daisy glared at him and said, 'We don't know that for sure. All we do know for sure is Mary Grey was always there at that time, and the bomb exploded at 8.45. Without a remote I don't buy it being a hit on Abdullah.'

'They're both dead, so we know Abdullah was punctual yesterday.' Farmer growled and asked, 'Can we trace the clock?'

Ernie shrugged. 'There's not much left, but you can try some of the top manufacturing jewellers. There's still a few old craftsmen working, one of them might recognise the work.'

Farmer nodded. 'Let's hope so. Can you get a batch of these photos over to my office? I'll put a team on it. Anything new on the victim, Len?'

Sandys, shaking his head said, 'Victims, Guv, we have two victims.'

Farmer snorted. 'I hear what you're saying, Len, one dead VIP and one unlucky lady who was in the wrong place at the wrong time. Let's concentrate on Abdullah.'

With another shake of the head, Sandys said, 'We've found nothing suspicious in his house which might explain why someone wanted him dead. We're trying to trace his movements after he leaves the mosque.'

'Anything else, Ernie?' Farmer said.

Ernie hesitated for a moment before saying, 'Well, there is something. I'm not sure if it's relevant. I've checked our records for precision mechanical timers and found something. During the seventies and eighties, a gang of safe-blowers used a clock like this. I can't say if it's the same but the description fits.'

Poker faced, Daisy asked, 'What was the gang called?' For the moment she thought it best not to mention the Delia file, particularly as she couldn't produce it.

Ernie thought for a moment before answering. 'No idea, there were never any convictions, so no names. We only keep records of methods and devices plus the crime reference number.'

'What about dates of the robberies?' Daisy asked.

'Yeah, sure, we have the dates, but I don't think...'

Smiling, she said, 'You know me, Ernie, you said it yourself once. I'm a picky SOB, but I do like to follow every little thing, no matter how irrelevant, one never knows where it might lead.'

Ernie protested. 'I don't remember saying that, Daisy, it must have been in the heat of the moment.'

'Whatever, please call me with the dates,' she said, handing him her card.

'Sure, I'll get on it straight away and call you within the hour.'

Slapping his arm Daisy said, 'Great, Ernie. I owe you a good lunch, I won't forget.'

Looking at the two of them Farmer growled. 'I suppose you both know that bribing a police officer is a criminal offence.'

Daisy laughed. 'I'll remember that, Commander, the next time we go to the Ivy.'

Raising an eyebrow Farmer said, 'Funny woman. Okay, we're done. Thanks a lot, Ernie, anything else you come up with rush it over to me.'

Ernie saw them to the door and shook hands with Farmer and Sandy.

Daisy hugged him and whispered in his ear. 'Send me a set of the photos, Ernie.'

'Sure, nice to see you again, Daisy,' he whispered. 'Try and stay out of trouble.'

CHAPTER 13

It was almost ten o'clock by the time Kaminski had found a pay and display parking space, fed the machine with coins enough for an hour and a half and walked the hundred or so metres to number 34 Symonds Street, W1. The brass plate advertised Dr Taleb, dentist, by appointment only. She pressed the intercom to be answered by a female voice.

'Doctor Taleb's surgery.'

'It's Mrs Kaminski, I have an appointment.'

The door lock rattled and the door sprung open, Kaminski stepped inside and closed it. She knew the dentist's surgery was in the basement but she had no interest in having any of her molars treated, instead, she waited in the wood-panelled entrance hall.

It had three unmarked doors, all closed. The one painted green she knew led to the dentist's surgery. Genuine patients were told to take this door. It reminded her of another green door which led to an execution chamber in her previous life in the StB. Unfortunates entered trembling in fear. Maybe some people feared a visit to the dentist in the same way. The thought amused her, and Kaminski was not the kind of person who was easily amused.

The door facing the entrance opened and a tall bearded man – she knew to be Pakistani – with cold black eyes and looking decidedly out of character wearing a grey double-breasted suit, beckoned her to follow him. Behind the door was another smaller hall and a staircase. Without saying a word, he pointed to a narrow table, standing against the wall.

Kaminski knew the routine. She didn't know if he was a mute or not but she had never heard him speak. She put her briefcase on the table and slipping her switchblade from her pocket, placed it beside it.

Opening the case, she watched as he checked each section. Satisfied, he turned to her and expertly frisked her. His hands were surprisingly gentle, she thought, but then she had also known torturers who were equally gentle up to a point. She faced him, maintaining a look of contempt during this procedure, which bothered him not one bit. Another nod indicated his approval. He stood back and waited for her to adjust her clothing and close the briefcase. She left the switchblade on the table and followed him to the first floor where he stopped outside a door and nodded again. She knew he would stand outside until her meeting was over.

She knocked and entered. Inside the man she knew only as the Mr Iqbal was at his desk reading *The Times*. Kramer had told her Iqbal had been a General in the Pakistan Army before politics forced his sudden departure and a change of allegiance. He was a small man for a General, she had thought when they first met, but he was of a type she was familiar with. A man who, by a combination of wile and ruthlessness always managed to succeed for a time but usually made too many enemies for a long-term career.

His piercing black eyes had the look of a fanatic and she knew he didn't like dealing with women, but Kramer only left Hampstead when he had to and insisted she be the go-between.

'Good morning Mr Iqbal,' she said, offering her hand which was ignored.

'Sit down, Mrs Kaminski,' he said as he put the newspaper aside. 'I take it you have positive news for me.'

Seating herself in the chair in front of the desk she said, 'Yes, the shipment arrived at Tilbury today. It will be cleared customs and in London by tomorrow. Our man in the customs service will see to it personally.'

'He knows nothing of the contents?'

'According to the manifest, it contains an aircraft compressor.'

'He believes it?'

Kaminski smiled. Shaking her head, she said, 'Of course not, the man is a senior customs officer and no fool. We pay him good money not to ask questions.'

'Excellent, what are the arrangements for the handover?'

'As I said we expect it to arrive in London tomorrow. Once we have it, we can make the final arrangements.'

'Good,' Iqbal said. 'I think that concludes our business, Mrs Kaminski. I look forward to our next meeting, good day.'

Staying seated, Kaminski leaned forward and put her hands on the desk, her eyes acquiring a look, which, in the past had unsettled stronger men than she thought Iqbal to be.

'Not quite, Mr Iqbal,' she said in an equally unsettling voice. 'There is the matter of payment. Mr Kramer has suggested I see the money before we proceed any further.'

Without answering Iqbal stood up and left the room. Kaminski heard him talking in a language she did not understand. Within a minute or two he returned carrying a slim leather briefcase which he snapped open on the desk and pushed towards her, saying, 'Here is the agreed amount, you can inspect it.'

Inside Kaminski saw five packets of violet banknotes, each with a bank wrapper indicating one hundred notes and there were two layers. Taking one of the packets she flicked through the notes, each of which was for one thousand Swiss francs, which besides being the highest denomination banknote available in the world, it was also the most easily concealable and a favourite of the criminal fraternity.

'Perhaps you would like to count them, Mrs Kaminski?'

'That won't be necessary, Mr Iqbal, I'll leave that pleasure for Mr Kramer.'

'Good, one more thing, in order to save time during the handover will you arrange to have the container open for inspection? We would not like to buy, as one says, "a pig in the poke."' His face adopted what he considered passed for a smile. It was more like a grimace.

'I'll see to it, Mr Iqbal.' Kaminski stood up and left the room. The bearded Walah was waiting in the corridor to escort her to the front door. She picked up her switchblade and left.

Gomez knew he was late. He had promised Veleta eleven and it was now thirty minutes past. He knew Veleta did not like tardiness. Gomez was not a coward, he was feared among his own kind, but there was something about this man Veleta that frightened him. He parked his car by the yacht and hurried up the stern gangplank and along the covered deck to the bridge.

The skipper, who was poring over charts, looked up. You're late, Gomez, you know he doesn't like people to be late.'

'The arrangements were not easy, with such little notice. Where is Señor Veleta?'

'In his stateroom, you know the way,' he said, unrolling another chart.

Veleta was seated in a pilot's chair looking out at the harbour, seeing nothing but Mary's face. On a low table was a copy of the *Daily Herald*; the front page had a photograph of Prince Abdullah in traditional clothes. There was no picture of Mary Grey.

There was a timid knock on the door.

'Come in.'

Gomez entered and waited in the middle of the room. Veleta slid off his chair.

Giving the visitor a cold look, he said, 'You're late, Gomez.'

Gomez, whose right eye gave a nervous tic said, 'Señor, we only had a few hours' notice. My men worked all night.'

Gomez was a criminal and in his business, Veleta had to deal with criminals, be they people like Gomez or dubious lawyers or bankers, even the police on occasion, it didn't matter which, but he knew the only way to keep him honest in their dealings with him was to add the element of fear and over the years he had developed a particular hard-faced persona to achieve this in a satisfactory manner.

Holding his hand out, Veleta said, 'Show me.'

Gomez opened his attaché case and removed a manila envelope and handed it to Veleta.

Taking a switchblade from his pocket, Veleta sprung the blade with a practised move, slit the envelope and dumped the contents on the low table: a wallet, airline ticket and a British passport. He opened the passport.

'Andrew Stafford, age fifty-four, height five-eleven, the photograph is good enough. Mr Stafford is being looked after?'

Gomez nodded eagerly. 'He'll wake up in thirty-six hours and be found wandering the streets without any bad memories.'

'You have his luggage?'

'Of course, one suitcase and a set of golf clubs.'

Nodding approval, Veleta said, 'Golf clubs, good, what time is the flight?'

'Six fifteen tomorrow morning, señor, from Alicante, you should be in Luton Airport at seven fifteen local time. A car will pick you up here at four thirty.'

'No driver, Gomez, you'll collect me.'

Gomez shrugged. 'As you wish, señor, it will be my pleasure.'

Veleta turned to a cabinet beside him and pulled a drawer out. Removing a thick manila envelope, he handed it to Gomez, saying, 'Good job, here's your money.'

Gomez took the envelope and put it into his attaché case, closing it with a sense of relief; praise from Veleta was rare indeed.

'Don't you want to count it?' Veleta asked.

'Señor, we have done business before. You have never tried to cheat me.'

'And I expect nothing less from you, Gomez… Your wife and family are well?'

'Thank you, they are well, señor.'

'Good, I hope they remain in good health.'

Gomez, protesting at the implication, said, 'Señor! I'm an honourable man.'

Veleta smiled grimly. 'You're an honourable thief, Gomez. There's an extra grand in the envelope for Mr Stafford, make sure you give it to him and his wallet, he deserves something for his trouble.'

'Of course, señor.' Gomez turned to leave. He was happy with the profitable business Veleta sometimes put his way, but there was always a worry when dealing with a man like that. Normally he would have pocketed the extra cash and give the pigeon Stafford nothing but in this case he would not.

Besides the skipper, Veleta had two crewmen for the yacht. They were both from the East-End of London, men to be trusted by the likes of Veleta. Each had his own reasons for living in this quiet backwater of Spain; for them Veleta's numerous contacts with the right people, including the police, offered them the security they craved.

The skipper, one Tony Diamond, was still poring over charts in the bridge when Veleta entered. Diamond – in his early sixties – was a former merchant seaman, who had been about boats since he could walk. The previous evening Veleta had explained what he wanted him to do.

Veleta asked, 'Have you worked it out?'

Stabbing a calloused finger on the chart of the English Channel, Diamond said, 'Yeah, I've chartered a fast boat from a yard, here, in

Gravelines. I'll lay up until I hear from you.' Pointing to a secluded spot on the Kent coast, he continued, 'I can pick you up within two hours, here at Romney.'

'Good, leave for Gravelines tonight. Is the sat-phone working?'

'Yes, they sent a replacement from Madrid.'

'I missed a call from Garcia yesterday, maybe the most important call I'll ever have. Get a spare.'

CHAPTER 14

After leaving Farmer, Daisy had taken the Tube from Elephant & Castle to Colindale in North West London. It was just after eleven when she was sitting in front of a motorised microfilm reader-printer at the British Library Newspaper Archives, which was located directly opposite the Tube station. Having shown the receptionist the dates of interest she was given a box of rolls of 35mm microfilm.

She knew it was going to be a tedious business, there being no method of automatically going to the page she was searching for, so she had to load each film within the date range and scroll through the pages until she found the one she wanted, more a job for methodical Alice, she thought, as she struggled with the clumsy controls.

Starting with the first story in the Delia file, she looked for the 5th of August 1962, and after a few misses she found it. The death of Marilyn Monroe and the date Mary was born. The question foremost in her mind was: if it was just a birthday souvenir why was it filed with a bunch of crime stories? If this was Gloria's file, whoever she might be, could it be the article on the hanged man she was interested in?

Finding the brief article was continued on an inside page, she read the story of the hanged man. His name was Sidney Vane, aged thirty-nine, with an address in Bingfield Street, Islington. He went to the gallows at nine a.m. on the morning of the fifth August. According to the hangman Mr Albert Pierrepoint, he was brave to the end. His conviction was for murder; the shooting dead of a police constable in the course of a diamond robbery. Vane was part of a gang who had blown the safe of a diamond merchant in Hatton Garden. In his defence he claimed he was not the one who fired the shot and no gun was found at the scene. The jury found him guilty of murder and the judge told him, as he was a habitual criminal with a number of previous convictions it mattered nought whether he had fired the fatal shoot or not. He was part of the gang, thus an accomplice before and after the fact, and duly sentenced him to death.

The Home Secretary refused to commute the sentence on the grounds that Vane failed to cooperate with the police and name his accomplices. Diamonds valued at one hundred thousand pounds were never recovered.

A gang of safe-blowers? Maybe this was the start of the Midnight Fox Gang, Daisy was thinking as she printed the story and went to the next date on her list. September 1976, fourteen years later. Another safe blown. This time in London Wall, gold coins and cash to the value of eighty thousand pounds stolen. If there was a connection with Vane's gang, why was there such a long gap between jobs? Maybe somebody was doing jail time. She went on to the next stories which confirmed what she remembered from Gloria's file.

Between 1976 to 1986 there were on average two high-value robberies a year. The MO was always the same. On the stroke of midnight, the safe or vault door was blown. Simultaneously a second explosion, thought to be a mixture of chemicals, made a deafening noise close enough to the robbery site to totally mask the vault explosion.

After the third robbery a newspaper wag coined the name 'the Midnight Fox' which immediately captured the public imagination. Over a ten-year period, there were eighteen high-value robberies.

She calculated the total sum stolen to be over two million pounds. Then there was the final job in October 1986. Ten thousand Krugerrands, each weighing one ounce of pure gold, was lifted from a vault. Worth a cool four million at the time according to the report.

The final story was dated two weeks after the gold robbery.

November 1986. A body found under a wharf in the Thames was identified as one Zar Brum, a Hungarian national. Brum was known to the police, having a previous conviction for robbing a jeweller.

A positive ID was made from his fingerprints. It was thought the body had been in the water for several days. The cause of death was inconclusive, but thought to be drowning.

Daisy finished just before twelve o'clock, took her collection of prints to the cashier and paid her fee.

Once outside she turned on her mobile and saw there was a missed call from Ernie. She was about to dial when he called.

'Sorry, Ernie, my phone was off.'

'No problem, Daisy, I have the dates you asked for.'

'That was quick, I owe you.'

Ernie laughed. 'For you, my love, anything. I'm looking forward to that lunch. You want the dates now or shall I email them?'

Fumbling in her briefcase, she retrieved her pad. 'I'll take them now but can you email them as well?'

'Will do, here they are, starting with the first robbery.' Ernie read out the list of dates and she wrote them on her pad.

'Any more on the timer they used?'

'The last robbery was twenty years ago, before my time here, but the timer was identified as a Messerlie gentleman's travelling clock, compact and accurate; had to be modified of course to include a switch, they'd have needed an expert watchmaker to do it.'

'What about yesterday's bomb?' Daisy asked. 'Do you think the piece you have today is from a Messerlie?'

'It could be, but until we have it positively identified I can't say.'

'One more question, Ernie, you were in Fingerprints at the Yard?'

'Yeah, before they moved everything here, why?'

'You ever come across the name Zar Brum?'

'Yeah, I know of him; his dead hands were brought in for identification during my first month on the job.'

'His dead hands?' Daisy asked, her imagination running riot.

'Sure, the hands were removed and sent to us for identifying, easier than moving a body about. They sew them back when we're finished.'

'Gross!' Daisy said. 'What do you know about him?'

'Not a lot,' said Ernie. 'Only canteen gossip. He only had the one conviction, which gave us his fingerprints, but apparently, there was a thick intelligence file on him. He was suspected of being a big-time trafficker in anything illegal that showed a big profit, drugs, arms, cigarettes. He was also suspected of being a big-time fence, and a murderer to boot. Several of his associates came to a sticky end. You name it, Brum had his finger in it.'

Daisy considered that before saying, 'There's no doubt about the fingerprint match, it was the man in the river?'

'None whatsoever, the fingers, thumbs and palms all were a perfect match to Brum's prints on file.'

'So, Brum is definitely dead,' she said, thinking aloud.

'As a dodo,' Ernie said. 'You should ask Arthur Casey. He works in your firm, doesn't he?'

Surprised at the question, Daisy said, 'Yes, Arthur's a partner, was he involved in the Brum case?'

'Must have been,' Ernie said. 'He was a DCI in the Flying Squad at the time, he'd have been involved.'

'Thanks, Ernie, I'll speak to Arthur. Did you send me the prints of the clock parts?'

'Yes, an hour ago, they should be on your desk by now.'

'Great, Ernie, I'll call you as soon as I'm done with this business.'

Within minutes she was on the platform at Colindale Station and saw there would be a train in four minutes. Finding a bench to sit on, she compared Ernie's dates with those of the cuttings. They were a perfect match. She called Alice on her direct line which was answered instantly.

'Hi, Daisy, you coming in?'

'Yeah, I need to run something past you, see you in about forty minutes.'

CHAPTER 15

When Daisy reached her office, she saw the photographs of the clock parts were on her desk as promised and looked at the enlargements under a magnifier. As Ernie had said, they looked precisely made, but her knowledge of mechanisms was limited to stripping her guns, so the photos told her nothing, although she did see there was a tiny mark on one of the wheels. Maybe the artist signed his work?

She'd better talk it through with Alice, pushing her intercom. 'Alice, if you're not into something I need a chat.'

Alice arrived with her tray and two cups of coffee. 'The coffee's just been made,' she said, pushing one over to Daisy, and seating herself on her usual chair she waited.

Daisy related the happenings since last evening; the visit to Mary's apartment, Frank Stubbs, and the missing Delia file. She followed with the information Jack Farmer had received from the Fisherman. The IRA were definitely not involved. As she spoke Alice, who was writing two columns of cryptic notes on her pad, looked up and interrupted.

'So, you're sure the IRA are not involved?'

Nodding, Daisy said, 'If the Fisherman says so I'll accept it and so will Peter Isaacs. It was never really a viable option.'

After tapping her pencil on her pad for a moment, Alice said, 'Agreed, and that lets you off Isaac's hook. He only wanted you involved because of your knowledge of the IRA. Let him find the bombers himself.'

Daisy sipped her coffee and thought about that. 'You're right of course, but I'm not so sure Abdullah was the target either. If he wasn't, it had to be Mary. So, while I still have Peter Isaac's authority, I can push my weight around and dig as much as I like and it's my intention to do just that. Whatever it takes I'm going to find out why anyone would want to kill her.'

Alice, eyebrows raised, said nothing as she waited, pencil poised.

Daisy knew the look. 'Okay then, listen and learn. I remembered the dates of the cuttings in the Delia file before I was interrupted, so I was able to reconstruct it. Incidentally, the folder was labelled Gloria 1986.'

'Who's Gloria?' Alice asked.

Shaking her head, Daisy said, 'I don't know yet,' and opened the folder of cuttings. 'You can read them later, they're copies I retrieved at the Newspaper Archives in Colindale, I've read them already.'

Alice pointed her pencil. 'So that's where you spent the morning. I tried to call you but your mobile was off.'

'You know what they're like in libraries about noise.'

Putting her pencil down, Alice said, 'Okay, I'm all ears, tell me what you've found.'

Holding up the full-page story of Marilyn Monroe, she said, 'This story dated 5th August 1962, is the day Mary was born.'

Alice shrugged. 'A conspicuous day, many people keep the front pages of their birth date.'

Pushing the page across the desk, Daisy said, 'I know, but look at this article.'

Alice read the article aloud. 'Sidney Vane was hanged in Pentonville Prison this morning at 9 a.m., despite a last-minute appeal to the Home Secretary for clemency. Vane was convicted of shooting dead a police constable in the course of a diamond robbery.'

Pushing the page back, Alice said, 'He was a Cop Killer, they always hanged them in those days.'

Folding the page and returning it to the folder, Daisy said, 'I know that. Vane was a professional criminal who specialised in safe-blowing. All the rest of the cuttings in the Delia file are related to high-value robberies carried out by a gang of safe-blowers.'

Alice scribbled something on her pad before replying, 'So, you're saying that because Mary Grey had a file on a gang of safe-blowers, yesterday's bomb was intended for her. I don't know, Daisy, these events happened years ago, why kill her now?'

Daisy sipped her coffee as she thought about it. 'Good question, maybe she got a lead on one of them. For her to have Gloria's – whoever she is – file, has to mean she was involved in some way.'

Alice considered that for a moment. 'She was twenty-four when the robberies stopped. She could've been part of the gang.'

Putting her cup down, Daisy said, 'Come on, Alice, you're forgetting there's ten thousand Krugerrands missing, plus the proceeds from all the other robberies which ran into millions. If you're that rich why work as a taxi driver?'

Alice smiled. 'Maybe she owns the taxi company, remember, she does live in the same apartment building as you, they must be worth big bucks these days, certainly not affordable on a taxi driver's earnings.'

Nodding her agreement, Daisy said, 'Right, I'd wondered about that, maybe she inherited it. Anyway that's what I want you to find out. Can you do a full profile on her, right back to her birth, the works? Put someone on it, top priority.'

Giving her a look, she made another note. 'On whose budget?'

Pushing the folder across the desk Daisy said, 'Mine, for the moment.'

Making another note, Alice said, 'Well, no doubt you can afford it. Anything else?'

'Yes, there is. Mary asked me to look up a company called Zentek Aviation; she told me she'd looked it up in Companies House, but found nothing. Can you check it out? It might be important.'

Alice wrote the name on her pad and said, 'No problem, I'll put Simpson on it.'

'Thanks,' Daisy said.

Alice looked at her jottings. Then opening the folder of cuttings, she said, 'This Delia file, it only contained the cuttings, no notes or anything like that?'

'Shit, I forgot. There were two photos: an old wedding photo which is still in the missing file and a photograph of Mary with a good-looking man standing in front of an expensive-looking yacht, called the *Lady Mary*, out of the port of Murcia. It should be registered somewhere, shouldn't it? Maybe give us a lead.'

Scribbling another note Alice said, 'It might. In Spain, every vessel over 2.5 metres must be registered. As we know the home port, you should call Manuel Sierra in Madrid, he should be able to track it down.'

'You're right, I'll do that later. Now I need to talk to Arthur, is he in today?'

Alice looked at her watch. 'He was, at this time he'll be in the Wild Boar.'

CHAPTER 16

The Wild Boar was less than ten minutes' walking distance from her office. A scruffy old pub situated a few streets away from the trendy Shepard's Market in Mayfair. Its décor was faded fifties with most of its fittings actually going back to that period, including the gilded ceiling. Nowadays it was a prime property for developers, but the owner was a canny Scot who knew its value and also knew it would fund a nice pension when he was ready to retire.

Today, Daisy saw it had perhaps a dozen or so customers, all of whom were locals of a certain age. She found Arthur, sitting alone at his usual corner table which was well chosen for the private chats he often had with his clients, it being tucked away in an odd bit of space near the fire exit and far enough away from the other tables to ensure privacy.

Arthur Casey was ostensibly Daisy's equal partner, as was his right, being the grandson of one of the founders of the firm. After thirty years' service in the Metropolitan Police – twenty of which he served in the Flying Squad – he retired in '92 with the rank of Chief Inspector and joined the family firm; to work alongside her father Henry Clowser.

When Henry decided to retire two years ago, Arthur – not wanting the responsibility of the top job – reduced his hours and passed the mantle to Daisy. Now age 65 and a widower, he liked a quiet life; with short working hours, allowing enough time for his leisure activities of golf and fishing.

Daisy understood this and arranged his work load – which was limited to managing their activities in positive vetting of personnel, both for the Home Office and FTSE 100 companies accordingly.

When he saw her approaching his table his face lit up with a broad smile. Standing up, he examined her face. 'Hello Daisy. In trouble again I hear.'

Returning his smile, she said, 'It was nothing, Arthur, just a fall and few stitches.'

Arthur shook his head in admonishment. 'From what I hear, young lady, it was lot more than nothing, you could have just as easily been killed.'

Patting his arm fondly, Daisy said, 'As you can see, Arthur, here I am, alive and well, so no worries. Now, I'm going to order some lunch, you'll take another of whatever you're drinking?'

Arthur lifted his glass. 'Thanks, I will, Old Speckled Hen.'

With a grimace she said, 'Sounds revolting, a pint?'

'Why not?' he said, holding his glass to the light. 'As can see, it's smooth, you should try it.'

Laughing, she said, 'I'll pass,' and went to the bar, soon returning carrying a tray with a lasagne and a Bud Light for herself and Arthur's pint. Putting the tray on the table, she settled herself in the chair facing him.

Arthur casually scanned the bar before saying, 'Much as I appreciate being seen lunching with a pretty woman, Daisy, I'm sure you want something. It can't be money, but as I hear you're involved with Peter Isaacs, it must be information.'

Her eyes rounding, Daisy said, 'Who told you I was working with Isaacs?

Touching his nose, Arthur smiled. 'A little bird, it doesn't matter, but let's finish our lunch and we'll talk,' he said, draining his glass and reaching for the replacement before continuing with his half-eaten steak pie and chips.

After they had both pushed their plates aside and speaking in hushed tones, Daisy told him everything: Mary's last words, finding the Delia file collection of news cuttings, including its contents and its disappearance, leading to her conclusion, that, with the absence of a remote and the IRA ruled out, Mary Grey could well have been the intended victim.

Arthur took a pull from his pint before saying, 'Did you discuss this with Jack Farmer?'

Nodding, she said, 'I did but I didn't mention the Delia file as I couldn't produce it at the time.'

'And what was his reaction? Did he buy it?'

Daisy laughed. 'Come on, Arthur, of course he didn't buy it, why would he? He had a dead VIP, much more interesting, then a lowly taxi driver. Not even after I pointed out that she was the only one guaranteed to be there at 8.45. Abdullah could easily have been a minute late.'

Arthur nodded. 'Which he wasn't in this case, but I get your drift, you're saying Ernie found no evidence of a remote?'

'None, no electronics, only a few pieces from a mechanical timer.'

Arthur's eyes roamed the bar before replying. 'If that's the case you could well be right. If someone wanted Mary dead, it would be the perfect set-up. If Abdullah also died, he would be considered the target. That would take all the heat. What do you want from me?'

Daisy paused, until a couple edged past their table, before saying, 'Let's start with the first name from the file. Sidney Vane, what do you know of him?'

Arthur thought for a moment before replying. 'That's going back a bit, Daisy, sure I remember the name. He was hanged in '62, just after I joined the force.'

'Yes, a long time ago,' Daisy said. 'But I know your memory is as good as ever, Arthur, now, what can you tell me about him?'

Arthur smiled and said, 'Flattery will get you everywhere, Daisy. As for Sidney Vane, not much. It'd be only gossip, remember I was a rookie cop at the time, just finished training at Hendon and walking the beat. It's mostly canteen chatter, but it was said at the time, he was the best Peterman in the business.'

Daisy's eyes rounded. 'Peterman, what's that?'

Arthur smiled. 'An old term, Daisy, to the uninitiated a safe-breaker; the safe being the Peter. He'd be an explosives expert and key man, someone who could open any door.'

'Got it,' Daisy said. 'Was he violent?'

Arthur shook his head. 'Definitely not, by all accounts an old-school thief, relied on skill and stealth, never had any need for violence.'

'What about the constable he shot?'

Shaking his head, Arthur replied, 'Nobody believed he fired that shot, probably didn't even know whoever did was carrying a shooter, or he wouldn't have been on the job.'

'He never said who it was?'

'Of course not, Daisy, as I said, old-school, he'd never squeal. All he said was he didn't fire the shot.'

'And he still went to the gallows.'

Arthur shrugged. 'He'd have been hanged anyway. In those days it made no difference who did it. He was an accomplice before and after the fact and therefore as guilty as if he had.'

Daisy considered that before asking, 'What about his known associates? Do you have any names?'

'Sorry, Daisy, can't help you there. As I said, before my time.'

'What about Albert? Would he have known him?'

Arthur laughed. 'Albert Grimes, yes, that old villain would certainly have known him.'

'Good,' she said. 'I'll talk to him.'

Draining the last of his beer, Arthur asked, 'You said you had three names.'

'Yes, the second's a criminal found dead in the Thames in 1986, name of Zar Brum.'

'That makes two dead men, not exactly a live inquiry is it?' Arthur smiled at his joke.

Returning his smile, Daisy said, 'Good one, Arthur, but Mary definitely said tell Harry, *he's alive*, and in her last breath, which was a great effort for her, she tried to utter a name which to me sounded something like Brown, but it could have been Brum, as he's mentioned in the file, maybe he's who she meant?'

Shaking his head, Arthur said, 'He's dead, Daisy, there's no doubt. Brum was of particular interest to me for a long time. We got a perfect match on his prints, and you know that fingerprints don't lie.'

Daisy was sceptical. 'So I'm told. Tell me about Brum.'

Arthur contemplated his empty glass for a moment before putting aside and saying, 'He was a real bad 'un. I've met a few in my time but Brum was in a class of his own, no redeeming features whatsoever. Claimed to be Hungarian, when he turned up in the UK in '56 as a refugee after the uprising in Hungary. He also claimed he had personally knocked out Russian tanks with homemade bombs. There was a big influx of refugees at the time and he, like many of them, was without papers, which means he could have been lying about his nationality. He drifted into crime, pimping to start with, then he blew a safe in a jeweller in Paddington. He was careless, left his fingerprints on the safe door. It's dangerous to try inserting a detonator with gloves on. He might have got away with it, as he didn't have a record, his prints weren't on file, but he went to the wrong fence to sell the jewels.'

'And there was a squeak?' Daisy said.

'Too right there was, he was nabbed and went down for five years. He was a model prisoner and got full remission, but the first thing he did on release was to settle with the fence who shopped him.'

'How so?' Daisy asked.

'His body was found in the Thames with his throat slit.'

'The fate of many a grass,' Daisy said. 'Was Brum charged?'

'No, we didn't have anything to link it to him other than motive and that wasn't enough.'

'And after that?' Daisy asked.

'He was watched, of course, but he never put a foot wrong. Before long he had a stall in Chapel Market selling costume jewellery and then after a couple of years opened a shop on the Caledonian Road selling watches and cheap jewellery. We suspected he was a fence among other things, but although he was raided several times, we never found anything.'

'Sounds pretty small-time,' Daisy said sceptically.

'It was for a few years, but then, about '76 he opened a bigger place in the West End, selling expensive stuff to the Toffs.'

'Hang on a bit, Arthur,' Daisy said. 'That was about the time the Midnight Fox robberies started.'

Arthur gave her a look. 'What do you know about the Midnight Fox?'

'Not much, only that it was the third name mentioned in the Delia file.'

'What exactly are you getting at?' Arthur asked.

Tapping the table for each name, Daisy said, 'Only that the three names in the Delia file, Sidney Vane, Zar Brum and the Midnight Fox, were all safe-blowers, which begs the question. Arthur, could Brum have been the Midnight Fox? The robberies stopped when he supposedly died.'

Arthur shook his head. 'Wrong, Daisy, the robberies stopped after they lifted four million quid worth of Krugerrands, maybe that was enough for them. And there's no "supposedly" about Brum being dead. The body in the river was his. His fingerprints proved it beyond doubt. As for him being the Midnight Fox, unlikely, he was older then, more experienced, but he might have been their fence, which amongst other things, he was. That and running a smuggling operation from the continent, drugs mainly, but M15 were convinced he was also a gunrunner, supplying RPGs and other weapons to the IRA. They were about to have us move in on him when his body was found. As I said, with Brum, there were no red lines.'

'Who verified the fingerprint match?' Daisy asked.

'In these cases, they always use two experts – they would both have to convince the coroner's court that they were completely satisfied the prints were Brum's.'

Daisy knew she was clutching at straws when she asked, 'Besides the prints, who made the physical ID?'

Arthur perused the gilded ceiling for a few moments as he recalled. 'Brum's body had washed up under a wharf, where it lay for more than a week. By then it had started to decompose and the rats had a field day on his face. His own mother wouldn't have been able to recognise him, but his clothes, wallet and watch were verified as his and fortunately his fingers were still intact so we were able to get a good set of prints.'

Daisy thought about it for a moment before asking, 'And the cause of death?'

'He had some head injuries which were probably inflicted while he was in the river, but according to the autopsy, although they found three times the legal limit of alcohol in his blood, the cause of death was drowning. Death by misadventure was the official verdict.'

'Wasn't there any indication as to how he came to be in the river?'

Arthur smiled grimly. 'You mean did he slip or was he pushed? With a man like Brum that was always a strong possibility. We interviewed his girlfriend, whose name was Henny Van der Meer.

Dutch, she was. Lived with Brum in a fine house in Hampstead. According to her she last saw him ten days before the body was found. He was meeting someone in the City Barge pub in Chiswick. His driver hadn't turned up for work that day, and as he didn't drive, she drove him as far as Kew Bridge, which is a few hundred yards from the pub. He told her he'd find his own way home. That was the last time she saw him.'

'Odd,' Daisy said. 'She didn't report him missing then?'

Arthur agreed. 'I asked her about that. Apparently, that wasn't the first time he's gone missing like that. She'd assumed he'd met someone, and shacked up with her. She was all right with that. It wasn't the first time and he usually showed up again in a few days.'

What was it in that scenario bothered her, Daisy was thinking, before asking, 'What about the missing driver, what was his story?'

Arthur again perused the gilded ceiling before answering. 'Billy Smirke, his name was. He went missing, didn't he. Billy had form. Did a five stretch for two smash-and-grab raids. He probably thought we'd try to pin Brum's death on him and made himself scarce.'

'Did you look for him?' Daisy asked.

With a shake of the head Arthur said, 'There was no need, was there, after the coroner's verdict of accidental death.'

Billy Smirke, a name she should remember, Daisy thought before saying, 'So all in all, a proper scumbag was our Mr Brum. What about his money? He must have died a rich man?'

Arthur gave a quiet laugh. 'You might think so. He had all the trappings. The house in Hampstead, a Rolls Royce, but when we looked into it, we found it was all a sham. There was a creditor's meeting after his death. Both the house and car were rented. The shop in Oxford Street was also rented and a lot of the stock hadn't been paid for. Whatever cash he had in the bank just covered his debts. If he was as wealthy as everyone thought, he hid it well.'

With a scornful laugh, Daisy said, 'It wouldn't be the first time a rich man showed up as a pauper after he'd safely stashed his loot away.'

Arthur, giving her a thoughtful look, said, 'Forget it, Daisy, Brum is dead.'

Dropping her chin, Daisy said, 'Okay, let's accept that for now, but Mary definitely said, "Harry, he's alive." Arthur, those words were so important to her that she used her last breath to say them. Someone is alive who is thought to be dead. I was interested in Brum because the Delia file had the newspaper report of his death in it. If you're sure Brum is dead then the only person left in the newspaper stories is the Midnight Fox.'

'And someone called Harry,' Arthur said.

'Yes, there's Harry. I'm sure Mary wanted me to tell him that someone they both thought to be dead is alive. If that's the case it's looking like whoever that someone is killed her before she could talk. Arthur, didn't you ever get a lead on the Midnight Fox? I mean over that ten-year period there were a whole bunch of high-value robberies attributed to him, didn't you ever get a squeak?'

Arthur cast his eyes upward and continued his examination of the gild on the ceiling for a long moment before replying. 'That was one of my biggest cases, Daisy, and my biggest failure. It was over thirty years ago when the robberies started and for the following ten years, I had a team of officers permanently on the case. Every known villain who had ever blown a safe was investigated and watched for signs of unexplained affluence, with no result. The final consensus was that this was a new gang, with no criminal connections, at least in the UK. I myself always thought they were a foreign gang who came over, did their work and disappeared back to wherever they came from afterwards. We even sent a team to the Costa del Sol, that being a natural habitat for English villains at the time as it is today. They stayed there for a year working with the Spanish police but didn't come up with a thing. All we ever got on the Midnight Fox gang was a good left thumb print at the scene of one of the robberies, which didn't belong to anyone who had legitimate access to the vault.'

'A thumb print?' Considering that for a moment, Daisy said, 'It obviously led nowhere, or there've been a result. What about the timers? Ernie told me they were traced to a Swiss clockmaker.'

Arthur nodded. 'Yes, after each robbery we found a number chalked on the safe or vault door, 1/20, 2/20 up to the last robbery which was 18/20. It was after the third Midnight Fox robbery when we got a line on the clock. We identified a piece from the decoy bomb to a clock made by a firm called Messerli, based in Bern. I visited the factory myself and was told that they had received an order and a banker's draft from a London jeweller and shipped their last twenty clocks of that particular model to a London address. As you might guess it turned out to be an empty shop off the Caledonian Road. All the paperwork was phoney.'

'Hang on,' Daisy said. 'Didn't you say Brum had a shop on the Caledonian Road?'

Arthur smiled and shook his head. 'No such luck, his shop was the other end, near King's Cross.'

'Okay,' Daisy said. 'So, including the Krugerrands there were eighteen robberies all with the same MO: A decoy bomb which used a Messerlie clock as a timer, that means there are two clocks left from the batch and according to Ernie the timer used in Wednesday's bomb was from a precision clock. It's too much of a coincidence, Arthur. If we consider that Mary was somehow connected to this gang, maybe one of that twenty was used to kill her.'

Arthur agreed. 'If that's what they needed to do, they would know that Abdullah's death would take all the heat.'

'Which is exactly what's happened,' Daisy said. 'But getting back to Brum for a moment, you said he was into smuggling.'

Arthur, his calmness slipping, said, 'Will you forget Brum, Daisy? He's dead, now, what's your point?'

Patting his hand, Daisy said, 'Sorry Arthur, but smuggling was one of his rackets, wasn't it? Maybe it's just another coincidence but Peter Isaacs has received intelligence about a big smuggling operation, involving a consignment of heroin and weapons coming into the UK, from Pakistan.'

Arthur asked softly, 'What kind of weapons?'

Daisy replied in little more than a whisper, 'Something serious, Arthur, for a Jihadist spectacular. Why?'

Arthur leaned forward. 'Well, Pakistan for a start. In my day most of the heroin from Afghanistan was usually taken overland to Turkey via Iran, before shipment to Europe. As for weapons, Narcos sometimes bring in some light weapons for their own use, but drugs are their business and they have their distributers in place for that, not arms.'

'You said Brum did both.'

'I told you to forget Brum, Daisy, even he cannot operate from the grave.'

Standing, she said, 'Thanks Arthur. You've given me a better feel for this. Now, I'm going to find Albert Grimes and see what he can add.'

Arthur smiled and said, 'Say hello to the old thief from me.'

CHAPTER 17

Thursday 5ᵗʰ September – Afternoon. Tilbury

Nizar and Karim arrived in London, the final leg of their long journey. A car was to meet them at the dockside in Tilbury, where they had disembarked from a freighter newly berthed from Karachi, their port of origin.

Standing on the dockside they were relieved to see that their driver, Rashid, a British-born Pakistani, knew both men, having trained with them during his stay at an al-Qaeda training camp in Koast, Afghanistan, earlier that year. For that reason, Rashid had been selected to be an integral part of their mission.

The men were complete opposites. Nizar, tall and bony, with cadaverous features, his black eyes sunk deep in his skull and Karim, the complete opposite – short and corpulent, with red hair, light skin and blue eyes.

Both men, who were in their mid-forties, came from Quetta on the Pakistan-Afghanistan border, a town known for its fierce fundamentalism and support for the Taliban and in their case, al-Qaeda.

Now, clean shaven – the lighter skin from former beards being almost unnoticeable – after their long journey. Instead of their traditional perahans, they were wearing two-piece suits made in Bangladesh and carrying their frugal possessions in a small canvas hold-all.

They had been chosen by Sheik bin Laden personally for two

reasons: one, they both spoke reasonable English, but more importantly, because of the special weapons training they had received from the CIA during the final years of Soviet occupation. As a two-man team they had successfully destroyed more than their share of the hated Soviet Hind gunships in the high valleys of their motherland.

After the Soviet withdrawal the two men had been fêted as heroes returning to their villages with gold and other rewards and were soon forgotten by the outside world. But they had not been forgotten by their wartime commander, Sheik bin Laden, who had sought them out, again, eighteen years later and told them that it was time to serve him again, promising them more gold than they could imagine to make this journey.

They were given money and instructed to make the long overland journey to Karachi where they were met by an agent of the Sheik who gave them western clothes and sterling.

Both had been given the doctored Pakistani passports of genuine merchant seamen – whose fate was unknown – and signed on as crew on the freighter bound for Tilbury. The ship's captain having been bribed to take them on for the round trip and facilitate their shore leave for three days when the ship docked. He was also warned not to question the men at any time about their activities, if and when they returned to the ship.

During the entire journey which had taken nearly two months, they had been treated with great respect by the guides who had moved them through the network. They were special men who had actually met the Sheik and had been hand-picked by him. Such an honour.

Driving a Volkswagen van, Rashid turned on to the A13 towards London. The two men, who were squeezed onto the bench seat next to him, listened as he explained his role in their mission. Soon they were to meet the Sheik's number one agent for Europe.

Not being familiar with the more direct route through the City of London, Rashid had to go the way he knew and endure a virtual crawl through traffic via the North Circular Road and Finchley Road, through Swiss Cottage. They arrived in Symonds Street just before five.

Rashid rang Dr Taleb's bell. When the receptionist answered he said only one word, 'Charon.' The electric lock buzzed and the door sprang open.

Iqbal's bodyguard quickly appeared. Ignoring Rashid, he bowed in a sign of respect to the two men before ushering them into the inner hall. Rashid left immediately, his job done for the moment.

Unlike Kaminski there was no attempt to frisk them. These two had special skills which were indispensable if the Sheik's plan was to succeed. They were to be treated with the utmost respect; they were heroes, men who had fought the Soviets alongside the Sheik, men to be trusted.

They would stay in the house for two nights while they were briefed on every aspect of the operation. They already knew their role in it. They would then be taken to the rendezvous where they would verify the equipment being shipped by the foreigners. They had three days to complete their mission and return to the freighter, which was due to sail on the evening of the eleventh for Karachi.

Daisy spent an hour trawling the Bayswater pubs she knew to be the haunts of a certain Albert Grimes. Albert, now in his mid-seventies was a retired thief, who throughout a long career as a burglar had spent half a lifetime in prison. Like the majority of his type, he had squandered any money he made from a life of crime as quickly as got it. Now he was living in a two-room council flat and surviving on benefits.

Daisy had used him from time to time, in the past, to confirm something she already knew. Albert was a mine of information about

London criminal's past and present. That is not to say he was a grass. He might be persuaded to talk in vague terms about active faces but he never named names.

They played a game whereby she would tell him what she thought and he would tell her if she was wrong but he would never actually confirm that she was right. He once told her life was too short already to be a grass. He was, however, quite happy to talk about past events and she was sure, if anyone knew who had been behind the Midnight Fox gang he would know.

Living in the area, she and her friends regularly frequented the same pubs so her presence was accepted without question. Carrying a copy of that morning's *Daily Herald* and using the excuse that she was looking for a friend, she gave each pub the once-over but there was no sign of Albert.

Daisy had not needed his help since she left the force but she made a point of buying him a drink whenever she met him. The last time had been less than a month ago so she was pretty sure that he was still living in the area.

It was not until the fourth pub that she saw a drinking pal of Albert's, one Micky Moore, sitting at a table with the racing pages open. Micky was a shabby little man who never did have much luck in life other than an occasional success on the dogs or ponies, which was his only full-time occupation.

Approaching his table, she asked, 'Hello Micky, how's your luck?'

Micky looked around, sizing up each face in the bar before acknowledging her presence. The wrong face and he would have ignored her.

'Not too good today, Daisy. I had three out of a four-way accumulator come up,' he said with a watery smile.

With a sympathetic smile she said, 'Bad luck, Micky, there's always tomorrow. Let me buy you a drink.'

Never one to miss an opportunity, Micky pushed his luck. 'That's very decent of you, I'll have a double whisky and a pint of Worthington to wash it down.'

Daisy smiled at the cheek, but every favour has its price, and went to the bar and ordered the drinks, and carried them to his table.

'I'm looking for Albert, is he coming in soon?'

Nodding his appreciation, Micky took a sip of the whisky before replying, 'Albert doesn't come in here much these days. He's taken to frequent the Redan; you know, the one the far end of Queensway.'

Daisy knew the Redan. 'Thanks Micky, I'll give it a try. Enjoy your drink.'

Sure enough, she found Albert in the main bar of the Redan, seated in his preferred position, at a table with his back to the wall, nursing a half-empty pint glass. He went through the same procedure as Micky whereby he scanned the drinkers' faces before acknowledging her and accepting her offer of a drink. The wrong face and like Micky she would've been blanked.

Putting her newspaper on the table, Daisy went to the bar and ordered the drinks – a pint of best and a double Scotch for Albert and a Diet Coke for herself – which she brought to the table and took a chair so that she faced Albert with her back to any curious drinkers.

'Cheers Daisy.' Albert raised the whisky, giving her an appraising look. 'Looks like you've had a bit of bother.'

Touching his glass with her Coke, she said, 'A bit, nothing to worry about.' Knowing Albert was susceptible to a bit of flattery, she said, 'Albert, I want to use your infallible memory about crimes gone by.'

'How long ago?' Albert sipped his whisky, his eyes giving the room a further scan.

Speaking in a conspiratorial whisper which she thought the occasion warranted, Daisy said, 'Twenty years ago, to be exact. The Midnight Fox, any ideas on who he might have been?'

Albert took another sip from his glass before replying. 'He was a very successful thief, a real master of his craft, that's who he was.'

'I know that already. I'm looking for a name, Albert, a clue as to his identity, even a whisper, there must have been whispers.'

'Sure, there were whispers aplenty, but no one knew anything. The Fox was too canny, never mixed with any of us crims. One or two big jobs a year, the loot must've been fenced abroad, nothing ever showed up in London. A real professional, he was, the Fox.'

Nodding, she said, 'What would you think, Albert, if I was to say the Fox was Sidney Vane?'

Albert spluttered his whisky, and looked around the bar to see if anyone had overheard. Satisfied, he took a long pull on his pint before answering.

'I'd say you was off your rocker, Daisy. Sid Vane was hanged in sixty-two.'

'I know that, but if he was alive, he'd fit the bill, wouldn't he?'

'Like a glove, Daisy, his MO was exactly the same, I've seen the safe doors.'

'How come?'

'They were sold to a scrap dealer who happened to be a friend.'

'You knew Sidney Vane?'

'Yeah, did a stretch with him in the Scrubs, decent fellow.'

'Not a Cop Killer then?'

Albert's head lifted. '*Never!* He was stitched up on that one. Sid was a cracksman, a skilled man, he never needed to use violence.'

Leaning forward, Daisy said, 'That may be, Albert, but he made mistakes, didn't he? Did some jail time.'

Albert shrugged. 'We all did, that was expected. Some little thing goes wrong, like the cops get to know your MO and stake you out until you make a mistake.'

'Okay, so, tell me Albert, explosives are dangerous and need the expert touch, you must be trained to use them. Was Sid in the army?'

'Yeah, he did war service in the Sappers, even got two medals for bravery.'

'And he became a cracksman after the war?'

Albert smiled. 'Sure. Like a lot of them, he came home a hero, with his gratuity and back pay, but it doesn't last and there wasn't any work as suited him, so he used his skills, got away with it for a few years but was a bit careless one time and got caught copped a five stretch, that's where I met him.'

'Tell me about Sid. Was he married?'

Albert's eyes widened. 'Too right he was. Gloria, her name was. Sid talked about her all the time, saw her once during visiting, real stunner she was.'

Finally, something, Daisy thought, as she pictured the neat handwritten label on the Delia folder – Gloria 1986 – it was Sid Vane's wife who collected the cuttings and the soldier with the medals must have been Sidney Vane, but why did Mary keep them hidden?

'Did they have any children?'

Albert nodded. 'Yeah, two, a boy and a girl. Henry, the son's name was, he was only twelve at the time of Sid's death.'

Henry, that could be Harry, Daisy thought. 'And the daughter, what was her name?'

Albert shrugged as he sipped his whiskey. 'Don't really know. Gloria was pregnant when Sid was hanged. Don't know if it's true or not but I heard that she gave birth on the same day.'

Mary was born on the same day, Daisy thought. There was now little doubt in her mind how Mary fitted in to all this. She had to be Sid Vane's daughter. 'Poor woman,' Daisy said. 'Do you know what happened to her after Sid died?'

'Yeah, she went to work for a jeweller.'

'Do you remember the jeweller's name?'

Albert thought for a moment, then pointed his glass. 'Yeah! Foreigner, he was. Brown's Emporium, his shop was called, on the Caledonian Road. Fancy name but he only sold cheap stuff, you know the type, chip diamonds, nine-karat gold stuff and cheap watches.'

'Do you know if he's still there?'

Taking a ritual pull from his glass before answering, he said, 'Nah, early seventies he opened a proper shop up West, real quality place.'

'That must have been about the time the Midnight Fox robberies started,' Daisy said, watching Albert for his lightbulb moment, as he considered this suggestion.

'Hey! You're right there, Daisy, never thought of that, great front for moving hot gear.'

'Did you know Mr Brown; did he have any form?'

Giving her a knowing look and tapping his nose, he replied, 'Oh, his name wasn't Brown, that was just for show, his name was Brum, I told you he was foreign.'

'Zar Brum?'

Albert nodded. 'The same.'

'Did you know him?'

Albert pulled a face. 'Sure, I met him inside, he was doing a five stretch for a safe job in Paddington.'

'You didn't like him.'

Shaking his head, Albert said, 'Nobody did, he wasn't a likeable man.'

'You said that you were inside with Sid Vane. Was Brum there at the same time?'

Albert nodded. 'Too right he was, Brum being a foreigner, could beat everyone at chess. Everyone except Sid, that is, they played a lot of chess.'

'Okay, Albert, I know what happened to Brum, but what about Sid's wife, what happened to her?'

Albert scratched the side of his face for a moment, then said, 'Don't know for sure. She worked at Brown's for a few years. I did hear that she went to live in Spain.'

'Do you know when that was?' Daisy asked.

After another moment of chin scratching, he answered. 'Not too sure, sometime in the late eighties I think.'

Interesting, Daisy thought. The last stories in her file, the Krugerrands robbery and Brum's death were dated 1986. Maybe it was time to retire?

'Do you know what happened to her son and daughter, Albert?'

Reaching for his glass, Albert said, 'I'm told that Henry, when was sixteen he was apprenticed to locksmith in Shoreditch. Don't know about the daughter.'

Other than Gloria being Mary's mother and Henry her brother, she was no further forward Daisy was thinking, when she asked, 'Albert, the Midnight Fox was obviously not just one man, but a gang of specialists. How many members would be needed?'

Albert eyes swept the bar occupants again before he answered. 'Good question, Daisy. I'd say five, minimum. To start with they'd need someone to deal with the alarms. They'd need a driver, maybe two drivers, there was a lot of gold to shift in that last job. A heavy to do the roof work. They always went in by the roof and the Peterman. He'd do the locks and blow the safe. Yeah, minimum five.'

'The locks?' Daisy thought about that. Albert had said that Henry Vane was apprenticed to a locksmith when he was sixteen. That would be 1966. If he'd stuck at it, he'd have had ten years' experience by the time of the first Midnight Fox robbery. More than enough. The question being, where was he now? And where were the other members of the gang, including the watchmaker and the Fence? Six or seven people who could identify the Midnight Fox.

At that moment something Arthur had said popped into her mind. Leaning forward, she said, 'One last question. Did you ever know a Billy Smirke?'

Albert, giving her a shifty look, replied, 'I might have, why?'

Daisy knew the look. Albert wasn't going to tell her much about Billy Smirke. She wondered why, as she said, 'He was Brum's driver, is he still around?'

Albert sniffed. 'Billy hasn't been around for a long time, Daisy. Rumour is he upset the wrong party and was parked, if you get my drift.'

Daisy got his drift and knowing that Albert was not going to tell her any more about Billy Smirke, she stood up. 'Thanks a lot for the chat, Albert. I must rush, see you,' and with a knowing look she slid her folded *Daily Herald* to the centre of the table.

'Take care, Daisy,' Albert said, putting the paper in his coat pocket, knowing that when he opened at page three, besides the shapely lady, he'd find the two crisp fifties as usual.

CHAPTER 18

Thomas was driving. Kaminski didn't know if this was because, despite his slow thought processes, he was an excellent driver with a native's knowledge of London, or that Kramer himself was unable to drive. She had never seen him behind the wheel, in London or elsewhere.

Seated next to her, Kramer spoke for the first time since leaving Hampstead. 'I've arranged for a boat to be made available for the handover and a safehouse by the river for us.'

'Does it have a boathouse?' asked Kaminski.

'No, but it has a small jetty and a secluded garden, and it's empty at the moment, it should suit us.'

The Mercedes passed Shepard's Bush Green and picked up the Chiswick High Road. Thomas drove at a stately pace along it and within minutes they had turned off the A4 roundabout and joined the road to Kew Bridge. Just before the bridge Thomas turned left into Thames Road.

Kaminski concluded that either Kramer had instructed Thomas as to their exact destination or they had been there before. Maybe that's where they disappeared to on Monday afternoon.

The double-fronted detached house was on a corner plot with a thick screen of unkempt conifers. The high iron double gates leading to the garage and the front of the house were locked. Thomas had a bunch of keys and after two attempts found the one that fitted and opened them. He drove in and closed the gate.

'Good spot,' Kaminski said. None of the neighbouring houses had overlooking windows. 'How come it's empty?'

Kramer, giving her an ugly look, said, 'The owner died a few years ago, nobody's made a claim on it, so it stands empty. There's dozens of houses like this in London. Some of them, like this one, stand empty for years.'

It may be empty but not unused, Kaminski thought, noting the freshly greased hinges on the gate.

Thomas used another key to operate the electric garage door. It was wide and deep, big enough for four cars in the front section, and there was a workshop in the rear. An access door led to the house.

'Excellent,' Kaminski said. 'There's no need to use the front door, we can come and go through here, a good place for a private transaction. Where's the access to the jetty?'

Leading the way to the rear, Kramer said, 'Through the workshop, I guess.'

Kaminski didn't believe there was any guessing involved, being by now being certain that Kramer had been in this house before.

The garage rear door led to the garden. Opening it, revealed a covered patio area and a York-stone path bordered by grass leading to a sturdy wooden gate at the bottom. The grass had been cut recently. The gate was secured by heavy bolts, top and bottom. Kaminski noted that they were also well greased and slid open easily. *Someone is looking after this house,* she thought.

Outside, she found a landing stage, big enough for a fifty-foot boat to come alongside. It was made of well-seasoned planks mounted on concrete piles which had been sunk into the mud. To the right a wooden guard rail, consisting of two four-by-two planks supported by uprights every six feet ran along the towpath. The tide was out, leaving a six-foot drop to the riverbed. Moss and water residue marks on the piles showed the water level came right up to the planks.

Perfect, Kaminski thought as she looked around. The site was located on a bend in the river, which meant the jetty was not overlooked by any of the neighbouring properties. With the tide out, the river had only a narrow passage in the middle navigable. At that moment its total traffic consisted of a rowing four and a twenty-foot cabin cruiser. She expected it would be busy enough at full tide, which was all to the good. What's one more boat among many?

'You satisfied?' asked Kramer.

Kaminski shrugged. 'It's good enough. What about the rest of the house?'

Giving her a sharp look, Kramer snapped, 'You don't need to see the rest of the house, we do the deal in the garage. You and Thomas bring the goods here when they arrive in London. We can arrange the meet with the Iqbal for Saturday night. Thirty minutes is all it should take for him to verify the goods and hand over the money.'

Kaminski shrugged. 'Suits me, I'd better take the keys.'

Turning towards the door, Kramer said, 'Thomas will keep the keys, now let's go.'

After leaving Albert, Daisy walked to Queensway Station, took the Tube to Leicester Square and walked into Soho where she found that London Quality Taxis occupied offices above a shop, the display window of which was shaded by a pink velvet curtain covered in signs of the Zodiac. The sign on the mirrored glass entrance door read 'Strictly Adults Only'.

She found a side entrance and climbed a flight of iron stairs to the first floor. The black lettering on the glass panelled door read: London Quality Taxis.

Pushing the door, which announced her with a *Ding Dong,* she found herself in a spacious room with three women seated at desks, two of whom were in front of a PC and wearing hands-free telephone headsets. The third woman, had a larger desk facing the entrance, which besides a PC had a unit beside it which held a laser printer/copier unit. All three of the them gave her a curious look, but before she could say a word Frank Stubbs appeared from a back office. Recognising her immediately, he beckoned her towards the office he had just vacated.

Daisy followed him into the sparse room which served as his office. The floor was covered in grey linoleum and the only furniture was a plain deal desk, which had an ancient wooden visitors' chair in front and an equally aged swivel chair behind it. Two grey steel four-drawer cabinets stood against the side wall. A poster-print of the victorious Arsenal football team, dated 2003-4, graced the wall behind the desk. *No evidence of hidden wealth here,* she was thinking.

Waving her to the empty chair before seating himself in the swivel chair which creaked as he settled himself, he said, 'Good day, miss, didn't expect to see you again so soon. I take this is not a social call.'

Daisy retrieved her pencil and pad from her briefcase, then easing herself cautiously onto the old chair calmly eyed Stubbs. 'I'm not here for a taxi, Mr Stubbs, I'd like to ask you a few questions about Mary.'

Stubbs's eyes narrowed. 'So you are a cop. I've already told them all I know.'

'You asked me the same question the last time we met,' she said. Then with a sweet smile she leaned forward and whispered, 'Do you have problems with cops, Mr Stubbs?'

Shrugging his brawny shoulders, Stubbs said, 'I run a taxi company, miss, so we get a certain amount of hassle from the boys in blue. I try to keep my distance, that's all.'

Daisy, whose instincts told her there might be more to it than that, did not press the point, instead saying, 'Well to set your mind at ease I'm not a cop, Mr Stubbs. I have been one, but now I'm private and this visit is strictly personal. Mary was my friend and if I can I want to find out who was responsible for her death. Can you tell me what questions the cops asked?'

Stubbs visibly relaxed in his seat. 'That's okay then, isn't it? And call me Frank. Two plain-clothes detectives came, just after eleven yesterday. They told me what happened, that Mary and Mr Abdullah were both dead.' As he said it, the big man's head fell and he was still for a moment. Then he repeated his actions of the previous evening and pulled out a coloured handkerchief and blew his nose violently. After wiping his eyes, he put the handkerchief away, mumbling, 'Sorry about that, you can image the shock that was to all of us.'

Daisy shifted in the uncomfortable chair, and gave him a moment to compose himself before asking in a low voice, 'What were you able to tell them, Frank?'

Looking at her with watery eyes, he replied, 'They wanted to know all about Mr Abdullah's arrangements with us, you know, timings, was he always on time, how long we knew him, that sort of thing.'

Daisy nodded and asked, 'And what did they ask about Mary?'

Shaking his head, Frank said, 'That's the thing, they only asked if she ever talked about Mr Abdullah, which she didn't. I told them Mary never talked about any of her customers. They wanted her next of kin, which I couldn't give them because I don't know any. That's all, it seems that Mary just had the bad luck to be Mr Abdullah's driver.'

Nodding agreement, Daisy said, 'That's everybody's thinking at the moment, Frank, their focus is entirely on the VIP, and maybe they're right, maybe not, only time will tell. Me, I don't want Mary to be just collateral damage. As I said, she was my friend and because of that, I intend to be very picky and check everything until I'm satisfied this had nothing to do with her. To start with I want to look at her work-sheets for the past month, can I do that?'

Frank stood up, and giving her a searching look he said, 'Yeah, no problem. I'll get our secretary to print them out.' Going to the door he called out, 'Jenny, will you print out Mary's work-sheets for the past month?'

The walls were thin. Daisy thought she heard sobbing from the other room. Frank shrugged his shoulders and went back to his chair. 'Sorry about that. Jenny's a bit emotional at the moment, she was very fond of Mary. We all were.'

Daisy believed him. 'I'm sure you were, Frank, as was I. How long did you say you knew her?'

'Since she joined the firm, eleven years ago.'

'Mary told me she was driving Mr Abdullah for about three months, is that correct?'

Frank nodded. 'Yeah, he used a couple of other drivers at first, but once Mary drove him, he wouldn't have anyone else.'

'So, every Monday to Friday Mary was waiting outside at 8.45, right?'

Frank nodded. 'On the dot. He was insistent about that.'

'Was he always on time?'

Frank shrugged. 'Pretty much, so Mary told me, give or take a minute or two.'

A minute or two, which in this case was a lifetime, Daisy thought, before asking, 'How many people would have known this arrangement?'

Frank's chair creaked as he leaned forward. 'How do you mean?'

'It's a simple question, Frank, who knew Mary would be in the mews at that exact time?'

'We all knew here, didn't we?'

'Have any of your staff left in the past three months?'

Frank laughed. 'Of course not. They get too well paid to leave, but why the question? Are you saying that someone was waiting for Mary?'

'As I said, Frank, I want to consider every angle. Has anybody been asking any questions about Mr Abdullah or Mary recently?'

Frank wrinkled his brow, then said, 'Not exactly questions, but now you mention it, Mr Abdullah's next-door neighbour called looking for a lady driver. Monday it was, Jenny took the call.'

'Man or woman?'

'A woman, Jenny said. She sounded foreign, wanted a lady driver to pick her up on Tuesday afternoon, said her neighbour told her he had an extremely reliable lady driver pick him up at 8.45 every morning.'

'And of course, Jenny told her that would be Mr Abdullah,' Daisy said.

Frank cocked his head. 'It had to be, hadn't. It's the only appointment Mary had at that time.'

'Did she give you an address?'

Frank shook his head. 'Didn't need to, did she, being that she was his next-door neighbour, Jenny just asked her if it was number 8 or 12 Shakespeare Mews.'

Trying not to sound how she felt, Daisy said, 'Of course she did, and what name did this foreign lady give?'

'Mrs Vereker.'

Writing the name on her pad, she asked, 'Did Mary collect her?'

Frank frowned. 'No, funny that, she called Tuesday morning, said she'd changed her plans, a friend was collecting her.'

'Yes funny,' said Daisy, thinking how easy it had all been for the bombers. It also confirmed her suspicions that Mary was the intended target. 'Did Jenny take her telephone number when she first called?'

'Sure, do you want it? It's in the call log.'

'I'll take it. Being a neighbour, she might have seen something,' she said, knowing the number would probably be as phoney as Mrs Vereker, but maybe not.

Starting to stand, he said, 'I'll go get it.'

Putting her hand up, Daisy said, 'There's no need, I can get it on the way out. Did anyone else call, any relatives or friends?'

The chair groaned as he leaned back. 'Not so far.'

'Mary must have given you someone to call in case of accidents'

'She did, and I called him. Her solicitor, a Mr Courtney-Hopkins.'

'Do you know him?'

Shaking his head, Frank said, 'No, Mary left his card with me, you know, just in case. Do you want to see it?'

Scribbling the name on her pad, she said, 'It's okay, I can look him up if I need to. What did he say when you called?'

'Not much, said he was sorry to hear it and that he'd take care of everything, funeral and so on.'

'Nothing about contacting her relatives?'

'Not a thing, just that he'd contact me with the funeral details.'

Cold-blooded sod, Daisy thought and asked, 'One final question, Frank, did you forget something when you left Mary's apartment last evening?'

With an expression of surprise, he replied, '*No*, I told you, I just wanted to look up her address book, find someone to call but as you had already done it there was no point, was there?'

'You didn't go back?'

'Definitely not,' he growled. 'Why would I?'

'Why indeed. Do you know if anyone else has a key?'

'Mary never said. She only left a set at the office because she lost her keys once and had to get a locksmith to open the door and change the lock.'

Standing up, Daisy put away her pad and said, 'Thanks Frank, is the printout ready?'

Frank stood and nodded towards the door. 'I'll see.'

She followed him into the main office where a red-eyed Jenny looked at her curiously before handing the sheaf of printout pages to Frank.

Taking them, Frank said, 'Jenny, that Mrs Vereker who called Monday, can you find her phone number?'

Jenny nodded and gave Daisy another curious look before hitting a few keys on her keyboard, and searching her screen. Finding the number, she wrote on a square of paper, which she handed to Frank.

'Thanks Jenny,' he said and handed the printout and the note to Daisy. 'You'll find a page for each day, which includes date, client's name, and address, start and finish times for each job.'

Glancing at the first page Daisy counted ten jobs, maybe two hundred during the past month, she guessed. *Let's hope one of these calls throws up something.*

'Thanks Frank, I'll keep in touch.' As they shook hands, she had the distinct impression that he was relieved to see her go. *Why?* she wondered and resolved to find out a bit more about Frank Stubbs.

Retracing her steps towards Leicester Square Daisy went into a Starbucks, ordered a latte and found a quiet table to make her call. Alice answered immediately.

'Hi, Daisy. You coming in?'

'Only if you need me, I've been walking around all day, and feel a bit worn, it must be the knock on the head.'

'Business-wise there's nothing that can't wait, but there is something for you.'

Daisy fumbled for her notebook and pencil before saying, 'Tell me.'

'Ian Wilson spent the afternoon searching family history records. He started with Sidney Vane.'

'And?'

'He was married in 1948 to a Gloria Grey. Interesting, eh?'

'Definitely. Gloria was the name on the Delia file. Any children?'

'Yes, a boy born in 1950, registered in the name of Henry Vane.'

'What about Mary?' Daisy asked.

'Born like you said on the fifth of August 1962, registered in the name of Grey by the mother, a Mrs Gloria Grey. Father entered as deceased. I would guess that could mean that Mary was Sidney Vane's daughter.'

'Yeah,' Daisy said, thinking that Albert had been spot on.

Alice sounded miffed. 'You don't sound surprised.'

'Sorry, I'm not, it confirms what Albert just told me.'

'Albert Grimes?'

'The same. He told me Sid's wife's name was Gloria and that rumour had it that she gave birth to a daughter on the day Sid was hanged.'

'It certainly looks that way,' Alice said.

'What address was on the certificate?'

'Bingfield Street N1, that's off the Caledonian Road. Wilson checked the voters register. She hasn't lived there since '88 and there's no record of her death, maybe she went abroad.'

'She did,' Daisy said. 'According to Albert she went to live in Spain in the late eighties. She'd be in her eighties now, maybe she's still alive. What about the son, Henry Vane, he'd be about fifty-seven now?'

After a pause, Alice said, 'Now much on him other than his birth. No death or marriage certificate.'

'According to Albert he went to work for a locksmith in Shoreditch when he was sixteen. Can you have Wilson check with HMRC for his work record, also the passport office on both of them?'

'Will do, anything else?

'Yeah, Frank Stubbs, the manager of the taxi company, check him out, will you? Including financial. I wouldn't be surprised if he lived in the same area as Mary.'

'I'll need to use Harrison for the financials. This is getting to be expensive, Daisy. I'll need it signed off.'

'Don't worry about the cost, Alice. Peter Isaacs has given me carte blanche on this. He'll be paying the bill.'

Alice laughed. 'Wow, nice going, Daisy. In that case I'll put everyone available on it. You'd best have an early night but be careful, whoever's behind all this is not going to be squeamish about another death.'

'Thanks Alice, I'll be in first thing.'

It was after seven when Daisy returned to her apartment. After feeding Heinz and letting him out on the balcony she thought about dinner. As usual when she was cooking for one, she relied on ready meals and her microwave. Tonight, it was to be a fish pie, topped with mashed potato. When it was ready, she opened a bottle of Dom Brial, put everything on a low table and dropped into the couch in front of it. Turning on the TV and the BBC news, she watched without seeing, absently eating the meal and sipping the wine, trying make sense of the day.

The phoney Mrs Vereker convinced her that Mary had been the bomber's target. But why? What she now knew about Mary's background suggested that it was to do with the stories in the Delia file. If Mary had recognised someone connected to the Midnight Fox gang, who didn't want to be recognised, that would surely have required her immediate silence. The killer also sought to make her appear to be an innocent victim during the assassination of Prince Abdullah. Whoever arranged her death wanted no investigation into Mary Grey's background.

Clearly, Mary wanted Daisy to read the Delia file – or as it turned out – her mother Gloria's file. So, was it the photograph of the boat or the news stories she wanted her to see? Maybe both. Two of the names from the news stories were clearly connected to her: Sidney Vane was her father and Zar Brum, who according to Albert Grimes, besides being her mother's employer for a time, did time with Sid Vane. Then there was the Midnight Fox. All three of them were handy with explosives and whoever killed Mary was certainly an expert. But, Vane and Brum, were dead. Vane without question and according to everyone she had spoken to Brum was also dead.

Therefore, of the three names, that only left the Midnight Fox, whoever he might be. If Mary had recognised him that certainly would be a motive for murder. Then, there was the photograph, was that what she wanted her to see? Daisy looked at the photo again. Mary looked happy, and the man, who was he? Could he be Harry?

Daisy took a 10X glass from the table drawer and looked at the face. Handsome enough, the touch of grey in the sideburns giving him a distinguished look, maybe in his fifties; the mirror glasses prevented any further attempts at recognition. Daisy turned the photo and looked at the 0034 number on the back – 34 was Spain. *There's only one way to find out.* She dialled the number.

CHAPTER 19

Friday 6ᵗʰ September

The Monarch Airlines flight from Alicante landed at Luton at 07.45, fifteen minutes behind schedule. As usual the landing was greeting with a round of clapping from the passengers. Then, the scramble for overhead lockers began. Veleta, who had a window seat, waited until half the passengers had disembarked before standing up. Gomez, who had arranged these things before, had advised him to be in the middle of the queue. That way the official would have gone through the first hundred people and already be bored. It was a package holiday after all and in the eyes of the official, all these people are dressed the same and even looked the same.

Veleta, dressed for his part in a sporty outfit: a beige cotton zip-up jacket, matching pants and Nike trainers – with luminous green stripes – carried an Iberia flight bag. He had no problems with the passport at Alicante and now, as it was his turn, he would see how close his appearance matched the true owner. There was no need to worry, the official looked at the document then at him, followed by the queue behind him and waved him through.

Veleta followed the throng to the baggage hall, grabbed a trolley and waited for the golf clubs and suitcase to arrive. He still had Customs to pass through and needed his props.

Frank Stubbs was waiting at the arrivals exit. Veleta saw him but showed no sign or greeting. While there was still a chance of a bust, they'd keep their distance. He found the left luggage booth and deposited the two items. Putting the receipt inside the passport he made his way to the exit.

Frank was waiting a hundred feet away beside his black cab. Veleta cast an experienced eye around looking for trouble, there was no need, he was in the clear.

Within minutes they were joining the M1 going towards London. The morning traffic was one continuous slow-moving line. Stubbs looked at Veleta in his mirror. They had not met in the year since he had visited him in Spain. His face, as usual gave nothing away, but he must be hurting, he wouldn't be human if he wasn't hurting. But he also knew the man to be single minded to a fault. He was here to do something. Best keep it on a professional basis.

'Things go all right, Harry?'

Veleta nodded. 'Smooth as silk, Frank, you got everything?'

'Sure, in the bag beside you, suit, shirts, underwear, shoes and socks all in the size you asked for.'

Veleta opened the bag and looked inside. 'And the file?'

'That's in the bag as well.'

'Good, you did well. Did you read the file?'

'Just the cover, to check it was Gloria's file like you said.'

Veleta nodded. 'Yeah, Mary found it in her possessions when she died. I told her to get rid of it but she insisted on taking it with her. It's best if nobody reads it.'

Frank concentrated as he moved the taxi into the outside lane to pass a container lorry. After pulling back into the centre lane he said, 'Don't be so sure on that, Harry, there was someone in the flat when I arrived, a woman, told me she was on police business.'

Veleta looked up sharply. 'A cop?'

'No, told me her name was Daisy Clowser, and she was a friend of Mary. Lives in the flat above. Blonde, real good looker and sharp with it. She wasn't fazed at all when I turned up.'

Veleta nodded. 'I know the name. She was a friend of Mary's. Did she say what she was looking for?'

Frank slowed, as the car in front braked. 'Yeah, the cops had asked her to look for next of kin. She wanted to know what I was looking for, insisted on seeing my ID. Like I said, no flies on her.'

'What did you tell her?'

'Only that I was doing the same.'

'Did she buy it?'

Frank shrugged. 'Hard to say, but she did say she was with Mary when she died, tried to save her, caught some injuries getting her out of the cab. Her face was cut, needed stitches. It didn't seem to bother her much.'

Leaning forward, Veleta asked, 'Did she say anything else?'

Nodding, Frank said, 'Yeah, asked me if I knew anyone called Harry, told me Mary had left a message for Harry.'

'Did she now?' Then, with a catch in his voice asked, 'Did she say what it was?'

Frank glanced at him in the driver's mirror and knew he was hurting. 'No, she said it was only for Harry.'

Veleta went silent as the taxi passed a long line of container lorries belonging to household names.

To ease the tension Frank said, 'Look at them, every morning it's the same on this stretch, bumper to bumper.'

Veleta stayed with his thoughts for another two miles before asking in little more than a whisper, 'How did you get the file?'

A relieved Frank replied, 'I waited outside until I saw the lights go on in her flat, then I went back, and took the file.'

'Anything else?'

'Yeah, Daisy Clowser, she came into the office yesterday.'

Veleta leaned close to the glass partition. 'What did she want?'

'She was asking questions about Mary.'

'What kind of questions?'

'About Mr Abdullah. Has Mary told you about him?'

'Yeah, seemed a decent guy.'

'He was. Anyway, she wanted to know all about Mary's timings with him. Seems to me she was more interested in Mary than Abdullah. She wanted to know if he was ever late opening the door.'

'Was he?'

'Yeah, like I told her, maybe a minute or two, but Mary was always there on time.'

'That's it?'

'No, she asked if anyone else had been enquiring about Mary.'

'Was there?'

Frank explained about the call from Mrs Vereker.

Veleta considered that for a moment before asking, 'What did she say about that?'

'Nothing, but as I said, she seemed more interested about Mary than the Arab.'

'Seems that way.' Veleta leaned back in his seat and was silent for another mile before asking, 'Have you made the arrangements I asked for?'

'Yeah, it cost a Monkey, we can get in during the lunch break. I'll stop at Scratchwood Services, you can change there.'

'How long from here?'

'In this traffic, twenty minutes.'

'Okay,' Veleta said. 'I'll leave a passport and the left luggage tag with you. Can you see that it gets back to its owner? We're not petty thieves. And, as we should be in London by ten, I want to go see Courtney-Hopkins.'

'No problem, Harry,' Frank said.

Veleta took the Delia file from the bag, opened it and looked at the wedding photo for a long moment. He then shook the file and riffled through the inserts before saying, 'There should be two photographs, Frank, one is missing.'

Shaking his head, Frank said, 'I'm sure nothing fell out, Harry. I took the file from the shelf and put it straight into the carrier bag.'

Veleta dumped the contents of the bag onto the seat beside and searched through the contents without success. 'Okay,' he said, 'it's not here. It must still be in the flat or else someone has read the file and taken the photo.'

Keeping his eyes on the road, Frank said, 'Like I said, Daisy Clowser might have read it. She asked me at the office if I'd forgotten anything when I left the flat. Could be she'd wanted another look and missed the folder.'

Putting the empty bag on the seat beside him, Veleta said, 'If she has read it, she already knows too much. Maybe that's why she's started nosing around. She called the restaurant last evening. Garcia took the call. She said she was a friend of Mary Grey. Garcia told her didn't know anyone of that name and hung up.'

'She told me she wasn't a cop, Harry,' Frank said.

'Yeah, I know. Mary told me what she knew about her. She told me about all of her friends. Daisy Clowser had a job in the Home Office for twelve years, before she joined the family firm, some type of high-class security company.'

'Like I said, Harry, a private cop. Discreet enquiries, that sort of thing, but remember, she told me she was on police business.'

Sitting back in his seat, Veleta said, 'I'll bear that in mind when I see her. How long to Scratchwood?'

'We're nearly there, five minutes at most.'

CHAPTER 20

Daisy awoke after eight hours of uninterrupted sleep. She knew it was past seven because Heinz was on the bed and his claws were digging into her arm. Feeling refreshed, despite a few aches in her bones and a mild throbbing from the wound in her forehead she got up and let Heinz on to the balcony. Following Alice's advice, she gave the street a long look, but saw nothing out of the ordinary to worry her.

By eight she had completed her new routine of showering, checking the wound on her forehead, which was healing nicely, and changing the dressing. Then, while letting Heinz in for his food, she gave the street another look, and saw nothing to worry her.

Making herself a breakfast of a lightly boiled egg, toast, coffee and a bowl of mixed fruit, she sat at the kitchen table. Propping Mary's work-sheets on the coffee pot in front of her, she glanced through them as she ate. Starting with Mary's last call on Tuesday, she worked backwards for a week. The calls were all journeys around inner London, with Victoria, Waterloo and St. Pancras stations being regular destinations. Maybe she was being dim this morning, she thought, but nothing stood out. Then she considered the unsatisfactory call she had made to the Spanish number on Mary's photo. She had the distinct feeling she'd been fobbed off. If so, why?

One way to find out, she thought, and went to the living room and found her Blackberry. Thumbing through the index, she found another Spanish number and called it.

Veleta changed his clothes in the men's room at the Scratchwood service area. The Austin Reed dark grey two-piece suit was off the peg but fitted him well enough. Set off with a pale blue fine cotton shirt, a tie which maybe had some history and black Church shoes. With his height, greying black hair and a permanent tan he made a commanding figure.

He paused at the newsagents and scanned the headlines. The latest on the bombing was already relegated to the inside pages. In truth there was no latest, only a rehash of earlier reports. He bought the *Daily Herald* and turned to Frank.

'It's too early to go to town. I haven't eaten since dinner, can you see what they have that's edible?'

Frank looked across at the buffet. 'You want the full English.'

'Good idea,' he said, smiling for the first time. 'Yeah, with two slices and a pot of tea, may as well go the whole hog.'

He took a table which gave him a view of everyone in the restaurant and started paging through the paper while Frank stood in line to collect the food.

They ate in silence, Veleta immersed in his thoughts.

As he wiped his plate clean with his last piece of bread before pushing it aside, he said to Frank, who had already finished, 'That brings me back. You remember the café we used to go to in Scrutton Street, what was its name?'

Frank smiled. 'Yeah, I remember, Mrs Burkes, it's still there.'

'Is it? All you could eat there for nine and sixpence, a long time ago.' The moment of nostalgia didn't last, the smile leaving his face when he thought of the reason for his visit. 'What do you think of all this with Mary? You're her link with the past. Did she say anything to you, like she was involved in anything, did she have any troubles?'

Frank shook his head. 'Not a thing, Harry, except that she was looking forward to her holiday. But I haven't seen her since Monday.'

'How come?'

'She signed off early on Monday and I was out all day Tuesday.'

'She didn't try to contact you?'

'No.'

Veleta lowered his voice. 'She tried to contact me, made two calls to the restaurant, Tuesday evening and the morning she died, both from her home phone. She's never done that before Frank, always called me from a payphone.'

'What did she want?'

'That's the thing, I don't know. I was out on the boat and the sat-phone was on the blink. Garcia told me she sounded anxious, needed to talk to me urgently, but when I got the message, she was already dead.' Tears welled and he went quiet. When he continued there was a catch in his voice. 'I was always there for her, Frank, except when it fucking well mattered.'

'I know you were, Harry, we all were. Is that why you didn't come the usual way?'

'Yeah, I sensed something wasn't right, Mary calling me like that, then being accidentally killed. I thought maybe someone is trying to flush me out.'

'Don't forget, Harry, Daisy Clowser told me Mary left a message for you.'

Veleta was silent for a long moment before saying, 'Yeah, I remember.'

Frank asked. 'What next, Harry?'

'We carry on as planned. First Courtney-Hopkins, then the hospital.'

Daisy exited the Tube at Green Park. The sky was blue and the air warm for September and she enjoyed the short walk along Piccadilly to St. James Street. By five after nine she was at her desk, checking her mail and messages. Finding nothing that couldn't wait, she buzzed Alice. Minutes later she came in with a buff coloured folder tucked under her arm and a mug of coffee in each hand.

Handing Daisy a coffee, she said, 'You're looking chipper this morning, had a good night?'

Taking the coffee, Daisy said, 'Thanks, I had a great sleep.'

'Good to hear,' Alice said. Taking her pad and pencil from the folder, she sat opposite.

Eying the folder, Daisy asked, 'What you got?'

Tapping the folder Alice said, 'The company you asked about and Harrison's report but bring me up to speed first.'

Daisy explained about the call to Spain.

'So,' Alice said, 'the Spanish number was a restaurant called La Gamba.'

'Yeah, I spoke to the manager, a Señor Garcia, he denied any knowledge of Mary.'

Alice deftly twirled her pencil between two fingers for a long moment before replying. 'You did say she went to Spain several times a year, maybe she just jotted the number of a good restaurant for future reference as we all do.'

Daisy shook her head. 'On the back of what seems to be a treasured photograph, I don't know.'

'Then you think Garcia was lying. Why, I wonder?'

'Good question,' Daisy said. 'I called Manuel Sierra in Madrid and asked him if he can trace the number, find La Gamba and take a look at it, maybe the man with the yacht is connected with it. I've also asked him to look into the Lady Mary, find out who owns it and where it's moored.'

'Good move,' Alice said and scribbled on her pad. 'What about your visit to Frank Stubbs, anything there?'

'Yeah, a big something,' Daisy said, and told her about Mrs Vereker.

Alice pondered that for a moment. 'Looks like you were right about Mary being the target. Anything else?'

'Not really,' Daisy said. 'I got a copy of Mary's work-sheets, but nothing stands out that might be relevant. Stubbs denied returning to Mary's apartment. I didn't ask him about the Delia file, didn't want him to know that I'd seen it.'

Alice raised an eyebrow. 'If he came back and took the file, he's hardly likely to admit it, is he?'

'That's what I thought,' Daisy said. 'I'm sure Frank Stubbs is not telling me everything he knows about Mary. I'll ask Jack Farmer to do a CRO check on him.'

Alice gave her a doubtful look. 'I shouldn't bother. If he had form, he wouldn't have a black cab licence. We have his birth certificate which shows he was born in Rufford Street N1, just a few streets away from where Gloria Grey was living.'

Daisy considered that and said, 'Then he must have known them. Everyone knew their neighbours in those days.'

'You're probably right, but where does that leave us? If Stubbs and Garcia are lying, who are they trying to protect?' Answering her own question, she continued. 'Maybe it's more like who are they afraid of? Although from what you've said, Frank Stubbs doesn't come across as the nervous type.'

'Definitely not,' Daisy said. 'What did you dig up on him?'

Alice opened the buff coloured file and pulling out a single page she said, 'I used Harrison. He's expensive, but he's the best and Peter Isaacs is paying, so no worries. Here's the gist of it: Frank Stubbs lives in Thornhill Crescent N1, off the Caledonian Road and only a few streets away from where he was born. He's been the manager of the taxi company since it started in '88. Including bonus payments, he makes about thirty-five thousand a year. He doesn't appear to have any serious debt, has a good credit rating, his bank statements show nothing out of the ordinary, regular income, with no unexplained credits. He married a Helen Butcher in 1972, two children, a boy, named Sam, born '74, and a girl named Jane born '78.'

'Bloody hell! Daisy exclaimed. 'You got all that in less than twelve hours?'

Alice smiled. 'Frightening, isn't it? There's more: as I said, Harrison and his group of nerds are the best. They have sources everywhere. All they need is the name and address you got from his driving license. According to the land registry, he bought his house in 1988, for one hundred and twenty thousand pounds. It's probably worth at least half a million today. What I find odd is that there are no entailments of any kind, there's never been a mortgage.'

Daisy considered that and said, 'Which means he paid in full. How did he manage that? Even back in those days serious questions would be asked if you tried to buy a house for cash.'

Alice shrugged. 'There are ways, all you need is an accommodating solicitor to do the conveyancing, have him launder the cash and complete the transaction with a solicitor's cheque. Remember Daisy, the Midnight Fox robberies stopped in '86. Could be Frank Stubbs was a member of the gang and began spending some of his loot. Maybe if we dig a bit more, we'll find more hidden wealth.'

Daisy, who knew that she trusted her instincts too much at times, was pleased that it looked like she was right about Frank Stubbs. 'You could be right, Alice, and if that's the case he'll know the identity of the Midnight Fox and everyone in the gang. He might even know who had a reason to kill Mary.'

'Anything's possible,' Alice said. 'From what you've told me he thinks Mary's death was just an unfortunate accident, which means he's not looking for reasons yet, maybe you should have told him your thoughts on that.'

Daisy, remembering Frank's two tearful moments, said, 'You're probably right, but I want to dig a bit more first.'

'Maybe that's best for the moment. Anyway, the company you

asked about: Zentek Aviation. Simpson checked it out and it's an American aircraft engine maintenance company, headquartered in Phoenix, Arizona, with operations in the middle-east, Asia and Africa. He called Phoenix and enquired if they had any recent events in London. They exhibited at Farnborough last year, but nothing since.'

'That's a bummer,' Daisy said. 'I'd hoped that might lead somewhere. Mary was so insistent, but if they don't operate in Europe, where did she see the name? Maybe someone's using it as a cover. I'll pass it on to Isaacs. Anything else?'

'Yeah, I also asked Harrison to do a search on Mary Grey's financials, thought it might throw up something.'

Daisy slapped the desk. 'Shit, I should have thought of that.'

Pulling another page from the folder, Alice said, 'You can't think of everything. Remember, you've had a knock on the head. Anyway, here are the numbers: according to her tax returns it looks like her only income is from her taxi which, over the past two years, averaged a thousand pounds a week gross. Apparently, that's about average for a London cabbie. Of course, fuel, maintenance, depreciation on her cab, which she owns, would mean deducting at least forty per cent. She also has to pay four hundred a month to London Quality Taxis for the radio service. That should leave her with around two thousand a month which more or less tallies with her bank deposits. Like Frank Stubbs there are no unaccounted deposits and she has a good credit score.'

Casting her eyes to the ceiling, Daisy said, 'Like you said, Alice, that Harrison is frightening. He must be breaking every data protection law in the book. What about Mary's apartment? Does she own it?'

Alice looked at her pad and said, 'Difficult to say. According to the land registry the property is owned by a company called Caledonian Investments, based in St. Helier, Channel Islands. They paid three hundred and thirty thousand pounds for it in '94. That was when Mary moved in, but other than the council tax and the utility bills Mary pays no rent or mortgage payments.'

'Which explains why she could live there on a cab driver's income. The question is, who owns Caledonian Investments?'

With a crooked smile Alice said, 'Being a Channel Islands company, it won't be easy to find out. They're worse than the Caymans.'

'Tell me about it,' Daisy said.

Alice gathered her papers and said, 'Is that it?'

'Yeah, I think we've covered everything, but it doesn't get us much further. We need definite connections to Mary. Maybe Wilson will come up with something.'

'Right,' Alice said. 'He's had enough time. I'll go see him. I'll send in a fresh coffee; do you want a Panadol?'

'No thanks, I took a couple before leaving the apartment.'

Alice got up and turned to leave when there was a tap on the door. Opening it revealed the tall gangly figure of Ian Wilson. With blond hair touching his shoulders, he wore jeans, emerald-green sneakers and a Saracens rugby shirt. Wilson looked exactly the part for his role as the computer genius and sometime hacker, which was his role in the firm.

Wilson was one of Alice's few favourites and seeing the notepad in his hand, she gave him a friendly smile and said, 'Speak of the devil, it's the lad himself. I hope you've got something for me, Ian?'

Returning her smile, Wilson said, 'Sure do, Alice, the passport and HMRC info you wanted.' Looking towards Daisy, he said, 'Hi Daisy, are you well?'

Daisy smiled, pointed to the plaster on her forehead and said, 'Well enough, Ian. As you can see, I'm still in recovery mode. Come in, let's hear what you've got,' and waited as Alice pulled over another chair and the two of them were seated.

Alice nodded to Wilson, who began reading from his notes.

'Okay,' he said. 'Passports: A ten-year passport was issued to Mrs Gloria Grey, in 1976 which was renewed in '86 and '96. A similar passport was also was issued to Mr Henry Vane, interesting enough on the same date in '76. His has only been renewed once, in '86.'

Nodding her appreciation Daisy said, 'Great work, Ian. Did you check out Henry's employment record?'

Eying his notes, Wilson said, 'I did, according to HMRC he was employed by a firm in Shoreditch named Blacks, from 1966 to '88. I checked them out. It was a locksmith but it's now closed. The owner retired ten years ago.'

Daisy pondered that input for a moment and said, 'What address did Gloria use for her application?'

Turning a page Wilson said, 'In '76 her address was given as Bingfield Street, London N1. Henry Vane used the same address on his application and it was used again for both of their renewals in '86, which doesn't tie in with what I found on the voters register. Gloria was living there up to '88, but, although Henry used the address for his renewal in '86, that's the last time he was on the register. Vane is not a common name, but after checking out all the London boroughs, I couldn't find him.'

'Interesting,' Daisy said. 'If he'd died, his name would be on the death register, maybe he changed his name. Gloria and Mary never used the name Vane.'

Wilson scratched the stubble on his chin for a moment before saying, 'It's possible but any name change would have to be declared and tagged to his original record if he wanted a UK passport.'

'Okay,' Daisy said. 'When you checked the register was Mary Grey's name on it in '86? She'd have been twenty-four then.'

Giving Alice a glum look Wilson said, 'Sorry, I only checked Gloria and Henry. I can take another look if you want.'

'No worries, Ian, leave it for now,' Daisy said. 'What about Gloria's renewal in '96? What address did she use?'

After glancing at his notes Wilson said, 'Apartment 4, Porchester Mansions, W2.'

'Mary's address!' Daisy exclaimed before asking, 'One more thing, Ian, can you do a HMRC search on Frank Stubbs' work history? He's older than Henry Vane, but he lived in the same area and their paths may have crossed workwise.'

Standing, Wilson said, 'No problem, Daisy, give me ten minutes.'

When he'd left the room, Alice laughed. 'Nobody's secrets are safe from that boy.'

Nodding agreement, Daisy said, 'Just as well he's working for us. The problem is, what we've learned is all past-tense. We don't know anything about the family after they all dropped out of sight in '88, other than Mary reappearing in '94, but what happened to Gloria and Henry?'

Alice didn't immediately reply and was clearly weighing her ideas as she played a rhythm on the desk with her fingers. Knowing her ways, Daisy waited.

Finally, Alice said, 'The robberies stopped in '86. The same year Brum died and Henry Vane renewed his passport for the last time. Two years later Henry left his job and hasn't been seen since. The same year Frank Stubbs bought his house, started his taxi business and according to Albert Grimes, Gloria moved to Spain in the late eighties. If they were involved in the robberies, two years would be a suitable cooling-off period, before they made any moves.'

'Makes sense,' Daisy said. 'But what does that tell us?'

Alice drummed her fingers for another bout of thinking before saying, 'From what you've told me the Midnight Fox gang used the same MO as Sidney Vane. Consider this: Gloria was married to Vane for long enough to learn his secrets. She also kept the file on the robberies and the article on Brum's death, so she must have known what was going on. Henry, was apprenticed to a locksmith, which would have given him the skills needed by the robbers to open doors.

They both disappeared two years after the robberies stopped. Maybe our Gloria was in this up to her neck.'

Smiling at the thought, Daisy said, 'A female Raffles, that'd be a first.'

'Based on the size of those robberies, very much so,' Alice said. 'But she must be dead, otherwise why hasn't she contacted someone about her daughter's death?'

Daisy was wondering about that when there was a knock, the door opened and Wilson, a broad grin on his face, waved a sheet of paper and said. 'Okay to come in? I have the info you wanted on Frank Stubbs.'

'That was quick,' Daisy said.

Wilson dropped into the vacant chair and pushed a page across the desk. 'I still had the search parameters set up for Gloria and Henry, so I only had to change a name.'.

Taking it, she began reading aloud. 'Frank Stubbs DOB 11/06/1945, employed as motor mechanic from 1961 to 1988 with Bentley & Sons, a Jaguar dealership, in York Way, N1.'

'Is the company still trading?' Alice asked.

'Yep,' Wilson said. 'I checked that out. Also, the location. Stubbs lived in Rufford Street N.I. at the time, which runs into York Way.'

'Good work, Ian,' Daisy said and waited until he left the room before continuing.

'That's a few streets from Bingfield Street,' Alice remarked. 'They were all neighbours.'

'Yeah, cosy,' Daisy said. 'Okay, that fills in more of the background, but we still don't know where Mary fits into all this.'

'Think about this,' Alice said. 'Mary only reappeared in '94 when she moved into Portchester Mansions, which was way beyond her means. She also had Gloria's file, so she must have known what they'd been up to, maybe even been part of the gang. Why else would she be rewarded with an expensive apartment?'

Daisy gave that some thought before saying, 'If she was involved with the gang, she'd have known some serious villains. Mary definitely said, "Tell Harry he's alive," and clearly wanted me to read Gloria's file. The question is, who is Harry and who's alive that she thought was dead? The only dead people mentioned in Gloria's file besides Marilyn Monroe, are Sid Vane, whom we know for sure is dead and Zar Brum the crime boss. All we've left to go on is La Gamba, the yacht *Lady Mary* and the mystery man in the photo. Let's hope they're not just taking a pose in front of a fancy yacht. I'll have to wait for Manuel Sierra's report on that. In the meantime, as Brum is the only one who could be alive. I'll go talk to Jack Farmer about him.'

Moments after Alice had left the room the phone rang on her direct line. Seeing who the caller was Daisy pushed the scrambler button before lifting the handset.

'Hello?'

Like herself Peter Isaacs had been born in Africa, and it was only over the telephone that his voice betrayed his origin. 'How are you feeling today, Daisy?'

'Just fine and dandy, Peter.'

'Good for you. Daisy, we need to talk, can you come in?'

'Of course, when and where?'

'My usual place, you should make it in an hour this time of the day.'

'Okay, I could do with some fresh air, in an hour then.'

CHAPTER 21

'M r Veleta to see you.'

Courtney-Hopkins was speaking on the telephone, and with a muttered, 'I'll call you back in an hour,' hung up, stood up and came forward hand outstretched. Veleta ignored it and waited for the secretary to leave.

The solicitor let his hand drop with the thought, *Should have known better, no manners these people, think they're God Almighty.* 'Sit down, will you? Can I get you something? Tea, coffee…'

Veleta, who remained on his feet, said, 'Have you done what I asked?'

'Of course, here it is.' Courtney-Hopkins opened a manila file on his desk, removed a single sheet and handed it to Veleta. 'A letter confirming that Señor Enrique Veleta is Miss Mary Grey's Trustee and has sole responsibility for carrying out her wishes according to her last will and testament.'

Veleta glanced at the letter and handed it back. 'Good. I want to bury Mary in Spain, do you see any problems in that?'

The solicitor shrugged. 'There are legal requirements but it will be done as you wish, I'll need your signature on some documents.'

Giving him a blank stare, Veleta said, 'I don't have time for that, I'll sign the blank pages, you can fill in the detail.'

The solicitor shrugged. 'Unusual, but in the circumstances, it's nice to be trusted.'

'Isn't it?' Veleta face smiled but his eyes were cold.

'Is there anything else?' Courtney-Hopkins tried to hide his nervousness.

'Yes, I want you to sell Mary's flat and contents. Frank Stubbs will remove any of Mary's personal items.'

'As you wish, the flat's owned by your Jersey company. I'll need your signature on several more documents.'

Signing more blank pages, Veleta said, 'There's one more thing. I need twenty grand in cash now, twenties and fifties.'

Without comment Courtney-Hopkins went to his safe and took out a wad of cash and a ledger. He counted out the money, made a note in the ledger and passed it to Veleta who signed it and passed it back. Putting the cash and the letter into his flight bag, he nodded to the solicitor and left the room.

Courtney-Hopkins slumped back into his chair, fumbled in the desk drawer for the half bottle of whisky he kept there, removed the cap and took a deep slug. *Jesus!* he thought. *Why do I deal with that man?* But looking through the ledger, the answer was clear – money, cash money, more than he could make out of any ten clients.

The whisky helped and he put the blank pages with Veleta's signature in the manila envelope. One doesn't tell a man like that to go somewhere else. He began speaking into his Dictaphone; the sooner the legalities of this totally illegal transaction were dealt with the better.

Peter Isaac's place was the Serpentine Bridge in Hyde Park. He preferred to conduct his more clandestine meetings in the open air, without notes, minutes or recording devices which allowed him complete denial without worries.

Daisy's taxi entered the park from the Bayswater Road entrance and as usual for the time of day the road through the park was jammed with slow-moving cars.

'Drop me by the bridge, will you Hassan?' she said. 'I have to meet someone for about ten minutes.'

'No problem, Miss Clowser,' said Hassan. 'I can wait just beyond, by the restaurant.'

As she got out, she saw Isaacs approaching from the direction of Prince's Gate. Immaculately dressed as usual in a two-piece grey suit he looked every bit the gent out for his morning stroll. *How appearances can be deceptive,* Daisy thought. He stopped when he saw her and waited by the bridge. Without a word they began to stroll towards the swimming area.

Satisfied that he was out of earshot he spoke as he walked. 'Good morning Daisy, how's your head? Brain still functioning, I hope?'

Daisy smiled. Tapping the plaster on her forehead lightly she said, 'My stitches are coming along nicely, Peter, and my brain received no permanent damage that I'm aware of, thanks for asking.'

Without looking at her Isaacs said, 'Good to hear. I spoke to Farmer this morning. He has no material progress to report. In fact, he's gathered all of his evidence but has come up with a big zero. He also mentioned that he hadn't seen or heard from you since yesterday morning, that is since he mentioned the Fisherman's confirmation that there was no IRA involvement, dissident or otherwise.'

Daisy waited until a youth had passed them on a skateboard before replying. 'You're prepared to take the Fisherman's word?'

Isaacs stopped in front of some ducks and surprised Daisy by removing a bag of corn from his pocket and begin the feeding ritual as he spoke. 'Yes, I am. I've spoken the him also and he told me that O'Grady has assured him that all known dissidents have been accounted for. You do remember O'Grady, don't you?'

Daisy winced. Even though ten years had passed, memories of the last time she saw Valentine O'Grady sent a shudder through her body. She replied, 'Yes, I remember O'Grady all too well.'

With his eyes still on the big mallard, Isaacs said, 'Thought you might.'

They both stood in silence for a long moment watching the ducks shunting each other for the food.

'I see you like ducks, Peter.'

Accurately tossing pieces of corn under the beak of an approaching mallard, he replied, 'I like all animals. Their needs are predictable. Humans, on the other hand, are the problem. If the IRA are out of it what can you do that Farmer can't?'

'You want me out, is that it, Peter?'

Isaacs's eyes stayed on the ducks. 'I didn't say that. I asked what you could do that Farmer can't?'

Looking directly at him, she replied, 'What I bloody well intend to do with or without your help is to find out who killed Mary. It would help me no end if you came clean and tell me what your intelligence was in the first place that got you involved and spare me the "chatter" bullshit.'

Isaacs threw the last of the corn to the jostling ducks as he considered her question.

'You remember Walker? I believe he was a friend of yours.'

Daisy watched the ducks scramble for the food and thought of the second man from the past mentioned. Unlike O'Grady, thinking of Walker gave her a warmer feeling. During his stint in Belfast, because of his swarthy appearance he was able to pass himself off as a playboy follower of the Aga Khan, a popular figure in Ireland, both North and South. And being neither Protestant nor Catholic he was able to move freely among both factions. He was in fact British, born in Herat, Afghanistan, where his father was a doctor from Surrey and his mother a high-born Afghan.

Taking her gaze off the ducks she looked at Isaacs and asked, 'He's alive then. I haven't seen him for a while.'

'Very much so, at the moment he's in Rawalpindi having recently spent two months travelling in Afghanistan with a band of smugglers.'

Imagining Walker in that situation brought a smile to her face. 'Passing himself off as what this time?' she asked.

'A Pashtun muleteer. Interesting choice, but he's quite good at that sort of thing, isn't he?' Isaacs said.

Daisy nodded and said, 'The best, what did he find out?'

Isaacs carefully folded his paper bag and put it in his pocket before replying.

'Besides their usual shipment of processed heroin, the smugglers carried two wooden crates from Kabul to Peshawar, which they took great care of. They were unmarked and wrapped in Hessian. Walker was unable to inspect either, but he learned that once they were safely across the border in Peshawar, the crates were to be delivered to an armourer in Darra Adam Khel to be serviced before being shipped to England for a forthcoming operation.'

Daisy watched the ducks finishing off the last of the corn as she cast her mind back to an all-night stake-out in County Antrim ten years ago, where to pass the time, Walker had told her about Darra Adam Khel. A town in the tribal area of Pakistan. Its only industry was making firearms. In the one street town every man Jack was a skilled gunsmith. Men and boys, using primitive tools were able to produce excellent copies of the AK47 and M16 automatic rifles, and anything else they could get their hands on, even RPGs with their grenades.

Give them any weapon, Walker had said, and they can produce the first copy in a week, and once patterns were made, could produce a steady supply.

Looking from the eating frenzy to Isaacs, Daisy said, 'It has to be something special to be taken to Darra, like maybe a Blowpipe or Stinger surface-to-air missile. I heard talk that a bunch of those that were supplied to the Mujahideen during the Soviet occupation have gone missing.'

Nodding his agreement Isaacs said, 'You heard right. The CIA supplied the Mujahidin with around six hundred Stingers. They've been trying to buy them back for years, but hundreds are still unaccounted for. Bin Laden must have access to some of them, because according to Saudi intelligence, his group made an unsuccessful attempt to smuggle SAMs into the Kingdom in '98.'

Daisy looked sceptical. 'I don't know, Peter, those Stingers must be twenty years old by now, well past their useful life.'

Isaacs nodded his agreement. 'You're right of course. Stingers only had a three- to four-year shelf life. I've been told that they would need new thermal batteries and expert servicing before they could be used. Darra Adam Kiel is definitely the place for that.'

'Did Walker find out what happened after Darra?'

'Yes, he stayed with the smugglers. Once across the border they had a truck waiting and delivered the crates to their contact in Darra. They waited there for two days until the work was done, after which the crates – still wrapped in hessian – were loaded back onto the same truck and delivered, together with the shipment of heroin to Rawalpindi. There the smugglers including Walker were paid off. He travelled back to Peshawar with them and discovered that the crates and drugs were to be taken by road to Karachi to be delivered to an established foreign trafficker, who had a safe route by sea to England.'

Daisy, remembering another thing Walker had told her, said, 'I was told that these people never trust anyone outside their extended family. Don't you find it odd that, if whatever was in those crates is so important to their operation, they would hand them over to foreigners?'

Isaacs gave her a thoughtful look as he considered this. 'Needs must, I suppose. If the traffickers have a safe route to the UK they would have to comply if they wanted to continue their operations in Pakistan.'

'Even when it involves supplying weapons to terrorists?'

Isaacs shrugged. 'Come off it, Daisy, they're Narcos, they'll do anything to protect their supplies. Do they worry that the junk they push costs thousands of lives? They bloody well don't, so what's a few more?'

'When was this?' she asked.

Not meeting her gaze, Isaacs said, 'Two months ago.'

'Two months! In that case, whatever it is, could be here already. Why all the secrecy, Peter, why couldn't you have told me two days ago?'

Isaacs raised his hands, saying, 'I hadn't connected the two. I've had Abdullah checked out. He's clean. Nobody has any reason to kill him. With the IRA out of the picture, what does that leave?'

'What I've been harping on all along,' Daisy said. 'It leaves Mary Grey. I believe she was killed because she recognised someone from her past, some serious criminal.'

Isaacs eyes narrowed. 'She had a criminal past?'

'I'm not sure, but she grew up knowing some serious bad guys and one of them may still be active.'

After a longish silence Isaacs said, 'Maybe there is a connection. If we're right about what's in those crates, whoever is bringing in this shipment are Narcos and these people don't think twice of using extreme violence, if they felt in any way threatened.'

Looking for a reaction, Daisy said, 'Peter, one thing is for sure, if the terrorists get Stingers into the UK and they take down an aircraft, there's going to be hundreds of casualties and some serious shit flying in Whitehall.'

Isaacs smiled. 'Succinctly put as usual, Daisy, and you're quite right, we can only hope that this particular lead you're following has some bearing.'

'So, you're asking me to carry on?'

'I am, and there's something else to bear in mind,' Isaacs said. 'Walker, has been ferreting about trying to find out more. He sent a message yesterday. Two specialists have been sent to the UK. Something big is planned – he doesn't know what or where – to take place in early September.'

'Which is any time now,' Daisy said.

'Correct. As I told you already, we have people in all the mosques and Islamic meeting places but there's not a whisper about an operation. It looks like it's being directed from outside. We have all of the known militants under twenty-four surveillance, other than that we can't do a thing.'

'So, it's down to me to save your ass again, Peter.' Daisy smiled as she saw him wince.

Isaacs started to walk towards the bridge. 'I don't have time for the niceties, Daisy, I want to find these people and neutralise them before they can act. I have the SAS on twenty-four standby. I need something to work with, just get me a name, that's all I ask.'

Neutralise? Daisy had seen that look in his eyes before and knew exactly what he meant by that word. *Definitely a worried man, is our Peter,* she was thinking, as she stopped and allowed a nanny in a green uniform to pass, before saying, 'Okay Peter, here's a name to be going on with. Mary asked me to check out a company called Zentek Aviation. We've checked it. It's an American aircraft maintenance set-up with operations in the Middle-East, Asia and Africa, but nothing in Europe. I don't know where Mary saw the name, but it may have been in connection with the person who killed her. My thinking is if Zentek have operations in Pakistan, the Narcos may be using their name as a cover for their shipment. Can you check it out with Customs & Excise, see if any shipment has been recently cleared in that name?'

Isaacs produced a mini recorder from an inside pocket and whispered into it before saying, 'I'll get on to it. When did you get this information?'

Guessing what was coming next, Daisy said, 'Wednesday morning.'

Casting his eyes towards the sky Isaacs said, 'You might have told me then, we could have warned Customs. As it is, if they have the name now it'll mean the shipment has already passed through.'

Giving him a cold look, Daisy said, 'Don't put this on me, Peter. I'd have told you if you'd had given me the full story in the first place.'

They walked in silence to the bridge where Isaacs said, 'See you, Daisy, I'll have Customs checked out immediately and call you.'

Daisy watched for a moment as he walked towards Princes Gate, his pace quickening, his mobile to his ear.

CHAPTER 22

Frank found the service road behind St. Thomas's Hospital and parked the taxi. Turning to Veleta he said, 'The mortuary is at the back, Harry. You'll find the entrance along the side. Ask for Mr White. He's expecting you at twelve. Do you want me to wait?'

'No need, Frank, I can use the Tube. Go back to the office, I'll call you if I need you. Mr White, you said?'

'Yeah, he's been paid.'

'Good, I'll see you later.'

Frank watched until Veleta turned the corner of the building before driving off.

The mortuary was one of several single-storey prefab buildings in the grounds of the hospital. There was a small reception with a nurse seated in a glassed-in booth. Veleta being tall and handsome warranted a smile and a softer tone of voice. 'Can I help you, sir?'

'My name is Veleta, Mr White is expecting me.'

'I'll tell him you're here.' Lifting the phone and speaking in the same soft tone, she announced the visitor.

Mr White was tall and thin wearing a white coat two sizes too large which drooped at the shoulders. He did not offer a handshake, instead held the door open for Veleta to enter the inner sanctum.

Veleta's only knowledge of mortuaries was gained in his youth from movies where corpses were stored in stainless-steel drawers, which were pulled out for inspection.

The room he entered was brightly lit, had a strong smell of

disinfectant and there was a wall lined with steel drawers.

Speaking in little more than a whisper Mr White said, 'You can only have a few minutes. I've arranged some privacy for you. I thought it might help. She's behind the screen.' He pointed to two bed screens which had been placed in the corner.

Behind the screen Veleta found Mary on a stretcher. Her body covered in a white sheet. Her face beautiful and relaxed in death, her hair carefully arranged in the way he remembered it. The face he had known and loved all his life. His hands clenched and tears welled. He reached under the sheet and found her hand. It was icy cold. What his brain had rejected when he first heard the news was reality. Mary was dead. He would never hear her chides and laughter again. He kissed her hand and placed it under the sheet. He leaned over and kissed her tenderly on her cold cheeks.

'It's not goodbye, Mary, I'll take you to a beautiful place where you can see the sea and the sun rising every morning.' He took a last long look, wiped his eyes before going to where Mr White was waiting.

'Thank you, Mr White,' Veleta said, slipping a wad of notes into the man's pocket.

Dropping his hand to the pocket Mr White said, 'But, Mr Veleta, I've been paid already.'

'I know you have,' Veleta said. 'But you've been considerate. I appreciated the screen.'

Veleta left without seeing the smiling nurse as he passed her.

Thomas drove Kaminski to the freight forwarders in Park Royal in a Ford Transit van, which he had assured her had been borrowed from a reliable source for cash on the nail and no paperwork. The company they were visiting had been selected by Kaminski for its reputation for integrity and quality of service, who in turn understood that they were doing business with the London branch of a well-known American Corporation, Zentek Aviation.

Kaminski had found it surprising easy to have the necessary letterheads and business cards printed and pass herself off as VP Europe for the Corporation. Even the hotel didn't question it when she was booking the Baird Suite. It was fortunate to her plans that Zentek had no operations in Europe.

Zentek Aviation had a maintenance facility in Karachi where it was a simple matter for her to have one of their personalised shipping crates stolen and delivered to Iqbal's people, for repacking the contents of their crates into. Together with authentic bills of lading, which were also stolen, the crate was container shipped via Tilbury to the freight forwarders in Park Royal. The goods were described as an aircraft engine compressor, being returned to the manufacturer for repair, to be collected personally by Ms Shelly Boy, VP Europe.

Because of the reputation of both companies involved the crate would normally have passed through customs without an inspection, but to be sure Kaminski used Tilbury as the port of entry, because there, she regularly used a crooked customs officer who would pass anything for a hefty payment in cash, providing the papers were in order.

Kaminski had been informed that morning that the shipment had arrived in Park Royal. Advised of the shipping costs she paid by cashier's cheque and watched, well pleased with herself as the crate was lifted into the Transit van.

Within the hour Thomas was reversing into the garage at the Chiswick house. Kaminski, eager to inspect the contents, watched as Thomas manhandled the rectangular crate until it was almost out of the van. 'Take one end,' he grunted to Kaminski. It was the first word he had spoken to her since they had left the house in Hampstead. Together they manoeuvred the crate onto two wooden trestles.

The crate had several labels of 'FRAGILE – HANDLE WITH CARE'. Kaminski inspected the shipping drop indicators and found them intact. She expected nothing less. The idea of this crate receiving a shock strong enough to break them, was something she preferred not to think about. The most likely outcome would be a large hole in the side of the ship and the loss of her large bonus.

'Open it,' she said, handing Thomas a screwdriver. He contemplated the tool, with its long shaft of steel, and gave her an apprising look. If it was supposed to be a threat it didn't have the slightest effect on Kaminski. She calmly met his stare and held it, while at the same time holding the haft of the switchblade in her pocket waiting for the lunatic to lunge.

Thomas looked away and began on the first screw.

'Get on with it, we don't have all day,' Kaminski said.

Thomas worked the screwdriver as slowly as his brain, but eventually he lifted the lid off and tore away the metal foil moisture proofing. Lifting the thick foam covering, Kaminski saw the two Grip-Stocks, two BCU units nestled in thick foam cut-outs. Under that she knew there would be another layer, containing two Stinger rounds in their fibreglass tubes.

'Right, everything seems okay. I've seen enough, put the lid back on, and let's go.'

Daisy went directly from her meeting with Isaacs to New Scotland Yard and was waiting at the reception for an escort to Farmer's office when DCI Sandys appeared.

'Sorry Miss Clowser,' he said with a friendly smile. 'The commander had to go to Belfast for the day. I'm afraid you'll have to do with me.'

Returning the smile, Daisy said, 'You'll do fine and forget the miss, I'm Daisy, and you're Len. You're in charge while the boss's away, right?'

As he signed her in and got her visitor's badge, he said, 'I am, but only the day-to-day stuff, no major decisions. You know what the boss is like.'

Pinning on her badge, she replied, 'That I do. Can we talk upstairs?'

Sandys led the way to the lift, which was already occupied by four burly men in plainclothes and a WPC in uniform, who all looked at Daisy with undisguised curiosity, thus stopping any further conversation until they reached the fifth floor and Farmer's office.

Without showing any signs of self-importance Sandys flopped down in Farmer's chair and an easy smile indicated to the chair beside it. 'Take the weight off your feet, Daisy, and tell me how I can help you.'

Daisy dropped into the chair and leaning forward, her hands on the desk, she gave Sandys a direct look and said, 'You know my position in all this, Len?'

'The boss said you were working for Peter Isaacs. I'm to give you our full co-operation.'

'*With* Peter Isaacs,' Daisy said. 'There's a difference, Len, not that Peter Isaacs would notice it.'

'Whatever, is there something I can do for you Daisy?'

'There is, but first, have there been any new developments?'

'Yes, two things,' Sandys said, and spun the dial on the safe built into the right pedestal of the desk. Removing a clear plastic envelope, he handed it to her.

Daisy saw it contained a crisp fifty-pound note.

'This bill was in Miss Grey's wallet,' Sandys said.

From the safe he picked out another clear plastic evidence bag which Daisy could see was stuffed with fifties.

Sandys explained. 'This is the three thousand, which was paid for the BMW. All in fifties as you can see.'

'There's a connection?' Daisy said.

'Yes, four notes out of the sixty in this bag are new and have consecutive numbers to the one in Miss Grey's wallet.'

Finally, something positive, Daisy was thinking. 'So, you're thinking that whoever supplied the cash for the BMW gave Mary the note.'

'The chances of any other explanation would be high, wouldn't you think?'

'Definitely,' Daisy said. 'This gives us a definite link between Mary and her killers.'

'Yes, the boss thought you were wasting your time on the girl but it looks like your thinking was ahead of ours.'

Daisy smiled. 'I hope so, Len. You said you had two new developments. What was the second?'

Sandys glanced at a single-page report on the desk and said. 'The timer. A jeweller in Clerkenwell identified the piece, apparently the scratch was a maker's mark, which positively identified it as a Messerlie movement, made in Switzerland. According to Ernie it has a history. We're following up on it.'

'A Messerlie?' Daisy said. 'Great, another connection to Mary. It's all linking up to the Delia file.'

Sandys stared at her blankly. 'What is the Delia file?'

Best be vague, Daisy was thinking, and said, 'It's a line of enquiry I'm working on which involves a long-dead serious villain named Zar Brum. Would there still be a file on him?'

Giving her a thoughtful look, Sandys said, 'I've heard the name of course, before my time and as you said, he had a reputation. I'll take a look.'

Going to a side table where there was a computer terminal, he keyed in the name and with a shake of the head said, 'No joy I'm afraid, as he's dead he's most likely been wiped from the system.'

Feeling a bit deflated Daisy said, 'That's it then?'

'Not entirely, there may be something in the old paper-based system.'

'Can we take a look?'

'Sure, but if he's been dead for twenty years, Daisy, what's the connection?'

'I've connected his name to Mary Grey. Brum only had one conviction back in 1958, for blowing a safe, and my line of enquiry involves safe-blowers. If he was suspected of serious criminal activities, there should be an intelligence file. I might find something in that.'

'Let's go,' said Len.

Daisy accompanied him to the lift which took them to a sub-basement, three floors below street level. It was dimly lit and stuffy. Banks of racks containing bundles of file folders covered the entire floor with the exception of a small office which was occupied by an overweight civilian who was eating his lunch and watching the news on a black and white TV. The arrival of a DCI did not seem to faze him in any way.

'Charlie, meet Miss Clowser, she's been seconded to Commander Farmer. Daisy, meet Charlie Burton, he's your original monster from the black lagoon. He never comes to the surface.'

Charlie grinned. 'Droll, sir, and it's not true, miss. I do go home in the evening and as you're only the second visitor this week I can get on with my studies.'

Giving him a friendly smile Daisy asked, 'What are you studying, Mr Burton?'

'Charlie to my friends, miss, I'm doing a PhD in random number prediction. When I finish, I can win the lottery and retire. Now what can I do for you?'

Daisy saw a glimmer of mischief in the big man's eyes. Maybe he was taking the piss but then she'd heard stranger stories from people in mundane jobs.

'I wish you every success, Charlie, and the name is Daisy. I'd like to see the file on one Zar Brum.'

'I know the name,' Charlie said. 'I thought he was dead years ago.'

'He is, but is there still a file I can see?'

Charlie, pushing himself out of his chair, said, 'Sure, there is, follow me.'

Charlie obviously knew his files like old friends. Without any referral to an index he led them to the correct rack and pulled a folder from it. 'Here it is, Daisy,' he said.

Taking the folder, she opened it and read the index. 'I see from this there were half a dozen folders on Brum. What happened to them?'

Charlie shrugged. 'They'd have been weeded over the years, him being dead these twenty years. This is all that's left.'

'It'll have to do; can I take it?'

Charlie looked at DCI Sandys, who nodded.

'You can book it out to me, Charlie.'

Charlie nodded and wrote the details in his log.

'That's that then,' said Charlie. 'Nice meeting you, Daisy, I'll get back to my reading.'

'One more thing, Charlie,' Daisy asked. 'What happens to that log?'

'I take it to the chief's office before I go home. He likes to know what's going on.'

Noting the year 2007 on the cover, she asked, 'There's a log for every year, right?'

'Right. We never fill it these days, things being as quiet as they are.'

'What about 1986, do you still have the log for that?' Daisy asked.

'Sure, we never throw away anything. I'll show it to you in a jiffy.' Charlie went into the bowels of his system and soon returned with the log. 'Here you are, 1986.'

'Can you see if the Brum file was logged out during August?'

Charlie opened the ledger on his desk and began flicking through the pages. He was a fast reader, his pudgy finger running down the pages.

'Here's one, twelfth August, 14:50 hours, logged out by a DI Ainscough, returned 11:45 hours sixteenth August.'

The date fitted, Daisy was thinking, and asked, 'Any more?'

Turning to the next page, Charlie said, 'Yeah, quite a few in September after Brum's body was found. Coroner's report was added.'

'What was DI Ainscough's job?'

Charlie looked at the log. 'He was assigned to the Fingerprint Department when he signed this.'

Convenient, Daisy thought. 'Is he still in the force?'

'No idea,' said Charlie with a shrug.

'He's probably long into retirement, but we can check the records,' Sandys said.

Giving Charlie a big smile and shaking his hand, Daisy said, 'Thanks Charlie., you've been a great help, good luck with your numbers.'

Back upstairs, Sandys saw her seated at Farmer's conference table with the Brum file, before leaving the room, saying he'd be back shortly. She was about to open the file when her mobile rang. Seeing the caller was Peter Isaacs she answered it. 'Hello?'

Without preamble he said, 'We've missed them, Daisy. Customs have confirmed a shipment in the name of Zentek Aviation was cleared at Tilbury yesterday and collected by a freight forwarder by the name of Blue Sky in Park Royal. They in turn have confirmed that the shipment, a crate weighing fifty-four kilos was collected from their Park Royal depot an hour ago.'

'Shit!' Daisy said. 'Did they say who collected it?'

'Yes, a Ms Shelly Boy, VP European operations, Zentek Aviation. She had ID and her name was on the shipping documents.'

'She's a phoney,' Daisy said. 'They have no European Operations!'

'Obviously, but it's the middle of the night in Phoenix at the moment, we'll have to wait a few hours for confirmation, not that it helps. They've got the bloody shipment. I've sent an operative with a photo-fit artist to Park Royal to get descriptions of Ms Boy and her vehicle. We're running out of time on this, Daisy.'

'Tell me about it.' Sensing the edginess in his voice, she said, 'Okay, let's think this through, Peter. They have to set up a meet and deliver the crate to the bad guys. They'll want to check the goods for damage first, so we'll just have to hope that gives us another twenty-four hours.'

'I can't take that chance, Daisy. You've got until 08.00 tomorrow to come with something positive. If not, I'll have to go public with the descriptions we get from Blue Sky, at least that might frighten the bastards off. 08:00 tomorrow, Daisy, not a minute longer. I'll await your call,' he said and broke the connection.

Putting her phone on the table, Daisy saw the clock on the wall read 12.20 and did some rapid thinking. If Isaacs went public Mary's killers would run and no way did she want that. But other than the fifty-pound note she had nothing to go on. Well, she thought, unless she found something in this damn Brum file, it'd have to do.

As she opened the file, Sandys came back carrying a laptop and asked cheerfully, 'Find anything we've missed, Daisy?'

Ruefully, she said, 'I haven't started yet, Len, I was interrupted by a call from His Highness.'

Sandys, a look of surprise on his face, said, 'The boss rang? He's supposed to be in a meeting in Stormont all day.'

'He probably is. No, it was just Peter Isaacs hassling me.'

Sandys laughed. 'Don't I know the feeling,' and went to Farmer's desk, sat in Farmer's chair and opened his laptop.

Daisy opened the file, which confirmed in official language exactly what Arthur had told her. Brum's body was found trapped under a wharf by a river police launch in the morning of the 8th November

1986. DI Jolly of the river police confirmed that the initial means of identification was from personal effects: a Rolex wristwatch and a wallet. Two experts from the Metropolitan Police Fingerprint Department gave evidence, and confirmed that the method of positively identifying Brum's body was by his fingerprints.

Fortunately, Brum had been wearing fleece-lined leather gloves and the fingers were still intact except for some water damage which they were able to deal with. They were in no doubt that the prints from his CRO record matched the dead man in every respect. There was no other means of physical identity, the body having been in the water for at least a week. Injuries to the face and head were put down to rats, any other means of identity, such as dental records were not used as the fingerprint evidence was accepted as conclusive.

The pathologist who performed the autopsy established the cause of death to be drowning. The injuries to the head and face were post-mortem. He also confirmed that the deceased had consumed a large amount of alcohol in the hours before his death.

The coroner returned a verdict of accidental death. *So much for that,* Daisy thought, pushing it aside and opening the fingerprint record. This consisted of ten 10 x 8 photographs, one for each finger and thumb. Each of the prints were marked with the points identical to the set on Brum's CRO. A minimum of sixteen points of identity were required as positive proof of identity. There was no doubt, as the experts had confirmed, each finger and thumb matched.

Brum's original Arrest Record dated 1958 was in the file. The offence was breaking and entering a jeweller's premises, robbery from a safe to the value of ten thousand pounds and illegal possession and use of explosives. His date of birth was shown as twenty-fourth of March 1938. *That would make him sixty-nine if he's still alive and that is the big if,* Daisy thought. The space on the rap-sheet for the photograph was discoloured from old glue but it was blank.

Getting up, she went over to Sandys and pushed the file across the desk. 'Len, shouldn't there be a mug shot in this file?'

'There should be,' he said, thumbing through the pages. 'Nope, it's been twenty years, Daisy. It probably fell out.'

'Or was taken out,' Daisy said. 'Well, there seems to be no doubt that the fingerprints match the dead man. The question is who was the dead man, Len?'

Giving her a curious look, he said, 'It has to be Brum, hasn't it? How else would the prints match?'

'That's the question, Len.' Daisy asked. 'How else? Could the records have been switched?'

Sandys smiled. 'There's always ways and means, Daisy. Unlike today, back then the fingerprint collection was paper based. No computers. Brum was drowned, wasn't he? In that case all he had to do was find someone with a police record who matched his height and general appearance, get him drunk, then drown him in a bath and throw him into the Thames.

'Before doing that, all he needs is a crooked cop, who has access to the Fingerprint Department to switch the dead man's prints with Brum's and Bob's your uncle. Piece of piss really.'

Smiling, Daisy slapped the desk. 'That's exactly what I thought, Len, that's the only scenario that would work.'

Sandys put his hands up. 'Hold on, Daisy, I was joking.'

'I know you were, Len, but it would make a lot of sense if it were true. You can't tell me that there's never been a dodgy cop in the Met.'

'It's pure fantasy, Daisy. Even if it were true, we could never prove it.'

'Why not, if we find Brum?'

'If the records were switched, the only fingerprints in Brum's file would be from the dead man. If it happened as you think and Brum is alive his prints are gone forever. There'd be no way to identify him now.'

'Unless we can ID the dead man,' Daisy said, thinking that Brum's missing driver Billy Smirke would certainly be a good name to start with. 'If there was a switch, Brum's prints should be in the dead man's file. That's possible, isn't it?'

Sandys dropped his shoulders and said, 'It's possible, we've had our bad apples in the past, but as I said it's only possible if Brum had someone with access to the Fingerprint Department.'

'Someone like DI Ainscough you mean?' Daisy said. 'He had Brum's file out a week before his death. He was attached to fingerprints at the time. So, what other reason would he have to take out a CRO file, which contains a copy of Brum's fingerprints, if it wasn't to replace it with a copy of the dead man's prints, after he had switched the original records in the main collection?'

Sandys smile disappeared as he considered the implication. 'Unfortunately, we won't be able to ask him. I checked with personnel, while you were reading. Ainscough died in a car accident in December '86. I suppose you think that Brum was behind that also.'

Daisy's fingers tapped impatiently on the desk as she thought about that, before saying, 'What's another killing among friends, Len? Brum would want to be sure he was free and clear, wouldn't he?'

Sandys' look was enough to tell her he was now thinking her way. 'If you're right there's Dr Abdullah and Mary Grey to be added to the list, what now?'

Daisy leaned forward, her hands on the desk and said, 'Okay, we have two definite leads. The fifty-pound note links the car bombers to Mary Grey. We have to find out who gave it to her. Then, there's the Messerlie clock, which according to Ernie, was used by the Midnight Fox gang for eighteen robberies. Brum was somehow connected to that gang, as was Mary, so she must have known him. Maybe he was part of the gang. Mary's last words sounded to me like *Brown, he's alive!* But it could have been Brum. Maybe he is alive and if she recognised him, he would want to silence her, and quickly, wouldn't he?'

Nodding agreement, Sandys said, 'So, where do we go from here, Daisy?'

'If Brum's alive and behind all this we need to find him, and quick. Can you brief Jack Farmer on what we've found?' I'm going to try finding the person who gave Mary the fifty-pound note.'

CHAPTER 23

Friday 6th September – Afternoon.

'**G**o straight in, miss, Frank is expecting you.' Daisy had called ahead. The secretary was still red-eyed and seemed ready to burst into tears at any moment. Seeing Daisy again was no doubt a painful reminder of recent events.

'Thanks a lot,' she said and made for the same office as before and found Stubbs at his desk. The cautious look he gave her was the same as before. No doubt he was probably reminding himself that she was a cop and there was a need to be careful, but why? Daisy wondered. In the light of the report on his financials she'd had Sandys check him out. He was clean, with not even have a traffic violation to his name. Still, she sensed that he was too cautious in his answers to be a totally innocent man. She felt sure he was holding something back and reminded herself again that just because he didn't have any form could also mean he had never been caught.

'Did you forget something, miss?' Frank asked, shifting his bulk in his chair until the springs creaked.

Daisy settled herself onto the chair in front of the desk and said, 'No, Frank, but I have a couple more questions. I've been looking at Mary's worksheets, it seems that most of her jobs were account customers, is that correct?'

Giving her a thoughtful look, he tapped his pencil on the blotter for a moment, before replying. 'Yeah, she was a real star with the regulars, especially the women, they always asked for her.'

'So, in that case she didn't do many jobs involving cash?'

Cautiously, he said, 'A few fill-in jobs, that's all.'

'Do you know how much cash she might carry?'

'It'd be a guess,' Stubbs said. 'Mary didn't go much outside West London. Most of her cash jobs would be under twenty pounds. I'd say she'd probably have about forty pounds in small bills and change.'

Daisy nodded. 'That figures. She had thirty-eight pounds and some change in her wallet, but also a new fifty-pound note, did she mention a big tipper?'

Stubbs nodded. 'Yeah, she did, as a matter of fact. Monday, it was. I'd given her a job, told her the caller was foreign, but talked posh, that she'd give a good tip. Mary didn't buy it, she said the posh ones are lousy tippers, but she took the job anyway.'

'Fifty pounds is a big tip,' Daisy said.

Stubbs nodded agreement. 'Yeah, I thought so as well.'

'Did she say why?'

'No, she didn't say much about that job.'

'Something on her mind do you think?'

'She just said I was right about the big tipper and signed off for the rest of the day, said she had something to do.'

Daisy proffered the work-sheets. 'Which job was it?'

Frank ran a finger down the Monday list. 'Here it is, Mrs Kaminski, pick-up at 34 Symonds Street W1, to the Palace Garden Hotel, in Kensington. Jenny was on her break so I took the call, she said she would be waiting outside at 10.45.'

Looking at the list Daisy said, 'This Mrs Kaminski, has she called for a taxi before this?'

Frank thought for a moment before shaking his head. 'No, first time. I'd remember a name like that, but I know number 34, it's a dentist's place. We get a few calls from there, probably a patient.'

'She'd have given a number, right?'

Putting his finger on the entry, Frank said, 'Sure, here it is.'

'You said she was foreign, any idea what country?'

Frank shrugged. 'No, you know, foreign like, London's full of them.'

'Did she sound anything like Dr Abdullah's neighbour, you remember her?'

Frank shifted in his chair. His face creased in thought for a moment before nodding enthusiastically. 'Yeah, now that you mention it, she did, very similar, but then these foreigners all sound the same to me.'

Great witness, Daisy thought. 'Thanks again, Frank, you've been a great help,' and stood up to go.

Stubbs eased himself out of his chair and stood close enough to be intimidating. Giving her a thoughtful look, he said, 'Why all the questions, miss? All I read in the papers is some Arab prince is killed, along with his driver. Some of the papers don't even have her name but you only seem to be interested in Mary, what gives?'

Holding his gaze for a moment she decided the whole truth was not in order yet. Backing away towards the door, she said, 'I'm asking these questions, Frank, because Mary was my friend, and I intend to continue asking until I find out who killed her. I'll keep you posted and thanks again.'

With two strides he was beside her again. 'Hang on a bit, miss, Mary's friend from Spain was here today. He's just arrived. I told him about you and he said he'd like to meet you.'

The man in the photo! Daisy thought, and said, 'I'd certainly like to meet him, what's his name?'

'Enrique Veleta.'

'Veleta,' she said. 'He's Spanish then?'

With a shrug, Frank said, 'I don't know, he could be. I gave him your card, that all right?'

Nodding, she said, 'Sure. Do you know where he's staying?'

'He didn't say, said he'd call you.'

'Good, maybe he can fill in some of the detail.' Taking two of her cards from her wallet, she said, 'Here's a couple more cards in case anyone else wants to talk to me.'

Kaminski pressed Dr Taleb's bell and after the usual introduction with the receptionist the lock buzzed and she pushed the door open and waited in the hall. As before the bodyguard appeared within a minute and without a word nodded for her to enter the inner hall. She gave him a look of feigned indifference as she was been frisked. 'He's expecting you, follow me.' It was the first time she had heard him speak, and it warranted a scornful smile from her. His high pitch made him sound like an excited girl.

Iqbal was at his desk reading what looked like a map. Giving her a disdainful look, he turned the sheet over and pointed to a chair. 'You again, where's Kramer?'

Sitting, she looked into his eyes and lied with a straight face. 'He's making arrangements for your delivery.'

Iqbal held her gaze, and said, 'May I remind you, Kaminski, that he's being paid a million Swiss francs for his efforts.'

Kaminski shrugged. 'That's the going rate for a job like this, the greater the heat the higher the price and this job has already generated plenty of heat.'

Kaminski felt Iqbal's piercing eyes were trying to look into her head. His voice changing to a tone meant to be intimate, he said, 'Tell me, Kaminski, how exactly have we been compromised?'

'It was Mr Kramer who was compromised, but it's been sorted, there's no need for you to worry.'

'Then that's Mr Kramer's problem, isn't it? Now what's happened to our shipment?'

Kaminski didn't like the man but she had to admit he was right. 'Your shipment is in London and ready for delivery. I'm here to make the arrangements for the handover, which, as know, means cash on delivery.'

'I know what it means,' he snapped. 'Tell me the time and the place.'

'Tomorrow night at nine thirty. The tide at Chiswick will be high enough then. A boat will pick you and your man up at Brentford Dock. It'll be quiet by that time. You can leave your transport there.'

'Men, Kaminski. There'll be four of us,' Iqbal said, pointing to the door. 'That's him outside, and two experts to check the shipment.'

'Okay. The boat will take you back to Brentford once the transaction is complete.' Handing him a folded sheet of A4, she said, 'This map is marked with the meeting place.'

Snatching it irritably, Iqbal examined it. 'What's the name of the boat and who is crewing it?'

Shaking her head, Kaminski said, 'You don't need to know that. The boat will be waiting at 21.30. The captain will find you.'

'You're not very trusting, are you Mrs Kaminski?'

'It's not a matter of trust. Mr Kramer wants it this way. It's a matter of security for all of us.'

Iqbal stood up, and again made direct eye contact with her. She held his gaze as she stood, thinking, not for the first time, this man was definitely not to be trusted.

'You know there can be no delays, Mrs Kaminski.'

Still holding his gaze, she said, 'There won't be any delays. We're as anxious as you to finish with this and be on another continent when your people get up to their tricks. Just bear in mind that we will have our security, so, let's do this in the spirit of gentlemen, with no tricks from either party. Good day, sir, our next meeting will be our last.'

Daisy's taxi stopped outside 34 Symonds Street which she saw was a Regency townhouse situated on three floors with Garret windows in the slated mansard roof. The ground floor had two sash windows to the left of the ornate front door and a basement surrounded with iron railings, painted black with golden spears. The basement windows were covered by beige vertical blinds.

She read the brass plate. *Dr Taleb. Dentist... By appointment only.* There was a phone number which she recognised as the one Mrs Kaminski had given to Frank Stubbs. There was only one bell, which she pressed and a woman's voice with a lilting South Asian accent answered.

'Dr Taleb's surgery. May I help you?'

'I'd like to speak to Dr Taleb. It's a police matter.'

'He's with a patient at the moment.'

'I'll wait.'

'Very well, push the door and take the first door on your left, the green one.' The lock buzzed and Daisy entered the hall. She wondered who occupied the rest of the house, but better find out if Kaminski was a patient of Dr Taleb first. If she was then the rest of the house was probably not important. Following instructions, she opened the green door which led to a flight of stairs going to the basement.

She followed the stairs to an open-plan reception area. A well-dressed middle-aged man seated on one of a line of chairs looked at her and smiled nervously. She returned the smile with what she hoped was a sympathetic response that showed that she felt the same way about dentists.

The receptionist seated at a desk looked up as she entered and they gave each other the onceover. Daisy saw a woman of about thirty-five, good looking, wearing gold-rimmed glasses with her hair severely tied back. Indian or Pakistani was Daisy's assessment. On the desk a black triangle with white lettering read *P. Patel.*

Guessing that P. Patel was a Miss, Daisy adopted a friendly approach and said 'Hello, Miss Patel, I'm WPC Denton. I must say this is a big house and there's only one bell, who lives upstairs?'

Miss Patel scribbled something on the file in front of her before replying, 'The upstairs is empty. The owner lives abroad.'

'Dr Taleb is the only occupant?'

Snapping the file closed she dropped it into a tray marked Out, and said, 'At the moment, yes. How can I help you?'

A bit of attitude here, Daisy was thinking. 'I hope you can, then I won't have to bother Dr Taleb.'

'You said it was a police matter?'

Daisy nodded. 'That's correct, it's just a routine inquiry.'

Holding her hand out the receptionist said, 'May I see some ID?'

'Of course.' Daisy produced a warrant card in the name of WPC Denton which she had obtained from DCI Sandys.

The receptionist gave it a cursory look and said, 'What would you like to know?'

'Can you confirm that a Mrs Kaminski is one of Dr Taleb's patients?' Daisy asked, watching the woman's eyes for a reaction.

There was none. The receptionist, holding her gaze calmly, said, 'Yes, I remember her, she was here this week.' Flicking through an appointment book, she said, 'Yes, Monday it was.'

'Was she a regular patient of Dr Taleb?'

'No, this was her first visit, she had toothache and needed urgent treatment.'

'Do you have her address?'

'Only the hotel, they sent her to us. It was her first visit.'

'Which hotel?'

'The Palace Garden Kensington. Why all the questions? Is she in trouble or something?'

'No, nothing like that.' Daisy knew when a lie was in order. 'I'm checking all the customers of a taxi driver who was a victim of a crime, as a matter of routine. Mrs Kaminski is one of over thirty I have to verify. I was hoping to speak to her but as this is obviously not her address I'll try the hotel. She might be still there or they'll have her address. Thanks for your help. I won't need to bother Dr Taleb now.'

The receptionist waited until a light on her entry phone told her that Daisy had opened and closed the street door before lifting her phone and dialling a number.

CHAPTER 24

Once outside Daisy took at more critical look at number 34. A big house in this location was worth a million or more. Yet the only sign of life was a dentist's surgery in the basement. Curious, but then London has many houses bought for investment rather than occupation.

She walked the short distance to the Edgware Road before hailing a taxi and within fifteen minutes she was outside the Palace Garden Hotel, which was off the Brompton Road, and wondered why Kaminski hadn't done the same instead of phoning London Quality Taxis.

She paid the driver and as she got out, saw the Porter hailing the first taxi in line, opening the door for a couple, and with a big smile and a smooth movement of hand to pocket with the tip, he touched his cap and closed the door.

Seeing Daisy arrive he smiled broadly and said, in his soft Irish lilt, 'Ah, Miss Clowser, lovely to see you, are you well?'

She'd known Pat Coffey since her days in S012 and knew that, in his position, the shaking of hands was not the done thing. However, a light touch on the arm and a friendly smile did just as well.

'I'm very well, Pat, how are you and the family?'

'They're all great, thank God; the oldest boy has just started university.'

'That's good to hear. Look Pat, I know you're always busy, but it would help me if you can cast your mind back to last Monday morning about eleven, were you on duty then?'

Pat's smile faded. He knew that she was connected with the police in some way, having helped her in the past and after a moment's thought said quietly, 'I was. This is about Mary Grey, isn't it? She was a lovely girl, always cheerful, a bad business.'

'Yes, bad,' Daisy said. 'She was also a good friend of mine.'

Nodding, Pat said, 'She was friendly with everyone. Is there anything I can do to help?'

'I hope you can. She dropped a woman here last Monday morning about eleven, do you remember?'

'Indeed, I do. We had a little chat; the woman had given a miserly tip. In Mary's own words, "There goes the last of the big spenders."'

'That's all?'

'Not at all. Mary doesn't work from the rank so she was about to drive off when she found the passenger had left a mobile phone on the seat. As I'm not allowed to leave the door she had to go and find her. She was gone about ten minutes and returned in a right sour mood, said she had to go traipsing all over the hotel to find her.'

'That's it?'

'Not a bit of it, she was getting into her cab when the woman came running up to her, they exchanged a few words, I couldn't hear what was said but it must have been a generous apology, because I saw Mary accepting fifty-pound note before driving off.

Bingo! Daisy thought. *That puts Mrs Kaminski right in the frame.*

'You've a great help, Pat,' Daisy said, slipping him a twenty which was deftly trousered.

'Any time, Miss Clowser,' he said, holding the door as she entered and headed towards the reception desk.

The receptionist looked at the warrant card with undisguised disdain, before asking, 'How can I help you?'

Daisy knew the type – charming to guests and haughty to underlings – and sharpened her tone. 'Do you have a guest named

Mrs Kaminski?'

With another superior look she looked at her screen, hit a few keys and shook her head. 'There's nobody of that name registered.'

'What about last Monday?'

A few more keys were hit and the screen checked again with the same negative shake of her head. 'We have no guest of that name.'

'Take another look, *Miss*,' Daisy snapped. 'I know for sure that she was dropped off here at about eleven o'clock on Monday this week.'

Miss, looking further down her nose, replied, 'Probably she just went to the bar or the restaurant. People come in all the time who are not guests.'

'Okay, then tell me, if a guest needs a dentist, whom do you recommend?'

'We have a list of local practices.'

'Can I see it?'

Miss gave her a look, which in Daisy's opinion warranted a smack in the mouth, but the list was produced. There were eight recommended dentists in the immediate area and she saw Dr Taleb name was last on the list.

It was getting dark when Daisy returned to her apartment. She fed Heinz and let him out onto the balcony. She had just poured herself a glass of Dom Brial when her phone rang. She grabbed it and slumped into her favourite chair. 'Hello?'

'Daisy,' Isaacs said. 'We've spoken to Zentek in Phoenix and they confirmed that they do have a maintenance facility in Karachi, but know nothing about any shipment to Blue Sky and definitely have no VP called Ms Shelly Boy. In fact, they have no executives in Europe at the moment.'

'As we thought,' Daisy said. 'Well, I've got something for you, I tried calling you but was told you were not to be disturbed. I have a name.'

'I was in a meeting and now I'm in a hurry. What name?'

'Mrs Kaminski – there's a definite link between her and the bombing.'

'What kind of link?'

'A certain fifty-pound note. It's a long story, I'll fill you in later, for now the name will do.'

'That's all, just a name?'

'Consider yourself lucky it's not Smith or Jones, it's unique enough to run it though your system, somehow I don't think that she's a first offender.'

'I'll get on to it, anything else?'

'Yes, have all the airlines checked, European and international, arrivals in the past month and departures for the coming week for Kaminski and any travelling companions.'

'This coming week! There's something you're not telling me?'

'Only I'm thinking there's been an almighty rush in all this. If Kaminski is just logistics I would think she will want to be well away from these shores before anything happens.'

'I'll get on to it, where will you be?'

'I'm not sure, my mobile will be on.'

'Good.' He hung up.

Daisy went back to her wine, and was contemplating her next move when her entry phone rang. She never had unexpected callers and ensured that her name and address were not listed in any directories. Maybe someone had pressed the wrong button. While she was thinking it rang again. This time she answered. 'Hello.'

'Miss Clowser, Miss Daisy Clowser?'

'Who's this?

'My name is Veleta. I'm Mary's friend from Spain, can we talk?'

That was quick, Daisy was thinking. Less than three hours ago

Frank Stubbs had told her a Mr Veleta had called. She had never heard Mary speak of anyone called Veleta, but now that she thought of it, Mary had never spoken of anyone outside their immediate social circle. She only had his word that he was friend of Mary. Best be careful.

'Of course,' she said. 'Come on up, third floor.' She pressed the lock release button and replaced the handset. Going to her bedroom, where she had a small safe built into her wardrobe, she removed the Beretta, loaded the magazine, chambered a cartridge and slid the safety on. Returning to the living room, she put on her jacket and slipped the gun into her belt where it nestled in the small of her back. If Veleta was the man in the photograph and a genuine friend of Mary's, packing a gun was not the recommended way to greet him. But there were some men she had known, dangerous men, in whose company she would always take such precautions. She had the feeling that her visitor might be one such man. She would soon find out.

She opened the door before the lift arrived and waited. The distance was no more than thirty feet, but it was enough to give her a chance of assessing her visitor before he got too close. When the lift opened and the man stepped out, she had no doubts that the man who stepped out was the man in the photograph.

He saw her waiting and walked lithely towards her. Now dressed, not in the polo shirt and chinos she remembered from the photo, but a smart new suit; in fact as she looked more carefully, she could see his whole outfit, from his shirt and tie to his highly polished shoes looked like they had just been bought that day. Maybe he didn't have time to pack, she was thinking, but on the other hand she'd known men with something to hide, who bought their clothes wherever they landed. Was Veleta such a man, she wondered? There were no pilot's glasses, this time, and when he was close enough, she saw he had a weary look about the eyes, which she couldn't decide was tiredness, or sadness. Maybe both, she thought.

Hand outstretched, he said, 'Miss Clowser, I was hoping you might be in at this hour.'

Nothing limp about his handshake either, she thought. 'Come in, Mr Veleta, I'm sorry we have to meet for the first time in such circumstances.'

Following her in, he said, 'So am I. Mary often spoke of her friend Daisy in the flat upstairs.'

His English was faultless. She tried to place his accent without success. Not for the first time she wondered why Mary had never mentioned him. After their chat in the taxi, she was sure that Mary had a thing going for Abdullah. If so, where did his man fit into her life? But looking into her visitor's eyes, she felt she knew.

They stood awkwardly for a moment in the centre of the room. She saw his eyes quickly take in everything. Then he looked at her face and said, 'Frank told me that you were with Mary when she died, that you were injured trying to save her. He didn't have any details so I was hoping you could tell me about it.'

'Of course, but we can't just stand here, sit down, can I offer you a drink?' She pointed to an armchair that would put her on the opposite side of the low table to him. *Best keep him at a distance,* she thought.

'What's that you're drinking?'

'Dom Brial, it's from a small co-operative near Perpignan. A friend brings me the odd case.'

Dropping easily into the chair he said, 'Sounds good.'

Daisy poured him a glass and topped up her own and took the chair facing him and asked, 'When did you arrive, Mr Veleta?'

'This morning. Frank called me with the news and as Mary has no living relatives, I figure it's up to me to make the funeral arrangements and help settle her affairs.'

So, Frank was lying when he said he didn't know anyone other than Mary's solicitor. She'd guessed as much.

Settling herself against a cushion to stop the Beretta digging into her back, Daisy related the circumstances of Mary's death, including their last moments together. When she had finished, his head dropped and his glass rattled the table as his hand shook. After a long moment he looked up, his eyes welled, and asked in a husky voice, 'Did she suffer? Was she in pain?'

Her own eyes welling as she relived the moment Daisy said softly, 'No, she was more concerned about me.'

He looked at her for a long moment before saying, 'That was beyond brave, what you did. You might have been killed yourself. I won't forget it.'

Taking a sip from her glass, she shrugged. 'It was a desperate situation. I knew I had to get her out of the taxi before the tank blew, which it did seconds later.'

Giving her another thoughtful look, Veleta said, 'You told Frank she spoke to you before she died.'

Daisy nodded. 'That's right, a few words only. For someone called Harry.'

'Mary always called me Harry. My name is Enrique, which is Henry in Spanish, but she always called me Harry.'

Looking into his eyes again, Daisy said, 'Mary's older brother was also called Henry.'

Veleta's hand rattled the glass again and his tanned face looked a shade paler before he said, 'Mary's brother Henry died nearly twenty years ago.'

And Harry Veleta was born, Daisy was thinking. Taking a sip from her glass, she was undecided. Should she trust him? Then, looking into his eyes, she had a clear vision of Mary's face and she was sure.

'I guess you must be Harry,' she said. 'Mary said I can trust you, so I'm going to. She was mortally injured and I think she knew she was dying when she spoke to me. These were her exact words: "Daisy, listen," she said. "You must listen. You must meet Harry – you can trust Harry. Tell him I heard his voice. He's alive." Then she said, "Delia... Delia..." I asked her who's alive, and her last whisper sounded to me like Brown, or it may have been just her last breath. Do the names mean anything to you?'

Veleta didn't answer for a long moment and when he did his eyes had welled again. Speaking in little more than a whisper he said, 'Not a thing. You're sure she wasn't delirious?'

'No, Harry, she was quite coherent.'

Veleta gave her a long look before saying, 'Mary told me you were some kind of private cop. Are you working with the cops now?'

'Yes, Harry, I am. Because of Mary plus the fact that I was almost killed in the bombing, I'm working with the cops and the intelligence services and I won't stop until I settle things for Mary. Let me explain something to you, Harry. I believe that Mary recognised someone from her past and she was murdered because of that. Who was she talking about, Harry, whose voice did she recognise, who's alive?'

Veleta leaned back in his seat, his eyes drilling into her for a long moment before he replied, 'I've no idea. Look, Daisy, Mary was a taxi driver, she knew a lot of people, and people talk in taxis. If as you say she was the target, she might have heard something she shouldn't have.'

Daisy shook her head vehemently. 'I don't buy that, Harry. If that was the case, why the message for you and why mention the name Delia, twice?' She was about to tell him that she already knew the answer, instead she asked, 'Who is Delia?'

Veleta, without any hesitation said, 'I don't know. I've never heard Mary mention anyone called Delia.'

Looking him squarely in the eyes Daisy said, 'I've learnt quite a lot about Mary in the past two days, Harry, including what happened to her father. I've been told her mother Gloria went to live in Spain, did you know her?'

Veleta fidgeted with his glass for a moment before replying. In a voice tinged with sadness he said, 'Yes, I knew Gloria. Sadly, she passed away two years ago.'

'Oh, I'm sorry to hear that,' Daisy said. 'And you've definitely no idea who Mary was talking about when she said, "He's alive."'

Veleta, shaking his head, said, 'Sorry, I can't help you on that.'

Won't bloody well help, you mean, Daisy thought. Remembering Frank Stubbs' aversion to cops, she was sure Veleta suffered from the same complaint and was also holding something back. She should have expected it. The question is, what?

It was only the comforting feel of the Beretta in the small of her back that gave her the courage to push further, saying, 'And I suppose you've never heard of a Messerlie clock either?'

Veleta may have been an excellent poker player, but even the best have their moments of weakness. Now she saw, it was his turn. Her question had brought the fleetest of startled reactions to his eyes and she was, in that instant, sure he knew all about Messerlie clocks.

Veleta's eyes were cold when he said, 'That's a strange question. What's a clock got to do with all this?'

'Twenty years ago, Messerlie clocks were used as decoy bomb timers, by a safe-blower called the Midnight Fox. The same type of clock was used to detonate the bomb that killed Mary.'

This time she got a reaction. Veleta drained his glass and stood up, his eyes looking a little sad when he said, 'Thank you, Daisy, for helping Mary, you've been a good friend to her. I won't forget it, but I must be off. I've things to do and not much time.'

Standing up but keeping the table between them Daisy said, 'One more question, Harry. Mary called you the evening before her death and again the following morning. Can you tell me what it was about?'

'I was out on my boat and missed the call.'

'She left no message?'

'Only to call her back urgently. By the time I docked it was too late. How did you know she called?'

'I dialled the last number Mary called. It turned out to be a restaurant.'

'Who did you speak to?'

'Garcia. He said he was the manager. I told him I was a friend of Mary Grey.'

'He told you he didn't know her, right? Garcia is discreet, never gives out information to strangers. I'll let you know about the funeral arrangements. It'll be in Spain. Goodbye Daisy and thanks again for what you did.'

'Before you go, Harry, consider this. I'm not interested in whatever happened years ago. I'm only concerned with the here and now. We believe the people who killed Mary are involved with terrorists and must be stopped before many more people die. Any help you and Frank can give us will shut the door on the past forever. Think about it, you have my number, and bear in mind that I can turn up the heat and make life pretty miserable if I find either of you are holding back information. I can assure you there'll be nowhere to hide.'

'Veleta gave her a vaguely amused look and said, 'Are you by any chance threatening me, Daisy? If so, it's been done before and by bigger people than you.'

Cheeky bastard, Daisy thought. Remembering the Beretta, she pressed on.

'I may not have the height, Harry, but I can assure you I carry a big stick.'

'I'm sure you do, Daisy and I'll think about what you said. Maybe we'll meet again, good night.' He opened the door and was gone.

Daisy waited to hear the lift start. It didn't, so he must have used the stairs. She went to the balcony and looked down at the street.

There were a few people going about their business in the early evening but no sign of Veleta and no car pulling away. Was he still in the building? *Maybe he's in Mary's apartment or has already been there before he came to see her. He could easily have gone out again to use the entry phone, better take a look.*

She had a feeling that Veleta could be a dangerous man and was nervous, but Mary's last words were: 'You can trust Harry.' Let's hope she was right. Nevertheless she moved the Beretta to a more accessible position in the front of her belt.

The stairs down to Mary's apartment were empty and the lift quiet. She heard only the normal sounds of life in the other apartments. With an ear against the door she listened for a long moment. There was no sound. She turned the keys in the two locks and pushed the door open. There was enough light coming through the net curtains to illuminate the room. It was empty.

Holding the butt of the Beretta, she thrust the door all the way back. There was nobody behind it. *Paranoid bitch,* she thought.

The room looked exactly as she had left it but going into the kitchen the first thing she saw was the Delia file, large as life back on the shelf. When she opened it, she found it contained exactly what it said on the cover – Delia Smith recipes. The cuttings were gone.

Somebody had done a good job of making her look a fool. *Wait a moment,* she thought. *I still have the photograph of Mary and Veleta on the yacht, or do I?*

She locked the door and hurried upstairs. She had left the photograph in the drawer of her low table exactly in front of where Veleta was seated but she had only turned her back on him when she served the drinks. She pulled out the drawer; the photograph was gone.

That's impossible, she thought. He couldn't have taken it. He only had a few seconds when my back was turned. *Somebody must have been here when I was out and the same person had been in Mary's apartment.*

She began to examine the room with a more professional eye and immediately noticed small differences to her previous memory of the scene. Someone had done a thoroughly professional job of searching the place. Her first thought was that Peter Isaacs was still checking her out, in his *trust nobody* way. But why would he take the photograph? It was the only item connected with this case. All the rest of the papers were in her briefcase and with her all day. It had to be Stubbs or Veleta.

She examined the locks on her door, and sure enough she found the fine scratches left by a lock pick. She had been well and truly turned over by a real professional. People who were able to open vault doors would not have had trouble opening her door; someone like the Midnight Fox.

She was about to take Veleta's empty glass to the dishwasher when she remembered something Arthur had said, which prompted her to find a plastic bag to put it in.

CHAPTER 25

Daisy had just finished her dinner of a microwaved chicken biryani when the phone rang. It was Peter Isaacs. This time there was no preamble.

'You asked about Kaminski. There's an Ursula Kaminski, origin Czechoslovakia on the watch list. Before the breakup, she was a Major in the Secret Police. You know what that means. She disappeared after the Czech Republic was formed. She was never charged with any offence. A person of the same name's passport was scanned at Heathrow, arriving on a British Airways flight from Karachi, four weeks ago.'

'Karachi!' Daisy said. 'That's the shipment's origin. She must be working with the traffickers. What passport did she travel on?'

'Wait, I'll check,' Isaacs said.

Daisy heard the line crackle as he put down the phone and waited.

After a few moments Isaacs came back on and said, 'Polish, date of birth twenty-first March 1953.'

'Okay,' Daisy said. 'Since she's using her real name, she must feel safe enough, we also have to assume that she's the Ms Shelly Boy who collected the shipment today, so have Farmer check every hotel, house rental agencies, car rentals. Somehow, I don't think B&Bs are her style. We have to find her, Peter.'

'She may be using her real name up to now, but if she's a professional, she'll have an escape passport. I'll get Farmer on to it right away,' Isaacs said and hung up.

It was after nine when Daisy re-entered the Palace Garden Hotel. She was now sure that whatever Mary saw must have been here when she returned Kaminski's mobile. Without stopping to consult the reception she took the lift to the level two basement which she knew was the base of the hotel security and CCTV.

Entering the suite which was an open-plan area, she saw two operators at their control consoles. In front of each was a bank of video screens. Daisy saw that every screen showed a different view of the interior of the hotel's restaurants, bars and public places and adjacent streets in high-definition colour.

There was a single half glass-walled office which she knew and went straight to it, throwing a smiling aside, 'Good evening, John is expecting me,' to the startled receptionist.

John Stone, a former Chief Inspector in the Special Branch, had worked alongside Daisy in the Midlands at the height of the Provo activity. Blocked for further promotion because of age he took his pension and gratuity and joined the Palace Garden as head of security.

Stone – seated at his desk – showed no surprise when she tapped the door and entered.

'Hi Daisy,' he said. 'Give me a moment while I lock away the valuables.'

Giving him a peck on the cheek, Daisy said, 'Droll, John, do you have a few minutes for me?'

Stone stood up and pulled a chair to the side of his desk. 'As many as you like, sit down, we're going through a particularly peaceful and boring time at the moment.'

Sitting, she said, 'I know just how you feel, there was a time when London was crawling with conmen and hotel thieves, now it's much easier to make a dishonest living by peddling the white powder.'

Nodding his agreement, Stone said, 'Tell me about it. How's your luck, business good?'

Daisy shrugged her shoulders. 'Can't complain, but there's one case at the moment that is causing me some difficulties, which is why I'm here.'

'If I can help, shoot.'

'Last Monday morning about eleven a taxi dropped a passenger named Mrs Kaminski here. The driver was about to leave when she found a mobile phone on the rear seat. This has been confirmed by Pat Coffey.'

'That's pretty commonplace, Daisy. You'd be surprised what's left in taxis.'

'I'm sure. In this case the driver, one Mary Grey, went in search of Mrs Kaminski, returned the phone and was given a fifty for her trouble.'

'Honesty paying off this time,' said Stone. 'So, where's the problem?'

'The problem is that there is no record of a Mrs Kaminski staying at the hotel. I checked at the reception.'

'I'll check it again for you.' He had a terminal on his desk and hit the keys with practised skill. 'Nobody of that name was a guest in the past month, she probably was meeting someone but we've no way of knowing if it was a guest or just someone in one of the bars or restaurants.'

Shaking her head, Daisy said, 'Pat Coffey told me Mary was only gone about ten minutes. That wouldn't have given her enough time to check all the bars and restaurants. She must have been directed somewhere. What about the conference suites?'

'I'll check.' He hunched over his keyboard again, checking lists. 'We don't keep list of visitors to the suites, only the organisers. Kaminski, you say?'

Daisy nodded. 'Mrs Kaminski, try also Zentek Aviation.'

'Zentek Aviation, got it. She hired the Baird Suite for Monday morning.'

'How did she pay?'

Stone looked up another page before saying, 'Interesting, the booking was made a month ago, payment was by cashier's cheque. Looks like Mrs Kaminski didn't want to leave a trail.'

'Right,' Daisy said. 'Was there a contact number?'

Stone stabbed a finger on the screen and said, 'There is, 31 20, that's an Amsterdam number.'

Probably a small shopkeeper or café that takes messages, Daisy was thinking, and said, 'These people are too careful to be honest, John. Zentek Aviation is a pukka company but it doesn't operate in Europe. They were using it as a cover. Did you provide any catering?'

Stone looked up another page. 'Tea and coffee, biscuits for five people, they only had the suite for a two-hour morning session, eleven 'til one.'

'Do you have CCTV in the suite?'

Adopting a look of feigned shock, Stone said, 'Come off it, Daisy! Of course not, do you think we spy on our guests?'

Smiling, Daisy tapped him on the arm, saying, 'Don't play the old soldier with me, John. I know you have CCTV on all public places.'

Stone agreed. 'Okay, but it's only for security, sometimes we have trouble with rowdy parties and the suites get trashed, but we don't have any sound and we never view them unless there's trouble.'

'Good, how long do you keep them?'

'They're wiped every week.'

'Okay, that means you'll still have the tape for the Zentek Aviation booking?'

Stone paused for a moment before answering, 'Yes.'

Seeing his reluctance, she explained. 'Look, John, for the moment I just want to see the faces. If it's needed, we can get lip readers. Now can I see the tape?'

Stone gave her another long look before saying, 'All right, strictly unofficial, I can show it to you, but the Data Protection Act prevents me from giving it to you without a formal request, signed by a judge.'

'I know that already. What can you show me?'

'Inside the suite and the corridor outside to the lift.'

'What about inside the lift?'

'Every lift has a camera for safety purposes.'

Daisy stood. 'Nice to hear, I don't like lifts much myself. Can you show me the suite and corridor on two screens for Monday morning?'

'Follow me,' he said, leading the way to nearest of the CCTV consoles. The operator, who was a trendy young man in jeans, with a U2 T-shirt and spiky hair, looked at Daisy with interest.

'Alan this is Daisy, a friend, I want to show her how efficient our set-up is. Can you take your break now?'

Dragging his eyes off Daisy, Alan smiled, gave Stone a knowing look and stood up, 'Sure John, anything to oblige the lady,' and walked towards the door. The operator of the second console, who was engrossed in whatever he was listening to on his headphones as he watched the half a dozen screens in his charge, didn't even notice their arrival.

Stone took the console chair, to the right of which was a carousel of tape cassettes and a bank of video recorders, saying in a low voice, 'Remember, I'll be looking for a job if this gets out.'

Daisy giving him a reassuring nod, said, 'No worries about that, John, we can always use a good man.'

Standing behind him she watched as he selected two cassettes from the carousel and loaded them into two recorders. Two screens on the console immediately showed the interior of the suite and the corridor outside.

The CCTV camera in the suite was well placed and gave a sharp, crisp image of the door, which was centred on the far wall, plus the area covering the polished wood round table and the eight chairs around it, one of which was bigger and plusher than the others. The Chairman's position.

On the table for each chair there was an A4 pad, pencil and a bottle of water topped with a glass. The recording showed the time to be 10:55. The date 02:09:2007. The room was empty.

'Not early starters, are they?' Daisy said. As she spoke a waiter entered carrying a tray containing cups and saucers, a plate of biscuits and two stainless-steel Thermos jugs. He placed the tray on a side table and left.

'Their refreshments order,' said Stone. 'The tape starts automatically five minutes before the booked time and stops thirty minutes after the end to allow for overruns.'

'How do you get away with this, John?' Daisy asked. 'These suites are used by business people, don't they ever scan it?'

'Sure, they do,' Stone said. 'Look at the decorative line of copper mirrored tiles around the room. The camera is behind one of them. It's not transmitting and so well shielded so it doesn't get picked up in a scan.'

After giving the tiles a good look, she said, 'Clever. When does the show start?'

'Right now.' The corridor screen showed a big man with tight blond curls exiting the lift and walking towards the door. The time clicked to 11:02.

On the suite screen, the door opened. The same man entered and began prowling around the table, lifting each chair easily with one hand like it was matchwood and inspecting the bottom. Satisfied, he went on hands and knees and inspected the underside of the table. Finding nothing to interest him he inspected the walls, disappearing for a moment as he went beyond the camera angle. The next view was full face as he stared straight at the camera. It was a face Daisy would not forget. Giving the room a last look, he left the room. The screen time showed 11:07.

'Somebody's Goon,' Daisy said.

'He's satisfied the room is clean,' said Stone.

The second screen showed the man face-on, walking towards the lift and entering it.

Stabbing his finger on the screen Stone said, 'The camera in the corridor is in a time-lapsed mode. It'll show the same scene until it detects movement.'

There was no movement until 11:12 when the scene changed and the Goon followed by a thickset man in a grey suit, exited the lift and walked, their backs to the camera, towards the door. The suite camera showed the door opening as they entered. Grey Suit took the Chairman's seat, mouthing an order to the Goon, who found an ashtray and placed it by his left hand before going out of sight of the camera.

Daisy remembered Brum's file said he was left-handed. The Chairman removed a gold cigarette case from an inside pocket and placed it and a matching gold lighter by the ashtray. The Goon then took up position by the door.

At 11:15 the corridor screen showed a woman exiting the lift and hurrying to the door. The suite screen showed her entering and hurrying over to stand beside the Chairman, who said something to her. The reply must have been satisfactory for he gave a nod in agreement. She went to the side table and began arranging the tray.

At 11:17 the corridor screen shows two men exiting the lift. One by his size obviously a Goon. The second, slim, medium height, with grey hair, wearing a beige cashmere coat, whose profile was vaguely familiar to Daisy as he stood by the door. She recognised him when the suite screen showed him entering. 'Sean Duffy,' Daisy said aloud.

'You know him?' Stone asked.

'Yeah, I know him, a former PIRA Commander and your guess is as good as mine as to what he's doing there.'

She watched as Duffy shook hands with the Chairman and the woman before taking the seat facing the Chairman. The two Minders took chairs close to their respective principles. The Chairman began talking. As she watched, without any sound, all Daisy could make of the scene was that it appeared to be convivial.

The corridor screen clicked to 11:20 when the lift opened and a woman exited and walked towards the door. Daisy felt her stomach knot when she realised it was Mary Grey. The suite screen showed the same time. The Chairman was in full flow when the door was pushed open. Mary entered and stood looking at them for a brief moment before she was noticed. She was holding a mobile phone and mouthed something as she held it up. Then she gave Duffy and the Chairman a long look. There was definitely a brief look of surprise, or was it recognition, on her face, which she quickly hid.

The woman left her seat and hurried over to Mary. Taking the mobile, she mouthed something and almost pushed her out of the room.

On the corridor screen, Daisy saw Mary – facing the camera – standing outside the door. 'Freeze that picture, John. Can you zoom in on her face?'

Stone's fingers moved expertly over the keyboard. The still of Mary's face filled the screen. 'She looks surprised,' said Stone.

'More like startled,' Daisy said. 'Like she's seen a ghost. Let's see what she does next.'

Mary stood by the door for a long moment before she shook her head in the way one might say 'impossible' and quickened her step to the lift.

Showing the same time, the suite screen showed the woman returning to the table and was about to sit, when Duffy said something to the Chairman, who nodded and barked an order at the woman, who by now Daisy guessed must be Kaminski. She nodded and hurriedly left the room. On the second screen they watched her, now facing the camera as she hurried to the lift, impatiently pushing the button until it came.

The suite camera showed Duffy and the Chairman in serious conversation. Duffy, stabbing his finger on the table several times to emphasise his points. The Chairman with a scowl, snapped his answers. This continued until the time on both screens showed 11:26.

The scene on the corridor screen changed and they saw Kaminski exiting the lift and hurrying to the suite door.

'She's been gone six minutes,' Daisy said, and watched as Kaminski appeared on the suite screen and hurried over to the Chairman to say something.

When she had finished speaking, Duffy stood up and mouthed something to the Chairman, before nodding to his Minder and hurriedly leaving the room. The corridor screen captured their faces clearly as they hurried to the lift.

The suite screen showed the Chairman's Goon now standing by the door and the Chairman and Kaminski engaged in what, by the look on their faces, seemed like a fraught conversation, which continued for some minutes before they hurriedly left the room.

Daisy, watching as they waited until the lift arrived and disappeared into it, was thinking, *The bastards knew they'd been compromised.*

Stone, breaking into her thoughts, said, 'Whoever that woman was, she certainly spoilt the party. Do you know her?'

Daisy, whose eyes welled at the thought, whispered, 'Yeah, I know her or should say knew her, she died last Wednesday.'

Stone grimaced. 'Not the car bomb?'

'The very one, John. I need to take this tape now, there's no time for a warrant.'

'The taxi driver, you knew her personally?'

'She was a friend, John.'

Putting his hand gently on her arm, Stone said, 'I thought so. Look Daisy, I'll give you the tape for the corridor and the lift. You can see all the faces in it. I can't let the tape on the suite leave this office. It's too risky.'

Squeezing his hand, Daisy said, 'Thanks John, that'll have to do, but don't wipe it. Has the suite been used since this?'

Stone went to his terminal and brought up another list. 'Yes, twice, why?'

Frowning, Daisy said, 'Pity, we might have got some forensics, too late now. Thanks again for your help, John, I owe you.'

CHAPTER 26

Friday 6ᵗʰ September – Evening.

Frank drove past the house in Chiswick. 'That it?'

Veleta looked at the gate. 'Yeah, park down the road we'll walk back.' Frank found a space, pulled in and killed the lights. They got out and walked.

Stopping at the gate, Veleta looked at the shuttered windows. 'Looks like it's been empty for a long time.'

The gate was locked. 'Open it.' Veleta stepped back and watched as Frank produced an oddly shaped tool which he inserted into the lock and began probing gently before he gave it a sharp twist and the lock sprung.

'You haven't lost your touch, Frank,' Veleta said and pushed the gate, which opened smoothly.

Frank grinned. 'I had a good teacher, Harry.'

Veleta nodded and pointed to the hinges. 'They've been greased recently.'

A quick look up and down the street and seeing it empty, they moved silently to the front door. Frank inspected the locks. There was a Yale and a Chubb mortice. 'No problem, Harry, but it'll take a while.'

'Maybe there's no need.' Veleta reached into a gunmetal overhead light shade and ran his fingers around the inside. 'Bingo. Brum used to say if it works don't fix it,' and handed a pair of keys to Frank. The door opened silently and they went quickly inside and closed it.

Once inside, they found themselves in total darkness.

'Those shutters on the upstairs landing must be light proof,' Frank said and produced a torch which lit up the hall, until he found a switch panel with four switches. 'Okay, Harry?'

Veleta nodded. 'Yeah, try it, those shutters were fitted for a reason, total privacy.'

Frank tried the first switch. After a single low-wattage bulb in a wall fitting illuminated the hall, he said, 'Someone's paying the lecky bill.'

Veleta opened a door marked 'Cloaks'. Inside was a wash basin and toilet. He ran the water until it became hot. 'Hot water,' he said. 'This house is being kept ready. Brum always had a bolt hole like this.'

With a puzzled look Frank asked, 'How come you know about this place, Harry?'

'It was one of Brum's houses, he bought it when he first shacked with Henny, you remember her?'

'Yeah,' Frank said. 'The tall blonde. Dutch, wasn't she? How could I forget her?' Then, looking approvingly at the oak staircase, he continued, 'A place like this must be worth a good few bob these days.'

Veleta agreed. 'Well over a million. Brum bought it cheap in the seventies.'

Frank laughed. 'Nice, he should have stayed in property instead of thieving.'

Veleta smiled grimly. 'Yeah, thieving from thieves you mean. Anyway, he shacked up here with Henny for a few years before moving to Hampstead, but he never sold it. According to his driver he used the place as his personal knocking shop.'

'His driver. Billy Smirke, I remember him, decent geezer, what happened to him?'

Veleta shrugged. 'I don't know. He did a runner after Brum's death. According to the papers the cops were looking for him.'

'Yeah, Brum's death *was* dodgy wasn't it? They'd have wanted to talk to anyone close to him with a bit of form.'

Veleta smiled. 'Billy had form all right. That's why we never used him. Brum employed him because of that and paid him peanuts.'

After a moment's consideration Frank said, 'A proper scumbag Brum was, but why's this place still empty?'

'I had Courtney-Hopkins check it out. Henny couldn't sell it because of some clause in Brum's will. After his death she went back and lived in it, before going abroad a few years ago. It's been empty since then. Mary kept an eye on it since then, but she never saw any sign of life. She even made inquiries with the local estate agents, asking if it was on the market. They told her there was a problem with succession, the owner had died and her will was being disputed.'

'You think Henny is dead?'

'She might be, people who got too close to Brum often ended up dead, or it might just be a ploy to keep the house empty without any questions being asked.'

'Harry, somebody's using this house, it's not for sale and not lived in, and has been like that for so long nobody takes any notice of it, but Brum is dead, isn't he?'

'Maybe not. Daisy Clowser told me the car bomb was detonated by a Messerlie clock and you know there was only two of them left.'

'Sure, Benny Shack was keeping them in his shop.'

'You and I and only one other person knew that.'

'Brum?

'Yeah, Brum, he bought all the clocks, and Shack modified them as and when they were wanted. Do you know if Shack is still around?'

'His shop is. Last time I was in Gospel Oak it was still there.'

'I'll pay him a visit in the morning. Let's look over this place and see if we can find anything connected to Brum.'

It was after nine when Daisy reached Arthur Casey's house in Maida Vale. Arthur lived alone, being a widower for five years. The door opened within moments of her pressing the bell.

'Come in, Daisy.' If he was surprised at her visit, he didn't show it. Arthur was a man who accepted situations as they occurred. Daisy rarely visited his house and when she did there was always a reason.

She followed him into his comfortable living room where she was greeted by his elderly spaniel, Jaffa, who insisted upon receiving the customary pat on the head and tickle under the chin before he settled back to his doze.

'Drink, Daisy?'

Nodding, she said, 'Thanks, just a small one. I need to keep my head straight. Scotch half and half would be lovely.'

'I'll get the water,' Arthur said and went to the kitchen, returning in less than a minute with a bottle of Evian. In his sideboard he found a bottle of Islay malt and two glasses.

Watching as he mixed the drinks she asked, 'Any luck on the drug shipment?'

Arthur screwed the tops back on the bottles before replying. 'I put out a few feelers, and a few names have been mentioned, but nobody seems to know anything definite. If there is a shipment, it's definitely not a London gang behind it.'

'We can only hope someone talks. I hope you still have a VHS unit? I've something to show you.'

Pointing to the TV, he said, 'It's in that cupboard under the telly, help yourself.'

Daisy was glad to see it was a model with freeze-frame and remote. She inserted the tape and switched on the TV.

Handing her the drink, Arthur said, 'What have you got there, Daisy?'

'It's a security tape from a West End hotel which shall be

nameless for the moment, you know how it goes, to protect the innocent etcetera. Sit down, I'll run it through and you can look at the faces without me prompting. Let's see if you recognise anyone.'

Arthur tapped her glass with his. 'Cheers, Daisy, let the show began,' he said and settled himself back in his armchair.

Daisy dropped down in the settee opposite and started the tape. Sipping her drink, she watched him, hoping for a reaction as each new face entered the scene. She was to be disappointed. He was watching intently, but completely deadpan. When it was finished, he was quiet for a moment, taking a sip of his whisky, before saying, 'Run it again, Daisy, I want to be sure.'

She rewound the tape and ran it. If Arthur had seen something, now was not the time to ask questions. As before when it finished, he was contemplative and took another sip from his whisky before putting the glass on the table and saying, 'I know the walk, Daisy. A man can change his face but never his voice or his walk.'

'Did you recognise someone, Arthur?'

Arthur nodded. 'Sean Duffy, of course, and as it happens, he's one of the names that was mentioned around when I was asking around. I'm told by a reliable source that Duffy is big time into drugs these days. Although nothing's been proven, he's suspected of being a middle-man between the Minihane cartel and the East Asian traffickers. The two women I've never saw before, but the boss man I'm pretty sure I know, not by his face but by his walk, pity there's no sound. I would recognise his voice in the dark.' Scratching his chin, he thought for a moment before continuing. 'You know, Daisy, I think the bastard may have fooled us all these years.'

'So, you think it's Brum?'

'It's a strong possibility. I arrested him more than a dozen times, never pinned anything on him, but had him in the interview room for long enough to learn every little move he made.'

Mary hadn't seen him walk, Daisy was thinking, and explained to

Arthur. 'The woman returning the mobile phone was Mary Grey. She had reason to know Brum, but he was sitting when she entered, so she couldn't have seen his walk.'

'If she heard him speak, she'd know. Looks like your friend opened the wrong door. Brum would not want anyone around who knew his past.'

'What about the other woman and Sean Duffy, wouldn't they know?'

Shaking his head, Arthur said, 'Unlikely, if it's Brum. He's had work done on his face, but his overall build can't be changed nor his way of walking. I wouldn't have recognised him without seeing him walk. He had a distinctive shuffling gait, with the toes of his shoes pointing inwards. If it is Brum, and I think it might be, he's been hiding behind a new identity for twenty years and I'm quite sure he wouldn't tie up with anyone who knew his real background.'

Daisy considered that before saying, 'There was a bomb involved and Duffy would know where to source bomb materials, wouldn't he?'

Arthur shook his head in disagreement. 'Duffy was probably there to do a drug deal. I don't think Brum would want him involved in anything else, too much explaining as to the why.'

'You're probably right, Arthur. If it is Brum, according to his record he knew enough about explosives to do it himself and the Messerlie clock goes back to his time.'

Arthur gave her a sharp look. 'What's this about a Messerlie, Daisy?'

'One was used to trigger the car bomb that killed Mary.'

Arthur's face was a picture of surprise. 'Bloody hell, Daisy why didn't you mention that yesterday?'

'I didn't know it then. A piece from the bomb was later identified as coming from a Messerlie clock.'

Arthur fiddled with his glass for a moment before replying. 'As I told you yesterday, Messerlie shipped their last twenty clocks to London in '76. Eighteen were used in the robberies, leaving two.'

Daisy nodded. 'One actually if you count the car bomb.'

Arthur took another sip from his glass before saying, 'You're right, but remember the clocks have to be adapted by a watchmaker to make them into timers. Unless he did all twenty at once, he must be still around.'

'He has to be,' Daisy said. 'All the others were set for midnight. Wednesday's bomb was set for eight forty-five.'

'Good point, Daisy, pity we never got a line on the watchmaker.'

'Tell me, Arthur, before '76, did you ever hear of clocks being used as timers?'

Looking into his empty glass and the bottle on the sideboard, he hesitated for a moment before putting it on the table and saying, 'Sure, the IRA used clocks for a time, as did most bombers, before electronic timers were available. The interesting thing is, during the Midnight Fox robberies, we searched the records and found that a decoy bomb was also Sidney Vane's MO. Maybe he was the first to use a Messerlie clock.'

Daisy considered this for a moment before saying, 'Brum did time with Vane and was suspected of being his partner on the job where the police constable was killed, rumour has it that he's the one who actually fired the shot that Vane hanged for.'

Arthur shrugged. 'Anything is possible with Brum. He was one evil bastard.'

Remembering Ernie's words, she said, 'According to Ernie Watters, after Vane was hanged there are no records of decoy bombs being used again for fourteen years until the Midnight Fox robberies started. The delay puzzled me, but maybe Brum needed the time to open his up-market jewellers, which would have provided the perfect front for disposing of stolen valuables. Do you think he was the

Midnight Fox?'

Fiddling with his empty glass Arthur gave a negative shake of the head. 'No, I never thought that. I'd say that after Vane was hanged, he lost his stomach for the sharp end, but I'd stake my pension he was involved as a fence. None of the stolen cash, gold or jewellery was ever recovered, that was more Brum's style.'

Finishing her drink, Daisy said, 'So, you think the man in the video is Brum doing a Lazarus?'

'Now that I know about the clock, it's more than likely. You say the girl knew him?'

'She knew him all right. Besides being Sid Vane's daughter, Mary kept a file of newspaper stories about all the Midnight Fox robberies and Brum's death, which apparently was collected by her mother Gloria.'

Arthur reflected on that for a moment before saying, 'If that's the case whatever Brum is up to can't be just drugs. That car bomb was hastily set up and bloody risky. He must have been desperate to silence her.'

'You're right. It isn't just drugs, Peter Issacs believes the traffickers are bringing in some serious weapons for Jihadists, to be used in an imminent attack.'

'I asked you the same question yesterday, Daisy, why the bomb? Why not just get her alone, knife her and pass it off as robbery?'

'Brum knew that Mary had recognised him and didn't want any investigation into her past that might lead back to him. Like Sidney Vane and the Midnight Fox, Brum liked decoys; in this case the murder of Abdullah was the decoy, Mary was to be simply collateral damage.'

'You could be right, Daisy, but he didn't figure on you being there.'

'No, he didn't. The question is, Arthur, now that we know who we're looking for, how do we find him?'

'I'd have Sean Duffy pulled in, he must be in contact with Brum. I'd sweat the bastard until he talks.'

Daisy shook her head. 'He's a tough nut, Arthur. It was tried before in Castlereagh. They gave him the full treatment and he didn't give them anything and besides, we have to find him first, he's probably gone to ground after the car bomb. He'll have guessed who was behind it.'

'The bomb won't bother him, if there's a big drug deal in the offing he'll stay close.'

'I hope you're right, Arthur. If he wants to hide, he'll use his old network, Noonan and Devereux, one of them will know where he is, probably holed up in Dublin or here in London in one of the Provo's safe houses. We never found them all.'

'Then, you'll have to go to the old haunts and sniff him out. Find him, Daisy, he'll lead you to Brum.'

The ground floor of the Chiswick House, besides the spacious hall and elegant oak staircase had two large reception rooms left and right. At the end of the hall was a door, behind which they found a staircase leading to the basement.

They moved from room to room using the light of the torch, checking that each of the rooms were shuttered and light proof, before putting on the light. Each of the rooms had a single bulb hanging from the ceiling as its only source of light. They were also completely devoid of any furniture or evidence of occupancy.

'There's nothing to see here, we'll look downstairs,' Veleta said and led the way down a flight of stairs. The house, dating from the time when the middle class could afford a few servants, had a large kitchen covering most of the area, off which was a fully tiled scullery with lines of marble shelves, all empty. Inside the scullery there was another door, which was locked by a Yale lock.

'Open it, Frank,' Veleta said.

'No access for the kitchen staff,' Frank said. Producing a strip of plastic, he slipped it between the jamb and sprung the bolt back. Behind the door they found a spiral staircase leading upstairs. Its cast metal frame and unpainted pine steps looked too modern to be an original feature.

'It's an odd place for stairs,' Veleta said. 'We'd better see where they lead to, but first let's take a look at the garden.'

The back door leading to the garden had a single lock and two bolts. The key was on a hook beside the door. Opening it, they crossed the covered patio and followed the York stone path to the back gate. A line of tall conifers running the length of the garden on each side provided a screen from prying eyes.

The gate opened on to a tow path running behind the houses. Directly opposite they found the jetty. Veleta looked at the river; the tide was on the rise, in an hour's time, the jetty would be accessible by a boat.

'There's nothing to see here, let's see where that staircase leads to,' Veleta said.

Veleta climbed first; the only light was from Frank's torch as he followed. They climbed more than twenty feet before reaching an exit. Veleta guessed they must be on the first floor. They were in a long narrow room with no windows or doors. An empty room.

Taking the torch, Veleta inspected the walls. 'Brum always said he had a place where he could lie low if the heat got too bad, this must be it.'

'It's empty, Harry, not exactly the best place to lie low.'

Veleta nodded. 'Yeah, like the rest of the house, it's not being used, and it looks like it hasn't been used for a long time. Maybe Brum is dead.'

'If the stairs are the way out but there must be a way in, Harry, there must be some sort of lever.'

Using the light from the torch, they both fingertipped the wall. It was Frank who found the lever.

'Something here, Harry, a metal strip, I'll pull on it and see.'

There was an audible click and a door-sized section of the wall sprung back. Frank pushed it open and they found themselves in a bare room lined with empty bookshelves. A section of one of the shelves formed the door to the hidden room. Finding themselves on the first floor they moved from room to room with the aid of the torch. There were four rooms and two bathrooms, all without a stick of furniture. A staircase led to two more attic rooms, and another bathroom also empty.

'There's nothing here, Harry, we've looked everywhere.'

'Except the garage.'

They found the garage could be entered through an entrance from the hall. By the light of the torch they saw a work bench and a wall mounted selection of tools, all of them in place designated by their painted outline. There was a long wooden crate sitting on two trestles and nothing else.

'What have we here?' Veleta walked around it until he found the consignment paper stapled to the wood and read it aloud. 'Karachi – London Tilbury consigned to Zentek Aviation, intermediate consignee Blue Sky, Park Royal London. Frank I'd lay odds that whatever is inside this crate is the reason for Mary's death, let's take a look.'

Frank went to the tool rack and selected two screwdrivers and handed one to Veleta.

'It'll be quicker if we do a side each,' Frank said, starting on the first screw.

Veleta was about to start when there was a whirr of an electric motor and he froze. The garage door was opening. Handing his screwdriver to Frank, he said, 'We got less than ten seconds, put them back.'

For four of those seconds he held the torch steady on the tool board until the tools were replaced. Then he swept the garage with light and saw there was a door to a rear section.

Veleta whispered, 'Follow me and for God's sake don't trip over anything, it's time for us to make like shadows, we might learn something.'

Veleta led, the light pointed to the floor. Frank turned and saw the lights from dipped headlights, then the bonnet of a car through the half-opened door before following close behind.

CHAPTER 27

Daisy had no idea how Peter Isaacs occupied his evenings. In fact, although she had worked with him for four years during the Troubles, she'd learned nothing about his private life. There's no biographical information in any of the directories. He once told her in his business the honours can come after he retires, for now he remains anonymous. But he also told her to call him any time, which she now did at eleven p.m., two hours after her meeting with Arthur.

In that time, she had made a number of calls to people she had not spoken to for a long time. For some it was a voice from the past, a reminder of old times. Others thought it was a call from the dead. In the end she located the present whereabouts of Sean Duffy and now needed Peter Isaacs' help to move forward.

There was no instant response, in fact she let the call go to twelve rings and was about to hang up when he answered.

'Hello?'

'It's Daisy.'

'I know who it is, you've caught me at an awkward moment, what do you want?'

Daisy's imagination was fertile but Peter Isaacs in an awkward moment? This was a first, but she was not prepared to ask the question.

'Peter, I need to interview Sean Duffy.'

'You assured me there was no Irish connection.'

'Duffy is involved in big-time drug smuggling. I have a CCTV tape of him in a meeting with Kaminski and another unidentified man. I can guess who this man is but I need to know for sure and Duffy can tell me.'

'So, that's what this is about, drugs?'

'We can't take that for granted.'

'Why should Duffy tell you anything, Daisy? We gave him the full treatment in Castlereagh and he told us nothing.'

'I know that, that's why I need you to talk to the Fisherman. I know he doesn't like drugs and he is the only one who can put the frighteners on Duffy.'

'How?'

'Through his enforcer Valentine O'Grady.'

'Daisy, you're way behind the times. O'Grady is now the proprietor of an upmarket art gallery in South Williams Street, Dublin.'

'I hear you, Peter, but my information is that nothing has changed with O'Grady, he still serves his master.'

'What do you want me to do?'

'Explain to the Fisherman that Duffy is close to the bombers. We want to rule him out and the only way to do that is to talk to him. In order to do that I want safe conduct to go to Dublin and I want O'Grady's cooperation in persuading Duffy to come clean.'

'Daisy this better be worth it. I don't have to remind you that the clock is ticking on this. I'll call you with the clearance to go. What name are you using?'

'Maggie Maguire, I still have the cover documents, credit cards, the lot and they're still valid.'

'That's bloody risky, Daisy, Maggie Maguire is supposed to be dead. If Dolan finds out you're in Dublin, he'd raise an army to find you.'

'Don't worry about Dolan. He went off his head in Portlaoise and currently is locked up in the Central Medical Unit for the criminally insane.'

'Let's hope he stays there. He was one copper-bottomed fanatic, even with him out of it, you'll need a minder, I'll arrange it.'

'No need, if you fix it with the Fisherman, I'll have safe conduct.'

'Don't worry, you'll have it.'

'Good, I have a feeling we must finish this job in the next twenty-four hours or whatever they're planning to do will be done.'

'Try not to kill anyone, Daisy. If things go pear-shaped, get rid of your documents and go to the rendezvous point. I'll send in a chopper.' He hung up.

Once behind the door, Veleta flashed the torch briefly and found they were in a small storage room, lined with empty Dexion shelving. There were no windows and no exits. Through the thin partition wall, they heard the door motor whirring come to a stop, followed by the smoother purr as an expensive car was driven into the garage. Then the whirr of the door being closed.

Veleta pressed his ear against the wall and heard the engine being cut and the car doors opening, followed by footsteps clattering on the concrete floor.

A rasping voice said, 'Leave the lights, Kaminski. It might show through the door, the car lights will do. Open the crate, Thomas.'

Veleta froze. He knew that voice.

The was a shuffling of feet, the sound of a big clumsy man. Veleta knew the type, big dumb and homicidal, definitely not someone he wanted to tangle with without a weapon.

He heard the sound of the screwdriver being pulled from its clip on the wall, followed by the satisfied grunt as each screw was removed and dropped into a tin. There were eight such sounds, then the sound of the crate lid being lifted off and dropped to the floor.

'Jesus, Thomas,' the man rasped. 'You want the whole neighbourhood to hear us?'

'Sorry, boss.' The muttered reply was almost inaudible.

'Here, give me the torch and we'll take a look.'

Veleta heard scraping sounds as something was lifted out of the crate before the man said, 'Looks like everything's here.'

'I told you there was no damage.' The female's accent was East European, Veleta thought.

'I know you did,' the man rasped. 'But I know Stingers and you don't. I had to be sure. I didn't want any screw-ups when Iqbal checks the crate. Remember, there'll be four of them to deal with.'

The female replied. 'There's nothing to screw up. If Bulger gets them to the jetty at ten o'clock, we should have completed the hand-over and be out of here in thirty minutes max. You've seen enough?'

'Yeah. Put the lid back on with a couple of screws each end. It'll save time tomorrow.'

Veleta heard the lid being dropped on, and the heavy breathing as each screw was inserted. Then the rattle of the spring clip as the screwdriver was replaced.

'Let's go,' said the rasping voice.

Veleta heard the garage door opening and the car doors close. The engine made less noise than the door motor when it started and reversed out. Within a minute the door closed again. He waited for fifteen minutes in the shadows before moving.

'Wait, Frank,' he said. Using the light of the torch pointed on the floor he entered the garage and went to the door where he listened for any sound outside; other than a car going by he heard nothing. They had gone, but better to be sure.

Leaving Frank where he was, he re-entered the house and silently mounted the stairs to the first floor. There from a window overlooking the street he had a view of the drive. It was empty. He looked carefully at the few darkened cars parked in the street. They all looked empty. Satisfied, he returned to the garage and found

Frank where he had left him.

Gripping Frank's arm, his voice shaking with emotion, he said, 'They've gone. That was Brum's voice I heard, Frank. I'm sure of it. The bastard's alive and he killed Mary and the reason is in that crate.' Pointing the light at the tool rack, he said, 'Let's see what this is all about, get the screwdriver.'

Veleta inspected the crate. The lid was now attached by only two screws at each end and two in the middle. Frank quickly unscrewed them and lifted the lid.

Veleta shined the light on the contents and removed the four-inch layer of packaging foam to reveal the two Grip-Stocks and BCU units, each pair in an individual foam cut-out.

Frank lifted one of the slabs of foam out and saw beneath it the olive-green fibreglass tube with US Army markings and said, 'Bloody 'ell, Harry, these are Stinger surface-to-air missiles.'

Looking at the tube, Veleta asked, 'How do you know that?'

'My son had a book called *Weapons of War*. It gives a full description of the Stinger.'

Giving the green tube a long look, Veleta said, 'Explain the basics.'

'Pointing to the Grip-Stock Frank said, 'From memory that green tube contains the missile which is attached to this. The target is sighted though the scope sight, when it's fired it goes after the heat signature of the target, jet engines. It locks on and chases the target. Its warhead has three kilos of explosives, enough to destroy an aircraft.'

'What's the range?'

'Three to four thousand metres. Look, there's two missiles and stocks, they must be planning two hits. Harry, this is serious shit, we're right in the Heathrow flight path here, and the planes are well under three thousand metres, these lunatics could kill hundreds of people.'

'We won't let that happen,' Veleta said. 'But I have to settle for Mary. We know their rendezvous time is ten o'clock tomorrow night. We also know they have a boat collecting the buyers at nine thirty tomorrow. We have twenty-four hours to come up with something. They don't know about us so that gives us an edge.'

Looking into the crate Frank shook his head and said, 'I don't know, Harry, why can't we just tip the cops and let them deal with it?'

Veleta leaned across the crate and gripped Frank's arm. 'Remember the oath we all swore thirty years ago when we started out, Frank. We'll never deal with the cops, never.'

Frank pulled his arm away and lifting one of the Grip-Stocks from the foam, he said, 'I remember, Harry, but this is different and we don't have to deal with the cops if we dump these in the river. They can't use the missiles without them.'

Veleta looked at the Grip-Stock for a moment before saying, 'That's a good thought, Frank, and we'll come back and do just that if I don't come up with a better plan that will fix the bastards, permanently. As I said we have twenty-four hours. Screw that down and let's get out of here. I have to find somewhere to stay tonight.'

'No worries there, Harry,' Frank said. 'You can stay with me; the wife is visiting her mother. I thought it best.'

'You thought right, best if no one sees me. Let's go eat something, is the New Bengal still there?'

'Sure, under new management, so nobody will recognise you, the food's still good.'

'Good, tomorrow is going to be a busy day.'

Daisy knew there was nothing she could do until Isaacs came back to her, or was there? She looked again at the list of events she had written, everything she considered relevant since the car bomb.

Dr Taleb's name was on the list. She had written 'Why?' beside it.

Why did Kaminski pick him, when he was the last dentist on the list, and the furthest away from the hotel? She also now knew that Kaminski was not staying at the hotel, although she could have asked to see the list when she was booking the Baird Suite, but why Dr Taleb?

There was no doubt that Kaminski had visited the house in Symonds Street. Mary had collected her there. So, if the receptionist was lying, and Kaminski had not visited the dentist then what was she doing at the house? She had to find out. The clock was ticking on this job and she didn't think the answer to that question could wait until morning.

She thumbed through her Blackberry and found the entry for Sid, who in his former profession was a keyman. An expert who could open any lock, now retired but whose services were called on from time to time by the security services. She dialled the number.

This time the call was answered on the second ring. 'Hello, who's this?'

'Daisy Clowser. Sid, you remember me?'

'Yes, it's past midnight, a bit late for a call, miss.'

Daisy quipped, 'I thought you only went to work after dark.'

'Funny, miss, you know I've finished with all that years ago.'

'A joke, Sid. I want to have a look over a certain property, just a look, nothing more.'

'Where is this property?' Sid became more business-like.

'In Symonds Street W1, number 34, a three-storey house with a Garret and a basement.'

'I know them. There's a service road running behind them. I've cased a few of those houses when I was in business. When do you want to go in?'

'It has to be in the next two hours.'

Sid gasped. 'Two hours! You're not asking much; you know I

charge double time for short notice.'

'You can charge whatever you want but it must be done now. Where do we meet?'

A short silence followed. Daisy was sure she could hear Sid's mutterings as he worked things out.

'We don't meet. Go to the property at one thirty. If I've found the house empty the front door will be unlocked. When you enter put the dead bolt on. I'll be watching. When you leave, I'll lock up after you.'

'What happens if you can't gain access, Sid?

Sid spluttered and said, 'What a question, miss, that's never happened.'

'I'm sure it hasn't. Thanks Sid, I'll have your envelope biked over first thing.'

'Remember, its double time.'

'No problem, Sid, you're worth every penny. See you for a drink sometime soon.'

CHAPTER 28

It was ten minutes past midnight. Daisy knew that Sid lived in Maida Vale and had a small anonymous car. He would need time to get his kit ready and dress for the occasion. Sid worked in the shadows and favoured dark clothing: black trousers a turtleneck, and rubber-soled shoes; clothing that would have him arrested if he was stopped by a patrol at one in the morning. Considering that a possibility she knew he also carried a yellow plastic worker's gilet, folded into a pocket-sized wallet, which could be donned if needed. Allowing thirty minutes for preparation, he could be in Symonds Street by a quarter to one. He would then make a careful reconnoitre of the house to ensure it was empty and at the same time finding the best way to gain access. Some locks take time to open even for an expert like Sid. One thirty seemed definitely doable. She would now make her own preparations.

She dressed herself in dark jeans, black shirt and jacket and found a pair of dark blue trainers which had seen better days. The Beretta, she fitted into a belt clip. It was close to one o'clock when she left the apartment with the thought of hailing a taxi on the Bayswater Road but decided instead to walk to Symonds Street which should take her no more than fifteen minutes.

When she reached Marble Arch, it was still busy with traffic. She could see Oxford Street ahead had the usual numbers of late night revellers. After passing the Cumberland hotel she found, by virtue of having no commercial activities at this hour, Symonds Street was virtually deserted. The only people who used it were residents and the odd cat.

Number 34 was in darkness. Daisy walked boldly to the front door. If Sid had done his job, the door would be open and the house empty.

She slipped on latex gloves and pushed the door. It opened without a sound. She entered and put the dead lock on as instructed. Deciding not to risk a light, she would have to rely on her Maglite.

Keeping the light focused on the floor she descended the stairs to Doctor Taleb's surgery where she found his door open and saw that the room had a street window. Flashing lights seen by some passer-by would soon have the police here. She quickly closed the door and began with the secretary's desk, who she thought, was in a perfect position to play a double game and control access to the house. Visitors could come and go at will, without anyone paying attention and who's to know if every visitor needed a dentist.

Doctor Taleb's appointments book was on the desk. Daisy turned the pages, looking through the entries for the previous week. She was not surprised to find there was no entry for Kaminski. Flicking through the Rolodex she found no entry for Kaminski but there was one for London Quality Taxis.

So, she thought, Miss Patel had probably called Kaminski's taxi from here. They both had foreign accents and to Frank Stubbs, an accent is an accent. Kaminski was here all right but it was not to visit Doctor Taleb. The question was, who was she visiting? Someone was running a slick operation from this house, but to what end?

She pulled out the desk drawers, they were all empty. The bottom of the drawers had no attachments. *Secretaries' desks are never as clean as this,* she was thinking. It would appear that Miss Patel, if that was her name, had terminated her employment, effective immediately.

Daisy put everything back as she found it. The secretary had made sure there was nothing to find. The absence of Kaminski in the appointments book was a positive, maybe the rest of the house would throw up something.

She went back to the ground floor and pushed the door to enter the inner hall. There was a hall table and an empty coat stand with a place for umbrellas. The table had a single drawer. Opening it she found among a clutter of cards for local tradesmen one for the Queen of Sheba Tandoori.

Opening the first of three doors she found a toilet with wash basin, both sparklingly clean. The next room was in total darkness. A quick flick of the torch showed the reason why. The windows were covered with heavy velvet curtains. She found the light switch. A chandelier lit up the room, which was a study. It had an ornate desk and leather chairs, with one wall taken up by a bookcase filled with books, colour coordinated and probably bought by the yard. An impressive marble fire surround with an equally impressive French-style mirror above.

There were no photographs on the mantelpiece, in fact the room was bereft of any personal touch, more like a Harrods display. The desk top was empty, save for a pen holder without pens and a blotter which she examined under the light; there were no indentions. The desk drawers were empty.

This room showed no signs of having being used recently, or it had been thoroughly cleaned. The fireplace had an ornate iron grate which was also empty, but she found a fine layer of fresh ash under the grate which indicated recent use.

Remembering that fragments of burning papers sometimes floated upwards with the rising heat, she stuck her head in the opening and used the torch to make a search of the chimney. Something reflected about eighteen inches from the entrance: a triangular piece of paper about an inch long was caught between two bricks. Managing to get a grip of one edge with her finger tips, she removed it carefully. Wiping the soot off her find with her glove, she examined it. The paper was stiff with a satin finish, printed paper of some sort and it was an edge piece, with a quarter inch of white border, and the rest printed green.

More importantly she saw there were four tiny printed numbers in six-point black type, maybe part of printer's number. It could have been any fragment that blew up the chimney but this piece could be gold, she was thinking. Maybe for once Lady Luck was on her side. She put it into her wallet behind her Visa card and went to the room opposite which was a dining room, complete with a rich man's idea of Regency. The mahogany table seated twelve. A matching sideboard stood against one wall. She found the drawers packed with sterling silver cutlery and the main body had shelves lined with cut glass glasses, but no wines or spirits.

Leading off the dining room was a spacious kitchen, again in showroom condition. The cupboards were bare, none of the usual accumulation of detritus normally found in a working kitchen. She opened the American fridge-freezer and found a dozen cans of Diet Coke and the same number of litre bottles of water. Again, no alcohol. This was definitely a dry house.

The back door was locked by two locks, a Yale and a mortice. *Sid's means of access,* she thought, and found the keys hanging on a peg beside the door. Opening it she saw there was a walled yard, and a basement well with iron stairs leading to a door which must serve the basement. *Access for Dr Taleb,* she thought, which meant there was no need for him to enter the rest of the house.

There were three wheelie bins against the back wall, one with a white lid and a label which read **Medical Waste**, one yellow and one grey. Set in the back wall was a wooden gate secured by two bolts. She opened it and saw there was a service road running behind the houses. *Easy access for people of Sid's profession,* she thought.

Closing and rebolting the gate, she turned her attention to the wheelie bins and lifting the lid of the yellow one she found it was stuffed with empty packets from dental supplies. In the grey bin she found a single black plastic bag which she pulled out and carried to the house.

Opening the bag on the kitchen floor she saw it was stuffed with empty Coke cans, water bottles and empty takeaway packs from the Queen of Sheba Tandoori. She counted enough empties to satisfy a couple of healthy eaters for the same number of days.

Asian food only and no alcohol, in her mind spelt Islamic in capital letters and in this case, considering the circumstances, Jihadists. Two or maybe three of them had been holed up here and now they were gone. To go where, and to do what?

Climbing the staircase to the first floor she reached a small landing with a palm plant in an ornate copper pot. The clay was moist and the plant looked healthy. She followed the stairs to the second floor where there was another landing with a similar plant, also with moist clay. At one end of this landing she saw a spiral staircase leading to the Garret. No doubt intended for the servants. She climbed the stairs.

There were three rooms in the Garret; the first door she tried set off an extractor fan. Its humming noise she was sure would not be heard outside the house. The room was fitted out as a bathroom, with a shower cubicle, wash basin and a toilet. A quick search revealed nothing, even the pedal bin was empty with a new plastic sack. She closed the door.

The second room was a sparse bedroom, with a single bulb hanging from the ceiling. A single bed with a thin mattress, a side table and a cheap matchwood wardrobe which contained blankets and bed linen. There was nothing to indicate it had been recently occupied.

The third room was larger, with two beds, each with a bare mattress. A larger wardrobe contained the blankets and linen neatly folded, but not washed recently. There was a distinct smell which Daisy immediately identified as gun oil. She found a towel among the linen and after sniffing it, had no doubt, that someone had used this either to wipe a weapon or wipe their hands after handling a weapon. She searched the room, including a careful examination of the two mattresses, but found nothing.

Taking the towel, she went down to the second floor. There she found two large bedrooms with en-suite bathrooms. The heavy curtains were closed, enabling her to use the light.

The beds, which were king size, had ornate mahogany headboards but no bed clothes or signs of use. Each room had two leather armchairs and a small desk. A large French armoire dominated one wall. She searched both rooms but found nothing to indicate recent occupancy. It was now all too obvious that she was too late. She cursed herself for not coming straight back to confront the receptionist after checking the hotel.

Dr Taleb's secretary had lied about Kaminski and cleared her desk. Mary had collected Kaminski outside this house. The food and drink containers proved that at least two people stayed here as recent as yesterday. One of those people was cleaning a weapon. Then there was the burnt piece of paper, that might lead to something.

She found the first floor laid out exactly the same as the one she had just searched. She knew that a search would throw up nothing, these people were too careful. The secretary had obviously warned them of her visit, giving them time to clean up and clear out, before she cleared out herself.

She searched the two bedrooms and again found nothing. It was nearly two thirty, she had told Sid she'd be out in one hour. Time to go. She opened the front door and looked up and down the street. It was quiet. Closing the door, she walked away. She knew Sid would be watching her, but after a careful peer into the shadows she didn't see a thing. Sid was a pro. She never understood how a man with such talent and meticulous eye for detail ended up in jail. She had asked him once and with a wry smile he told her, 'Lady Luck has a habit of swinging both ways.'

CHAPTER 29

It was 3am when Daisy reached her apartment and called Peter Isaacs. This time the call was answered on the first ring. Maybe he was a night reader and a plain common or garden insomniac. She was never to find out.

'Yes?' his voice was calm.

'Have you spoken to the Fisherman?'

'I did, and he didn't take kindly to being disturbed at such a late hour. He made some calls and came back to me within thirty minutes. O'Grady will see you in his shop.'

'Who is he expecting?'

'I didn't give a name, only that the visitor was known to him.'

'Good,' Daisy said. 'There's been a development which needs your immediate attention. I want a house in Symonds Street W1 put under immediate surveillance.'

'The number?'

'Thirty-four.'

'I'll get on to it right away. Anything else?'

'Yes, I'll need to get an early flight to Dublin and I have something to show you, so we must meet before I leave. Jack Farmer should be there also.'

'You don't have the time for a commercial flight. The meeting will be in Farmer's office at eight o'clock, I'll arrange for a jet to take you to Dublin after the meeting. Sleep tight, Daisy.'

'Sleep tight,' she said to Heinz who was snuggling her leg. 'And I suppose you think it's morning already and want your food.'

Putting down his food, she opened the windows to the balcony. It was a warm night so she left them open. Before falling into bed, she arranged for a taxi for seven fifteen.

Within less than a minute she was in a deep, dreamless sleep but it seemed only another minute had passed when she was awoken by her alarm three hours later. That was the moment she promised herself to sleep for a whole twenty-four hours when this was over.

Before the taxi arrived, she had time to shower and change into the Marks & Spencer outfit Nurse Hollis had bought her which was eminently more suitable for her Dublin persona. A double espresso from her De Longi and a microwaved croissant kickstarted her brain and she began thinking of her story for Valentine O'Grady who was by now well aware that the Maggie Maguire he knew in Belfast was a British agent. Fortunately, in the chaos of that last night when her near lifeless body was airlifted out, her cover was never blown. Maggie Maguire was the only name he ever knew her by and she wanted to keep it that way.

Daisy reached Farmer's office at five to eight. Farmer and Isaacs, each with a mug of coffee, were seated facing each other at the conference table, waiting. Both of them looked at her expectedly when she arrived.

Without preamble Farmer nodded to the empty chair at the head of the table and said, 'It's your party, Daisy, help yourself to a coffee.'

'Morning Jack, Peter,' she said. Placing the white plastic bag she was carrying on the table and her briefcase by her chair, she filled her mug with coffee from a Thermos jug and took her seat. Removing the piece of paper she had found in the chimney from her wallet, she passed it to Farmer and said, 'Before I start on the detail, I want this analysed. Look, there's part of a printer's number on it.'

Both men looked at it and nodded in unison. 'It's thick enough to be a map,' Farmer said.

'Thanks, Jack, that's what I thought,' she said. 'I know it's only two alphas and two numbers, but if I remember rightly there's a database for analysing printer's marks, can you get your experts on to it?'

Farmer went to his desk where he put the paper in an evidence envelope, pushed a button on his intercom and waited for a WPC to appear.

Handing her the envelope, he said, 'Take this to Harris in Technical and have him try finding out what it is. We need a copy here, top priority.'

'I hope that you have more for us than a scrap of paper,' Isaacs said.

Daisy smiled and taking the towel from the plastic bag she handed it to him. 'Well, Peter for a start, I have this smelly towel for you.'

Isaacs took it with a look of disdain and sniffed it cautiously. 'Gun oil does have a distinctive smell. Where did you get it?'

Daisy didn't answer, instead she turned to Farmer and said, 'I take it Kaminski hasn't been found?'

Farmer shook his head. 'I've put everybody available on it – hotels, car rentals, airlines the lot, nothing so far.'

'And Len has briefed you on my visit yesterday?'

'If you're referring to the fifty-pound note, yes.'

'That's all?'

Giving her a puzzled look, he said, 'Nothing else, I haven't seen him this morning.'

'Okay then, I'll start with the note.'

'What fifty-pound note?' asked Isaacs.

'There was one in Mary Grey's wallet, the serial number of which was consecutive with four of the notes taken from the dealer who sold the BMW used in the bombing. To me it was a connection and the only positive lead I had.'

Isaacs raised an eyebrow and said, 'Tenuous, to say the least but do go on.'

Daisy knew Isaacs well enough to see he was interested and continued. 'I got Mary's work-sheets from London Quality Taxis and found a lot of her calls were account customers with no cash involved, other than maybe a couple of pounds for a tip. She had a habit of dropping her customer and calling in from that location for her next call, usually within a few minutes.'

'You're losing me, Daisy,' Farmer said. 'You haven't explained exactly why Mary Grey's calls are significant to this enquiry.'

Giving Farmer her full attention, she said, 'Okay, let me explain. Mary said a few words to me before she died which didn't mean anything at the time, but that evening I found what she wanted me to find in her apartment and started to look into her background. I was soon convinced that, in the course of her work she must have recognised a serious criminal from her past, who didn't want to be recognised. The car bomb was a setup, not for Abdullah but to kill her.'

'Well, if that was their intention they certainly succeeded,' Isaacs said. 'Are you saying that we've expended a huge amount of resource for some kind of common gangster hit?'

Glaring at him, Daisy said. 'It was no kind of common hit, Peter. Mary was my friend, and certainly not common. Now, can I get back to the fifty-pound note?'

Isaacs shrugged. 'I suppose you'd better, but keep it simple, we don't appear to be too bright this morning.'

'Mary had only one delay between calls on Monday, that was when she dropped one Mrs Kaminski at the Palace Garden Hotel, in Kensington. She was there for almost fifteen minutes. I thought that odd. The fare was a short one, from number 34 Symonds Street, which is close to Marble Arch, so I decided to check out the house, where I found a dentist had his practice in the basement. His secretary told me that the rest of the house was unoccupied at that moment. The owner lived abroad. The dentist Dr Taleb was a friend of the owner.'

'So, Kaminski was his patient?' Isaacs said.

'According to the secretary, she had an appointment on Monday morning at ten o'clock, for toothache, and choose Dr Taleb from the hotel list of dentists.'

'Which you confirmed?' Isaacs said.

'I confirmed that she was lying. Dr Taleb is on the hotel list, but he's the last name and the furthest from the hotel. It got me thinking that Kaminski had some other reason to visit that house and the dentist was only a cover.'

'What about the fifteen-minute delay?' Farmer asked.

Before checking the dentist list, I spoke to the doorman who knew Mary well. Apparently, Kaminski had left her mobile in the taxi and Mary went to return it. According to Pat Coffey, that's the doorman's name, she was gone about ten minutes. When she was about to drive off, a woman, who must have been Kaminski hurried up and spoke to her. The doorman saw the fifty-pound note change hands.'

'Maybe Kaminski was just happy to get her phone back,' Farmer said.

'No, I think more likely she wanted Mary's name, she already knew the taxi company.'

'I'm sure you're going to tell us why,' Isaacs said.

'This will tell you why,' she said. Taking the VHS cartridge from her briefcase she handed it to Farmer. 'Can you play this, Jack?'

Farmer took it and went to a side table where there was a TV and VHS unit. He put the tape in and returned to his seat.

They watched the tape without a word; when it finished Farmer was about to eject it when Daisy stopped him. 'Play it again and I'll give you a voice over. As you can see it starts at 11:02 hours.'

They watched the Goon exit the lift and go into the suite. 'The Goon is checking for bugs,' Daisy said.

As the time changed to 11:07, they had a full-face view of the Goon leaving the suite and returning to the lift.

The screen read 11:12 when the Goon and man she was now sure was Brum, exited the lift and entered the suite. 'Who's he?' Farmer asked and froze the frame.

Knowing Farmer, she knew she'd be forever and a day explaining just how Brum fitted in, now wasn't the time. So, best keep it simple, she was thinking and said. For the moment, I've named him Mr B. Run the tape, Jack.'

At 11:15 Kaminski leaves the lift, hurries up to the door and enters.

'That has to be Mrs. Kaminski, Mary Grey's fare,' Daisy said.

'How can you tell?' asked Isaacs.

'Wait, and you'll see.'

The corridor was empty and the screen showed 11:17 when another two men left the lift and stopped at the door. One slim, with grey hair and wearing a cashmere coat paused at the door, his face in profile. The second, an obvious heavy.

'I know him,' Farmer said. 'Sean Duffy.'

'The same,' Daisy said. 'He's the drugs connection.'

The screen showed 11:20 when Mary appeared. She paused at the door, knocked and entered.

'That's Mary Grey, you can see that she's carrying a mobile phone, the one Kaminski left in her taxi.'

Both men nodded, but said nothing.

Less than a minute elapsed before Mary reappeared, paused outside the door for a moment, then shook her head and walked slowly towards the lift.

'Now that's a worried look if ever I saw one, wouldn't you agree?' Daisy said.

'Seems like it,' Isaacs said, shifting in his seat.

'There's more,' Daisy said.

Mary had just disappeared into the lift when they saw Kaminski hurrying out of the room and going to the lift.

'She's obviously following Mary,' Daisy said.

It was five minutes before she reappeared and went back into the room.

'Time to catch up with Mary, give her the fifty and get her name, maybe even find out that Mary had a regular early call, Monday to Friday. I found out from the taxi company that a foreign lady, who must have been Kaminski, called them and conned them out of Abdullah's address.' Daisy looked at their faces and knew they were convinced.

The screen read 11:27 when Duffy and his Goon came out of the room and hurried to the lift.

'Duffy doesn't look happy,' Farmer said.

The corridor was empty for another four minutes when they saw Mr B. leave the room followed by Kaminski and the Goon.

'The meeting is adjourned, I think,' Isaacs said. 'You may be right, Daisy, Mary Grey barged into their meeting and recognised either Duffy or the man you call Mr B. Kaminski she already knew and we can rule out the two Goons.'

'She did seem puzzled when she came out,' Daisy said. 'Like she had seen a ghost. Maybe she did, but I'd rule out Duffy. If she'd recognised him, he wasn't in any compromising situation. It was just a meeting. No, my money is on Mr B.'

Isaacs smiled and said, 'Come on, Daisy, you're not saying that he's a ghost, he didn't look in any way supernatural to me.'

'Metaphorically speaking, Peter, to her he's a ghost from her past, a dangerous criminal she and everyone else thought to be dead.'

'She had a past? Tell us.'

'It's a long story, Peter, one that can be told when we have the time. For the present, the fact that she recognised Mr B. signed her death warrant. Her arrangement with Dr Abdullah made it all that easier for them to use him as a smoke screen.'

'Okay, enlighten us, Daisy, just who is this Mr B?' Farmer asked.

'I've no proof, but it seems likely that he's a serious crim who somehow faked his death and was declared legally dead over twenty years ago. Name of Zar Brum. I searched what's left of his file with DCI Sandys yesterday and he also thinks it's a definite possibility. Mary Grey knew him and was killed because she recognised him. The last words she said to me were: *"He's alive."'*

Giving her a look of disbelief, Farmer said, 'Bloody Hell! How sure are you on this?'

'Pretty sure. Arthur Clay saw the video last night. He was a DCI in the Flying Squad and knew Brum well. He recognised him from his walk.'

Isaacs shifted in his seat and said, 'If as you say it is this man Brum, Daisy, just where is all this leading us? What are we looking at here?'

'Connections, Peter. One: Pakistan. Your source said that the Jihadists were using a drug trafficker to ship their weapons from Pakistan. We know Zentek have a facility in Karachi and one of their crates was used for a shipment they know nothing about. We also know Kaminski was in Karachi recently. Two: Narcos. My information is Duffy is part of the Minihane Drugs Cartel. Kaminski and Brum were meeting him in the hotel. What else could they have been talking about? Three, Jihadists: Kaminski was meeting them in Symonds Street.'

Isaacs lifted an eyebrow and looked from Farmer back to Daisy before replying. 'It was three o'clock in the morning when you asked me to put a watch on the house. May I ask why the delay?'

'I wanted to have a look inside the house first.'

Farmer groaned. 'You're not telling us you broke in. For God's sake, Daisy, have you forgotten all about due process?'

'There was no time for due process in this case, Jack. Anyway, I didn't exactly break in. I had a keyman facilitate my entrance.'

'We're not hearing you, Daisy, but go on,' Isaacs said.

Daisy shrugged and continued. 'I started with Dr Taleb's surgery. As I expected the secretary's appointment book had no mention of Kaminski. Whoever she had visited in the house, it was not the dentist. Searching her desk, I found all the drawers empty. I guess the secretary won't be turning up for work today. My visit must have spooked her.'

'You searched the rest of the house and found what?'

'Every room empty, Peter, as if they hadn't been used for months. I found ashes in the study chimney, which is where I found the piece of paper. No sign of occupation except for a bedroom in the Garret. I would swear it had occupants in the past day or so, that's where I found the smelly towel.'

'Did you find anything else to confirm that?' Farmer was leaving Isaacs to ask the questions.

'There was a dustbin in the yard full of takeaway containers from the Queen of Sheba Tandoori, empty Coke cans and water bottles. The fridge had packs of Diet Coke and mineral water.'

'Asian food and no alcohol, interesting, your assessment being what?' asked Isaacs.

'Taleb's secretary was a sort of gatekeeper to the house. She knew the rest of the house was empty and she had the keys to the upper part. There would be a continuous stream of genuine patients during the day to be directed downstairs, while by arrangement special visitors would probably be met in the hall.'

'Neat arrangement,' Isaacs said. 'Anyone watching the house would just see every visitor use the intercom and ask for Dr Taleb.

What about the dentist, is he in on it?'

'It wouldn't make any sense to involve him, would it? They only had to plant the secretary on him and use the house whenever she told them it was safe to do so.'

'The secretary, did you get her name, nationality?' Issacs asked.

'Her name is Miss Patel; my guess would be Pakistani.'

With all the secrecy we have to assume the worst case, Islamic terrorists were using that house, for their meetings,' Isaacs said.

'So, is that it?' Farmer growled. 'All you've got for your trouble is a smelly towel and a piece of paper. The safe house is blown and the birds have flown. Nice going, Daisy.'

'That's about the size of it, Jack,' Daisy said. 'But we know Kaminski was one of the special visitors which makes Brum and maybe Duffy connected to whatever they are planning.'

Isaacs shook his head and said, 'Unfortunately we'll never know just what Duffy was up to.'

'I'm sure O'Grady can persuade him to tell me, Peter.'

Isaacs smiled and said, 'If you can, it'll be a first. Duffy was shot dead in his home in Dublin in the early hours of this morning.'

Slapping the table, Daisy said, 'Jesus! Peter when were you going to tell me this, when I was on the plane?'

Giving her a cold look, Isaacs said, 'I'm telling you now. You can forget Duffy, he was in a bad business. Maybe he got too big for his boots, or maybe he was tied to the wrong mob. There's been a spate of tit-for-tat killings in Dublin during the past few months.'

Daisy's mind raced as she considered this unexpected turn of events. The only plus she could think of was she didn't have to risk meeting O'Grady.

Breaking the silence, Farmer said, 'You're holding the ball, Daisy.'

Turning to him, she said, 'We can only use what we have, Jack. To start with we need stills made from the video to circulate these faces to the Border Force. At least we can try and stop them leaving the country. With Duffy out of the picture, our only hope is to find Brum, Kaminski or Miss Patel from Symonds Street. I suggest we talk to Dr Taleb first, he may be able to give us a line on Miss Patel. There's also that piece of paper I gave you. I know it's a longshot, but can you put a rush on it? We need a break.'

CHAPTER 30

Saturday 7ᵗʰ September

Awatery dawn was brightening the sky when Rashid, Nizar and Karim left the modest semi-detached house in Hounslow, where they had stayed since the previous evening. For Rashid, who had been renting the house, which was directly on the flight path to Heathrow, this had been an unexpected development. Iqbal had ordered the move from Symonds Street, *'for security reasons'* he had said, insisting to Rashid that they stay with him.

A short drive took them past New Brentford Cemetery and into Lampton Park. It was just gone 06:00 when Rashid parked the van and waited. He had checked out the park at this hour, several times during the past two weeks, and each time had found it empty.

Satisfied that today was no different he said to the two men, 'We can walk from here, it's not far.'

Rashid led the way to a play area partly screened by a high laurel hedge which had a slide, a climbing frame, a toddler's waltzer and a couple of bench seats. Indicating that they should sit, Rashid said, 'This is on the direct flight path to Heathrow. The international flights start arriving from six fifteen every morning.'

Nizar looked at the empty sky and said, 'Iqbal showed us a map of the flight path.'

Rashid laughed derisively and said, 'You can see Iqbal's never been operational. Never trust a map, you have to see for yourself, that's why I've brought you here, all the flights will pass over our heads.'

'The target must be American,' Karim said.

Looking at his watch, Rashid said, 'Two American flights will be passing in the next ten minutes, an American Airlines flight out of Nairobi and a United Airlines flight from New York. Tomorrow will be the same, you can take your pick.'

They sat, in silence, looking at the sky for five minutes before they saw the first glimmer of lights approaching. In less than a minute the plane was passing over their heads.

'That's a British Airways flight,' Rashid said.

Nizar, watching its path with professional interest said, 'How can you tell?'

Rashid answered proudly. 'I've been watching here for the past two weeks and memorised the tail markings. The next one should be United Airlines.'

Obviously impressed, Karim said, 'You've done well, Rashid.'

Pleased, Rashid said, 'Like I said, you've got to check the details. Here it comes now, right on time.'

Nizar stood and watched the approaching plane. Nizar stood behind him in his number two position. Both were assessing the trajectory of their target. When it passed overhead both men pivoted as one and followed its path.

'I checked it out,' Rashid said. 'It's an Airbus 300.'

'It's big,' Nizar said, 'much bigger than a Soviet gunship. To succeed we must fire the two missiles.'

'Two big hot engines,' Karim said. 'We can hit them both.'

'Can you do that?' Rashid asked.

'Yes,' said Nizar. 'When there are two gunships, you must take them both or the survivor will kill you.'

'Good, that's it then,' said Rashid. 'Tonight, I'm to take you to Brentford Lock to meet Iqbal and his bodyguard. A boat will take you to verify and collect the weapons. Once we have them in my van,

Iqbal and his bodyguard will disappear and I'm in charge of the operation. My job is to get you here tomorrow morning to do your stuff, and get you back to your ship afterwards.'

Seeing the look on their faces Rashid laughed and said, 'Don't worry, chaps, this is no suicide mission. The Sheik values your skills. I have a plan, but first we'll go to my cousin's restaurant in Southall for something to eat. Afterwards we'll come back here and I'll show how we're going to get clear of this place.'

Veleta and Frank were finishing off what passed for an English breakfast in a café on the Caledonian Road.

Pushing his plate aside, Veleta said, 'Thanks, Frank, that's probably the last decent meal I'll have for a while.'

Frank carefully wiped the remains of his egg with a piece of bread before replying. 'If you're still not sure what to do, Harry, maybe tipping the cops would be best, we know exactly when they'll be at the house.'

Veleta shook his head. 'You know we don't deal with cops, Frank. We've spent too long getting clear. If we deal with them now there's a good chance we'll be the ones banged up and Brum will give them the slip. I can't take that chance. Brum has to settle for Mary. It'll be dangerous so it's okay by me if you don't want any part of it. You've done enough already.'

Leaning forward, Frank said in a low voice, 'No bloody way, Harry, we're in this together, like always. What's your plan?'

Veleta took a sip from his cup and looked into it for a moment before replying. 'Okay, from what we overheard the boat is arriving at ten o'clock tonight. It'll be dark enough on the river by then and the tide will be right to land a boat at the jetty. We get into the house before they arrive and wait. When the boat leaves it'll mean Brum's completed his deal. That's when we hit them. We can handle it, there'll be only three of them.'

Frank's eyes widened as he said, 'What about those missiles, Harry? Those bastards are planning to take down an aircraft and kill an awful lot of people, we have to do something about that.'

Veleta put his cup down and said, 'Don't worry, Frank, I know what we've got to do and I have a plan that should take care of business, but we'll need someone to cover our backs. I was thinking of Daisy Clowser, if she'll play ball. She acts like she can handle herself and she's not exactly a cop.'

A relieved Frank nodded enthusiastically. 'Yeah, you're right. She did say she wouldn't stop until she settled for Mary. Maybe she'd welcome the chance; either way we'll need hardware. This is no knife or cosh job.'

'That's for sure, what can you get?'

Frank lowered his voice and said, 'I have a couple of sawn-offs stashed away. We have to get close for this, so they'll be just the job.'

'What about shells?'

'I've a box of number two.'

With a grim smile Veleta said, 'They should take care of business. What in God's name are you doing with that kind of hardware?'

Frank grinned. 'I had a bit of bother with a gang of Toerags, trying to sell me protection, so I persuaded them to go elsewhere.'

Pushing back his chair and standing, Veleta said, 'I can imagine. Okay, right now I've got things to do. First I'm going to visit Shack in Gospel Oak.'

With a worried look Frank said, 'Benny's an old man, Harry, you're not going to…?'

Veleta smiled. 'No, Frank, I'm not going to do anything to him. He must have set that clock and he's going to tell me what he knows about all this. After that he's going to set the last clock for me. Later, I'll need a space to work. Do you still have that garage in York Way?'

A relieved Frank said, 'Yeah, I keep two limos in it and service the taxi.'

'Good. When I've done with Shack, I'll do some shopping in Camden Town. We need to change into dark clothes like the old days. I'll buy something for myself and a couple of balaclavas at Millets. Then I'll need you to take me to Leytonstone, to visit the chemist, he'll have what I want. We'll meet back at the office. I'll call you with the time.'

'I'll be waiting, you need the taxi now?

'No, I'll take the Tube.'

An hour later Veleta stood in front of the shop in Gospel Oak. The façade and window display had not changed one iota in the twenty years since he last saw it. Faded gold lettering announced the premises of Benjamin Shack established 1918. The same old collection of clocks and clock mechanisms, including a couple of silver fobs and one nice half hunter, was there.

It was nine-thirty when Veleta pushed the door and entered. A loud bell signalled his arrival. The shop was empty. He pushed the deadbolt and flipped the sign from open to closed. The smell of old wood and polish permeated the shop. In every available space there was a clock, either attached to the wall or free-standing, grandfathers and grandmothers, the combined ticking of which merged into a definite drumming. He paused for a moment to look into a slim wall-mounted display case containing a collection of old fob-watches, complete with chunky silver chains.

There was a glass-topped counter which also served as a display case, full of old watches and mechanisms. Veleta knew that the room behind was a workshop and he was probably being watched through the one-way mirror attached to the wall. He also knew there was no exit at the rear of the premises, nowhere to run, so he stood in front of the counter, hit the customer bell and waited.

Benjamin Shack the Third eventually shuffled out of the workshop door and stood behind the counter, staring at him through steel-rimmed glasses. He was a shrivelled-up old man, well past his seventies, but his eyes were like gimlets. If he was afraid of what he saw he hid it well.

'Harry, is that you?'

Placing his gloved hands flat on the counter, Veleta leaned forward and said, 'Take a good look, Benny, *be sure*, it's been a long time.'

'It's you all right, Harry,' said Shack, stepping back from the counter. 'What do you want this time?'

Without answering Veleta went over to the display case of fob-watches and slipped his hand under the bottom to find the release catch. The unit was hinged and swung smoothly away from the wall to reveal an alcove with four dusty glass shelves, three of which were empty except for age-marked outlines of previous occupancy, each one an identical rectangle of dust. On the fourth shelf there were three outlines and a single carriage clock. Veleta took the clock and placed it on the counter, saying in a low voice, 'I've come for my clocks, Benny, there should be two left, where's the other one?'

Shack shook his head. 'There's only one left, Harry, you know that I delivered one to you last Tuesday. I watch the news, Harry. I know what happened. That was a bad business.'

Veleta replied in a voice little more than a whisper, 'You're mistaken, Benny, you delivered nothing to me. Last Tuesday I was fifteen hundred miles away.'

Shack shuffled his feet uneasily. 'The woman, Harry, she told me you sent her.'

Veleta shook his head emphatically. 'I never sent any woman, describe her.'

Shack, eyes widening behind his glasses, tried another backward step but was stopped by the wall.

'She came in on Tuesday morning, she was waiting for me to open, told me you had sent her. She wanted one of your clocks. A foreign bird, black hair, black eyes, a lot taller than me, she had an accent, east European, I'd say.'

Veleta gave a harsh laugh. 'Would you? Everyone's taller than you, Benny. What exactly did she say?'

Shack's watering eyes swept the ceiling for a few second before answering in a faltering voice. 'Her *exact words,* were: Harry sent me for one his Messerlie clocks, there should be two left.'

Veleta nodded, then, taking the clock from the glass top he walked around the counter and stood by the workshop door a few feet from Shack. 'You don't look too good, Benny. You'd better sit down.'

Shack, with the resigned look of a man going to the gallows, shuffled uneasily past him, into the workshop. Veleta followed.

Shack's workshop, which was about half the size of the shop, had a workbench running along one wall. Mounted on it were a lathe, a drill press and a number of precision vices. The remainder was clear space covered in green linoleum except for an inspection magnifier-lamp. Dozens of delicate hand-tools were attached the wall. The only furniture in the room was an old wooden swivel chair, in front of the bench, two equally ancient high-backed dining chairs, which stood against the wall opposite and several grey steel cabinets which stood against the end wall. Veleta placed his clock on the bench, then crossed to the chairs and pulled them into the centre of the room. 'Sit down, Benny,' he said, pushing one of the chairs towards Shack, before sitting himself on the other.

A wary Shack moved his chair out of arm's reach and sat.

Veleta smiled at the old man's caution. 'Relax, Benny, I'm not going to bite you, now tell me, what time did you set it for?'

Shack, his hands gripping the seat of his chair, said, 'Like she told me to. I set the contacts for eight forty-five exactly. You remember, Harry, that with the Messerlie, that would serve for a.m. or p.m. I thought that a bit odd, but that's what she insisted on, to the second, she said.'

Veleta leaned forward on his chair and said, 'You know what the clock was used for, don't you Benny?'

Shack shifted in his chair and nodded. 'Yeah, I do now, the eight forty-five wasn't p.m. for a robbery, like she said, it was for that car bomb last Wednesday morning.'

Veleta stood up abruptly and stood over the old man. 'That's why I'm here, Benny. You remember Mary, don't you?'

Shack, whose watery eyes widened, replied, 'Sure, I remember Mary, she came in for you a couple of times. Lovely girl, she was.'

'Mary was driving that taxi.'

Shack's head dropped and he swayed in his seat. What little colour that was left drained out of his face, his voice just a whisper when he said, 'God in Heaven, Harry, what have you done?'

Thinking Shack was about to faint, Veleta leaned over and gripped the old man's shoulder. 'It wasn't me, Benny,' he said. 'I've told you already, last Wednesday I was fifteen hundred miles away.'

Shack looked up, confused, and muttered, 'Then *who* sent her, Harry? She knew exactly what she wanted. Nobody knew about those clocks but you, me and Brum and he's been dead these twenty years.'

Veleta held Shack's shoulder until he was steady in his seat. 'That's what we all thought, but it looks like he fooled us all. You'd recognise Brum's voice if you heard it again, wouldn't you Benny?'

Shack with a puzzled look replied, 'His voice? Too right I would. I'd know it if I heard it in the dark.'

'Right, and so would anyone who knew him well. A man can change his face but not his voice, and Brum has a distinctive voice. Last evening, I heard Brum's voice again and it wasn't a ghost. The bastard's alive. It was he who sent the woman for the clock. When did she collect it?'

Still seated, Shack said, 'That same afternoon, she took the clock and gave me a grand in fifties. Then she said to me, 'You remember the rule, keep your mouth shut.'

Veleta went over to the bench and regarded the clock for a moment, then taking it in his hand he said, 'Whose rule was that, Benny?'

'It was Brum's rule,' Shack said, standing up shakily. 'You know like*, all squealers die*, were his exact words.'

'If I'm right about the voice and he's behind all this, Benny, my advice to you is to close the shop today and disappear for a while. If the cops got to know what you've done, you'd die inside. It's not a good place to be for an old man, Benny. That's if Brum doesn't get to you first.' Veleta lifted the clock from the bench and said, 'This is number twenty, Benny, the last one. Before you go, I want you to set it for me.'

Daisy, accompanied by Farmer and DI Sandys, went straight from the meeting to Symonds Street. Farmer's driver double parked outside. Letting them out, he went to find parking. They were standing there as Dr Taleb approached the door. Daisy had never seen him before that moment, but for some reason he matched her image of a dentist.

He was a neat man, slim, medium height of middle eastern appearance. Maybe Egyptian or Jordanian, she thought. He wore a good suit and his shoes were highly polished. He looked at Farmer and Sandys, both sizeable men, now crowding him, with some apprehension before addressing Daisy. 'May I help you?'

'Are you Doctor Taleb?'

Nodding, he said, 'I am.'

'Dr Taleb, I'm WPC Denton, this is Commander Farmer and Detective Chief Inspector Sandys from New Scotland Yard. We would like to ask you some questions about this house.'

Dr Taleb looked at them calmly. 'May I see some ID, gentlemen?'

Warrant cards were produced, which were carefully scrutinised. Nodding his satisfaction, he said, 'They seem in order, but we can't talk in the street, can we?' and pressed the intercom.

The four of them crowded the door for a long moment before Taleb said, 'That's strange, Miss Patel is always here before me.'

Daisy, who would have been more surprised if Miss Patel was there, asked, 'Do you have keys?'

'Of course,' he replied, producing them from a pocket in his attaché case and opening the door.

They followed him down the stairs, to the windowless reception – which was in darkness. Taleb switched on the lights and found chairs for them before seating himself behind the receptionist's desk. 'Now perhaps you will tell me what this is all about. Miss Patel is never late and she said nothing to indicate she would be late; it's a nuisance. I have my first patient at nine-thirty.'

Farmer settled his bulk in his chair and nodded for Daisy to proceed. Sandys remained standing.

Daisy took the chair directly in front of Taleb and said, 'Dr Taleb we are investigating a double murder and we believe one of your patients may be involved.'

The doctor's eyes rounded slightly, before asking in the same calm voice, 'Which patient?'

Daisy was expecting more reaction, but then she thought, *This man is a dentist, isn't he? Therefore remaining calm would be his stock in trade.* 'A Mrs Kaminski, she was here last Monday.'

Taleb looked at each of them in turn before replying, 'I'm afraid you're mistaken. I don't have any patient of that name.'

'Are you sure?' Daisy asked. 'Do you know all of your patients?'

Taleb shrugged. 'Not all but, if, as you say, Mrs Kaminski was here four days ago, I would remember, it's an unusual name.'

'Then, how is it that your secretary Miss Patel confirmed to me yesterday after consulting her appointments book that Mrs Kaminski was a patient and that she was here on Monday at ten o'clock?'

'Then she made a mistake. Look.' Taleb reached for the appointments book and flicked impatiently through the pages. 'Monday, here you can see for yourself, no Mrs Kaminski.'

Daisy, who didn't need to see what she already knew, decided to test him further and said, 'Look, Doctor Taleb, we know for sure that Kaminski was in this house on Monday morning because she ordered a taxi from here.'

Snapping the appointments book shut, Taleb said, 'If you know that, why are you asking me?'

'I wanted to see if you knew, Doctor, and I'm now satisfied that you didn't. When does Miss Patel normally arrive for work?'

Taleb looked at his watch before saying, 'Nine o'clock, she's very reliable.'

Daisy squinted at her watch, saw it was nine-fifteen and said, 'But not today. Did she say she might be late today?'

Taleb shook his head. 'No, she definitely did not.'

'Can you call her? Find out if she's on her way.'

'Of course,' Taleb said. 'Is she in some kind of trouble?'

'She might be, but we need to speak to her urgently.'

'Just a moment, I'll find her number.' Taleb riffled through the Rolodex, checked a card then the one before and the one after before saying, 'Her address is missing.'

No surprise, that, Daisy was thinking. 'Do you have her personnel file?'

'Of course, it'll be in the accountant's drawer.' He crossed over to a grey steel filing cabinet and pulled out the middle drawer and fingered through the folders; there were only about six folders and he checked each one.

'It's not here,' he said, shaking his head with a puzzled look. 'It was here yesterday. The accountant would've needed it to enter her wages details.'

'How long has she been working for you?' Daisy asked.

'About eight weeks, she was a friend of my previous secretary who vouched for her.'

'Why did your previous secretary leave?'

Dr Taleb put the folders back in the drawer and slammed it, harder than needed, before answering. 'She had to return suddenly to Pakistan, there was some family crisis.'

Family crisis my foot, more likely orders from someone too dangerous to refuse, Daisy was thinking as she said, 'Dr Taleb, Miss Patel lied to me about Kaminski, which can only mean that she herself was involved in the criminal activity that was going on in this house.'

Dr Taleb's eyelids flicked nervously. 'Criminal activity? That's impossible. Besides myself, the house is empty for eleven months of the year.'

Farmer cut in. 'We'd like to verify that for ourselves. Who is the owner?'

'Mr Karim Said, a business man based in Amman, Jordan, also my cousin and I can assure you that he is not involved in any criminal activity and neither am I. Now I have my first patient due in ten minutes and I must call the agency for a temp.' As he spoke the sound of Farmer's old police car bells filled the room. Farmer found his phone and answered. After listening for a moment, he nodded and said, 'Yes, good, fifteen minutes, call Mr Isaacs.'

Standing up he said, 'Thank you, Doctor, I don't think you'll be seeing Miss Patel again. We have to search the house as a matter of urgency. Do we need the bother of a search warrant?'

Dr Taleb, obviously relieved, replied, 'Of course you don't, Commander, there's nothing to find. I assure you.'

'Good, we'll need a key to the front door, no need to bother you further.'

Producing his keys, Taleb said, 'Take mine, I have a spare set.'

Farmer gave them to DCI Sandys, saying, 'Len, stay here and get a forensics team in upstairs. Tell them not to bother the doctor, but check Miss Patel's office and desk for prints.' Turning to Daisy, he said, 'We need to go.'

CHAPTER 31

When they returned to Farmer's office, they found Peter Isaacs examining an A2-size map he had laid out on Farmer's conference table. It was coloured in shades of green and yellow. Looking up, he said, 'There's no doubt that this is where your piece of paper came from, Daisy. The material and the printer numbers match.'

'What is it?' Farmer asked, leaning over it.

'It's a noise-tracking map for all westerly flights landing at Heathrow,' Isaacs said, running a finger along a path from Chiswick to Heathrow Airport. 'See, it's coded in shades of yellow, light green and dark green, each shade indicates the aircraft's altitude on its approach.'

Daisy, leaning over the map, said, 'I get it. Yellow is above 6,000 feet, light green 3,000 to 6,000 feet, dark green is below 3,000 feet. Why in God's name do they issue such information? Look, anywhere between Kew Bridge and Heathrow the flights are below 3,000 feet.'

'According to the notes that came with it, it's produced to satisfy house buyers, estate agents and environmentalists,' Isaacs said.

'And your would-be Jihadist who has access to a surface-to-air missile,' growled Farmer.

'Yeah,' Daisy said. 'Thanks to Kaminski and Brum, they now have them.'

'If the Symonds address was used to house the shooters until last night, forensics should find some trace,' Farmer said.

'It's never that easy,' Daisy said. 'They must have been planning to move out anyway. Patel must have panicked when I called. She tried to be too clever mentioning the referral from the hotel. She should have known that I'd check it.'

'You took your time about checking it,' Farmer growled. 'A few hours earlier and we might have nabbed them.'

'You're absolutely right, Jack, no excuses, I blew it, but the whole set-up looked so damned respectable.'

'No point in apportioning blame,' Isaacs said. 'We have a major threat and I don't see a way forward other than going public on this and hope it might frighten Brum and Kaminski enough for them to abort the handover. I'll have to report to the PM. We'll need thousands of troops in order to police the flight corridor.'

The four of them looked at each other in silence as they contemplated that prospect before Daisy's mobile broke the spell. She didn't recognise the caller's number when it flashed on her screen, but answered it and said, 'Hello.'

'It's Veleta, we should meet.'

Aware that all eyes were on her she lowered voice and said, 'I'm busy at the moment, is it urgent?'

'I know you're busy, we need to talk about Brum.'

'When and where?'

'Twelve o'clock at Whitley's in Queensway, wait outside Costa. Come alone.'

'I'll be there, alone.' The line cut.

The two men looked at her, waiting.

'Hold off on the PM, Peter, there's a third party involved in this that I've neglected to mention so far. I had a feeling he knew more than he was saying.'

'Who is he?' asked Farmer.

'Who he is, is not important, Jack. It's what he might know that is. I'm meeting him in thirty minutes.'

Daisy entered Whitley's through the south entrance, just around the corner from the Bayswater Clinic she had been taken to only three days ago. *Let's hope this is not going to end up in a return visit,* she thought.

She was familiar with the layout of the mall. In fact, she could remember when Whitley's was an old-fashioned department store. If Veleta had taken a position on the upper floor he could watch her approach and ensure she wasn't being followed.

It had just gone twelve. The place was busy with Saturday shoppers. Every nationality under the sun seem to be represented in the Bayswater area and from the look of the faces in the mall that morning half of them must be here, she was thinking. She found Costa, but there was no sign of Veleta.

She waited by the door for all of five minutes thinking that she must look like some hopeful waiting for her date. She was looking in the wrong direction when she felt a touch on her elbow and Veleta was beside her. She saw he was wearing the same suit as before but had changed his shirt for a lighter shade of blue which looked like it had just come out of the box.

'You're alone, no cops?' She saw something in his eyes, something which was not so apparent on their first meeting, which made her shiver.

Nodding, she said, 'I'm alone.'

'Good, go inside find a quiet table.'

Fortunately, at the time of day, although the food restaurants were busy, it was a quiet enough period for Costa. Daisy found an empty table far enough away from its nearest neighbour.

Veleta took the chair facing the door and said nothing until she had ordered two mugs of coffee, brought them to the table and sat facing him.

Taking a sip from her drink, she looked at him expectantly.

Veleta returned her stare, his eyes seeming to search for some sign, then taking a sip from his mug he said, 'You've been a good friend to Mary, but she always thought that you were some kind of cop.'

'Is that such a bad thing, Harry, being a cop?' she asked.

'In this case, yes. What are you, Daisy?'

Looking at him, she was thinking this was one of these times when a lie was in order and said, 'Never a cop, Harry, military intelligence, but that was years ago, now I'm private.'

'But you're working with the cops now, why?'

'Like you said, Harry, Mary was my friend and like I've already told you I won't stop until I settle for her. Isn't that reason enough?'

Giving her a thoughtful look Veleta nodded and said, 'Reason enough.'

Lifting her mug, Daisy said, 'You've got something to tell me, Harry?'

Veleta's eyes swept the restaurant before replying. 'How much of this have you figured out already?'

Daisy took a deliberately long sip from her coffee before putting the mug down and saying in a low voice, 'I'm not telling you anything, Harry, until I get something from you.'

Veleta leaned forward and whispered, 'Trust me. I can give you a big something. Now, tell me what you know.'

Looking into his eyes and speaking in what she hoped was a menacing tone she said, 'You'd better have something big, Harry. The reason Mary was killed is that Zar Brum is alive and she recognised him.'

'That's all you know?

'I know a lot more, Harry. Brum is doing some weapons deal with a group of Jihadists. With him is a woman named Kaminski, who is a professional smuggler and there's at least one heavy.'

'And?'

'The Jihadists have left the house they were using, in a big hurry, either something spooked them or it could also mean they are ready to act'.

'How did you find out about Brum?'

'I read Mary's Delia file, or should I say Gloria's file, before Frank arrived to collect it and followed up the stories in it. Forensics found a piece from the bomb timer which was identified as coming from a Messerlie clock. Digging in the files and asking the right people I found out about Mary's family background, which convinced me that Mary was the bomber's target. I followed the route she took last Monday. She saw Brum at the Palace Garden Hotel. I managed to get some CCTV footage of the scene. Brum was identified by a colleague of mine who had dealings with him in the old days. He had no doubts it was Brum. You don't have any doubts either, do you Harry?

'No, I don't,' Veleta said. 'I was close to Brum last night, heard him talking, it was him all right. To be sure I visited the watchmaker this morning, he confirmed it.'

'Harry, there was another man with Brum in the video, one Sean Duffy. He was shot dead in Dublin last night. That may be nothing to do with Brum but if it is and he's removing witnesses, the watchmaker might be next.'

Veleta's eyes bored into her as he said, 'I've already warned him. You've done well, Daisy; the question is can I trust you?'

'Mary trusted me. She wanted me to read Gloria's file, Harry, and her last words were that I could trust you. Look Harry, as I've already told you, I'm only interested in the here and now, the past is dead and as far as I'm concerned and if there's a good outcome from this it'll stay dead.'

'I hear you, Daisy. As you said Brum is supplying arms to the Jihadists. The deal is to be done tonight and I know the where and the when.'

'Russian SAM missiles, right?'

Shaking his head, Veleta said, 'Not Russian, American, Stingers. You know a lot, Daisy.'

'I know they're planning to down one or more passenger aircraft on the flight path to Heathrow. There could be hundreds of lives at risk. For God's sake Harry, you have to tell me.'

'It'll be your job to stop the Jihadists, Daisy, Brum is my business. I don't want any interference from the cops.'

With a brittle laugh Daisy said, 'This is my party, Harry. I've been given a free hand. My priority are the missiles and the Jihadists, just give them to me and you can deal with Brum, any way you wish, that is if you're sure you can handle it.'

'If you can keep your end up, Daisy, I can handle it.'

'Tell me what you want me to do.'

'Okay. The house, where the changeover will take place, backs onto the river. It has its own jetty. Brum has arranged for a boat to bring the Jihadists to the jetty at ten tonight. There'll be four of them. Brum will be in the house, waiting to hand over the crate containing the missiles. They'll do their deal, then carry the crate to the boat. I want you to let them get to the middle of the river before you take them.'

'I know they're armed, Harry, there might be some noise.'

With a grim smile, Veleta said, 'I was counting on that.'

Daisy smiled and said, 'You like decoys, don't you?'

'You're a smart woman, Daisy. Can you arrange for an intercept boat to be in the vicinity of Kew Bridge at nine?'

'That I can. What about the house? Brum's house, is it?'

Veleta ignored the question. 'Do you know the Baghdad Café in Praed Street?'

'No, but I can find it.'

'Be there at eight o'clock, come alone, we'll go to the house together. Do we have a deal?'

Looking at him over her mug she said softly, 'Yes Harry, we have a deal.'

Veleta gave her a not unfriendly smile, drained his mug and stood up. 'That's it then, wait five minutes before you leave. Until tonight then.'

CHAPTER 32

It was two fifteen when Veleta pushed the door and entered Shack's shop. The door alarm momentarily drowned the sound of the ticking clocks. The shop was empty. Hitting the bell on the counter, he waited. This time nobody came. He hit it again. The only sound came from the clocks.

The hairs on the back of his neck warned him of trouble, maybe big trouble for him if he didn't act fast. Going to the street door he flipped the sign from open to closed before springing the lock's night bolt and pulling the blind down. No time for surprise visitors. He'd wipe the front of the door for prints before he left.

He found Shack slumped in a chair by his workbench, his hands, grasping at his chest were covered in blood, his mouth open with half his lower denture protruding, his eyes had the puzzled look of sudden death.

Veleta had seen knife wounds before. This one had been done by an expert, who knew exactly where to thrust the blade for instant death. Shack wouldn't have felt a thing. He felt the dead man's neck; the skin was still warm. Shack had said come at two. If he'd been on time, he might have saved him. *Too bad for Benny,* Veleta was thinking. Then the thought struck him – maybe he had interrupted the killer, maybe the killer was still here. He looked for something to use as a weapon and found a claw hammer on the bench. Holding it in front of him he went to the back of the shop, where he found a closet-sized room with a WC and wash basin. It was empty. There was nowhere else for anyone to hide and no back door.

Wiping the hammer, he put it down and began looking around. Benny had said it would be ready. He found it in the roll-top desk. It was small and tightly wrapped in multiple layers of duct tape. A short steel wire ending attached to a key ring and four coloured wires stripped at the ends were the only protrusions. Attached to it by a rubber band was a square of white card. Veleta read what were probably Shack's last words: 'Same colour codes as always, connect them to your stuff. Pull the ring, the contacts make in three minutes.'

Kaminski watched all of her clothes, down to the skin, that she was wearing at the watchmaker's, burn on the garden barbecue. 'That's the second set I've had to burn this week, this job is beginning to get expensive.'

'Don't forget the knife,' said Thomas.

'It's already in the dishwasher.'

'If Iqbal tries any tricks tonight, you'll need more than a knife.'

'Don't worry, I have something. Did you bring down the cases?'

'Yeah,' he said. 'They're on the kitchen table.'

Nodding for Thomas to follow, she went into the kitchen and opened the first aluminium case, which had three automatics, magazines and two boxes of cartridges in their foam cut-outs. She selected a SIG Sauer P226 and handed it Thomas, saying, 'This is chambered for .40 Smith & Wesson, it should do.'

Thomas weighted the pistol in his hand and nodded approval before putting the items on the table. 'What about Kramer?'

With a snigger she handed him a .32 Colt. 'This is his. It won't stop much but it makes him feel brave carrying it.'

With a dark look Thomas snatched the gun and growled, 'Up close it'll do the job, he likes its size, it's light and easy to conceal. What about you?'

Kaminski opened the second case and removed the Scorpion

machine pistol from its foam cut-out. Caressing her fingers over the matt-black casing, she almost purred when she said, 'This little beauty is real killing machine. A single burst can cut a man in half.'

'You know how to use it?' Thomas asked dubiously.

Ignoring the question Kaminski took a leather shoulder sling from the case and fitted it to the butt of the Scorpion. When she slipped it on her shoulder, the pistol hung level with her hip, allowing her hand to come naturally to the grip. With a swift movement she lifted the gun, pointed it in Thomas's direction and said, 'This was my service pistol and it's seen action.' Seeing the look of alarm in his eyes, she let the gun drop by her side and with a wicked smile said, 'See, hanging like this it's always ready and easily concealed by my coat. Where's Kramer?'

'Inside watching the cricket on Sky. Barbados are playing.'

Putting the Scorpion on the table she said, 'Poor bastard, he works so hard.'

Thomas smirked. 'As he keeps telling you, he finds the stuff, you just smuggle it. Without him, you'd be nothing.'

'That's what he thinks. If we get through tonight, he'll be able to watch the cricket live in Jamaica in a couple of days. Are you all packed?'

'Sure.'

'Be bloody sure,' she snapped. 'Don't leave a thing and clean up your room. I'll be with Kramer.'

Besides money, and a regular supply of young whores, cricket seemed to be Brum's only interest in life. He was engrossed in the match when she entered the room. Looking at the screen, with the spectators in their whites and panamas, the cloudless sky, a colour blue she never saw in Europe, Kaminski felt a sudden urge to be far away from this place.

Without taking his eyes from the screen Kramer asked, 'Is it done?'

She said harshly, 'It's done, the old man could have fingered me, and that's not a risk I like to take.'

Kramer turned and gave her a thoughtful look before saying, 'You brought it on yourself, Kaminski, none of this would have been necessary if you hadn't called that taxi, I won't forget that.'

Giving him a withering look, she replied, 'Maybe, if you had bothered telling me you had issues with taxi drivers in London, I'd have left them alone altogether.'

Kramer ignored the comment. Instead, speaking in low menacing voice, which she knew was his practiced method of intimidation, he said, 'It wasn't clever, was it, Kaminski, to make the call from Iqbal's place? That Patel woman called while you were out. The cops have been snooping at Symonds Street. They were asking about you by name.'

Kaminski snorted. 'That doesn't mean a bloody thing and you know it. They'll probably be checking every fare on the driver's log. What did she tell them?'

'What else? She covered for you, didn't she, told them you were a patient, but Iqbal wasn't happy. For him Symonds Street is blown. They've cleaned up and moved the two specialists to another house in Hounslow. Does that change things?'

After a moment's thought she said, 'No. The arrangements are the same. Bulger is picking them up at Brentford Dock at nine thirty and will make his way down river to the jetty to be there at exactly ten. We need to be at the house by nine thirty.'

'Good,' Kramer said. 'We'd better be careful with Iqbal, he might want to take the goods without paying. Remember, we're scum in their eyes.'

'It's your deal, Kramer,' Kaminski said. 'Thomas and I will stay in the background and be ready. I have the Scorpion. We should be finished by ten thirty, then we can meet with Duffy and get away from here.'

'You can forget Duffy. I had a call from Dublin an hour ago. Duffy was wasted last night.'

'Jesus!' she gasped. 'How?'

Kramer shrugged. 'Shot as he was arriving home. Minihane knows who did it and said he'll deal with it.'

'What about our deal?'

'It's to be rescheduled for Amsterdam. You'll have to deal with it.'

'Minhane's okay with that?' Kaminski said. 'Fuck it Kramer! Before, he insisted you be here, no one else would do. That's why we've had all this trouble.'

Kramer gave her a hard look and said, 'He has to be. I told him I wasn't coming back. I've had it with this place. Now, when can we leave?'

'Tomorrow morning at the latest. I've an open ticket on the Euro Tunnel. We just have to park the weapons and get our stuff.'

'Passports?'

'If we need them, I have Irish for yourself and Thomas, Dutch for me. The car has Dutch papers.'

Kramer, whose voice had lost some of its menace said, 'Good, a few more hours and we'll be clear of this. We must be careful, Kaminski, no more mistakes.'

'Yeah, we must.' She wasn't going to tell him her plans for the future didn't include him. There was only one safe route out of this mess and she planned to take it.

'Excellent, get Thomas to pack my things and clean up my room,' he said, turning his head in dismissal and returning to the cricket.

CHAPTER 33

The Baghdad Café was a Turkish kebab restaurant. Deep and narrow, it had one line of tables pushed against the wall with a small bar in the rear. Daisy wondered if the dim lighting was meant to encourage a mood for lovers or provide the privacy drug dealers craved. She could just make out Veleta and Frank Stubbs seated at the end table.

After taking her seat a waiter put a bottle of what she saw to be a thirty-year-old Arafat brandy on the table and three crystal glasses. Frank poured three healthy shots. Nobody touched them. Veleta looked at his watch. Daisy saw it was a Rolex Oyster.

'We have two hours,' Veleta said. 'Brum won't go to the house any sooner than he has to. He'll wait for some darkness to cover his arrival. We need to get into the house before nine.'

'How far is this house, Harry?' Daisy asked.

'Near Kew Bridge, you'll have your heavies in place by nine?'

'Plain-clothes SAS troopers in a fast boat will be at Kew Bridge and a chopper will be waiting in Kew Gardens.'

'I'm impressed, you must carry a lot of clout, Daisy.'

'It took some persuading; they wanted to saturate the area with armed police. We have to succeed on this, Harry, or my name is shit.'

With a grim smile Veleta said, 'Don't worry, Daisy, there's three of us and only about seven of them.'

For the first time she saw him smile. Maybe he did have a human side, she was thinking and said, 'I like your idea of odds. Harry. These people have already killed two people.'

'Three,' Veleta said. 'They killed the watchmaker, this afternoon, just fifteen minutes before I arrived at his shop.'

Frank shook his head in disgust. 'Benny is dead. Jesus, Harry, why did they want to kill an old man like that? He'd have never talked, never, Brum knew that.'

'I'd say Brum is a frightened man,' Daisy said. 'That makes him even more dangerous.' Looking at the canvas cricket bag on the floor by their feet, she asked, 'What are you guys carrying?'

'Two sawn-offs,' Frank said. 'It's all we could find.'

'Meaning twelve-bore shotguns with barrels and stock cut down, right?'

Frank nodded. 'Right. Good enough for close work, what about you?'

Daisy patted her jacket and said, 'A Beretta with ten rounds of point 40 Smith and Wesson in the magazine, plus a spare. How are you going to play this?'

Holding out his hand and no longer smiling, Veleta said, 'I'll explain your part when we reach the house. Now I'll take your mobile.'

'Why?'

'You know why. I'll give it back when you need it.'

Handing him her mobile, Daisy said, 'You don't trust me a bit, do you Harry?'

Taking the phone, Veleta said, 'Mary trusted you and that's good enough for me. It's the people you work for I don't trust. They can track you with this phone. Is this the only one you have?'

'Of course it is. Did you expect me to wear a wire?'

'You'll stand a search when we get to the house?'

Daisy shrugged and said, 'I will, but it will be the end of a beautiful friendship, Harry.'

Harry smiled. 'We can't have that, can we?' Handing her the mobile, he said, 'Take it, but keep it off until you need it.'

Daisy smiled and pocketed the mobile before saying, 'I take it you have a plan, Harry, one that might work?'

'Sure, I have a plan, let's drink to it and get out of here.' They knocked back their drinks and left.

Frank parked in a parallel street, a safe distance from the house. Removing the canvas satchel from the boot he said, 'There's a cut through over there that comes out close to the house, Harry.'

They followed him down past a line of lock-up garages, then along a high fence at the bottom of some gardens to emerge almost opposite the house, which looked dark and empty.

The young couple, arms linked, who were just passing them on the opposite side, did not give them a second glance.

'So, this is Henny's house,' Daisy said.

'You knew about this?' Veleta's voice had an edge to it.

'Only since this afternoon. I have an assistant called Alice who's been tracking all Brum's assets. Brum bought this house at auction in 1972 but registered the deeds in the name of Henny Van der Meer, his common-law wife. How did you find it?'

'Mary found it the same way you did. Henny is either dead or lives abroad.'

'Either way,' Daisy said. 'It's now in the hands of a management company, who checks it from time to time and pays the bills. They in turn are paid by a company registered in Lichtenstein. I would say that this house is where Brum does his deals, him or Kaminski. Is that right ,Harry?'

Shaking his head, Veleta said, 'Maybe only this deal. We've searched the house, it's completely empty other than the crate in the garage. You got any other little surprises for me, Daisy?' If you knew about the house you didn't need me to show you.'

'True, but we have a deal, Harry, remember, I promised, no cops. To me a deal is a deal. After all it might have been the wrong house. Now can we get started. Tell me what you want me to do.'

Veleta looked at her for a long moment. She met his stare and waited.

'Okay,' he said. 'We go in through the front door.' Taking the canvas satchel from Frank, he said, 'Get the gate.' His hand held Daisy's arm as she went to follow.

Daisy watched as Frank manipulated his lock picks. In less than thirty seconds the lock sprung, and the gate was open.

'Come on,' Veleta said.

With one hand still on her arm and carrying the canvas satchel in his other, they crossed the street like the perfect couple.

Frank took the keys from the lamp shade, opened the front door, and returned them to the lampshade. They went quickly inside and closed the door on the Yale lock.

'Follow me.' Veleta led the way into the kitchen. Putting the canvas satchel on a table he turned to Frank and said, 'Keep a look out from upstairs.'

Frank nodded and left the kitchen. Veleta went to the back door and unbolted it.

Alice had shown Daisy photographs and plans of the house and garden that afternoon, so she knew exactly what to expect as she followed Veleta. Two mature trees, an apple and a pear stood out as shadows. After the covered patio, there was a narrow York stone path to the back gate. They walked together in silence. Veleta unbolted the gate.

The jetty showed up as a grey outline, becoming clearer as their eyes adjusted to the gloom. 'Not much light, that's good,' Daisy said.

Pointing, Veleta said, 'There's some good cover in those bushes over there.'

They stood on the jetty and looked at the river. The tide was full with the water almost level with the planks. The far side of the river was just a shadowy outline in the gloom. A cabin cruiser, lights twinkling passed slowly upriver, otherwise it was quiet.

'Nice and peaceful here, Harry,' Daisy said. 'Romantic even, but it's getting late. Any time you're ready, I'm waiting to hear your plan.'

Veleta looked out at the river for a moment before replying. 'Brum is using a riverman called Bulger to bring someone called Iqbal and three others to the jetty at ten o'clock. Frank knows the boat. It's a forty-foot work boat and operates like a river-taxi. It's a regular sight on the river carrying passengers and general cargo.'

'I think I've seen it,' Daisy said. 'An old boat, painted blue, with a forward wheelhouse, and an open deck with a derrick. The stern sits low in the water.'

'That's the one. There's a cabin under the wheel house for the passengers, so they'll be out of sight until it reaches the jetty.'

'For someone who's just arrived from Spain, you know an awful about Brum, and the shadier side of London, don't you, Harry?'

'I overheard him talking here last night, and like you, Daisy, I'm also a bit of a ferret and did some checking this afternoon.'

'When they land does Bulger stay with the boat?'

'I'd expect so. He'll not want to know what's being moved, would he? The clients will go into the house, check the goods and bring the crate to the boat.'

'And you overheard all this last evening.'

'How else would I know it?'

'I can't imagine,' Daisy said.

'When they're leaving Bulger will want to be underway immediately. That's when you call in your men. Tell them that when

282

the boat reaches the middle of the river, you've arranged a signal.'

'What kind of signal?' Daisy felt that her *raison d'être* was about to be explained.

'A timed explosion, powerful enough and very noisy, like a stun grenade. A chemical mix dreamed up years ago. It'll disorientate everyone on board for a few minutes and maybe even disable the boat.'

A Sidney Vane special, Daisy was thinking as she said, 'Just how do you plan to get this device on board, Harry?'

Veleta leaned towards her and said in a low voice, 'That's where you come in.'

Daisy couldn't see his eyes clearly in the gloom but she thought she glimpsed a hint of a smile and said, 'You know, I thought you might say that. You want me to get onto the boat while they're in the house and plant the bomb. Is that it?'

'Not quite,' Veleta said. 'I want you to put the bomb on the boat, but not while they're in the house. There's no way of knowing how long they'll be inside and the bomb is set for three minutes. Just enough time for them to reach the middle of the river and be headed upstream, but close enough for the explosion to be heard a long way.'

'So, you're asking me to get on the boat after they've finished loading the crate.'

'You catch on fast, Daisy.'

'I could just as easy call in my men while they're loading the crate.'

Shaking his head, Veleta said, 'That's not part of our deal, Daisy.'

With a knowing nod Daisy said, 'I get it. You need the explosion, the deafening noise, don't you Harry, just like the decoys in the old days, to give you an edge with Brum.'

'I don't know what you're talking about, Daisy, what old days?'

Time for a bluff, Daisy was thinking and said, 'Harry, my company has one of the best intelligence teams in the world, we have associates in every major country. In addition, I have the full cooperation of the police and SIS. I knew when we first met that you were not just Mary's friend from Spain. I've had people around the clock taking a keen interest in you. I know all about Harry Veleta – or should I call you Harry Vane? – who up until now I was sure was the Midnight Fox, but only this afternoon I received a report, which included a very interesting photograph from my agent in Madrid about your activities. As a result, I now believe the Midnight Fox was more a family affair.'

Harry's teeth flashed as he laughed in the gloom. 'Now you're getting fanciful, Daisy. I never heard of the Midnight Fox until you first mentioned it.'

'Come on, Harry. You're Sid Vane's son. Gloria was your mother and Mary your sister. My Spanish is a bit rusty but doesn't Veleta translate to a weathervane? Not a very original alias, but it shows you had some loyalty to the family name.'

In a voice little more than a whisper, Veleta said, 'What else do you know?'

'When your father was hanged, you were twelve years old. Zar Brum was your father's partner in crime and my sources tell me that it was Brum who fired the shot that killed the police constable. Unfortunately, Sid was caught and as was the criminal's code in those days, he took the rap and went to the gallows. His silence ensured that his widow and children would be looked after. Is that how it was, Harry?'

'You're telling the story, Daisy.'

Looking at him in the gloom, Daisy was thinking how bigger and more dangerous he now seemed. Better blunder on.

'Sid would have made sure your mother knew the truth about who fired the shot and she was able to hold this over Brum. So, in order to save his own skin, he supported the family, for fourteen years, isn't that right Harry?

'It's a good story, Daisy, maybe you should become a fiction writer, but I'm curious, why fourteen years?'

'It was fourteen years later, in 1976, that the first robbery attributed to the Midnight Fox took place. I saw Gloria's wedding photo, Harry, and besides being beautiful she looked to me like a strong and capable woman. A woman who would want payback for her husband's premature death. Fourteen years was time enough for her to ensure that you grew up with a hatred for the cops and for you to become an expert locksmith. Time enough for her to pass on Sid's method of blowing safes and vaults. Being your father's son, you probably inherited a natural aptitude for the work.'

Pausing, she waited for a reaction from Veleta, who was watching her impassively but he said nothing, so she continued. 'I believe that Gloria was the planner. Brum the fence, while you and your band of thieves, of which I am sure Frank Stubbs, after seeing his prowess with a lock pick, played a prominent role, were the sharp end, opening the vaults and setting the decoy bombs. You were extremely successful for ten years, the seventeen jobs you pulled of netted a nice few million. The police were baffled. Then there was the last job, all that gold. What happened? Did Brum get greedy, want it all for himself, is that what happened?'

'I thought you knew it all, Daisy.'

'I do know it all, Harry, and I can prove it.'

'How so?'

'Two things, Harry. One was a careless moment in an otherwise faultless career when the Peterman left a fingerprint on a safe door.'

'So?'

'So, you left me a nice set of your dabs on the wine glass you used in my apartment, Harry.'

Veleta turned and looked at the river for a long moment before asking, 'What was the second thing, Daisy?'

'A photograph of your mother's grave arrived from Madrid today. The inscription on the headstone read: **Gloria Grey, 1923-2005 – Beloved Mother of H&M – Adios La Bella Zorro**[*]. Need I say more?'

Veleta turned to face her and said, 'I think you've said enough, Daisy. Now are you with us on this or not?'

'A final word, Harry. Whatever Brum did, must have been treacherous enough for him to want to fake his own death and disappear. Whether he got away with your gold is of no concern of mine, but what he's doing now, supplying missiles to the Jihadists, is, and he must be stopped. You're a thief, Harry, maybe even retired now, free and clear with your life in front of you. Somehow, I don't think you're the killing type. Why not leave it to the professionals?'

Moving closer to her, Veleta said, 'You're still not listening, Daisy. Brum killed Mary and old Benny. It has to end this way. Now enough of the questions. Maybe I'll tell you my story some other time if we live through this. Right now, we have to finish this tonight and whether you're in or not, you're not going anywhere until it's over.'

With a brittle laugh Daisy said, 'Don't worry about me, Harry. I wouldn't miss this for the world. I'm in and we don't have much time. I'll need to find a place to hide. Now where's your bomb?'

'You'll do it.'

'Of course, I'll do it, but let's get on with it before I've time to change my mind. Where's number twenty?'

'Sorry, I don't understand.'

Daisy snorted. 'Harry, don't take me for a fool, there were twenty Messerlie clocks. The gold robbery was number eighteen, number nineteen was used by Brum to kill Mary which means there's one clock left and you went to see the watchmaker today.'

---

[*] The Beautiful Fox

286

Looking at her for a long moment, Veleta said, 'You know, Daisy, I'm glad you weren't around twenty years ago, you must have been one smart intelligence agent. Maybe I'm asking too much.'

Daisy held his gaze. 'Maybe you're the one taking on too much, Harry. I repeat, being a thief is one thing. Killing people, even scum like this lot is another matter. Let me call in the specialists, Harry, let them deal with Brum.'

Veleta stepped back and said, 'No, we'll forget about the bomb, it's too dangerous for you. Frank and I can manage without it.'

Daisy shook her head. 'No, you bloody well can't. It's not the first time I've faced danger, Harry. It's a good plan. These fanatics are armed and happy to die for cause. The explosion should give my men the edge they need, so enough talk, Harry, let's go and get number twenty.'

CHAPTER 34

Veleta removed the bomb from the canvas bag and handed it to Daisy. Its size and shape were that of a house brick, completely wrapped in layers of Duct tape with a steel ring attached to a short wire on one side. Daisy held it gingerly, hefting it in her hand to get a feel for the weight if she had to throw it.

'It's wrapped in foam so it should be safe enough to drop it a few feet but no further,' Veleta said.

Examining it, she said, 'Safe enough? As I remember it, Harry, detonators don't respond well to a sudden shock.'

'It's the best I could do in the time. When you pull the ring, you have three minutes.'

'OK,' she said. 'Let's do it. Come, you need to bolt the gate behind me. They'll expect that.'

They walked in silence back to the jetty where they stood for a moment in silence.

Veleta, a tall shadow without a face, said, 'Daisy.'

'Yes Harry.'

'If this goes against me and Frank, you'll have your gang take care of Brum.'

Touching his arm, Daisy said, 'Harry, Brum has added to his criminal activities by being a traitor, there's only one thing in store for him and you know it.'

Harry looked at her for a long moment in the gloom before saying, 'Good luck.' He turned and went back through the gate.

Daisy heard the bolts sliding home and started examining the jetty in more detail. She saw it was little more than a planked construction some twelve feet wide running along about thirty yards of the riverbank. She could make out wooden upright posts which would allow several small craft to tie up. A wooden fence, consisting of two four-by-two planks supported by uprights every six feet ran along the waterside. Moving closer, she saw two boat hooks with rusted iron hooks and thick wooden shafts leaning against the fence beside the landing stage. The planking felt solid underfoot. At one end where there was a bend in the river, the jetty jutted over the water. Upriver, fifty yards along the tow path she saw the outline of an iron gate. This was private property which suited her purpose. There would be no unexpected strollers.

Now, all she had to do was to make like the invisible woman. For that purpose, she was suitably dressed, black jeans and trainers, with a light turtleneck, also black. She pulled a black woollen beanie over her blonde hair, found the darkest shadow and settled herself into the comfortable squat she had perfected in Northern Ireland when a stakeout might last many hours.

Veleta watched the street from the first-floor window. The odd car passed and a few people went up and down. It was five minutes to ten, a time on a Saturday night when most people would be either indoors eating their dinner or already out to their favourite pub or restaurant. He had stationed Frank at a window overlooking the garden, where there was good view of the river. The door of Brum's secret room was open, ready for them to conceal themselves in the unlikely event of a search.

It was getting close to ten o'clock. Veleta was beginning to wonder if Brum was going to show when the silence was broken. Someone had turned the key and opened the front door. He heard muffled voices and footsteps in the hall. He had been watching for their car but had missed their approach completely from his view. Fuck it, he'd messed up already.

He heard a door open. *They're going into the garage.* He waited, listening, before moving. Then, treading a step at a time, testing each floorboard for squeaks, he made his way to where Frank was waiting.

Frank held his hand up in the gesture of wait and pointed down several times. When he was close enough Veleta whispered, 'They came in the front door, no car, that means they'll go out the same way. We can nail them in the hall.'

'What if they come up here?' Frank's mouth was close to Veleta's ear. As he spoke, they heard footsteps in the hall and then the sound of the bolts on the back door. From the window they saw a figure walk to the back gate and open it.

'That's a woman, must be Kaminski,' Veleta said. 'She'll wait there until the boat arrives, that leaves only Brum and his Goon in the garage. They won't be doing any searching. We wait and we watch.'

Daisy, whose eyes had become accustomed to the conditions, heard someone at the gate. It swung open and the figure outlined in the opening paused for a moment before stepping out and onto the jetty. It was a woman and she was only a few feet away.

It must be Kaminski, Daisy thought, and slipped the Beretta out of her satchel. She was ready.

She watched as Kaminski stood, facing the river and lit a cigarette. Daisy saw the woman's face clearly in the flame of the Zippo. *Bad move, girl, showing yourself like that,* she was thinking, when she heard the throb of a powerful diesel engine coming from upriver. Her instincts sharpened as they always did before an action, thinking, *This party is about to begin.* From her crouched position she had no view of the water. The sound of the engine was getting ever closer.

The boat pulled smoothly alongside the jetty; its bows to the incoming tide. A figure appeared from the wheelhouse door and a rope was tossed to Kaminski. Her cigarette hissed as she tossed it into the water and deftly caught the rope, slipping it over the mooring post. The boat held. The figure stepped onto the jetty and attached the stern rope and returned to the wheel house. The engine was throttled back to little more than a hum.

Daisy counted four figures as they joined Kaminski, who said something in a low voice and led them through the gate. The gate was closed, but the bolts were not thrown. It was exactly ten o'clock. Daisy speed dialled a number on her mobile, which was answered on the first ring.

'Delta One,' a voice rasped.

'The boat's at the jetty, move to position two.'

'What's the opposition?'

'Four plus the boatman.'

'Copy that, we're ready.'

Daisy put the Beretta back into her satchel, slung it on her shoulder and in a low crouch slowly approached the boat. There were no riding lights and wheelhouse was in darkness. She hoped that Bulger would be watching the house and not the stern of his boat.

Staying low she slid over the side and onto the deck. The heavy boat hardly moved in the water with her extra weight. She lay prone, for long enough to see if there was any reaction from the wheelhouse. There was none. Crawling to the stern she flashed her mini Maglite for a second, enabling her to see, among a jumble of ropes, car tyres and general rubbish, a long wooden chest pushed flush against the stern.

Lifting the lid, she flashed her torch again. Inside she saw what she was looking for. Bundles of ropes of various sizes, one of which was just what she needed. A roll of thin, but strong-looking synthetic cord. She tugged at a length to feel its strength, it would do. Lying beside the chest she listened. All she could hear was water lapping against the hull and the hum of traffic on Kew Bridge: from the house she heard nothing. Her watch told her that four minutes had passed since they went inside. How much time before they returned was what mattered to her. It might be a quick exchange of money for goods or there might be an argument. To be safe she had to be off the boat in minutes. She would have to risk her light to deal with the bomb.

She had already discounted Veleta's idea of tossing it on the boat as it left the jetty for two reasons: one being that in her experience detonators did not like shocks, the bomb could explode on impact; added to that she had witnessed Kaminski dealing efficiently with the mooring ropes and likely as not she would be there to help them cast off.

Using the light, she saw that the rope chest had two lengths of two-by-four – an inch clear of the bottom – supporting the sides. Finding another short length of rope, she tied the bomb securely to one of these. Then she tied one end of the cord to the ring. A good pull would remove the ring and activate the timer.

Feeding the cord carefully out of the chest she closed the lid – which was warped and not a tight fit – giving sufficient gap to allow the cord to move freely. Then, still crawling, she carefully fed the cord along the back of the stern to the side of the boat. Slipping back on to the jetty she continued to feed the cord loosely until she reached a mooring post. After tying the cord to it and dropping the slack into the water, she crept back into the shadows and surveyed her work. There was nothing to be seen and unless she had the worst of bad luck it would not be noticed.

Sitting in the shadows, she waited. There was no sound coming from the house. The boat, still an outline in the darkness. The low hum of its engine blended with the sounds of the distant traffic on Kew Bridge. For a few moments the engine noise – of another boat passing upriver – rose above it, then, just as soon it was gone.

She removed the Beretta from her satchel and performed a blind check. The gun was ready. Was she? It was ten minutes since they went into the house. She would soon find out.

CHAPTER 35

Inside the garage Iqbal, Karim and Nizar and Brum crowded around the crate. Iqbal's bodyguard, standing behind his master, kept a malevolent eye on Thomas and Kaminski.

Looking into the crate, Iqbal said, 'There should be two Stinger rounds, two Grip-Stocks and two BCU units.

Nizar nodded and viewed the contents for a brief moment before lifting one of the Grip-Stocks from its foam cut-out and examining it. With the exception of his partner, whatever he was looking for was a mystery to the assembled group. He appeared to be satisfied and handed the unit to Karim who repeated the inspection and nodded his satisfaction. The procedure was repeated with the second Grip-Stock until Nizar said, 'They're good.' Then he removed one of the two BCU units and carefully scrutinised it. 'These look new.'

'They are,' Iqbal said. 'They were stolen from the Pakistan Army.'

Returning the two Grip-Stocks and BCU units to their cut-outs he carefully lifted the two slabs of foam out and placed them on the bench. He then lifted one of the Stinger rounds from its foam bedding below. Inside the reusable fibreglass tube was the three-inch diameter by five-foot Stinger round which contained all the missiles' fire and forget guidance systems, plus 3kg of high explosive, enough to blow them all through the roof.

'They've been serviced in Darra Adam Kiel by an American-trained armourer who's set up shop there,' Iqbal said. 'I have the serial numbers of the rounds,' and produced a sheet of paper. 'Read them out.'

Nizar read out the sixteen-digit alphanumeric to which Iqbal said, 'Good, check the other one.'

The other serial numbers checked out. 'I'm satisfied,' said Iqbal. 'Put everything back and screw the top on.' Nizar repacked the crate and looked for a screwdriver.

'Just a minute,' Brum growled. 'There's the small matter of payment.'

Iqbal handed him his attaché case. 'Here is the amount we agreed, you can keep the case, it's genuine goatskin made from my own goats.'

'Most kind of you,' Brum said and passed the case to Kaminski. 'Count it and be quick, we need to finish this.'

Kaminski took the case to the work bench and opened it.

Nizar had found two screwdrivers and while he and Karim began attaching the top. Thomas and Iqbal's minder regarded each other like a pair of dogs sniffing the air before a fight.

'It's all there, boss,' Kaminski said, and closed the case.

'Excellent,' Brum said. 'A satisfactory conclusion to our arrangements. The boat will take you back to Brentford. See them to the jetty and lock up, Kaminski, I'll take the case.'

Daisy heard a noise, maybe a footstep, and moved deeper into the shadows. The cloud cover had shifted and the sky had turned a shade lighter, making her available cover thinner.

The gate opened and the figures, just darker shapes against the grey, slipped through. She counted five; the trailing pair were carrying a coffin-shaped crate between them.

She could make out Kaminski, who stood on the jetty and spoke to one of the men in a whisper. The man nodded and gestured something to the others. The box was lifted aboard, and pushed up against the wheelhouse.

'Best cover it,' Kaminski said.

Daisy put her accent as East European, which tallied with what Isaacs had said about her being Czech. She saw a cover being unfolded and secured over the box.

'Stay inside until you reach the dock. I'll cast off,' Kaminski said.

Immediately the figures entered the wheelhouse the engine increased a pitch. Kaminski released the bow and stern ropes and threw them aboard. The boat swung out into the river.

With her restricted vision Daisy concentrated her hearing, and thought she heard a snapping sound as the cord became taut and the ring was pulled. Maybe it had broken maybe not, either way it was too late to do anything about it. If it worked, she would know in three minutes. Time to call her backup. She speed dialled the number and whispered into her mobile, 'Three minutes, Captain. It's your deal now, you've had your orders.'

'I hear what you're saying. Over and out.'

A minute passed and Kaminski stood watching the river. Her Zippo flamed, as she lit a cigarette. As she did so, a burst of gunfire came from the house. Kaminski froze, her hand holding the Zippo, its flame illuminating her face.

Five shots, three clearly the sharper crack of a pistol and two from a shotgun, Daisy reckoned, and definitely not part of the script. Up until that moment she had not decided what to do about Kaminski. One thing was sure, whatever was going on in the house didn't need Kaminski's help.

She crawled out of the shadows and stood up, her right hand by her side holding the Beretta, and moved slowly along the guard rail.

Kaminski, still at the water's edge, had turned to look towards the house. The clouds had become more scattered and a watery moon gave improved visibility.

Daisy was within three yards of her, the Beretta still by her side, when a twig cracked under her feet.

Kaminski turned, saw her, and calmly said, 'And who the fuck might you be?'

A cool one, Daisy was thinking, before saying, 'I'm Daisy. That boat won't get far, Kaminski, and neither will you. I'm arresting you for the murder of Mary Grey.'

Giving her a long look, Kaminski took a drag from her cigarette, and flicked it into the water.

Daisy's eyes followed Kaminski's hand for the split second it took to do this. A bad move, she would later recount, for when she looked again, Kaminski's left hand was pointing the Scorpion at her head.

'Your hands, Daisy. UP and EMPTY or I'll shred you,' Kaminski said.

Daisy, recognising the extended magazine of a machine pistol, knew she was outgunned. Slowly extending her hand, she dropped the Beretta, at the same time cursing her stupidity for letting Kaminski get the drop on her with her simple cigarette trick.

Transferring the Scorpion to her right hand, Kaminski said, 'Good, now kick it towards me.'

Taking a step towards the guard rail Daisy kicked the Beretta and as she watched it spin in Kaminski's direction, her mind was formulating a desperate plan, part of which was to keep Kaminski talking.

Counting down the seconds as she spoke, Daisy said. 'You heard the shots, Ursula. The house is full of armed police. Fire that weapon and they'll have you.'

Kaminski, holding the Scorpion steady, its muzzle pointing directly at Daisy's chest, looked at her for a long moment of indecision before saying, 'If that's the case, Daisy, whatever you name is, you're my ticket out of here.' Then pointing her left hand in the direction of the wrought-iron gate, she said, 'Now start moving towards that gate. Any tricks and I'll kill you and take my chances.'

Daisy, still counting down the seconds, shifted onto the balls of her feet, but moving wasn't part of her plan. 'You're wasting your time, Ursula. I'm not moving and if you fire that weapon, you're finished. Better run while you have the chance.'

Even in the dim light she saw the hate in Kaminski's face. Keeping the Scorpion on Daisy, she moved to pick up the Beretta.

Her bluff had worked, Daisy thought. Kaminski was going to run, and she was ready for the moment.

Kaminski had the Beretta in her hand when Veleta's bomb exploded.

Like a thousand screaming banshees, the noise tore at her ears. Even louder than she had expected, Daisy thought, as she saw Kaminski stagger, shake her head and turn sharply to look for the source of the pain.

Ignoring her own ringing ears, Daisy sprang towards the guard rail and grabbed the boat-hook. Then, holding it two-handed like a quarter staff she lunged forward and smashed the iron hook into the side of Kaminski's head.

Kaminski screamed, turned and looked at her with unfocused eyes. The Scorpion was still moving in her hand when Daisy hit her again, hard on the temple, with the other end of the shaft. Kaminski slumped to the ground, her feet kicking for a moment, and she was still.

The last echoes of the explosion had died away and for a few moments the river was eerily quiet, to be broken again by several bursts of automatic gunfire. The SAS had located their target and would be following out their orders. Daisy then, remembering that she had neglected to inform Harry exactly what Peter Isaacs orders were.

She bent down and easing the Scorpion from Kaminski's fingers, unhooked it from its lanyard and put it aside. Checking Kaminski's carotid, she found a pulse. She was alive and she wouldn't be out for long. She needed something to restrain her.

Going to the mooring post she pulled at the cord until she retrieved the end. The ring was there. Attached to it was a short wire and attached to that was the piece of plastic which kept the contacts apart. It had done more than its job. The bomb, probably devised by the long-dead Sidney Vane, had just saved her life.

There was enough of the cord and she reckoned it was strong enough. Going to Kaminski she turned her face down on the deck and tied her hands, the thin cord biting into her flesh. It would probably stop her circulation, but then this woman was due a bit of pain, Daisy thought as she pulled her feet up and tied them to her hands.

Turning her on her side so that she could breathe, Daisy inspected her handiwork. The term trussed up like a chicken came to mind. She was satisfied. Kaminski was going nowhere.

Picking up the Scorpion she examined it and decided it was much like any other machine pistol. Recalling her instructor's words regarding fully automatic weapons: *hold it firmly, girl, point it, pull the trigger, spray and pray*. If there was real trouble in the house, it should give her an edge. Finding her Beretta, she stuck it into her belt. Her mouth felt dry and her hands trembled. *Christ,* she thought. What wouldn't she give for a drink right now.

The house had been quiet since the first burst of gunfire. Soon the area would be crawling with police. She had to be quick and careful. Whoever was still alive in there would be expecting Kaminski to return.

Keeping to the shadows and off the path she reached the back door and cautiously entered the kitchen, sweeping it with the Scorpion. It was empty. She paused at the door into the hall and listened. Someone was groaning, then there was a fit of coughing, then silence before she heard Veleta.

'Watch the door, Frank, it's not finished yet. Brum's woman is still out there.'

She called, 'Harry, it's me, Daisy, I'm coming in.'

Frank was watching the door. The barrels of his sawn-off, pointing in her general direction, dropped when he saw her. The low-wattage lamp and the thick smell of cordite made the whole scene look surreal. Thomas was lying at the garage door, obviously dead, his face a mask of blood.

Veleta was holding his gun on another man. Daisy recognised Brum from the CCTV. He was slumped on the floor, his back positioned against the front door. Going closer to stand beside Veleta she saw there was a bloodstain on Brum's shirt just above the heart. His eyes, alert and malevolent, showed surprise when he saw her.

Showing him the Scorpion, she said, 'As you can see, Mr Brum, Kaminski's not coming, and if the gunfire is anything to go by, your clients are either in custody or dead. What happened, Harry?'

'Brum decided to wait for Kaminski in the car, we had to jump them.'

'And?'

'We had them covered from the stairs, bang to rights. Then the Goon went crazy. He punched the light switch and started shooting in the dark. Frank and I fired at the garage door. After that, silence. We waited. Someone was coughing and groaning by the front door. When I hit the light, I found this.'

Daisy looked at Brum's shirt; the bloodstain was spreading. 'That's not a shotgun wound. He's been hit by a stray bullet. Bad luck, Mr Brum.'

Wiping blood from his mouth with his left hand, Brum snarled, 'Fucking Thomas, the crazy bastard's done for me, Harry. Who's the bitch?'

Daisy smiled grimly. Then pulling the Beretta from her belt she put the barrel an inch from Brum's head, thumbed back the hammer and said, 'This is hardly the time for insults, scumbag, but for you, I'll make an exception. I'm the justice you should have had twenty years ago.'

Putting his hand on her arm, Veleta said, 'Don't, look at him Daisy, he's finished, he'll be dead soon enough.'

Seeing the fear in Brum's eyes, Daisy smiled, lowered the Beretta, stepped back and placed the Scorpion on the kitchen table.

Veleta let the sawn-off fall to his side and turned to face her, the weary smile on his face quickly changing to a look of surprise and then fear as she mouthed, 'Jesus, Harry,' and brought the Beretta up, straight armed, and fired a single shot.

'What the...?'

'Bloody hell! Harry,' Daisy said. 'Don't you know you never turn your back on a prisoner?'

Veleta, white-faced, turned and saw Brum had fallen sideways, eyes staring at the ceiling, a hole in his forehead seeping blood, in his left hand he held a black snub-nosed pistol.

Dropping the Beretta to her side, Daisy said, 'He was planning to take you with him, Harry.'

A shaken Veleta put his sawn-off on the table and his look encouraged Frank to do the same, both of them giving Daisy a wary look.

'What now, Daisy?' asked Veleta.

Realising their discomfort Daisy put her Beretta beside the sawn-offs and said, 'Did you ask Brum why he came back?'

'Yeah, I did. He said Minihane insisted on him being here to do the drugs deal.'

Putting her hand on his arm, she said softly, 'I know it's no conciliation, Harry, but Brum being here, and Mary walking in on their meeting, has saved a lot of lives.'

Veleta's eyes were cold when he said, 'Yeah, at the cost of her own, Daisy. The only conciliation is that by killing Brum you settled for Mary and saved my life. I owe you for that.'

'You owe me nothing, Harry,' Daisy said. 'Without your help this would have ended badly.'

The three of them stood facing each other in the kitchen. Then the brief silence outside was broken by the sound of sirens.

Shifting uneasily on his feet Veleta said, 'I'm sure you can take care of things now, Daisy.'

Daisy nodded. 'Yeah, you'd better slip away, soon this area will be swarming with cops. Do you have a safe route out?'

'I'll be okay. What will happen to Frank?'

'Nothing, neither of you were here tonight.'

'Then, we'd best be off, Daisy.'

'That would be best, Harry. If you leave your address, I'm sure the director would like to send you a letter of comfort.'

'We're not into the letter business, Daisy,' Veleta said.

Daisy shrugged, and picking up the case at Brum's feet she snapped it open. Recognising the violet-coloured Swiss banknotes, she said, 'These are thousand-franc notes, Harry, maybe you can take care of them? Brum must owe you that much.'

Taking the case, Veleta smiled and said, 'Happy to oblige, Daisy. Tell me, what happened to Kaminski?'

'She's still alive, for the moment, but what happens to her now is not up to me anymore.'

'And the men on the boat?'

'Bulger's boat unfortunately blew up when it was carrying a cargo of fireworks. There'll be no survivors.'

Veleta looked at the remains of Brum and Thomas. 'You're able to deal with all this and Kaminski?'

'Nothing happened here tonight, Harry. The cleaners will be here soon. There'll be no headlines tomorrow. That's how the director likes these things to end. It makes the opposition nervous, you know, not knowing what happened, what went wrong.'

Giving her a strange look, Veleta said, 'There was never any intention of taking them alive, was there, Daisy? For a moment there I thought I was in for the same treatment.'

With a tired smile Daisy said, 'Don't say I actually scared you a little, Harry?'

He didn't answer as he pushed Brum's body to one side and opened the door. The sirens were closer now. Frank gave her a nervous smile and hurried out. For a moment Harry stood by the door looking at her; for once he seemed stuck for words. 'What about the wine glass, Daisy?'

'Don't worry, Harry, the glass will go in the dishwasher when I get home. The file on the Midnight Fox will be closed forever.'

He touched his forehead and said, 'Ciao, Daisy,' and was gone.

Printed in Great Britain
by Amazon

54418685R00179